THE BURIED LIFE

Buried Life artfully sets a whodunnit murder mystery
lystopian underground city filled with dark politics
oul secrets. It's a gripping read from start to finish,
two clever female leads and a delightfully colorful
More, please!"
h Cato, author of The Clockwork Dagger

Regency-era sensibilities and Agatha Christie's flair
e subtle conundrum, Patel's debut novel introduces
rs to a subterranean city of the future, centuries after
s dubbed 'The Catastrophe', and beautifully manages
the   licate balance between entertainment and social
con   entary. The subtly fantastical story is resplendent
wit   urprisingly deep villains, political corruption, and a
gri]   g whodunnit feel."
1   ishers Weekly (starred review)

"*Tl   uried Life* is a dark, imaginative steampunk gem –
tai   nade for mystery fans and history nerds alike, with
pl(of cops-and-robbers to keep you on your toes. This
is   ry fine contribution to the genre."
rie Priest, author of Boneshaker *and* Maplecroft

"V   ely steampunk-ish but not quite classifiable, *The Buried
Life* is recommended for readers comfortable straddling the
border of fantasy and sci-fi; dedicated fantasists and hard
sci-fi fans may want to go down another hole."
Books, Brains & Beer

"The setting was fascinating — an underground
a group of rulers that are more dictators than any
societal rules, and, of course, murder and mayhem
main characters here were all quite fascinating – nua
layered, realistic. It was a great read."

In Case of Survival

"I like a novel that challenges you AND gives you en
information to figure it out. I loved this novel and
forward to Ms Patel's next."

Koeur's Book Reviews

"Carrie Patel has conceived of a dark steampunk-esque
futuristic world filled with anachronisms that, despite that,
work well together. And there's a library to die for – what
bookaholic could resist?"

Popcorn Reads

"I really enjoyed the novel, Patel's descriptions are strong
and evoke Recoletta quite clearly. The narrative builds up
to a clear climax… I can't wait to return to Recoletta. If you
enjoy your SFF a bit off the beaten path or genre mashups in
general, then I highly recommend giving Carrie Patel's *The
Buried Life* a shot."

A Fantastical Librarian

"While the story begins as a routine mystery, it quickly
develops into something else entirely. The story sets up
a promising storyline and an interesting world, and I'll
be curious to see how the things develop in the city of
Recoletta."

Bookaneer

CARRIE PATEL

The Buried Life

ANGRY
ROBOT

ANGRY ROBOT
An imprint of Watkins Media Ltd

Lace Market House
54-56 High Pavement
Nottingham
NG1 1HW
UK

angryrobotbooks.com
twitter.com/angryrobotbooks
Underground, overground

An Angry Robot paperback original 2015
1

A catalogue record for this book is available from the British Library.

ISBN 978 0 85766 520 1
Ebook ISBN 978 0 85766 522 5

Set in Meridien by Argh! Oxford.

Printed and bound by Printondemandworldwide.

To Hiren Patel

PROLOGUE

In a firelit study half a mile underground, Professor Werner Thomas Cahill sweated and reddened under a councilor's beady stare.

"It's a wonder," Cahill said, "bigger than we ever expected." His hands rested, palms down, on the massive cherry wood desk in front of him, and he licked his lips, searching for words to convey scale. Towering walls crowded around him and disappeared in the darkness above. He felt like a rodent in a viper pit.

The owner of the desk drummed long, slender fingers across it, and Cahill marveled at how clean it was. A councilor of his standing should have a lot more clutter.

Councilor Ruthers leaned forward. "Professor Cahill, you are aware of what this means?"

"Yes, sir."

"And I trust that you've been discreet?"

"You're the first person I've told, sir." Perspiration condensed on the polished wood under his hands.

"Then you know the complications that would arise if this were to surface." The words came out like the first sigh of snow in the autumn air, unexpected and chilling. Cahill took the councilor's meaning and shivered.

"Of course, sir."

Ruthers paused, waving a hand in the air. "That isn't all I'm talking about." What frightened Cahill most was not that Ruthers would threaten his life, but that this was, apparently, least among their shared concerns. "This is your life's work – your dream. It's the same for an odd three dozen as well."

"Actually, sir, it's about twice that if you count–"

"I don't."

Cahill swallowed. Working with other people was hard enough. But conniving and backstabbing? This was why he tried to avoid collaborative efforts. And politics.

The chair beneath him whispered as he shifted on the velour upholstery. Councilor Ruthers smiled in what he must have thought was a reassuring manner.

"Werner, don't worry about this. Your job is research – let me handle the politics. Agreed?"

Cahill nodded. That was all you could do when Councilor Ruthers asked if you agreed.

"Excellent. I want you to begin taking inventory. Prepare a preliminary report for Dr Hask, including an estimation of time and manpower. We'll start next week."

"Next week, sir?"

"Phase two." Councilor Ruthers pulled an inch-thick, bound folder from under his desk and slid it to Cahill. It seemed out of place on the otherwise immaculate surface. Cahill took the folder, feeling slick leather under his thumbs. The cover bore one word.

Prometheus.

CHAPTER 1

THE INSPECTOR & THE LAUNDRESS

The smugglers fled to the surface. Sooner or later, they always did. An underground city only offered so many places to run.

Liesl Malone's feet pounded a rapid tattoo on the cobblestones, an up-tempo echo of the two sets of footsteps half a block ahead. The smugglers had been faster at the start of the chase, but now they were tiring. And, from the sounds of their clipped grunts and curses, panicking.

Malone's long breaths filled her with the odors of soot, sweat, and desperation. She hadn't wanted to move before next month's clandestine cordite shipment, but the smugglers had recognized her. Someone had tipped them off. If they got away, the contacts she'd spent months grooming wouldn't just be useless, they'd be dead.

The chase had started in the subterranean labyrinths of the city's factory districts, where torch smoke choked the tunnels and obscured the murals and carvings left by thief gangs, rowdy youths, and immigrant factions. The factory districts bred criminals the same way sewers bred rats, and she'd spotted the smugglers in a knot around a jewelry fence's stall. She could just see the whites of their eyes in the flickering torchlight as they squeezed between laborers from the nearby rubber mill. But when a murmur rippled through the crowd about the ghost-pale woman in the black overcoat, the smugglers had noticed her and bolted.

Unfortunately for these two, Malone's feet were just as sure in the tumbling, jagged passages as theirs were, and her sharp elbows parted crowds as quickly as their girth. The smugglers had drawn their weapons, but she knew they wouldn't dare fire. Most of the passages in the factory districts were as tight as they were twisted, leaving little open ground for a clear shot. Only the most desperate of fugitives would open fire in the melting pot of gangs and ruffians there. Even the lowest newcomers made allies, and everyone had a long memory.

Above the crowded tunnels and warrens of the underground city, the moonlight and shadows must have promised concealment, and the midnight chill must have tasted like escape. For whatever reason, a fugitive on the last leg of flight almost always made for the surface the way a wounded rabbit crawls to the bushes to die.

And now Malone pursued them through the stone forest of verandas, entrances great and small to the city below. These crumbling shacks listed toward one another, throwing sweeps of ancient brick and concrete into the street. The ones that still stood in this part of the city were especially small, barely big enough for three or four people to stand in. She would not have trusted the rusting chain-winch lifts and staircases within most of them for a seat on Recoletta's ruling council.

Just ahead, one of the smugglers stumbled and nearly tripped on the cracked cobblestones. Deep trenches from years of carriage and wagon travel gouged the streets in this neighborhood. The air stank with factory smoke, which billowed into the night sky from outlets above the mills and foundries. Malone hoped that a stray wind wouldn't send the chemical-blackened fumes their way to add to the darkness.

The first smuggler dashed behind a sawtoothed brick wall. His redheaded partner wasn't as nimble. He smashed into the opposite structure, his pistol clattering into a nest of rubble, before he pivoted and dashed away. She rounded the corner just in time to see him speed ahead. Malone tracked the smugglers' flickering movements in the moonlight as they wove between half-standing walls.

Reaching a jumble of tumbledown construction that looked more like a ruin than a city block, the smugglers predictably split up. Malone followed the man who had dropped his gun as he peeled off to the right and into a rubble-strewn alley. The smuggler glanced over his shoulder long enough to see her and bent to pull something out of his boot as he loped ahead. She ducked into a scarred crevice between two walls before he could turn again.

She scaled the weathered sandstone building in front of her, digging her hands and boots into jagged pockmarks. She crouched atop it and watched the smuggler five feet below back further into the alley, his eyes scanning for the black-clad inspector. Her polished black boots made nary a sound as she squatted and side-stepped just over the smuggler's head. He continued to squint into the alley, but when a bank of clouds slid away from the moon, Malone's shadow appeared at his feet, and he stiffened.

As the smuggler whirled, derringer raised, Malone kicked a foot out and sent a spray of loose sandstone and grit into his face. He clawed at his eyes and fired high, and Malone slid from the veranda in a rain of debris to land behind him. He turned, blinking frantically as her foot sailed toward his outstretched arm and sent his gun spinning to the ground.

He grasped at his hip with a shaking hand, drew a knife, and rushed at her.

She retreated to the end of the alley and into the cross-street behind it, hoping that he would notice her revolver and reconsider. He hurled the knife instead. As Malone dodged left, the knife wheeled past her elbow and a bullet whistled by her nose. She saw the other smuggler out of the corner of her eye and heard a click as he thumbed back the hammer on his revolver. A quick release of sweat cooled her scalp. Malone dove back into the alley, knocking the redhead off his feet. She drove her elbow into his stomach and rolled past him, kneeling between him and his fallen derringer as he gasped for air. She pocketed it while he struggled to his feet.

"Back out of the alley. Hands behind your head," she said, making sure he saw the grinning "O" of her revolver's muzzle.

He coughed, rising slowly. "He'll shoot me."

"So will I." Malone pointed her gun at his right kneecap.

The smuggler's face went white. "You can't do that!"

"I never miss at this distance."

"But I'm unarmed!"

Malone flicked her revolver at him. "Hands up. Slowly." He took shuffling steps backwards, his lips working wordlessly and his face flushing in alternating shades of rage and panic. "You two must not be close," she said.

The smuggler glanced up from his feet. "Anjoli thinks with his gun, that's all."

"He's still armed. What's that say about you?"

He glared at her. "Says I got other skills."

"Like knife throwing?"

The smuggler's nostrils flared and his jaw clenched, but it was the sudden flicker in his eyes that Malone was watching for. She spun, rolling to the side as a muzzle flashed at the other end of the alley. The redheaded smuggler howled behind her. Malone squeezed her trigger twice, and the figure standing thirty yards away collapsed. She turned back to her recent acquaintance on the ground, hunched over his thigh.

"I'm bleeding," he said, looking up at her.

She tossed him a pair of handcuffs. "Use these."

The man winced, taking a sharp breath through his teeth. "What are those supposed to do?"

"Keep me from using this," Malone said, wagging her gun. She turned back into the alley, pointing her revolver into the dimness. At the other end, Anjoli slumped against a bank of fallen masonry, pawing for his fallen pistol with a mangled hand. Blood poured from two stumps on his right hand and onto the gun's slickened grip. More pooled under his leg, painting the jagged paving stones a shiny black in the moonlight. Anjoli looked up at Malone with dull eyes and slid the blood-wet gun to her feet.

A shadow fell across the alley from the crooked avenue beyond Anjoli. "That was a problem built for two, Inspector Malone."

She holstered her revolver and patted a derringer snuggled against her thigh. "I've got my own pair."

Inspector Richards stepped over the rubble, circling around to Anjoli. He snapped a white handkerchief out of his pocket and grasped the smuggler's hand in it, examining the stumps. Anjoli groaned, and Richards left the bloodied rag in his hand. "Pinch it here and hold tight." Richards straightened and turned back to Malone. "Surgical shot, Malone. Dare I ask the what-ifs?"

"When a contract is eight months old, one less smuggler is the least of our worries. If prisoner transport doesn't show up soon, though..."

Richards glanced over his shoulder. "The welcome wagon's a few blocks back. The driver doesn't know what to do on the surface roads here, if you can call them that, and never mind the subterranean routes. Plenty of time to get these guys patched up and taken to the station."

Malone buttoned her long black overcoat against the night air. "You got here fast."

"You're easy to find," Richards said. "I just follow the gunfire. Or the curses. You have an effect on people." Anjoli moaned again.

Malone leaned against the crumbling wall behind her. "Is that why you always show up after I've passed around the cuffs?"

Richards smiled, a glint of white in the moonlight. "Oh, leave it. I know you wouldn't have it any other way. Besides, Recolettans need to know who keeps their city clean."

She shrugged, looking back down the alley. The hunkered shadow at the other end raised his arms, showing her a pair of glimmering handcuffs.

Richards followed her gaze. "Is that the better half?" Malone nodded. "How'd you know?" he asked.

It was Malone's turn to grin. "He told me." The only reason that Anjoli would have come back for his partner was if he knew about their networks and safehouses. Anjoli would never be safe with his partner in the hands of the Municipal Police, which meant that the other man either had to escape with him or die. The redhead's fear of his partner told Malone that he knew this, too.

A wooden carriage pulled up outside the alley with a clopping of hooves and the groan of wheels. Heavy bars crossed the narrow windows along the sides of the carriage, and the team inside traded muffled orders as they prepared to

bind the smugglers' wounds and load them up. "Since you've
got it from here, I'll walk back to the station," Malone said. "I
can finish my report in a few hours."

"That won't be necessary." Richards turned back down the
alley as four uniformed officers jogged from the carriage. "The
chief has other plans for you," he said, his voice lowered. She
followed, silent. "Break-in at 421 East Eton. One casualty."
Malone met Richards's gaze, not bothering to ask why her,
and why now, after an all-night manhunt.

"Just outside the Vineyard," he said. "Obviously, the chief
wants you to take a look at this as quickly and quietly as
possible. It could be nothing." The edge in his voice suggested
this was too much to hope for. Little crime occurred near the
Vineyard, and for a good reason. It was home to the whitenails,
the most powerful men and women in the city, and the only
thing more formidable than their wealth was their mercenary
sense of justice. Any criminal in that neighborhood would
only hope for the Municipals to catch him first.

To Malone, the Vineyard was even worse than the factory
districts. If something had gone wrong beneath those pristine
marble verandas, it would in no way be a simple matter.

As if reading her thoughts, Richards looked down at the
patterns his boots had scraped into the grit. "There's something
else," he said. "The victim is named Cahill. He's a historian.
Was a historian."

Malone stalked out of the alley, her coat swishing against
her black slacks and knee-high boots. Within a quarter of an
hour, she had left the factory districts for the straight, broad
surface avenues that most Recolettans knew. As if aging in
reverse, the crumbling ruins gave way to towering structures
marking various residences and businesses, whole and austere
and gleaming blue in the moonlight. It was a wonder they had

been so carefully crafted, particularly when city-dwellers spent most of their time underground. Pressed against one another in the fashion of a crowded metropolis, the monuments took on the character of gruff, mustachioed old men, huddled together in their dress coats and frowning upon passersby.

Malone found a hansom cab at the corner and showed her inspector's seal to the driver, giving him an address just beyond her destination. If discretion was imperative, it wouldn't do to travel too close to the Vineyard in the wee hours with a chatty cabbie watching.

As the carriage clattered from the less impressive zones toward the Vineyard, the old men lining the cobbled streets evolved, growing in stature and spreading their arms over tiled avenues. Whether they opened their arms to welcome or to snatch depended entirely upon one's relationship to them.

Recoletta, like all modern cities, had been constructed around the two values that society prized most: security and privacy. Even hundreds of years after the Catastrophe, people still lived underground. Crude shelters had developed into shining palaces and rudimentary tunnels into yawning halls lit by fire and mirrors. Ornate verandas declared the locations and the prestige of their owners in the flashiest manner affordable. Even the larger structures, some of which could easily house several families, never functioned as actual living or workspaces. The real business went on below, hidden from common scrutiny.

This observation became truer as one traveled from stone to marble.

The hansom came to a halt, and Malone walked half a dozen blocks further to a neighborhood seemingly hewn from fine, veined stone. She found herself alone in the surface streets, grateful that the neighbors were too wealthy to be out at this hour. Malone stopped in front of a tall, narrow building of jet-black with a single elevator cage inside. Whereas the neighboring edifices were polished to a sheen that flashed in the moonlight, the one in front of Malone was worn rough and mottled with lichen. Three steps led to a rusty black gate. It was bowed outward, she noticed, and shards of glass and metal trickled from the upper steps to the perfectly aligned cobblestones below.

Boots stomped in the street behind her with dull, crunchy thumps. She turned to the older man trudging toward her. He also wore Municipal black, but his coat was frayed at the edges and faded at his elbows and shoulders. Inspector Carlyle glowered up at her from beneath thick eyebrows.

"I was wondering when our ghost inspector would appear," he said through sagging cheeks.

"Richards sent you," Malone said. She wasn't surprised that Richards had neglected to mention this.

"Over an hour ago. Someone had to keep an eye on things while you were running around." He pushed a lantern into her hands.

Malone caught a whiff of whiskey sourness on his breath. "Smells like you had company." Stepping over the debris, she lit the lantern and called the elevator to the main residence. Carlyle followed close behind. They squeezed into the elevator cage together, and his breath filled the space for the eleven seconds of their descent.

The elevator settled into the bottom of the shaft, presenting them with a wooden door still hanging ajar. Malone took a grateful breath of fresh air. Her pulse slowed ever so slightly as she stepped into the darkened entryway. Dust motes swirled in front of her lantern, and a faint illumination flickered further down the hall.

"You know, this would be a lot easier if you'd flip the gaslights on," Carlyle said.

Malone kept her gaze trained down the hall. "Were they on when you showed up?"

He grumbled something indistinct.

Malone followed the winking light and a wine-colored carpet to a study, a musty affair of bookshelves and worn leather.

It was almost a relief to see the crime confined to one small room. Four books were massed near the door of the study in an assortment of positions, fanned pages folded beneath the weight of their covers. A lone candle resting on a desk in the far corner lit a crumpled corpse slumped next to one shelf and the pile of fallen books at its feet.

Carlyle stood in the doorway while Malone crossed the study.

The shivering light animated the broken body as if it were still struggling to live, and the man's hand, still warm and limp, also suggested a tenuous grasp on life. Bending over the dead man, Malone could just make out the shadow of a bruise at the base of his skull.

"Messy old bastard," Carlyle said. "I thought these fancy folk were supposed to be well kept."

"Does he look like a whitenail to you?"

"Not much I can see without the damn lights."

The deceased was fully dressed in stained and rumpled clothes that he must have worn for several days, unusual for a member of high society, though not for an eccentric workaholic.

The study yielded further evidence that the victim had been less of the former and more of the latter. The patterned wool rugs, though obviously expensive, were threadbare in places and compounded with dirt and spills that had never been cleaned. Some of the volumes lining the walls appeared to be falling apart, and a coating of dust blanketed everything but the books.

Carlyle sneezed. "This guy ever heard of a broom?"

"Looks like he was busy."

"Doing what?"

"That's what I'm here to find out."

Malone hovered over the lit candle. By the substantial pool of warm wax at the base, she guessed it had burned all night. The lid had been removed from the inkpot, and the wet and balding quill lay discarded on the desk, which was otherwise clear. There was every appearance of serious business having taken place throughout the night, but no evidence of the finished product.

She pushed past Carlyle, ignoring his sigh when she finally flipped on the gaslights, and poked around the rest of the house. She might as well have searched in the dark for all the good it did her. A thorough survey of the rest of the house uncovered no other clues: no upturned furniture, no ransacked closets, and there was money and a few valuables left in plain sight.

Malone returned to the study and knelt by the victim. She pulled from his pocket a wallet that, like everything else he owned, appeared well used and ill cared for.

The doorjamb creaked as Carlyle leaned against it. "Any money left in there, Inspector?"

She found his credentials on coffee-stained cardstock that felt soft with age. Werner Thomas Cahill, seventy years old, Doctorate of History. As rare as they were, Malone had never met a historian, but with his disheveled attire and unkempt gray hair, Cahill looked much as she would have expected.

"Any connections?"

"Directorate of Preservation," Malone said, reading from Cahill's papers.

"Obviously. Who else can hire historians?"

"The Quadrivium." Malone held up an ID card from Recoletta's premier university.

Carlyle threw his hands up and turned halfway into the hall as if demonstrating his exasperation to an imaginary audience. "This guy was a couple of blocks from the richest quarter in the city, he worked at two of the top institutions, and yet he lived like a tradesman."

Malone's eyes flicked up to the shelves. "Not everyone likes pretty manners and parties."

Carlyle shivered and tried to cover it by shoving his hands violently into his pockets. "Rich weirdos. You tell me what a history-reading geezer does like. More importantly, tell me when you're done." He marched back into the hall, and moments later couch springs sighed in the parlor.

For all of the luxuries Cahill lacked, he'd owned more than a few things that even the Vineyard dwellers would never have, and they all sat on his bookshelf. As she skimmed the spines of the books lining the room, her heart jumped. She raised her lantern and squinted at the shelves. Nestled among the ancient and modern fiction classics were a handful of titles concerned with history, or at least theories about it. Most historical records had been lost or destroyed in the period immediately following the Catastrophe. The Council restricted the serious study of antebellum history, and any archives and accounts were guarded within the vaults of the Directorate of Preservation.

Seeing history books on display sent Malone's gut roiling. Cahill must have been important to have permission to keep history books at his home. Surely he had permission? Even as she wanted to hide the volumes, to push them deeper into the shelf, she caught her hand creeping toward them, her fingers itching. Perhaps, she thought, they might reveal something about Dr Cahill's mysterious work. She considered this even as she listened for Carlyle's return.

Malone stopped herself. Had these books been relevant to the crime, the assassin would have taken them, too. And if they weren't relevant, then there was no professional reason for her to open them. Fingers tingling in midair, she dropped her hand and stepped back from the shelf. Even a scholar such as Dr Cahill would not keep history books of real danger in his home, and if he did, well, such matters were not among the concerns of the Municipal Police.

She let her gaze wander to the other books on the shelves. Beside and beneath their titles were familiar, reassuring words: *Novel. The Collected Poetry of... Essays and Anecdotes. Short Stories.* These were the kinds of books that appeared in schoolhouses, public libraries, and the salons of the cultured. Censorship didn't feel as bad when you kept the sweetness and light. History and the darker vignettes, on the other hand, remained under the lock and key of trusted authority, like some virulent epidemic. Above all, such powers feared releasing into the air whatever secrets had nearly destroyed the world so many centuries ago.

Malone turned her back to the bookshelves. For all her searching, Cahill's desk was still empty, and she had no way yet of knowing what had filled it a few hours before. Carlyle snored in the next room. It was nearly seven when she blew out the candle and returned to the parlor.

She coughed, and Carlyle jerked awake.

"What now?" he said.

"I go back to the station."

"And me?"

"You wait here for the morgue cart." Malone headed back to the elevator.

Sunlight barely reached the elevator shaft from the veranda's tall windows above. As Malone stepped into the cage, she noticed a faint glimmer between her feet. She reached between the bars of the bottom grating and dug into a crumbling line of mortar in the stone flooring, retrieving a layer of grime and a small key just before the elevator began its ascent. As Malone turned the key between her fingers, her mind spun in quick, concentric circles.

Upon reaching the surface, she tested the key on the gate and found a match. Malone noticed for the second time that the inside of the building was clean, with all of the broken glass on the steps and the avenue just outside. She tucked the key into her pocket, reached her conclusion, and made her way to the station downtown.

Halfway across the city, in more modest quarters, warm, astringent water licked at Jane Lin's elbows as she searched the washbasin. One black pearl button the size of her thumbnail; that was all she needed to save her job. Work with the whitenails would dry up if word got out that she was a butterfingers, or, worse, a thief.

A wool frock coat hung against the opposite wall, its empty buttonhole glaring back at her. She had steamed it to crisp perfection and spot-cleaned it with a toothbrush, yet this somehow made the button's absence even more conspicuous. Now, as she picked through the linen garments in the basin with exaggerated delicacy, trying to find a small, dark button amidst the soapsuds felt like trying to find a thimble on a crowded railcar. Assuming it was there at all.

A knock at the door brought her to her feet with a swift,

startled jump. Wiping her hands on the front of her skirt like a kitchen thief, she unlatched the door for a dour, balding man whose expression suggested that he had just caught a whiff of something awful.

"Mr Fredrick Anders?" he said, his eyes fixed on some point over her head.

"Jane Lin, actually," she said, suddenly conscious of her damp, wrinkled skirt and the drooping bun into which she had tied her dark hair. She straightened, shifting to block his view of the coat hanging against the far wall. "Mr Anders lives one over. Number 2C."

The impeccably dressed man twitched, appearing unaccustomed to anything like a rebuff. "Thank you," he managed. Jane shut the door and turned back to the washbasin in the middle of the floor, where it sat ringed by puddles and suds. She began twirling the clothes inside with a pronged wooden dolly, finally accepting that the priceless button, wherever it might be, wasn't in the basin.

About ninety seconds later came another knock, this one rapid and irregular. Before she could start toward the door, a tall, wiry man bounded in without preamble.

"Jane, what on earth are you doing? Haven't you heard?" he said, breathless. "There's been a murder!"

The way he said it, as if announcing a grotesque exhibit at a street fair, surprised her more than what he said. "A what?" The dolly's wooden handle slipped from her fingers. "When, Freddie? And where?"

"Only last night," he said, a little calmer, "just outside of the Vineyard." His eyes twinkled as he waited for her reaction.

"That's impossible. How…"

"No one knows yet, but trust me, you'll be the first to know when I get word."

Jane mopped a few stray locks away from her forehead. Leaning against the washbasin, the dolly suddenly looked sharp and sinister. "Do you know who died?"

"The Municipals aren't saying much, but it looks like some shriveled government scholar was choked with his own mothballs."

"That's terrible, Freddie." She frowned, pausing for decency before the necessary follow up. "Did you get the assignment?"

His buoyant expression fell, and he ruffled his sandy-brown hair with one hand. "Blocked again by Chiang, the editor with a vengeance." He balled a wad of paper from his pocket and flicked it through an imaginary target and into the fireplace behind Jane. "Or maybe just out-bribed by Burgevich. But I will be covering the grand society ball next week! Take a look at this pair of shoe-shiners." His green eyes sparkled again as he brandished two sheets of vellum adorned with flowing calligraphy.

"Sounds like one of your editors likes you." Jane rubbed the smooth material between thumb and forefinger. "Hardly seems fair that those go to you, though. I'm in that part of town every day of the week." Though short of a miracle, that would soon change.

Fredrick beamed again as Jane grabbed the dolly and returned to her wash. "One of the many perks of career journalism. That's actually what I came by to tell you." He rolled the sheets and tucked them back into his coat. "That, and to invite you along, of course."

Jane stopped mid-press, her fingers tight around the handle. "That's very kind," she said.

Fredrick laughed. "You know me, I'm not doing it to be kind. I can't suffer through all those speeches on my own." He watched her slow, methodical strokes in the basin. "Don't tell me you already have plans."

She stared into the filmy water. "Of course not."

"Then I'm sure you'll clean up fine in whatever you put together."

Jane straightened her back and rested a hand on her hip. "Freddie, I fix clothes for a living. That's the least of my worries."

"Then whatever the hell is it?" Freddie had circled around her and now stood just a few feet from the damaged frock coat.

Jane's eyes flicked from the coat to Freddie. "No offense, but *you*. My clients will be there. And I'll be there with you, a reporter. I don't want to give any of them the wrong idea." It was true, and it was easier to explain than the missing pearl. The last thing she wanted right now was to add Fredrick's hysteria to her own worries.

Fredrick rocked forward and threw his head back. "Oh, Jane, you and your precious reputation."

"And my precious commissions."

Fredrick held up his hands, but his voice carried the tone of an argument already won. "Look, no snooping at the party. Just straight reporting. Besides, most of your clients don't even know what you look like. Unless all the Vineyard housemaids are there, your good name and your good jobs will be fine."

Jane looked down at the linens, unwilling to refute him. "It would be nice to visit the Vineyard without my laundry cart."

"Not to mention without looking like a servant."

"I'm not a servant," she said in a quick monotone. Not yet, anyway. "But I'd like to see whitenails at one of their fancy parties, with all their coattails and ball gowns and gentility." Washing fine clothes for Recoletta's upper crust engendered the desire to see people actually wear them.

"They're not half so endearing as you seem to think," he said, "and they're twice as dangerous."

"I'm sure they're dangerous to someone who makes a living off their secrets." Her eyebrows flicked upward as she gave him a skeptical grin. "But I'm a little more discreet. Not to mention charming. What's the occasion, anyway?"

"A delegation from South Haven is coming by train next week, no doubt to arm-wrestle over farming communes. Naturally, no expenses will be spared." He spread his hands in the air, framing an imaginary canvas. "Brummell Hall, in the heart of the Vineyard, with a sumptuous spread of prime rib, shrimp the length of my finger, pastries light as clouds, and velvet-smooth wines." His eyes took on a wistful glaze.

"This is a celebration in their honor?"

"On the surface, yes. Making an impression, that's what these affairs are really about. The Vineyard is known for its sour grapes."

A kettle filled with a starch mixture whistled from the stove, and Jane went to remove it. "Well, you haven't handed back your invitation. I'm sure it'll be fun, even for a jaded old grouch like you." Though Fredrick was barely in his mid-thirties, he was still a full decade older than Jane and ripe for teasing.

"Let's get one stiff cocktail in you and we'll see who's laughing. But not to worry, I couldn't ruin this for you if I tried." Jane winced inwardly, reflecting that Freddie wouldn't have to try at all if the missing pearl button led to a falling out with her clients.

He glanced at his wristwatch. "I really should get to the office. The paper has to pay me for some kind of work, after all. Ta, Jane." With an exaggerated bow, he backed out of the door.

Alone again, Jane surveyed her den, lined with piles of clothes. With the quiet years she had worked to build a hopeful life here, it left a sluggish ball of dread in her stomach to imagine that it could all disappear after one day's mistake. She was in the habit of glancing through her commissions upon receipt, but she'd been in a hurry when Director Fitzhugh's housekeeper had shoved the bundle into her arms. Now it was impossible to say, and impossible to prove, whether the button had disappeared in her care or before. And it was equally pointless to wonder whether this was an unfortunate accident, an act of sabotage by a housekeeper who'd always stared at Jane's scuffed shoes a little too pointedly, or a convenient mishap arranged by an employer looking for an excuse to hire someone else. One heard of such incidents from time to time.

As plain as it was, Jane's apartment was a private haven. She had a bedroom to herself, a small workroom for her tailoring, and space enough to entertain her friends. She knew every nook and cranny and had swept every corner thrice, and the button wasn't here. The question was, should she confess the problem to Mr Fitzhugh and hope for mercy or try to find a replacement at the market? Not real pearl, certainly, but a near enough approximation?

The question dissolved when Jane recalled a childhood in halls of peeling paint and mildew and nights in crowded, flu-ridden bunks, when she remembered that she lived not half a mile away from the swarming slums and noxious air of the factory districts. She set off for the market. She would save sympathy for a last resort.

CHAPTER 2

THE SUBTLE ART OF EAVESDROPPING

As the sun burned off the early morning chill, Inspector Malone approached the gray marble pavilion of Callum Station, the headquarters of the Municipal Police. Officially named for a famous and respected police chief over three centuries ago, the station was more colloquially known as Calumny Station to anyone who didn't work in it. With their head-to-toe black garb and their reputation for prying, the Municipals caused weeks of gossip for anyone unfortunate enough to receive a visit. Sniffing out smuggling operations and quelling factory district unrest was a thankless job, indeed.

However, this had the side effect of making Malone's final approach agreeably solitary. If they could help it, most pedestrians would walk an extra block rather than pass next to the station. Set in the outer ring of downtown and its respectably cheerful verandas distinguishing high-end shops, offices, and town houses, Callum Station loomed like a pallbearer at a card party. The entire structure radiated gloomy impassivity, from the smooth columns to the broad steps and the steady arches of the roof. The building's one unique feature perched above the drab, gray structure: a beacon inside a narrow tower, lit at all times to symbolize the perpetual vigilance of the Municipal Police.

With one sleepless night behind her and a full day ahead, Malone reflected that this was more apt than ever.

She descended a broad stairway to a spacious underground rotunda lit by the clean, white light of radiance stones that seemed unnecessarily bright this morning. The chemically treated crystals glowed like white-hot fireflies and could, after a few hours exposed to the sun, light a room for days or weeks on end. They preserved some of the natural wavelengths of sunlight, allowing for the lush gardens in the wealthier areas of town. Here, however, they threatened to give Malone a headache.

Several wide corridors sprouted from the rotunda. Malone marched through the largest of these, marked by a pair of grim lion statues and two equally stone-faced guards gripping bayonets.

She followed a pair of burning trenches set high in the passage's walls. Chemists had invented various powders, pastes and oils to enhance the luminosity of flame, extend its life, and even alter its color, and these compounds roiled in almost every fire in the city. With sophisticated mirrors and lenses crafted from mineral and glass composites, no corner of the underground had to remain dark.

Deputy chiefs' offices, conference rooms, and smaller corridors leading deeper into the station lined the hall. Next to one of these stood a young man wearing Municipal black. He was handsome, in an eager, boyish way, with jet hair, a caramel-brown complexion, and a disarming smile. Malone knew the other hundred-odd inspectors by name, and she was acquainted with most of the support staff, but not with this man. Nevertheless, his eyebrows rose in recognition as she approached.

"Inspector Malone! Good morning. You must've just come from Cahill's domicile."

She nodded.

"Excellent. The sweeps who reported the incident are already here. Didn't want to talk to them until you arrived, naturally. I'm sure we'll want to compare notes." The young man tapped his forehead. "Of course. You must be wondering what I'm on about. Chief's assigned me to work with you on the contract."

Malone's muscles tightened as he fumbled in his coat pockets, producing a shiny, newly minted inspector's seal and handwritten orders marked with Chief Johanssen's stamp. "Richards told us he'd sent you, said you should be back within an hour. Or two." For what seemed to be the first time since his rapid introduction, the young man stopped talking long enough to breathe, his eyes wide with expectation.

Malone looked at the orders, half expecting to see him assigned to morgue duty for the day. The two things Malone knew about trainees and junior inspectors were that they rendezvoused on the bottom level of the station and that they never worked with her. Yet it was her name, scratched in blotted black ink, staring back at her. "And you are?"

"Me? I– Oh! How careless. Inspector Rafe Sundar, ma'am." He gave a short chuckle of embarrassment, his graceful features momentarily absurd.

Malone studied him. Extending an arm, she squeezed her lips into a smile. "Pleasure."

A broad grin warmed his face, and he pumped her hand rapidly. His left hand gently pressed her arm into the handshake. Malone preferred the crisp efficiency of a brief, dry squeeze, but Sundar had her in an extended vice grip of friendliness. "The honor is entirely mine, Inspector," he said. "I have to say, I'm thrilled to be working with you. You have quite the reputation around here."

"Yet I know nothing about you. Tell me about your background, Inspector." She eyed him as she pronounced the last word, sounding it out. He blushed.

"I completed my training the week before last with a batch of five other recruits. Top marks in procedure and investigation." He hesitated, shifting on his feet.

"And?"

"Studies in murder and assault cases. Naturally."

"Before that."

Sundar massaged a spot on the floor with his toe. "My background is, you could say, a bit unorthodox. I'm not sure it's particularly interesting, Inspector."

"I'm not asking for conversation's sake."

"Ah. Well, in that case, I came from a four-year career in theatre."

Malone's eyebrows shot up and her lips tightened. "Why the career change?"

Sundar stopped fidgeting. "Too much memorization. I'd gotten into it for the improv."

"I see." She paused, considering him. "Our first order of business is to question the sweeps. Richards will have detained them in the east wing." She trailed off, tapping a black-gloved finger to her chin as she began to turn.

"Yes, the holding lobby on level four. Follow me, please." He nodded and led the way down the narrow hall. She scowled at his back but, with a sigh, allowed him to lead her through the station she knew so well.

The smaller corridor's plain, gray walls tightened around them. The hall curved steadily, concentric with the rotunda, a line of eye-level gas lamps visible for a dozen yards at a time. Passing offices and branching hallways, Sundar began briefing Malone.

"I monitored them until I came to meet you, and I don't think they're involved. They were working on the same schedule as usual – their supervisor came by, and I checked that with him, of course." The inspectors took a left and descended a short flight of stairs. "They've been pretty quiet, but not too quiet, if you know what I mean. Anybody left to their own thoughts in one of those holding rooms would be." He glanced at her, hoping for agreement. "They've done a number on the tea and biscuits we left them, and I haven't caught any fidgeting or whispering. Really, I think they just happened to be at the right place at the right time. For us, I mean." The inspectors entered a small, cluttered room with a downward-facing window built into the far wall. "They didn't show the usual signs of trying to hide something, Inspector."

Malone gave Sundar an appraising glance and glided over to the window. It was common for sweeps and other groundskeepers to stumble upon crime scenes. Wandering all corners of Recoletta at any given hour, day, and especially night, the groundskeepers formed a veritable army of maintenance men and women who emerged from their homes in the poorer districts in shifts, cleaning public spaces, relighting torches, and charging and replacing radiance stones as needed.

Unfortunately, with the exception of whitenails, groundskeepers were the most difficult to interview. That they reported such a high percentage of crimes often cast them in suspicion. That they received the lowest wages in the city only deepened public distrust. The groundskeepers heartily returned these sentiments, but criminal penalties against failing to report a crime, not to mention the knowledge that such an omission would only worsen their precarious reputation, compelled them to grudgingly come forward.

Two grimy men with circles under their eyes and haggard expressions sat twitching their beards in a bare, colorless chamber. The combination of artful lighting and a one-way mirror concealed the observing window, and Malone watched as the sweeps sipped from mugs of lukewarm tea and chatted in monosyllables, their eyes hooded by the lights and their exhaustion.

She folded her arms and looked at Sundar's reflection in the glass. "Show me your top marks in investigation."

"Of course." He ducked out of the observation room and reappeared in the door of the holding room a few moments later. Malone started; though she had seen that same uniform, the same neat slick of hair, and the same rounded eyes, less than a minute earlier in the observation room, the man beneath them seemed taller, older, and quietly assertive.

The groundskeepers looked up at Sundar, pulling the mugs between their propped elbows. He strode to the table where they sat, shook their hands, and addressed them with polite warmth. He seemed transformed from the nervous and excitable young man in the hall, a confident smile underlining his every word.

"Gentlemen, thank you for your time," Sundar said. The groundskeepers watched him silently. "You must know that we appreciate your assistance. Your reports contribute greatly to the peace and stability of Recoletta."

One of the groundskeepers sniffed.

"Of course, I also know that you don't have any choice but to be here. If you weren't, some goon with a bad attitude and a blackjack would be at your door, giving you hell and halitosis. You'd end up here anyway, and probably with an extended stay at the Barracks," Sundar said, referring to the headquarters of the City Guard and its infamous prison on the western end of town.

One of the sweeps plunked his mug onto the table, crossing his arms. "You got questions or what?"

Sundar nodded at the mug. "Yeah. How's the tea?"

"Horse scat," said the same man, and the other laughed. Sundar smiled.

"You're not kidding. They gag us with that stuff every morning. Part of the daily briefing." The sweeps didn't laugh, but concessionary grins slid across their faces, and Malone saw their postures relax as they slumped more comfortably in the stiff chairs. "Between you and me, though," Sundar said, settling into a seat across from them, "I know you've got nothing to do with this. Someone was going to stumble across the veranda sooner or later, and it just happened to be you two. So, why don't you just tell me what you saw?" Slipping into the interrogation, Sundar asked them about their routine and their findings that morning, and they answered amiably, gulping their tea and thumping the table as they talked.

After half an hour, Sundar shook their hands again and walked them to the door. "That addresses all of our questions, but we'll contact you if anything else comes up. I'll have someone see you out."

Sundar and the two sweeps disappeared from the holding lobby and, two minutes later, he returned to the observation room. For all of the acting talent he'd shown in the chamber below, he hid his triumph poorly.

"Passing grade," Malone said, her eyes still lingering on the room below. "Barely. You forgot something."

"What's that?"

"You interrogated them together."

Sundar nodded once. "I know we usually separate witnesses upon arrival, but, respectfully, I thought I could get more information from them this way." Malone tilted her head, and Sundar continued. "If they wanted to make up a story, they had plenty of time to rehearse it on their way to the station. A little goodwill can go a long way, and I'd rather have them lie freely to me together than clamp shut in separate lobbies."

Malone felt her own jaw clamp tight. "As long as you can tell the difference."

"Respectfully, ma'am, I think I can."

She pulled a silver pocket watch from her coat. "Meet me in Chief Johanssen's office in five minutes. I'll cover what I found at the scene."

She reviewed Sundar's notes from his initial observation. To her disappointment, they were neat and thorough. If she was going to get a reprieve from babysitting, she'd have to talk to Chief Johanssen directly.

Malone returned to the main hallway and followed the fiery trenches to its end. A shallow alcove framed a wide, solid door. Malone pushed it open to reveal a familiar scene: Farrah, the chief's buxom assistant, drowsily scanning several pages and twirling a pen in her free hand. She looked up with a characteristic half-smile.

"Go on in," the redhead drawled, leaning back in her chair. "Chief's waiting for you."

Malone crossed the threshold into a second, grander office, paneled with oak and furnished with green leather chairs. Chief Johanssen, a thickset man in his late fifties, sat at a handsome desk opposite the double doors, a roaring fire warming his back. Brass lamps lined the walls.

"Malone. He nodded in her direction. "Come in. Sundar." Malone followed his gaze to a point just behind her right shoulder where the younger man had materialized. Sundar smiled in greeting as they both moved toward the desk. Johanssen rose and shook their hands, his warm, coarse paws enveloping theirs.

"Glad to see you both." He settled once again into his armchair. He gestured to the two seats in front of his desk, and the inspectors lowered themselves into the squeaking leather. "Malone, Sundar tells me the sweeps were clean," he said with a wry grin, "but tell me what you found at the address."

"Broken gate, sir, just like the sweeps said. Cahill was dead; his study showed signs of the struggle, but nothing else was disturbed."

The first stray worry lines cracked across Johanssen's forehead. "Your analysis?"

"Murder with intent, sir."

Johanssen folded his hands, and Malone waited for the inevitable opposition. "No question about a break-in," he said. "But this sounds like a struggle and an accident. At Cahill's age, it's all too easy."

Malone understood the chief's hesitation. Violent crime outside the factory districts, populated with the more desperate types, was uncommon. Except for the occasional poisoning or duels between rivals, they grew exceedingly rare as one approached the Vineyard and the neighborhoods that rippled out from it.

"Doubtful, sir," she said. "There was bruising at the base of his skull."

Sundar rubbed the curve at the back of his own head. "Below the bump? That would be hard to hit accidentally unless he fell backward into a desk or shelf or something."

"Right," Malone said, cutting Sundar off and continuing before Johanssen could protest further. "And Cahill was slumped against the wall when I found him. No blood, skin, or hair on the furniture. That suggests a blunt instrument, something that the murderer took with him. No bruising around the wrists or forearms. No attempt to restrain him."

Johanssen's lower lip pushed into a momentary pout as he sucked his teeth, thinking. "The motive?"

"Theft, sir."

"Of what? Cahill's street is filled with merchants and bankers. All more tempting targets."

"The murderer wanted information, not valuables. Dr Cahill was a historian, and he was working on something before he was killed." Malone described the scene in Cahill's study, and the corner of Johanssen's mouth twitched when she mentioned the history books and the empty desk.

"If I may," Sundar said, clearing his throat, "the sweeps mentioned the broken gates, but according to them, the gates were bent outwards, and they said they saw shattered glass on the steps outside. Isn't this the opposite of what would happen if someone broke in?"

"If someone broke in," Malone said. "No one had to." At that, she produced the key she had found near the elevator.

Johanssen squinted at it. "Go on."

Malone crossed one leg as she continued, putting the key on Johanssen's desk. "How the murderer got this is the real question, but it tells us that he planned. It also tells us that he's not a professional. Whether he panicked or stumbled, he dropped his key on the way up the elevator, and he couldn't take the time to return for it. Or couldn't see it in the dark. The gate was rusted enough for him to break it open with a few good kicks or a couple blows from his weapon. He only had to break out."

"Why not leave through the subterranean door?" Sundar asked. Every business and residence had one, whether or not it had its own veranda. Recoletta, after all, was built around its subterranean thoroughfares and warrens. "He wouldn't have had to break that one to open it from the inside, would he?"

"Have you ever been to East Eton? The subterranean avenue is one of the main roads into the Vineyard, and Cahill's domicile is twenty yards from a railcar stop. The assassin would be in plain view for three or four blocks with nowhere to hide."

"Easier to slip among the buildings on the surface," Sundar said.

"Obviously."

Exhaling, Johanssen furrowed his brow. "And all this for a stack of papers?"

Malone laced her fingers, waiting.

"What concerns me is where the murderer got a key. Assuming you're right," Johanssen added. "You know how people are about security, especially on that side of the city. There's hardly a locksmith in Recoletta who would've made that."

He scratched a cheek with his knuckles. "Farrah should have the contract by the end of the day, Malone. In the meantime, Sundar will assist you."

The moment she'd been waiting for. "Respectfully, sir, getting the bureaucrats to talk will be hard enough without a rookie in tow." She sighed. "No offense."

"None taken." And he looked like he meant it.

The chief stared down at his desk for a long moment. "Sundar, wait outside."

The younger inspector disappeared behind the double doors. Chief Johanssen turned his gaze to Malone.

"I know this isn't how you'd have it, but make an exception for this contract. He needs your experience, and I need to know where that key came from." Johanssen leaned forward, shadows pooling under his heavy brows. "Besides, Inspector Sundar has a few talents you don't. People skills are chief among them."

She gritted her teeth. "I've noticed, sir."

He nodded. "You also know that we don't see murders in Dr Cahill's district. Expect that charm to come in handy."

Malone rose and bowed. "Yes, sir." She left and followed Sundar into the hall, noticing Farrah's hopeful gaze in his direction.

"The coroner's report won't be ready until tomorrow," Malone told her new partner as they paced toward the rotunda. "In the meantime, we should try to locate some of Cahill's old acquaintances."

"Don't we need to wait for the Council to approve the contract?" The Municipal Police received contracts from the Council to investigate crimes, petty theft and serial murder alike. They provided the formal authorization to proceed.

"It's not that strict," Malone said. "We don't wait on a case like this. One of the benefits of not working directly under the Council is that we can be more efficient."

"That's what separates us from the City Guard, right? They take their orders from the Council, and we just liaise?"

"That, and most of them have scat for brains," Malone said, relishing Sundar's discomfort. And that's why we're the investigators and they're the muscle, she thought.

"Oh." Sundar paused, digesting this new information. "We could start with the Directorate of Preservation."

"Getting information out of the directorates is a nightmare, and Preservation is the worst. We'll need the contract and, probably, additional signatures from half a dozen councilors."

"Can we afford to wait?"

"We don't have a choice."

He smiled, fixing his eyes down the hallway. "If you'll allow me, Inspector Malone, I think I can handle this."

She glanced sideways at Sundar. Casual confidence wafted off of him like a scent. Nurtured, she guessed, by all the entitlements of expensive schooling, attentive parents, and easy good looks. She resigned herself to this one concession. Either he'd botch this and the chief would finally have to listen to reason, or he'd succeed and they'd get something useful.

"Alright, Sundar. Show me what you can do."

News of the murder uptown had already seeped through the city, and the Municipals' secrecy only fueled the rumor mill. Jane's central concern, however, was replacing the pearl button before her evening deliveries.

She worked her way toward the center of town. At Tanney Passage, the capillary tunnels opened into a cavernous conduit. Her walkway overlooked a window-speckled chasm. Homes and offices were built into the chasm walls below her, where silhouettes bobbed behind windows and laundry fluttered over the abyss. It all looked so precarious.

She drew back from the gulf. A notice board in the passage advertised the Cahill murder on a garish red sheet. The shreds of crimson hanging around the announcement suggested that someone, most likely in the City Guard, had already removed several installations of the same. She pressed on.

Arching bridges spanned the chasm ahead of her, and railcar tracks punched through the rock below. The railcars dove through soot-blackened boreholes in the stone like great metal worms, and the lights in the nearest windows blinked whenever they thundered by. She boarded one bound for the Spine.

When the railcar finally wheezed to a halt, Jane emerged at Recoletta's central thoroughfare.

Almost half a mile in diameter and stretching from one end of the city to the other, the Spine always left her feeling small. Eight different avenues lined the Spine's curving walls, and a network of railcars and trolleys ran along it. Unfortunately, she was realizing that even something small could create a big problem. She quickened her pace, moving in and out of pools of light from the skylights above.

She took a lift to a higher street and passed one of the fire-lined trenches carved into the tunnel. The trenches didn't stand out this early in the afternoon, but at night, they glowed all the way from the edge of town to the Council's seat at Dominari Hall. They looked like burning ribs, as if some serpentine behemoth had swallowed them all. Jane preferred the evening view near the top, where suspended radiance stones mirrored the eclipsed night sky.

As she drew nearer to the center of town, tiny arbors and gardens sprouted from the wide walkway at the bottom of the Spine, and the gleaming threads of cable cars spanning the tunnel grew more numerous. She turned into a warren of smaller passages that wound through the market.

Jane came to a large cave amidst the tunnels and saw the tiers, stores, and stalls of the market proper, spread over three levels: raw materials and tools on the bottom level, wrought goods on the second, and foodstuffs on the top, where the ventilation drove the odors of fish and cheese quickly to the surface. Hope quickened within her as the hubbub reminded her that one could find almost anything here.

The wares on display came from near and far: from her own neighbors and from cities whose names she could not pronounce. Here, Jane could find dyes made in the factories near her home, buy fabrics woven in cities hundreds of miles away, and browse, if not purchase, jewelry from lands separated by waters and mountains. It was the closest she, and most other city-dwellers, got to travel.

Goods on the top level originated closer to home. Foodstuffs came from the farming communes, settlements established dozens of miles outside the cities, where people lived aboveground and cultivated the plants and animals that nourished most of civilization. For such a vital link in Recoletta's economy, the farmers themselves were notably absent. Their only contact with city-dwellers came in the trade that followed the railroads. In the minds of most Recolettans, farmers were little more than figments, and given the general disrepute with which city-dwellers viewed surface-dwellers, most were glad to keep it that way.

Jane found the bead and button stalls quickly. Forcing her eyes to slow down, to comb each bin and display, was an act of sheer willpower. Her mind was focused on a carefully rendered image of the remaining buttons, and each specimen she saw in front of her was an inferior imitation. Too light, too opalescent, too fake. Goaded by the double edges of hope and dread, she ventured to the jewelers' stalls. Even there, she realized that none of the specimens resembled the missing button closely enough. It was a small relief to be free of a solution she couldn't afford.

She was leaving the jewelry stands when she saw two overcoats of a similar cut and quality to the frock coat hanging in her apartment. The men wearing them were getting closer.

Moving toward her through the crowd were two men dressed in inconspicuous but spotless suits. Their stride set them apart, as did the manner in which people instinctively created passage for them. Arguing in hushed voices and gesturing privately, they were attempting discretion, though not successfully, in Jane's opinion. She knew before looking that their hands would be impeccably manicured, the nails trimmed to a fashionable length a half-inch past the fingertips. Jane wondered what whitenails were doing in the market when they had hordes of servants to run their errands for them. She sidled up next to a turquoise stall and pretended to examine the wares while she listened.

"Of course I'm concerned; the man was slaughtered in his home last night," said one.

The second voice followed in more controlled tones. "Don't be ridiculous. That was a complete anomaly. An accident."

"Can you honestly believe that? You know as well as I that this was no accident."

"All I am saying," said the second man, "is that he was old, certainly a tad eccentric, and in poor health as it was." His voice adopted a harder quality. "More importantly, he was not in the same position as you or I. You need not worry yourself about this."

The first voice returned, sounding more subdued. "I'm just beginning to wonder..." He paused.

"Wonder?" There was quiet menace in the second man's voice, like the muted hiss from a covered pit of serpents.

"...if this is such a good idea after all." The first man trailed off, and his companion cut in quickly.

"Not a good idea?" he said, raising his voice. "Not a good idea? You have picked a most inopportune time to articulate your doubts, Phineas." He nearly shouted at his fellow.

"Not so loudly, please! Anyone could–"

"You are the one who requested this little soiree in the first place. And I have already told you, there's no one here to listen." He swept an arm at the passing currents of people, gesturing as though they were little more than livestock milling about them.

"We're much safer discussing matters here than we would have been in the Council chambers or the directorates," the second man said through clenched teeth. As if to prove a point, he gave a cursory glance around the booths. Haggling merchants and encumbered pedestrians paid them no heed. In fact, the cacophony of voices, the rattle and clang of goods, and the gritty shuffle and thump of a hundred footsteps all around them drowned their voices beyond a radius of a few yards. The second man looked past Jane and continued speaking.

"The decision has already been made," he said to the man called Phineas, "and it's too late to undo this. Besides, you recall well the other misfortune." He leaned close to his friend. "And as I remember, you had no qualms with that incident," he whispered silkily.

Jane saw both men clearly, now, and there was something familiar about the pair that she could not quite place. Phineas was a short, round, balding man with a swab of white hair behind his ears and tiny spectacles that he kept adjusting with unsteady hands. Shining with perspiration and rocking anxiously in place, he looked like an oversized, frowning egg. His companion was a tall, thin man with curly white hair crowning his head and gracing his chin like a dollop of cream. For his arched nose and assertive strut, he reminded Jane of a rooster. The rooster cocked an ear at the egg.

"Yes, I remember that," said Phineas, avoiding the rooster's beady stare. "And maybe it was the wrong thing to do. But you're right, we're beyond the point of second-guessing ourselves – on both counts – and I suppose I would not really be in favor of halting everything anyway. It just concerns me, that's all I meant."

The other man straightened his posture again and rubbed his pharaoh's beard. "I am well aware, and let me assure you again that you do not need to worry. Even if what happened last night is at all related to us, and allow me to say again that such a coincidence is highly improbable, it cannot touch you or me. We are perfectly insulated." The rooster almost cooed the last word, smiling.

Phineas grinned. "Yes, I'm sorry for carrying on like this. It was just the shock, really." He hesitated and looked up at his companion. "But, look, I don't think there will be any need—"

"I won't breathe a word of this to the rest of the Council. We can, as you said, chalk this up to shock."

"Yes, shock. Good..."

The taller man guided Phineas by the shoulder, leading him once more into the sea of people. As she watched them go, Jane saw the rooster give his companion what could have almost been a reassuring pat on the back.

CHAPTER 3

THE DIRECTORATE OF PRESERVATION

If the Spine was the backbone of a long-dead monster, the bureau district was its cold, hardened heart. The passersby here were few and discreet, ducking in and out of featureless doorways and offices with their heads down. In their black attire, the inspectors blended in. Uniformed members of the City Guard with rifles and polished short swords stood at every corner. Their dead eyes scanned the pedestrians and lingered on the two inspectors. Malone glanced at Sundar, who looked like a young bloodhound on a scent.

It was easy to forget how close the bureau district was to the opulent Vineyard. Even the councilors and other whitenails who oversaw the directorates seemed to shed their colors here, like butterflies turning into moths.

The inspectors turned a corner, approaching a fifteen-foot high rectangular tunnel set in a plain rock facade at the end of the street.

Malone searched Sundar's face. "Let's hear this plan of yours." The dank air clung to her skin.

He smiled. "Charm and invention, Inspector Malone. With the right measure of both, you can worm your way into – or out of – anything."

It sounded like an audition strategy. Malone thought of the other possible leads, Cahill's neighbors and friends, their usefulness melting into fear and forgetfulness while she and Sundar wasted time. Knots formed at the corners of her jaw. "Don't tell me this is how you got by in your procedures class."

"One chance, Inspector. If I don't get us in, you won't hear another peep from me for the rest of our investigation."

Indeed, Malone thought.

Proceeding in silence, they reached the subterranean entry to the Directorate of Preservation.

Sundar stopped and lifted a hand, motioning for Malone to wait. Frowning, she watched as he slipped off his gloves, pocketed his seal, and buttoned his overcoat, obscuring his fitted black shirt. He looked up, and Malone followed suit. Nodding, he pulled a pair of wire-rimmed spectacles from his breast pocket and adjusted them on his finely arched nose, affecting a studious air. It was all Malone could do to repress a sigh.

"Are you serious?"

He winked. "Trust me."

The dim hallway ended in a small reception room where an elderly secretary scrawled behind her desk in the faint gaslight. Miraculously, she was surrounded not by armed guards, but by cracked walls and decades-old gas lamps. It amazed Malone that even the most mysterious directorate in Recoletta carried a whiff of mundane bureaucracy. Every office lobby in the world must feel the same. The secretary looked up at the sound of their boots, blinking her mole-like eyes at them.

Sundar clasped his hands and rested his forearms on the desk, and Malone glimpsed a thin, red cord hanging to the side. A panic alarm. Sundar would have only one chance to bypass her, and he would have to choose his words carefully.

And he predictably began with polite nothings. "Good day, ma'am."

The secretary squinted at him. "Your business?"

He swallowed. "You'll kindly pardon my confusion, but we're looking for the Directorate of Preservation. Could you, by chance, show us the way?"

"You're standing in it," the secretary said. Malone bit her tongue and hoped that Sundar had more to his act than this.

"How fortuitous. Not too many markings on the streets in this area, I'm afraid."

"Most people who come here know where they're going."

Sundar flashed a radiant smile. "Never said better." He reached up to scratch a spot behind his ear. "Now, to business. We're here as–"

He did not finish. A shining disk arced through the air between them, landing somewhere below the secretary's desk. Malone winced, waiting for the secretary to dive for the panic alarm.

"My lens!" Sundar felt the empty space in his frames. "How terribly embarrassing. I knew I should have had these mended. I do hope you can find it down there, I'm positively helpless without my glasses." Malone caught the thespian's flourish as he recited his lines. It felt like Sundar was overdoing it, but, even so, the secretary didn't seem to notice.

Busied and thrown off balance by the distraction, the secretary bent over the floor, patting it for the missing lens. Malone peered over the counter and looked at her ledger.

At last the secretary stood up again. "Here." Sundar slipped off his glasses and gave them to her. When she had pressed the lens into place, he leaned forward to allow her to slide the glasses onto his face.

"Thank you so much," Sundar said. "I'm afraid I can never see straight to pop it in myself." The secretary's hand brushed his cheek.

"But my, what soft hands you have," he said.

Malone could not believe her ears.

"However do you manage?" he said. "All that paperwork must suck the moisture right out."

To Malone's astonishment, she saw blooms of color rising in the secretary's wan cheeks, and she realized that the woman was falling under the persuasion of that graceful nose and those delicately curved lips.

"Almond oil and beeswax." She smiled. "I keep a little jar of it under my desk."

"Too clever! And it's those little acts of inventiveness that say so much about a person, don't you think? Well, I'm sorry to have gone on so," he said. The secretary didn't appear to mind. "But we're here for research. I'm Professor Stewart, and this is my supervisor, Professor Donner. I believe we have an appointment?"

The secretary shifted through her papers, frowning. "You're not listed anywhere."

"I'm afraid this whole matter was rather last minute," Sundar said. "I don't mean to seem difficult, but this appointment is quite crucial to our trip here, and, as we're obligated to return tomorrow, we really won't have another opportunity." The secretary glanced up, a doubtful expression creeping back into her face. "We're visiting from South Haven, you see," he added.

Recognition flashed in the secretary's small eyes. Seizing the advantage, Malone jumped in. "If you'll check with Councilor Hollens, or with Dr Hask, I'm certain one of them could clear this up for us."

The secretary pursed her papery lips, wavering. After a moment's hesitation, she rose. "Wait here," she said. "Ten minutes." She scuttled through the door beyond her desk and disappeared with a quickness that belied her age. Not wasting a moment, Malone darted behind the desk and skimmed the directory. An instant later, she motioned for Sundar to follow her toward the elevators.

"Good work," she murmured. "How did you know to mention South Haven?"

He shrugged. "A hunch. The Council's hosting a delegation from South Haven at the gala next week, so it seemed as reasonable as anything. Why do you ask?"

"There's a party here from South Haven."

"Really?"

"No one's scheduled to visit today, but there are five appointments throughout the week." She looked at Sundar's wide eyes. "You might have noticed if you hadn't been busy flirting with the secretary."

He smiled. "But then you wouldn't have gotten to peek behind her desk."

"Anyway, all of these delegations meet with Dr Charley Hask." They stopped at the end of the hall.

"Where can we find him?"

"Level 4. Straight down."

Sundar started toward a stairwell, but Malone whistled and pointed to the elevator shaft. Empty as it was, the inspectors could see the bare stone walls, ribbed with steel tracks and pocked with access tunnels. Producing a collapsible metal lever, Malone pried open the safety gate as Sundar watched, mouth agape.

"Is that regulation, Inspector?"

"The Directorate will post guards on every landing of

the stairway, and they won't be as gullible," she said before leaping into the shaft and grabbing the cable. "I'd put those gloves back on if I were you."

"Are we supposed to be doing this?"

"We're supposed to get answers. Besides, you just impersonated a foreign official and lied to a directorate representative."

Sundar gave Malone time to slide down several feet before jumping in after her.

"By the way," he said, attempting not to wheeze as he adjusted his hold on the cable and wound his legs around it, "how'd you know to mention Hollens?"

"He's supervised this directorate for years," she said. "That's where the experience comes in." Loosening their grips, the two slid down the cable, their hands protected by the long black gloves.

As she reached the fourth floor, Malone slowed to a halt. She leaned and stretched her arm, grabbing one of the rungs just below a small service shaft, and swung toward it. Crawling into the narrow chute, she heard the elevator below lurch into motion. Sundar dove for a rung and, smacking gracelessly into the wall, pulled himself into the shaft with a grunt. After a short crawl, they reached a deserted corridor and extracted themselves from the ductwork, brushing the dust from their coats.

"We have maybe five minutes before the secretary realizes we're gone," Malone said.

Sundar nodded, still catching his breath from the crawl. "Then does she come looking for us or assume we gave up?"

"If she starts a search, that's another five minutes, tops." The room just beyond their hall was almost silent, but the draft puffing around the corner suggested a large cavern and, both inspectors knew, much to search.

"How lucky do you feel today?" Sundar said.

"In a place like this, not at all." Turning at the end of the hall, they reached a cavern partitioned by bookshelves. Men and women bent over hardwood desks, skimming texts and scribbling notes while their lips mouthed silent words. In fact, the only noises were the scratch of quill on paper and the whisper of ancient pages. The austere white lighting, undecorated walls, and straight corners contrasted with the stacks of books: colorful and chaotic-looking rows framed by ladders.

"Not a good place for firelight," Sundar said. Malone snorted. "I still don't get it, though," he mumbled.

"What?"

"A place like this. You'd think they'd have a little more security up front, right?"

"They don't need to. How many people do you think wander into the bureau district, let alone this directorate, without a good reason?"

"I see your point."

"Not all of it." Malone picked up a slim hardback from the table nearest her. She thrust it out at Sundar, who instinctively stepped back and pulled his hands away.

"Afraid of a paper cut, Inspector?"

"The penalty for owning unauthorized books..." He trailed off, his eyes widening. Other than the murder of a whitenail, the possession of unedited, unapproved texts was the most severely punished, and certainly the rarest, crime in Recoletta.

"Never mind that you're an inspector on an investigation," Malone said, "your response is automatic. Now imagine that for everyone who doesn't have a silver seal."

No sooner had the inspectors taken stock than slapping footfalls and shrill wheezing broke the near-silence.

"Just what are you doing down here? This is a confidential study, no visitors allowed!"

"Roane and Rodriguez. We've come to see how the work is progressing," Malone said, cutting him off with a cold stare.

The man's face underwent a staggering series of transformations as he flipped between apology, confusion, and suspicion. "I had no idea you were here, Doctors. Pardon me, but we were not expecting you until–"

"Yet here we stand," said Sundar, relishing his new role. "And as you are aware, we're on a tight schedule. Now, if you please." He gestured vaguely down the stacks.

The man bobbed his head. "Many apologies, sir and madam. Allow me to take you to Dr Hask, who must be expecting you."

Falling in behind their escort, Sundar leaned close to Malone. "Not too shabby yourself, Roane. Or are you Rodriguez?"

"Quiet."

As they passed between the desks and inhaled the room's strange, musky perfume, Sundar craned his neck to see the scholars and their books. Even Malone was surprised. These were not the anemic, fusty bookworms one usually envisioned, cramped between parchment stacks and chamber pots. They looked lean and driven. She glimpsed a few titles in recognizable script: names like *Behemoth*, *Art of War*, and *Heart of Darkness*. As they continued, Malone fixed her eyes down the hall, monitoring every bend and corner in their path. Sundar's lingered just a little longer on the mysterious titles.

The bookcases reached from the floor to the ceiling, where chain link gates hung. Expressionless supervisors with lists and medieval keyrings manned the shelves, and whenever a scholar requested or returned a book, the nearest supervisor jotted a note. Malone pitied the overseer whose job it was to account for every book at the end of the day. She turned to their guide.

"I hope that Cahill's death will not impede progress unduly."

"His loss will be felt, since he was heavily involved with the project. But I doubt that this inconvenience will cause too many setbacks."

"What are the chances of this sort of 'inconvenience' happening again?"

"Well, ma'am, I guess that depends on who you ask. The higher-ups are assuring us that this is just a nasty coincidence, but, between you and me," he said in a lowered voice, "a few people look worried."

Sundar glanced around the tables. "They look pretty calm to me."

"Hm? Oh, most of them don't know the half of it – not yet. It's some of the upper echelon that's looking real twitchy."

"How is the directorate going to cooperate with the authorities?" Malone asked.

"You mean the Municipals? I wouldn't know about that. That's a question for Dr Hask."

Footsteps approached again, rapid and determined. Pages rustled and flapped as the newcomer and his palpable rage drew near.

"Badge, badge, badge, Gowlitz! Do you see a visitor's badge? On either of them?" The interloper's mustache was waxed to a thin pair of upward-pointing clock hands.

"Sir, they're part of the panel from Sou–"

The smaller man rounded on him. "It's a rhetorical question, you idiot. That means no talking from you. Or perhaps you'd like to explain this to Dr Hask?"

Gowlitz's guilty silence only enraged him further. "Back to your desk, and keep your mouth shut."

Ashen white, the researcher mumbled a vague formality and retreated. The furious man returned his attention to the inspectors, his eyes popping.

"This is all quite unnecessary. I'm Dr Rodriguez and this is my colleague, Roane," Sundar said. "We're here from South Haven to meet with Dr Hask."

"Not a chance." The words came before the angry man could open his mouth again. The speaker, a woman with a melodious but controlled voice, had materialized in the midst of the confusion, and she regarded the two detectives with a gaze every bit as unflinching as Malone's. "But I shall be eager to learn how you managed to get down here in the first place, as poor liars as you both are," she said. Sundar looked offended.

Malone shrugged. "Then as inspectors of the city, we demand to speak with Dr Charley Hask." She presented her seal.

The woman gave it a cursory glance. "I'll have someone see you out."

Malone took a step forward. "I'd hate to make the kind of exit that would upset your researchers. I'd really hate to tell them about my current theory regarding their colleague's death. Perhaps Dr Hask could clear things up for me. We won't take much of his time."

The woman looked as if she had bitten into a lemon. "I am Charley Hask. Follow me to my office and we can sit down."

Charley Hask looked young, particularly with her petite stature and short blond coif, but Malone estimated that she couldn't be a day under fifty. From her perfectly linear stride to her serene expression, Dr Hask radiated confidence and calculation. She also looked like the type of woman who could deliver a withering insult with a pleasant word and a smile.

When they reached her office against the back wall, Dr Hask opened the door and motioned them inside. "VERITAS" was inscribed above it, the recessed letters filled with gold paint. Malone looked at Hask.

"What is 'veritas'?"

She smiled. "Our directorate's motto. It means 'truth', Inspector."

Sundar peered at her. "With a big 'T' or a little one?"

Hask gave him a languorous head-to-toe twice over. "You're clever for eye candy."

The office was organized and well lit. A gaunt, older man was already standing inside, now gazing at the newcomers in puzzlement. In his arms he carried long, bundled rolls of paper, like baguettes. Seeing the inspectors, he clutched his papers a little more tightly against his chest. Hask turned to him.

"I apologize, but we'll have to continue our discussion at a later date. Dominguez, please escort Mr Fitzhugh to the surface," she said to the mustachioed man.

Fitzhugh and Dominguez brushed past the two inspectors, the latter with a final contemptuous glance over his shoulder.

"Now," Hask said, sitting behind her desk, "I take it you have a few questions for me."

Malone took Fitzhugh's empty chair. "We're investigating the death of Dr Werner Cahill."

"Of course. Yes, Cahill worked under my direction until his untimely death. We were all much grieved to hear of it," Hask said, her placid eyes unblinking.

"Then he worked here, on this floor?" Sundar asked.

"Typically, yes."

"And the rest of the time?"

"Cahill was one of our senior researchers. His work occasionally called for light travel," Hask said.

"What did he do here?" Malone said.

"Why, he did what we all do in this directorate," said Hask, her palms open. "We reconstruct the past, using clues from what texts we have managed to recover."

"The state of Dr Cahill's study suggests that he was working on something just before he died." Malone said. "What was it?"

She crossed her legs. "Only he could have told us that."

"Why would he have been working so late and away from the office?"

Hask said, "I think I will have to give you the same answer."

"You're not answering me at all."

Hask's eyes narrowed. "Inspector, let me be frank. I don't know what Cahill was working on, and I couldn't tell you if I did. You saw the study where he died; what did you find there?"

"Nothing. Whatever he was working on was gone when I arrived." Hask blanched and folded her hands. Malone continued. "What kind of project could have incited a murder, Dr Hask?"

"Separating the truth from fiction is a dangerous labor, Inspector," she said.

"Veritas," Malone said.

Hask smiled again. "Precisely. As I said, it's our motto."

Next to Malone, Sundar sighed and rolled his eyes.

"Could this be the work of someone within your directorate?" Malone said.

"Absurd. What would give you an idea like that?" Hask dismissed the idea with a wave of her hand, but she inclined toward the inspectors.

Malone decided not to mention the key, and she silenced Sundar with a quick look. "The rumor mill is already churning,

Doctor. This incident has disturbed some of the other scholars. Why, if there's no connection?"

"They spend their days in a cave filled with books, trying to make sense of old stories about murder, deceit, and war. What else would you expect?"

"I would expect you to be more cooperative, Dr Hask, seeing as we serve the same authority. Would you rather help me solve this or allow someone else to steal your secrets?"

Hask leaned into her chair's padded headrest. "As always, you Municipals assume that there is some hidden agenda, some paramount evil that demands your attentions. It's a tired story, and I'm afraid I've read it before."

"All the same, I need to see what Cahill and his colleagues have been working on."

"That's confidential information," said Hask, "which you would need a warrant to see. In fact, you will need one to continue this conversation. My time and patience for a courtesy interview have quite expired. Dominguez." The haughty man reappeared in the doorway. "Please escort our guests to the surface." Dominguez nodded and began marching the inspectors out of the office. Sundar elbowed past him.

"Someone's got you on a short leash if that's the best you can give us."

"I'm in the business of giving orders, not answers. This is a bureaucracy, boy. Get used to your place."

A silent Dominguez led Malone and Sundar to the surface, where he left them with a disdainful sniff. The sky had begun to darken, and clouds bruised the horizon.

"Well, that was anticlimactic," Sundar said, looking over the skyline.

"I didn't expect her to tell us anything."

"I'm a little fuzzy on that. Why bother to talk to us in the first place? Did she even have to pretend to cooperate?"

"She wanted to know what we know about Cahill's late-night project. Once she realized that the documents were taken, she was done."

Sundar scratched under his collar. "Don't know about you, but I feel used. What exactly did we get?"

"We know she's scared. Did you see her face when she heard that Cahill's work was gone?"

"Paler than yours."

"She didn't do it, and she isn't helping whoever did."

"Odd to think of her scared. For such a small woman, she knows how to throw her weight around," Sundar said. A long breath whistled through his teeth. "Looks like I've got a bargain to fulfill. Not another peep out of me for the rest of the investigation."

Malone watched their boots scrape across the cobblestones. "Top marks," she said.

Sundar looked up.

"We were never going to get answers out of this one," Malone said. "But you got us farther than I could have on my own. Partner."

Sundar coughed, a blush rising from his neck, and Malone continued walking.

"Hask isn't going to give us anything without the word of someone higher up, so we might as well start there tomorrow. Unfortunately, it's too late for anything but dinner tonight. I'll buy, if you can stomach something in Turnbull Square," she said.

Sundar grinned. "You may be at the top of your game out here, but don't think you can outdo me at the dives. I've survived them all."

"Once again, you're going to have to prove yourself."

"Challenge accepted, Inspector."

"Call me Malone."

The pair strolled through the deserted surface streets of the bureau district in the waning light, before darkness swallowed them.

Sundar's beer mug left a shiny, dark ring on a bar already stained with dozens of them. He set it back down with a heavy thunk, and the foamy beer inside sloshed up to the lip but didn't quite spill. Nevertheless, Malone noticed that his tongue was still as nimble and his voice as clear as it had been when he interviewed the sweepers that morning.

"It's not that different," he said, rubbing the layer of moisture on his glass with a thumb. "Acting and inspecting, I mean. Is that what you call it? Inspecting?"

Malone shrugged, tilting her head back for a gulp of crisp, spicy, pale ale.

"Anyway, they're not that different. You're just tricking different people."

Malone sat her own glass on the bar with a barely audible clink. "Except we fail when we're found out. Your audience knows they're being tricked."

Sundar tapped a triumphant index finger on the bar. "But they still laugh. They still cry. We fail if they remember we're actors." He took another swallow from his amber-tinted pint. "No, there is a difference. The stakes. But don't let my old company hear I said that."

Malone snorted. "Heaven forbid."

Sundar tilted his head. "I dunno, Malone. Don't get me wrong, I wouldn't go back for all the mansions in the Vineyard, but consider their point of view. They have a successful night, and a hundred people may go home a little happier, a little kinder, a little more aware. But if we have a good night, what do we do? We send someone to the Barracks."

"A criminal," Malone said.

"And we make someone unhappy. We may give someone else satisfaction or justice, but we don't make anyone happy."

"We do what's necessary," Malone said, tightening her grip on her glass.

Sundar nodded. "But what's more effective? Keeping people happy or keeping people satisfied? Won't happy people be peaceful people?"

Malone raised an eyebrow. "I guess we could all join the players and find out."

Sundar grinned wryly. He traced the Venn diagrams of mug stains on the bar with long, tapered fingers. "What would you rather have?" His brown eyes met Malone's for a moment. "Happiness or satisfaction?"

Now Malone focused on her glass and on the thin layer of bubbles floating at the top of her ale. She turned the glass in her hand, staring into the golden liquid. The other patrons behind and beside them built a wall of sound, but Malone could only hear a piercing ring coming from her own inner ear.

"I know what I'd pick," Sundar said, taking another drink. "But for now, I'll settle for another one of these." He slid his empty mug to the bartender. "One for you, Malone?"

She nodded, a faint sigh of relief escaping her lips.

Sundar pushed another pale ale toward her. "So, you know what got me into the black coat. What about you?"

Malone took a sip. The truth was, nothing else had ever occurred to her, but that answer made her uncomfortable for some reason she couldn't place.

"It's my best color," she said.

Sundar snorted, a jet of liquid spurting from his nose. He swiped at it with the back of his sleeve. "Seriously, though. A righteous hunger for justice? Family in the Municipals?" He lowered his voice, grinning and looking at the tables around them. "Family in the Barracks?"

"All of the above," Malone said. "At one point or another." Sundar nodded, staring into his beer, and she guessed that he was, once again, searching for a new topic.

As it happened, one found them, crashing into the bar between them. A heavy man with a doughy face and a bald spot on the back of his head looked up at them, his eyes heavy with accusation. "You'd better watch where you're going," he said, each syllable colliding into the next, "or I'm gonna hafta show you whose bar it is."

Malone's hands were already on the cuffs linked to her belt. She and Sundar both wore their black coats, but so did half of the citizens of Recoletta. The only thing that clearly marked them as inspectors were the silver seals pinned to their lapels, and Malone doubted that their interloper would have noticed if they'd been covered in them.

"Back to your table," Malone said, her fingers tensing over the cuffs.

"This is my table," the man said, "and you better watch your tone with me." Malone saw how it would unfold. She'd warn him again, he would get aggressive, and she and Sundar would have to haul him to the station to sober up under lock and key. The night would be over for all three of them in the next thirty seconds, but hopefully without any broken bones or missing teeth.

Apparently, Sundar had other ideas. "Sorry about the mixup, friend. Next one's on me." He signaled to the bartender, who slid a glass of water down the counter.

Sundar's hand came to rest on the drunk's shoulder, and a light touch guided the man to his vacated barstool. The muscles in the man's face had already started to relax, and the color that had started climbing his neck was subsiding. One of his hands was opening and closing over the bar, and Sundar nudged the glass of water into it.

The drunk took a sip. "Thanks, it just… Wait, this isn't mine." He looked at the glass as if it had grown out of the stained wood.

"Whoops, sorry." Sundar whistled and waved to the bartender again. Another glass of water slid his direction, and he switched it with the one in the drunk's loosening grip. "Here you go. Cheers." Sundar took the first glass of water, clinked it against the one in the drunk man's hand, and they both tilted their heads back and gulped until the bottoms of their glasses held no more than a dewdrop. Sundar slapped his new friend on the back, clearing his throat manfully. "Damn good. Another?"

The drunk shook his head, looking almost bewildered. "I've had enough. It's just… I just…" He sighed. "It's so hard."

Sundar nodded as if he already knew what the man was talking about. "Tell me about it." And the man did. For almost an hour.

By the time it was over, Malone knew more about the man, his wife, his mistresses, and their demands, than she cared to, and Sundar was still nodding with encouragement. The man's story wound down, like many such stories, with rambling deceleration. The bartender had already sent for a carriage and, glad to have avoided a scene, was happy to pay the fare to send the man home. After an hour of drinking nothing but water, Sundar's new friend seemed able to remember his address, at least.

When they had sent the man home to recover and, hopefully, confess his crimes, Malone again sat next to Sundar at the bar, feeling more exhausted than she had by their visit to the Directorate of Preservation. The bartender served them another pair of pints on the house, and Malone accepted hers with relief.

"I think we answered your question," Malone said. Sundar looked over at her, a swallow of amber in his throat and a question in his eyes. "Look around. What do you see?"

"The same thing we saw when we arrived."

"No broken tables, no black eyes." Malone took a sip of her ale, the taste cool and crisp on her tongue. "You may not have sent him home happy, but you sent him home clean."

CHAPTER 4

A STRANGER IN THE HOUSE

Dusk settled, and Jane made her way through the streets, pushing a bulky cart filled with the evening's deliveries. At the bottom was the frock coat with its orphaned buttonhole. One way or another, it had to be delivered tonight. She wheeled her bundle into a gaslit railcar and set off for the Vineyard, determined to enjoy the visit as if it were her last.

Jane pushed her cart out of the railcar. Even after countless trips, Recoletta's finest district took her breath away. The illusion of surface life was almost complete here, where broad underground avenues lined with lamps proceeded past hand-carved and gilded walls bedecked with greenery.

While homes and offices in most parts of town shared walls with their neighbors on two or three sides, the residences here enjoyed the dual extravagances of open space and landscaping between them. It was as if the underground had sprung up around the mansions, rather than their having been carved from it. Jane soaked up every fluted column and flowering shrub, aware that she might not be welcome in this neighborhood after tonight.

In the evening, groundskeepers fed the lanterns aqua-blue powders to complement the soft glow of the moon and stars from the skylights above. Jane passed whispering couples and cheery gangs, all out for an evening promenade or a leisurely dinner, as she made her stops.

On the second to last stop of her circuit, Jane came to a long facade of light gray marble with jade accents. An iron gate separated her from the tranquil garden and the paneled door within. Jane pulled the cord suspended in front of the gate, and at the bell a bird-boned maid came out to meet her. Lena rarely said more than a dozen words on any of her visits, and even so, Jane realized that she would miss their quiet routine. Lena led her down a curving garden path lined with radiance stones that glowed like fireflies. Leaving her cart just outside the door, Jane followed up the steps and through the back door of the Hollens residence.

Alfred Hollens was the only councilor with whom Jane had any connection. They had met in person a few times, and he had managed to be courteous without condescending, a feat for which few councilors were known. Mostly, however, Jane dealt with the domestic staff as she did now, continuing with Lena through the entry hall. As Jane passed a sitting room, she could just make out two voices: Hollens's smooth rumble, which she recognized, and another, which she did not. It was strangely accented and carried dark tones, bringing to mind cut obsidian. Tilting her head, she saw Hollens, a mahogany-skinned man in his mid-fifties, reclining in a plush armchair, one side of his face illuminated by the flickering firelight. Half of the room was in darkness, and Jane could not make out the stranger folded within it.

Lena took the bundle of folded and mended jackets from Jane and turned a corner into a service stairway, disappearing.

As Jane watched her go, a ragged sigh escaped the sitting room. Edging closer to the corner, Jane could barely catch snatches of conversation from the firelit room. Though a discreet employee, particularly in the guarded company of the Vineyard, she found her curiosity aroused for the second time that day.

"I really don't know what to think." This was Hollens speaking, and Jane could hear concern in the councilor's normally strong voice.

"I've said it before. Something like this was inevitable." Here was the man with the obsidian voice, murmuring in a strange accent that massaged his vowels and torqued his syllables.

"This will cost us weeks. If we're fortunate."

"It's simply a matter of containment. Setbacks are to be expected." The unfamiliar man punctuated his statement with a quick slosh, a hard swallow, and the swashing sound of pouring liquid.

"This is more than a setback. It's unprecedented."

"So is Prometheus." Jane detected amusement in the other voice.

"Enough," said Hollens. "More than ever, discretion is imperative. And if I'm not mistaken, that's your area of expertise." Jane heard the tinkling of ice in a glass, followed by a sigh. "What worries me is that dossier. He had it. Now it's gone. Whoever has it knows what we know."

"A third of what we know."

"More or less. But does it contain the location? That's the real question." Ice and liquid chimed again as Hollens took a drink.

"No."

"Did you see his copy? Are you sure?" Hollens asked.

"No. But Ruthers is, and he gave it to Cahill. If you're unconvinced, I'm sure you could speak with him yourself."

Jane waited through a long pause. When Hollens spoke again, it was with the forced coolness that a man of his standing reserved to mask extreme distaste. "If you've already spoken with him, I'll take you at your word."

Their voices faded beyond Jane's hearing. Pressing still closer to the corner, she picked up the conversation again.

"...nothing but a fluke. You will see to that, won't you?" asked Hollens.

"It is what I do."

"Good man. You've proven yourself on many occasions, and you know how we rely on you. Now..." Hollens cleared his throat, and the men spoke in whispers that Jane had no hope of overhearing. Moments later, Lena returned with another bundle of suits and Jane's payment. Guilty and startled, the laundress stifled a gasp, but Lena did not appear to notice that her attentions were focused elsewhere.

"The first one has a drop of wine on the front, and the second is frayed at the hem. Councilor Hollens will need them by Wednesday."

Before Jane could respond, a muted thump and a cry of surprise sounded from deeper in the house. Lena's eyes followed the direction of the noise, her lips parting in a small sigh. "Wait here."

Jane murmured in assent and, with the bundle in her arms, turned back into the hall. It was not until she nearly collided with someone that she looked up.

Shrouded in a spicy-sweet smoke and leaning against the wall just outside of the sitting room was a tall, broad-shouldered man whom she presumed to be the stranger she had heard conversing with Hollens. Dressed in a loose-fitting black dinner jacket and idly smoking a cigarette, he was the embodiment of upper-class carelessness or middle-class coattail-riding. Even for an informal house call, his manner in the councilor's home was cavalier, which led her to suppose the former. His jacket was a size too large, his ascot hung askew around his neck, and his pants were wrinkled. She then noticed that he was watching her with interest, his dark blue eyes shining behind black, chin-length hair. She blushed.

"Red becomes you, my lady."

Jane hesitated, thinking that there wasn't a scrap of red anywhere on her dress or jacket, but she took his meaning and felt another wave of heat flood her face.

The stranger smiled. "I don't believe we've met. Roman Arnault." Arnault pushed away from the wall, facing her.

"I'm the, ah, laundress."

"I'm sorry?"

Jane blinked, more uncomfortable than ever. "The laundress. I wash clothes for Councilor Hollens. Specialty items, mostly, since he has a staff, but..."

"I didn't catch your name."

"Oh! It's Jane. Jane Lin." Her fingers dug into the bundle in her arms.

Arnault gave her the kind of smile that looked as if he must have practiced it many times before. He peeled one hand from the bundle and kissed it. "A pleasure to meet you, Jane Lin, laundress."

He said her name slowly, as if trying it out. Jane flicked her gaze downward, noticing his hands and their clean but trimmed nails. After a few moments, he followed her eyes to the cigarette between his fingers. "Cloves," he said, holding it up for her inspection. "Care for one?"

"Oh, I wasn't... No, thank you, Mr Arnault."

"A lady of modest habits."

Jane had found that when whitenails and their ilk chose to make pronouncements on her station, bearing, or character, it was best to offer nothing but the tacit confirmation of a small smile, which she did now.

Arnault's mild tone kept what came next from sounding like a rebuke. "Miss Lin, do I look like a man who enlists the services of specialty laundresses? Or whose recommendations on the same would be trusted?"

Arnault paused, and Jane, whose repertoire of etiquette offered no guidance for this kind of conversation, listened hopefully for Lena's footsteps. "You can disagree with me, especially if I'm so pompous as to make sweeping generalizations about you, someone I have known for all of two minutes." He took a deep breath, and Jane felt herself do the same. "So, Jane Lin, are you ready to tell me what you really think?"

Jane heard the words come out of her mouth before she knew what she was saying. "It's easy for you to say so when you can get away with visiting a councilor dressed like that."

Arnault's expression changed slowly, his eyebrows lifting and his lips drawing back.

"I'm sorry," Jane said. "I shouldn't have said that."

But he looked amused. "Speaking your mind is nothing to be sorry for, Miss Lin. I find a little honesty refreshing, especially in this neighborhood. So, how does a nice girl like you end up in it?"

"Everybody has dirty laundry, Mr Arnault."

He chuckled, but in a way that suggested a private joke. "How right you are."

"And you, sir? What kind of business are you in?"

"There's no need to 'sir' me, Miss Lin. As for the business…
I suppose you could say that I'm in the same line of work that
you are." He took another drag on his cigarette.

Jane looked him up and down, taking in his outfit again.
"If we're being candid, Mr Arnault, I find that hard to
believe."

"It's a metaphor, Miss Lin."

"Should I be honest again?"

"Always."

"It sounds like a bad one."

Arnault considered the clove cigarette between his fingers.
"To return to your modest habits," he said, holding the cigarette
in the air between them, "you avoid these because…?"

Jane blinked. She didn't want to mention that a habit
like that was absurd for someone on her income. "They kill.
From the inside."

"So do a lot of things," Arnault said. "And people. And just
like your dirty laundry, some things are best kept private."

He said it with a twinkle in his eye, but the memory of
the overheard conversation sent flutters through Jane's
stomach. "Are you always this friendly with the domestic
help, Mr Arnault?"

"I'm not friendly with anyone."

"Then I have grossly misinterpreted our brief encounter."

"That's because you're a good influence, Miss Lin, and you
should stay for tea."

Jane could not begin to fathom the reaction were she to
have tea in Councilor Hollens's home at Arnault's invitation.
"I thought you'd already enjoyed some with the councilor."

"We shared a stronger beverage. But with a nice young lady
like yourself, I'd have tea."

The image of the frock coat in the laundry cart and the unpleasantness that awaited at the next stop pierced her thoughts. "Actually, I should be going now. I've got a few more errands before the night's over."

"You do more business in the Vineyard?" Arnault asked.

"I do."

"And whereabouts, my lady?"

"Just a few streets over, a bit north of here." Jane shrugged.

Before he could press her further, Lena reappeared, a nervous scowl on her face. "Mr Arnault, you know the councilor doesn't like you smoking in here. I'll just show Miss Lin out, and I'd be obliged if you'd put that thing out in the meantime."

Roman took one more long pull on his cigarette. "Better yet, I can accompany Miss Lin to the gate and finish it there. Apologies."

"Now, sir. What with recent events, I've got to lock the gate after her."

Roman's back was already to her as he walked Jane to the door. "I'm sure I can figure it out." Lena returned to the stairway while Roman led Jane to the garden, his palm barely resting on the small of her back. It was the kind of touch that Roman seemed to offer without much thought but that made her think about her posture and the placement of her hands.

Jane stole a sidelong glance at her escort, more curious than ever about the man and his mysterious visit. What kind of man called on a councilor in such a state of dishevelment and accompanied the domestic help to the gate? Jane thought herself a keen observer, but between Arnault's flippant charm and vague purposes, he seemed a man submerged beneath dark waters, isolated and imperceptible. The firefly lamps in the garden glowed with a new mystique, like tiny sets of eyes watching with an unblinking gaze. Everything in the night now seemed just beyond her grasp.

They reached the gate and Roman turned toward her again. Even in the semidarkness, she could clearly see his face, the olive tones shadowed by something more than the hour. He placed one hand on the gate. "I hope we meet again, Jane."

"If you continue to visit my clients while I'm making rounds, then I suppose we will."

"If you continue to eavesdrop during said rounds, I'm certain we will."

Jane started, taken by surprise and wondering if she should also feel frightened. So this was why he had accompanied her. "I wasn't..."

"Of course you were; I can see it in your face. Don't look so upset. In your place, I would have done the same."

She did not find this reassuring, but it seemed pointless to argue. "How could you tell?"

The look on his face, and the memory of her blush, suggested that this was a silly question. "By your expression, Jane. When you rounded the corner."

"I almost ran into you."

"It wasn't the surprise, it was the recognition. And the guilt. You gave yourself away," he said, smiling faintly.

"I was waiting for Lena to return with my next commission. I couldn't help overhearing you in the next room."

"Then you heard what we said?"

"Some of it."

"I would advise you not to repeat any of it. There are more dangerous ears than mine."

A chill tickled her spine. "I promise, I'm always discreet with my–"

He laughed. "Don't worry, Jane, that wasn't a threat. An inquisitive little laundress is no concern of mine."

"Not your dirty laundry, you mean."

Roman looked into the street. "It's late, Miss Lin. Perhaps you should finish your errands tomorrow."

The only thing worse than continuing to Director Fitzhugh's house would be delaying the errand any longer. "A gentleman needs his clothes. I doubt the hour will excuse me from deliveries if I want to keep my commissions."

"Surely it would if your client is indeed a gentleman."

Hearing such solicitousness from a man who had walked a fine line between threatening and warning her moments ago prickled. "I do this almost every evening, Mr Arnault. Tonight is no different."

"I don't doubt your ability, I only refer to the unfortunate events of last night. With a murderer on the streets, you might be safer inside at this hour."

"As I recall," she said, angling her head up at Roman, "the victim died in his own house. In that case, I'm much better off out here."

"Perhaps so. Take care of yourself, though. Yes?"

Jane answered with a civil bow. Roman elbowed the gate open for her, and she found herself once more in the streets and a little relieved to escape his commanding nonchalance. Her face burned at the idea that he was possibly still watching her, but she suppressed the urge to look back until she reached the intersection. When she did, she saw only Councilor Hollens's garden, still but for the twinkling of tiny lights.

Despite her unease, Jane found herself hoping that he was right, that they would meet again.

Not that it was likely after her next stop. She continued through the underground streets. The merry flocks and tender pairs of earlier had vanished, leaving the only movement to the lamps which now burned a deeper, pensive blue.

Director Fitzhugh's street was, if possible, even quieter than the others at this hour. She approached his door and tapped. Mr Fitzhugh lived alone, his scant domestic help boarding elsewhere. Unless Mrs Lefevre, the housekeeper, had stayed behind to witness her humiliation and pass final judgment on her plain shoes, Jane would have to face Mr Fitzhugh himself.

In the silence that followed, she decided. She would tell Mr Fitzhugh about the missing button. Someone would eventually notice the absence, and better to explain herself now than live in apprehension.

And yet no one came to the door. Returning home now was out of the question. Jane knocked again, harder, and the door groaned open.

No one was on the other side. A chill rippled through her, and she nudged the door open further. Mr Fitzhugh or a guest must have accidentally left it ajar. She ventured inside, calling softly, "Mr Fitzhugh? Are you there, sir?"

Something tinkled across the floor as she crossed the threshold. She followed the sound and picked up something small and cold, holding it near the door. A cuff link. Real gold. Valuable enough that it might make up for the missing button. Jane advanced into the blackness.

The darkness in the hall sucked up the faint blue glow from the street. She remembered his residence well enough to navigate through the pitch black, so she tiptoed through the entry hall and into the parlor, feeling more and more like an intruder. Patting the walls for a gaslight control, her fingers came to rest on a switch. She thumbed it several times without igniting even a flicker. Above her head she heard the sound of a faint creaking, like a tread on the ancient, wooden floors. She whispered again in the darkness, searching for Mr Fitzhugh.

Jane considered the awkwardness of her position. Suppose he was sleeping and awoke to find her rummaging around in the dark, uninvited. How would that look? Yet suppose he had had an accident and needed help. Maybe, she thought, he had left the door open for her. How then could she explain herself if she left? She pressed on, realizing that, more than anything, she simply wasn't willing to turn back now that she'd made up her mind about the button. Somewhere above and closer now, the rhythmic creaking continued.

Stretching out her hands and feeling her way through a doorframe, she crossed into another indiscernible room. Unexpectedly, her foot caught on something on the floor and she stumbled, falling to the ground with a gasp. She twisted off of her stomach and felt for the lump that had caused her fall. Her fingers alighted on something big: a bulky cloth bundle that yielded to her touch. Grasping blindly at its extremities and beginning to appreciate the length of the pile, she had a capricious fancy, which started, unwelcome, to materialize into something more concrete.

Feeling from a firm, tapered section a few feet in length, she grabbed an odd shape that felt like polished leather. She pictured the object in her mind's eye and envisioned its liquid shine. Jane reached further and felt a hard surface beneath it and, pulling back, touched strings. Laces. A shoe. Which meant...

Still brushing her fingers cautiously along the pile, she touched what was, unmistakably, a human hand. Running her hands further, she came to the neck and gingerly felt the bald pate, hooked nose, and long face of what she had every reason to believe was Lanning Fitzhugh. No pulse, but the body was still warm. He could not have died long ago.

Several things occurred to Jane at once.

The first was that the footsteps above had stopped. Through her mind ran belated admonitions for not having some inkling of the situation sooner, for having so rudely entered uninvited in the first place, for not listening to Roman Arnault, and, most of all, for not knowing what to do next. Mercifully, these thoughts were soon stifled by instinct.

In the split seconds of silence as she knelt, listening, she wondered if perhaps the intruder above her had already left through the surface exit. Maybe he had never noticed her. Her gut gave a sickening twist as she decided that this was unlikely. If he had not heard her knock, he would have heard her call. If he had not heard her call, he would have heard her tumble. Or would he? The merest glimmer of relief appeared as she reasoned that she might even have scared him away.

These feeble hopes crumbled when she heard the footsteps resume overhead.

With mounting horror, Jane realized that the footsteps were moving toward the stairs. As their doomful cadence drew closer, her ability to run was sapped. The adrenaline pumping through her system buzzed and prickled her nerves, but her legs felt weak and shaky. Besides, she was not even certain that she could make it to the door in time, assuming that she could navigate the halls again in the dark and then outrun the other visitor in the streets.

Shuffling on carpet: the intruder was halfway down the stairs. Thinking back to the dim avenues, she did not remember seeing anyone out after leaving Hollens's residence. Even if she made it out the door, what then?

Silent tears blurred her eyes as she groped at the mantel beside her, searching for some form of aid. The tread was just outside the room. Her fingers closed around a heavy candlestick, which she brought close to her chest, clutching it in her nearest imitation of a defensive posture. Backing away from the body, she tiptoed to a corner.

At that moment, a hand wrapped around her neck and something sharp pierced her skin. Mental blackness advanced seamlessly from the dark and overcame her.

CHAPTER 5

INDEFINITELY

When Jane opened her eyes again, it was heavily and with abstract confusion. A spot on the back of her head throbbed and, as she moved her arm to touch it, she felt the fresh softness of new bed sheets. The movement left her head reeling, and she squinted and grasped the sheets to steady herself. Opening her eyes more widely and looking around, she saw much that she did not recognize, but, fortunately, one thing she did.

Fredrick stood in the corner of a clean, bright hospital room, watching Jane. As her gaze lighted on him, he smiled and approached the side of her bed.

"You're awake. You've been in and out since you got here, but you hadn't so much as batted an eyelash for an hour. You had me worried."

"Where am I?" The words felt thick and cottony in her mouth.

"You're in the hospital. They brought you in late last night."

"Last night? What time is it now?"

"It's Saturday morning. You've been here for almost seven hours, Jane, but that wouldn't surprise you if you could see the knock on the back of your head. You should be just fine, but the doctors wanted to keep an eye on you, not to mention keep you away from further harm." He broke off and regarded her. "Do you remember anything?"

A jumble of images and sensations rushed through her mind as she tried to recall the events of the previous night. "The Vineyard. A laundry run. But you're looking at me like there was something else. What happened?"

Fredrick looked grave and completely unlike himself. "I'd better let them talk to you about it. You stumbled upon a murder, Jane. And by the bruises on your hands and knees, quite literally."

At that statement, the disorganized thoughts tangled in Jane's subconscious rose to her waking mind and arranged themselves in disturbing rank and file. She pushed herself upright in her bed as Fredrick disappeared and returned with two unfamiliar visitors.

The first was a woman with short, platinum hair and an androgynous face that looked like it had been hewn from marble. She took a seat next to the bedside while the other – a handsome young man with friendly, graceful features – stood a short distance away with Fredrick. Both wore black overcoats with silver badges.

Even sitting, the lady inspector seemed tall. What struck Jane most, though, were her pale blue eyes. In a dark room, Jane would have expected them to glow. Her voice was only a little softer than her gaze. "Miss Lin, I'm Inspector Malone, and this is my partner, Inspector Sundar. How's the head?"

"Alright, I guess." Jane could feel the distant echo of an oncoming headache, but she estimated that she had a few hours before it hit in earnest.

"I'd like to ask you about last night," Inspector Malone said, watching Jane.

"Yes, ma'am."

"You went to the Vineyard."

"Yes," Jane said.

"Your purpose?"

"My work."

"As a laundress."

"Yes, ma'am." Jane expected Malone to pull out a pen and notepad at any moment to record her answers, but doing so would have required the inspector to break her frozen stare, and that did not appear forthcoming.

"How often do you go to the Vineyard?"

"Four or five days a week, sometimes more."

"How many clients do you have there?"

"Twenty-three households." Jane hesitated. "Twenty-two now. I can give you the names."

"Later. You work for an exclusive lot. How did you get those jobs?"

Jane shrugged. The motion was strangely painful. "You start with one or two and get a reputation."

Malone blinked for what seemed like the first time. "Most of them keep domestics."

Jane was having a little trouble distinguishing Malone's questions from statements of fact. "Not everyone keeps a full staff – some like their privacy even more than service. Some won't spare the rooms. Besides, I'm a specialist. Houses with full-time domestics don't send me the everyday things, like towels or unstained clothes, but whatever requires finesse goes to me."

"What kind of laundry requires finesse?" the young inspector, Sundar, asked from the door.

"Delicates, Inspector. Whitenails like a lot of fine materials – chiffon, lace, and the like – and those don't do well in your standard wash. Beyond that, I can remove stains, fix tears, and resize garments. Most importantly, though, the whitenails trust me."

Malone nodded, signaling for Jane to explain.

"As you can imagine, they don't allow just anyone into their homes, and they're picky about who goes through their dirty laundry... if you know what I mean. They pay well for discretion." Out of the corner of her eye, Jane saw Inspector Sundar perk up at the word, like a terrier scenting a rat, but Inspector Malone remained cool.

"Do you know something dangerous about these people?" Inspector Malone said.

Jane shook her head. "No, nothing like that. But you can tell a lot about a person by their dirty clothes. I have several clients with some, ah, unusual hobbies."

"Please elaborate."

"It's nothing illegal, of course, just things they wouldn't want the neighbors to know about." These were secrets that a less scrupulous employee might sell for a handsome price. But not a price that would make up for the loss of business. "I can't tell you who, but I have a few who are pretty active in their evenings, if you catch my meaning. I also serve a couple that goes walking in the wilderness on the weekends. Spending that much time outdoors and away from the city would be scandalous enough for you or me, but can you imagine as a whitenail? You can't explain grass stains to the neighbors."

From his spot near the door, Inspector Sundar smirked.

"You don't understand," Jane said to him. "Some in that crowd are so traditional that they never even use the surface streets, no matter what the underground traffic's like. I've met a lady who keeps her nails six inches long. Silly, I know, but that's the world my clients live in."

"Understood, Miss Lin," Malone said, giving her partner a brief, steadying glance. "Now, it's time to discuss the attack." She looked at Jane as if this were an invitation rather than an imperative.

"OK." Jane took a deep breath, the air cold in her lungs.

"Very good. Sundar," Malone said, and the young man began to escort Fredrick out of the room.

"Wait," Jane said, "I'd like him to stay. It'll help me," she added, searching the inspectors' expressions. Sundar looked at Malone and nodded.

Malone seemed to repress a sigh. "Whatever makes you comfortable," said she. "Tell us what happened, beginning with the moment you left home last night."

Jane took another steadying breath and began her story. She described everything in as much detail as she could remember, taking the detectives with her from house to house along her route, through the railcar tunnels, and to the Vineyard.

Inspector Malone looked on, her expression unchanged. "At Fitzhugh's, how many sets of footsteps did you hear?"

"Just one."

"When did you first hear it?"

"Hard to say, but not long after I entered the house. Maybe half a minute. I didn't think much of it at the time." Jane imagined Inspector Malone chiding her about her imprecision.

"And when did you hear the footsteps stop?"

"Well, after I saw the body," she said, "I panicked, and whoever else was there must have heard me. That's when I stopped to listen. I thought for a moment that the stranger had gone, but that quickly changed." Jane shuddered at the memory.

Malone leaned in, homing in on the details. "Did you hear the footsteps enter the room where you were hiding, Miss Lin?"

Jane's brow furrowed. She didn't remember that, but after a while it had been difficult to hear over the pounding of blood in her ears. "I don't *think* so."

The inspector's eyes shone with mysterious significance. "What happened to the footsteps?"

The closer things got to her moment of unconsciousness, the more jumbled and mangled the memories seemed, like a crashed railcar accordioning at the point of impact. "I can't remember. After a point, I lost track of everything. The footsteps got to the stairs. Then I heard them outside the room. After that, I just remember waiting in the darkness."

Malone nodded and relaxed her focus. "You said the door was open when you arrived."

"Yes, ma'am."

"Why did you leave it open?"

"I didn't."

"Are you certain?" asked Malone, showing the first sign of misgiving.

"Yes," Jane said. "I know I shut that door behind me. It was what caught my attention in the first place."

Malone shifted in her chair. The lack of clarity seemed to unsettle her. "The domicile was dark. You would have seen better with the door open."

Jane shook her head. "Not really. The light from the streetlamps didn't make a real difference a few feet into the hall. It seems foolish now, but, at the time, I was more worried about someone else following me in." She looked from Malone to Sundar. "Is this important?"

"That's how you were found, Miss Lin. Your laundry cart was overturned and the clothes scattered over some two hundred feet. A resident followed this trail to the wide-open door of Fitzhugh's domicile."

Jane gazed at the edge of the bed sheet, digging deeper for some forgotten detail. Coming up dry, she finally looked up and shrugged at Malone, who continued.

"Do you know of anyone who has reason to harm you?"

"Of course not."

"Everyone has enemies, Miss Lin."

"Everyone important, maybe." Still, Jane considered the question. "No one I know of."

Malone pressed her lips together and nodded. She started to rise, and Jane understood that she meant to leave as suddenly as she'd come.

"Wait," Jane said, looking at both inspectors. "Isn't there something you could tell me? Now that you're done with me I've got to return to a normal life."

Malone paused, and her partner again gave her a prompting look. "I believe you were in the wrong place at the wrong time. Lanning Fitzhugh was the victim of a murder, and you stumbled upon it while the attacker was still present. You became a liability. I don't think you're in any further danger, but I'll send an officer to keep an eye on your residence."

Jane frowned. "How can you be sure? That I'm not in danger, I mean."

This time, Sundar spoke, pushing away from the door. "We're not. But whoever it was took care to knock you out."

"Took care? There's something the size of an egg on the back of my head."

Sundar held up his hands. "Yes, and there's a mosquito bite on the side of your neck. A drug of some kind, and probably too much, but the knot on your head came from your fall, not a blunt instrument."

He picked a piece of lint from his coat. "Besides, you said yourself that the domicile was dark – so dark you didn't see your attacker coming. He knows that. And he knows something else. By noon today, Fitzhugh's death will be all over the city, and I get the feeling that's just fine with him. So, why would the killer risk his cover by coming after you? He may not even know your name. Assuming, that is, your friend here is as discreet as you are," he added with a nod at Fredrick. Fredrick, looking up from his notepad, fooled no one with his innocuous shrug.

Jane felt the first small swell of relief, but something else occurred to her. "Am I a suspect?"

Malone finally smiled. "No. Your hands are too small to have made the marks around Fitzhugh's neck."

Jane nodded, but there was a still more pressing question on her mind. "Inspector, do you think he – or she – meant to kill me?"

"I think he meant to keep you from interfering with his escape. And I think he's capable of killing when he means to."

Jane felt a chill. She also felt a strange urge to laugh. Whatever her problems were now, a missing pearl button was not among them. "Thank you, Inspector."

Malone gave her another rare smile and handed her a clipboard and paper. "The names, please."

Jane complied, passing the list of her Vineyard clientele to Malone, who gave it to her partner. Then, the lady inspector rose from the chair, and she and Sundar walked to the door.

"I appreciate your cooperation, Miss Lin. Please visit Callum Station if you remember anything else," she said, pausing. "One more question. You said that you heard Alfred Hollens and Roman Arnault talking. Did you hear what they said?"

"A little," Jane said, blushing again. She wondered about the professional consequences if word of her indiscretion got out. But not for long.

Malone smiled, looking actually pleased for the first time. "Go on."

"They were speaking very quietly, so I couldn't catch all of it," she said, and she repeated the fragments that she had heard.

"Prometheus?" Malone said. "Do you know anyone – or anything – by that name?"

"No, Inspector. That was the first time I'd heard it."

Malone nodded and turned to leave. "Thank you again, Miss Lin."

Jane spoke up once more. "Inspector? Do you think this murder is related to the one found yesterday morning?"

A flicker of hesitation crossed Malone's face. Her partner looked at her with raised eyebrows before she spoke again. "Yes. However, I would ask you to exercise your famous discretion. Good day." With that, the two inspectors donned their coats and disappeared. As soon as they were out of sight, Fredrick approached the bedside again with a conspiratorial grin and a wink.

"Wonderful, Jane," he said. "Did I ever tell you that you're a first-rate interview? A true-to-life breathless, wide-eyed heroine!"

"You're really going to write it? After the bit about discretion?"

"Technically, she said that to you, not to me." He looked away as Jane continued to fix him with a dubious stare. "Come on. People are going to figure that one out whether I write it or not. Or do you mean to tell me anyone's actually going to believe that two back-to-back Vineyard murders are unrelated?"

Jane sighed. "Consider us even after the ball invitation. But I don't want my name anywhere in your story," she added.

He gave a thoughtful shrug. "Fair enough. Anyway, the main focus will be what you saw, not who you are. No celebrity for Jane."

She sighed and stared at the foot of the bed for a few moments. "You know what I do want?"

"I'm dying to hear it."

"Food. Bowls and platters of it."

"Well, then, we'll have to get you out of here. They're serving bowls and platters of something down the hall, but I wouldn't call it food."

Jane laughed, taking his proffered arm and sliding out of bed. "Seems they gave me a private room. Maybe they have something special in the kitchen, as well."

"Don't count on it. You only got your private quarters because you were the imperiled and valuable witness, which, by the way, made you a devilishly difficult person to look in on."

"They didn't accept your credentials?"

"No," he said with a sniff. "Clearly no one here reads the news. Anyway, I finally had to dig out my old sponsorship papers to prove our connection."

"I'm touched that you still have them."

He waved a hand. "Point being, now that you've survived and delivered your testimony, they'll choke you on the same gruel they feed everyone else. Now, that's nothing to laugh about. Get changed so we can get out of here."

Jane slid behind a dressing screen where her clothes from the night before waited. She slipped out of a plain cotton gown and into her dress and finally pulled a corduroy coat, rumpled and dirty after her adventure, over her arms. Fastening the buttons around her waist and torso, she stumbled back to Fredrick's waiting arm.

"Easy. Off we go," he said. They were out of the door and down the hall, his left arm serving as an anchor while his right steadied her shoulders. "It doesn't count as walking if you can't do it in a consistent direction."

"We'll see how you do after *your* brush with death," Jane said. All the same, she stared at the ground in front of her feet in fierce concentration.

They were almost clear of the hall and its suspicious odors of burnt oats and lard when trouble approached from behind. "Where are you two going?"

Fredrick decided to answer the challenge, turning his charge and himself to face the speaker. A nurse, shaped like a potbelly stove, stood several feet away with her hands on her hips. "So glad you should ask. My young friend here is ready to take some fresh air and a meal. Unless you're nose-blind to the... revealing odors of this place, I'm sure you'll agree that both of those objectives are best accomplished outside of your fair hospital."

The nurse's eyes narrowed, and her knuckles made an odd cracking sound as she flexed them. "She doesn't look like she's ready to go anywhere, sir."

"Ah, but there we disagree. She's awakened from her candlestick-induced slumber, provided her testimony to the proper authorities, and expressed her wish to depart. So, considering the facts, she's quite ready." Jane nodded her agreement in a diagonal fashion. Despite Fredrick's flip manners, and what often appeared like a more-than-casual detachment from reality, she knew her friend had steel where it counted. Even against a nurse with arms the size of his neck.

"Sir, you'd better put her right back where you found her or I'll have to prepare a hospital bed for you, too."

"I'm not sure what to make of that, but you're clearly more imaginative than I. Let's see, I'm sure I have something here that we can all agree on." He fished the aforementioned sponsorship papers out of his pocket and handed them to the nurse. She barely finished the first three lines when her eyes shot back to his.

Fredrick rolled his eyes. "Yes, that's me, but that's not my real birthdate."

"You're Fredrick Anders? The Fredrick Anders that wrote about the rise of whooping cough in the factory districts?"

"The same."

"I don't know what to say. I'm sorry, I thought you were a creep."

"Glad to have convinced you otherwise."

"And to think, not only a champion of the working class, but you've sponsored this poor girl!" The nurse paused, admiring the picture of social conscience and charity before her. She brought her hands together with an audible crack. "You're a good man, Mr Anders."

"Can I quote you on that?"

The nurse finally turned her attention back to Jane. "OK, there's not much else we can do for her now, except keep an eye on her. I normally wouldn't allow this, but, under the circumstances, I'll let her go with you as long as you promise to check in on her regularly."

"On my honor."

"Every few hours," she said, shaking a blunt finger at him. "At the first sign of any drowsiness, dizziness, or abnormal behavior, bring her back to us. Understood?"

"Completely."

"Wonderful." She whipped hear head around in the direction of a contingent of frantic nurses and hollered, "Open bed in 382! Next one in!" With a long-suffering shake of her head, the nurse retreated down the hall. Jane and Fredrick looked at each other.

"Well, Freddie, at least one of us has some celebrity."

"I'd settle for not looking like a creep."

Jane patted his arm. "Don't take that one to heart."

The corners of Fredrick's mouth and eyes twitched up in well-meaning mischief. "Speaking of looks, when are we going to find a nice, non-creepy type for you?"

Jane exhaled something between a laugh and a sigh. "Careful, or you'll really make my head hurt."

"Someone like that nice young inspector. He was rather attractive, wasn't he?"

A little surprise of a grin tripped over Jane's lips. "Now that you mention it, he was."

"Yes. Too bad he's sleeping with the older one."

"Don't be ridiculous."

"Just because you don't like it doesn't mean it's false."

"And just because it's juicy doesn't mean it's true."

"All due respect, Malone, but is that your idea of a bedside manner?" Sundar said. Malone looked over at him with the closest thing she had to a casual glance. "You make the killer look friendly by comparison."

"She's fine. We needed answers, and we didn't have time to waste."

The inspectors were on the surface street above the hospital. Sundar leaned against the smooth marble of a veranda. "We did get answers, anyway. She definitely isn't hiding anything."

"No."

"What do you think about the door, though?"

Malone folded her arms and scanned the streets around them. "Witnesses make mistakes like that all the time."

"What if the murderer left through that door?"

"He fled to the surface last time. It would have been safest this time, too."

"Lin said the underground streets were empty."

"No moon out last night. The Vineyard underground is better lit. Anyway, I think she didn't shut the door, or at least she didn't shut it properly."

"Maybe the killer broke it on the way in."

Malone shook her head. "Every door, every lock was intact."

Sundar bit his lip, frowning. "Getting a key to Fitzhugh's would be even harder than getting a key to Cahill's."

"I know."

The young inspector sucked his teeth. "So, we really are assuming this was the same person. That it wasn't a coincidence that two prosperous citizens were murdered in their homes in or around the Vineyard without any apparent break-in."

"I don't believe in coincidence."

Sundar nodded. "For someone with a key, he has a conspicuous way of making an exit. Think about the overturned laundry cart."

"It's interesting." Malone spent a few moments in silent thought before shrugging. "A stray dog could have done that."

"Maybe, but the clothes weren't torn or dirtied or anything. Just scattered. And quite meticulously, at that."

"Drunk partygoers, then."

"You think someone would have seen the open door and walked right past it? Besides, this was in the Vineyard. I don't get the idea that there are too many hooligans running amok."

"You'd be surprised at what goes on there."

Sundar considered it. "Is it possible," he said, "that whoever attacked Lin left a trail of clothes to the open door on purpose? So that she'd be discovered, I mean."

Malone began to walk. "You think the killer was looking out for her."

"He did knock her out," he said, following.

"The murderer has preyed on two defenseless old men. I don't see him going out of his way for anyone."

They walked in silence for several paces, watching the Saturday morning traffic before Malone continued. "Miss Lin's account doesn't tell us much about the killer, so we'll have to look for those answers elsewhere." She turned to Sundar. "Next steps, Inspector?"

"We can check on the coroner's report if we return to the station now," he said. "I don't know if he'll have anything definitive, but it's worth a try."

"The chief will also want to know what we found this morning."

A brisk walk from the hospital and its immaculate, white veranda brought them to the station's familiar pavilion of impassive gray. A drop down the stairs, a turn from the rotunda into one of the smaller hallways, and a short march to its conclusion brought them to the coroner's office. Malone knocked and the elderly man let them in, wearing crisp whites and a multicolored smock that had originally been white too. The coroner's eyes lighted with recognition on Malone, and he pumped her hand with surprising vigor, the corners of his mouth forming a crinkly smile.

Malone's own mouth melted into a grin. "Good to see you. Dr Brin, this is my new colleague, Inspector Sundar."

Sundar extended his own hand in greeting. "Nice to meet you." Stepping forward, he caught a whiff of something pungent. "Wow! I didn't know that you embalmed specimens in your office, Doctor."

Brin's smile dropped. "I don't."

Sundar frowned. Malone could tell that he was entering dangerous territory, but the young inspector was oblivious. "Oh. Where's that formaldehyde coming from, then?"

"Young man, that is not formaldehyde." Brin turned his back on the pair and marched toward his desk. Before Sundar could press the issue further, Malone elbowed him. *Aftershave,* she mouthed. Now it was his turn to blush.

"Please, Inspectors, have a seat." Dr Brin put on his spectacles, two thick wedges of glass connected by a flimsy-looking wire, and lifted a sheet of paper. "I doubt I'm telling you anything new," he began, "but here's what I found: Cahill suffered a blow to the head, just below the base of his skull, after which he fell, breaking his neck. Death was instantaneous."

"With the blow or with the break?" Sundar asked.

Dr Brin did his best to ignore Sundar while answering the question. "With the break. Any surprises here, Inspector Malone?"

"Helpful as always," she said. "Any way this could have been an accident?"

"Oh no, Inspector Malone," he said, raising his eyebrows. "This was intentional. The attacker struck with great force and precision."

"And the attacker? Did you discover anything about him?"

"Nothing conclusive, I'm afraid. Simply that he or she was strong and agile enough to overpower a seventy year-old man. And right-handed. There were no hair fibers, snatches of clothing, or foreign materials on the corpse or at the scene which could help us identify the attacker."

"So it was a naked bald guy," Sundar said.

"That's all we need, Doctor," said Malone. "Can you estimate when you'll complete your examination of the second body?"

Dr Brin's brow furrowed. "The second body?"

"Lanning Fitzhugh. The victim discovered this morning."

"Oh, him," he said, removing his spectacles and polishing them on his oddly stained smock. "I'm afraid we don't have it."

"What do you mean? The City Guard had already removed it from the domicile when we showed up."

Brin puffed on the lenses. "It was my understanding that they were keeping it for their own examination."

"And then?"

Dr Brin shrugged. "Cremation. The courier didn't give me details."

Sundar blinked. "There must be some mistake, Doctor."

Brin scowled as he replaced his glasses. "Young man, I may be funny-smelling, but I'm not hard of hearing. The courier said we would not receive the body."

Malone stepped in. "Has something like this ever happened before?"

"No, but there's a first time for everything, including a murder chain in the Vineyard. I've lived long enough to know that much."

"I see. Well, thank you for your help."

"Of course, Inspector Malone. Always a pleasure to work with you." He gave Sundar a pointed look.

Their first appointment thus concluded, Sundar and Malone continued to their next, where Farrah informed them that the Council had not yet signed the contract. Entering the chief's domain, the detectives greeted Johanssen and laid out the new facts.

"And the victim?" Johanssen asked. "What do we know about him?"

Sundar stepped forward. "Mr Lanning Fitzhugh was Master Architect of the city, sir. He worked on planning and design in Recoletta for thirty years, and then he took charge of the Bureau of Architecture about a decade ago."

"What about recent projects?"

"His specialties were sustainability and tunnel excavation. Looking through some of his certificates, it appears that he worked on a good deal of the southeastern districts in his younger days, though he seemed a little less active of late. Then again, he was sixty-two, sir," Sundar added. He looked to Malone, who nodded and made no further comment.

Johanssen sighed. "I'm going to venture a guess that you think these two murders are related."

"We do," said Malone.

"And the motive this time?"

"The same, sir," she said. "Someone is looking for information."

Johanssen's hands came down heavily on the desk. "Do you have anything to support that theory? Beyond the Vineyard connection?" The tone of his voice, not quite agitated, but not far from it, told the inspectors everything they needed to know about his enthusiasm for the idea.

"Well, there are the obvious valuables and money that the assassin passed over," Sundar said.

Johanssen waved an open hand over his desk. "Any sign of disturbance? Any upturned book stacks or rifled desk drawers?"

"None, sir," Sundar said.

"Then while I'll agree that this was no ordinary burglary, how do you know the killer was looking for information? If he had a key," Johanssen said, a grimace crossing his heavy features, "he could have gotten what he wanted at any time. That these two men are dead suggests something more."

Malone nodded to Johanssen and pushed her open palm down next to Sundar, signaling him to wait. "That's why we believe the killer targeted these men based on shared knowledge," she said. "Since dead men don't talk, they can't tell us what it was."

"Shared knowledge? And how to you figure that? One was a reclusive historian and the other an aristocrat and an architect. They moved in different circles."

"Not entirely, sir. Lanning Fitzhugh was in Charley Hask's office at the same time as us," Sundar said. "At the Directorate of Preservation, where Cahill worked." Malone inclined her head toward him, recalling their visit.

The chief sighed. "Sundar, you're new at this, so let me explain something. We maintain a delicate working balance with the Council and its directorates." He held out two flat palms in demonstration. "Contracts, like everything else in the city, go through the Council because the Council's in charge. The Council assigns them to us because we're independent. And they dislike working with us because we're independent. But they really dislike getting dragged into scandals and rumors, even if only by suggestion. I'm not ready to make our relationship any more difficult based on a hunch."

"Sir, are you saying that we shouldn't investigate this contract?" Sundar asked, his brow wrinkled.

"I'm saying that the Council, and, more broadly, the whitenails, don't like any attention that they don't direct. So before you get too bold with these theories, I want to make sure you know what you're talking about."

"We're sure it was Fitzhugh, if that's what you're worried about. We saw him clearly," Sundar said. "Dr Hask dismissed him by name when we arrived."

Johanssen massaged his temples and the skin around his thick, ridged sockets. Malone pursued the advantage. "This murder was cleaner than the last, sir. From Miss Lin's story, it seems that he possesses a detailed knowledge of the victims' domiciles... one might even call it 'familiarity'."

Johanssen clamped his eyelids shut. "That's what worries me."

Only the crackle of the fire and the sound of Johanssen sighing broke the silence of the office, and Malone continued. "When we saw Fitzhugh at the Directorate of Preservation, he had rolls of papers with him – blueprints, maybe."

"You think the killer took them?"

Malone rested an elbow on Johanssen's desk. "Impossible to say – we didn't get a good look at them. But, whatever they were, it tells us that Fitzhugh was visiting Hask for business. And he took papers with him. I don't think that too many things leave that directorate under Hask's eye." Malone paused, watching the chief's expression as he considered her words. She continued in the same tone.

"After observing the latest scene, I'm convinced that the murderer has copies of the victims' house keys – we saw no broken locks and no evidence of tampering."

"Despite the open door," Sundar added.

Malone's eyes rolled back to the chief. "This means the murderer has an accomplice among the whitenails – assuming he isn't one himself."

This last remark pushed the chief over the edge, as Malone had anticipated. His forearms came down on the desk with a weary thud, but his eyes betrayed the energy of purpose. "Make no mention of this conversation, Inspectors. Continue with this contract. I'll give you every authorization and reinforcement at my disposal, just keep your heads down." His eyes rested on each of them briefly. "You may be on to something, but watch where you sling these accusations – those people are almost as sensitive as they are suspicious. I don't want the city thrown into an uproar over this. We haven't had a flurry in the upper ranks since the Sato incident," he said. "And you know what happens when panic breeds from high up."

Malone nodded. "It floods down, sir. We were hoping to follow up at the Bureau of Architecture, where Fitzhugh worked," she said. Wordlessly, Johanssen pulled a sheet of paper from a desk drawer and signed a warrant for the detectives.

"Just don't ruffle any feathers. I expect regular updates on this contract, Inspectors. Consider it trouble if I hear about your exploits from anyone other than yourselves." This time, his eyes darted to Malone.

"Yes, sir."

"Dismissed."

Sundar started out of the office, but Malone paused again. "Sir, do you know anything about Roman Arnault?" she asked.

Johanssen rubbed his hands together thoughtfully. "Moves in the upper circles, foreign born, comes from money. Eccentric. A loner. Why?"

"Lin overheard a bit of conversation between Arnault and Councilor Hollens. Not enough to tell us anything, sir, but she made it sound interesting."

Johanssen pondered a moment. "I'll keep an ear out for any unusual talk in the higher circles, and I'll let you both know if I find anything. Until then, Malone, close this contract."

"Sir," she said, departing with a bow.

Once again traveling the subterranean streets, Malone and Sundar discussed their plan of attack for the Bureau of Architecture. Sailing over the underground passages in suspended railcars, they agreed that, warrant in hand, their approach today could thankfully be more direct. Even without the signed contract from the Council, Malone could not imagine any trouble from the Bureau of Architecture. That bureau was to the Directorate of Preservation what a locket was to a bank safe: fewer secrets and fewer fastenings. Besides, decapitated as the bureau now was, the remaining staff would be too hungry for answers to be tight-lipped.

They returned to the bureau district to find the underground streets bustling and approached the Bureau of Architecture via the surface avenues, where the view was even more impressive. Though the Directorate of Preservation was little more than a hole in the rock face, designed and placed to be inconspicuous, the Bureau of Architecture was a monument to its purpose, with needle-like spires and smooth planes soaring over the avenues, like the projections of a Gothic cathedral. Though it radiated the same forbidding austerity as the rest of the area, the two detectives strode undaunted through the wide, arched doors of the veranda.

A quick descent brought them to the lobby, where another beady-eyed receptionist waited. This man appeared younger and livelier than his female counterpart at the Directorate of Preservation, but he gave them the same appraising eye as they approached.

"We need to speak with your director," said Malone, sliding the warrant across his desk.

He ignored it. "Mr Fitzhugh isn't in."

"Of course he isn't."

"Excuse me?" The words came out more like a suggestion than a question. The receptionist had already lost interest in the two inspectors and turned his attention to more compelling affairs behind his desk.

Malone eyed the man, uncertain. Beside her, Sundar's face was a mask of impassivity, and only his eyes, darting to hers, expressed his bewilderment. "He's dead," Malone said.

This caught the receptionist's attention. He looked them over, from the buckled boots rising to the knees, to their slim, belted pants, black shirts, and loose coats. His face suddenly pale, he took the warrant in one manicured hand and perused it before meeting their gaze again. "Is this some kind of joke?"

"One we got our chief to sign off on?" Sundar asked. "Trust me, he likes his job a lot more than you seem to like yours."

The receptionist recoiled. "Pardon me. It's just that I don't know–"

"We know you don't," Sundar said. "But someone else in here does. Just take us to him."

"Follow me, please," the man said, leading them across the marble-tiled floor.

Malone was surprised that no one had informed the receptionist of such a drastic change in his department, but, given the Council's penchant for damage control, it was plausible. The authorities might have chosen to keep the news of Fitzhugh's murder under wraps until learning more about his death and designating a successor, but there was little time before the murder became common knowledge.

They descended a wide spiral staircase to the floor below, where the receptionist brought them to an oaken door. He knocked twice and was admitted after a few brief moments by an unpleasantly familiar figure. The receptionist glanced at his toes more than a few times.

"Inspectors, sir. They've come with a warrant." His role concluded, the receptionist retreated to his post, leaving Dominguez to glare sourly at Malone and Sundar.

"Let me see that," he said, making a grasping motion with his open hand. He scrutinized the document, his face reddening as he searched it. Dominguez handed it back, looking up ever more sullenly at the visitors.

Malone stepped forward, looking into the office behind Dominguez. "Satisfied?"

"Let's get this over with as quickly as possible. What do you want?"

"Take us to your leader," said Sundar, obviously savoring the moment.

"Master Architect Lanning Fitzhugh is the director, and he is indisposed."

"That's why we're here," said Malone, and the reproachful look on Dominguez's face suggested that this was not news to him, either. "Who runs things now?"

"I do," he said. The corners of his mouth began to curl upward.

"For how long?"

Dominguez shrugged in a manner that was anything but casual. "Indefinitely."

"We need Fitzhugh's records. We want to see every project, completed and in progress, that he worked on before he died."

"I'm afraid I can't do that," he said, feigning reluctance.

"Oh? And why is that?" asked Sundar.

"I'm only the interim director, so I don't have access to confidential information. That being the case, I certainly can't give access to it."

Sundar rolled his eyes. "How long until the Council makes a permanent appointment?" Malone asked.

"Oh, the necessary paperwork may take months. Formalities upon formalities." He sighed with an unctuous grin.

"Direct us to the documents," said Sundar, "or we'll have to arrest you for obstruction of justice."

"How?" Dominguez chirped. "That's not within my power, no matter what's written on your permission slip." Viperous triumph gleamed in his dark eyes.

Malone tapped a finger to her lips. "This puts you in an unfortunate dilemma," she said, her mirror-blue eyes studying him. "You've benefited overnight from Fitzhugh's murder. You've succeeded him for, as you say, an indefinite period of time with the possibility of keeping the job. And now you have immunity in that you are in no position to provide us with the information we need – information that may incriminate you. This makes you the prime suspect. If we don't get the information we require, we will have to arrest you and hold you at the station – indefinitely, of course."

At first, Dominguez's jaw flapped and his eyes again bulged from their sockets. His face colored crimson and his cheeks puffed with rage. Then, he deflated. The fury drained from his face and disbelief replaced it. One look at Malone's still features convinced him, and he moistened his lips in a lizard-like fashion before continuing in a more diplomatic tone.

"Inspectors, I believe there's been something of a misunderstanding. Despite my every wish otherwise, I truly cannot accommodate your needs myself. However, I trust that you will allow me to present you to the Honorable Councilor Ruthers, who oversees this bureau. He can give you what you need." In the patchwork of authority that bound the Council and the Municipal Police, even a seasoned bureaucrat like Dominguez had to cede some ground now and then.

"Good enough," Malone said. Dominguez bowed with uncommon graciousness and led them further down the hallway.

Malone knew of Ruthers, though she had never expected to meet him. He was the unofficial leader of the oligarchic Council, a man whose personality was composed of equal parts cunning and force. Like all councilors, he governed a number of Recoletta's bureaus and directorates, holding ultimate responsibility for their smooth and successful operation and occasionally directing their activities for political advantage.

Councilors were typically uninvolved in the daily proceedings of most directorates, leaving the majority of the business in the capable hands of the directors, such as Hask and Fitzhugh, that they appointed. After all, one could not be expected to personally manage the work of as many as five or six directorates, particularly when all-encompassing issues of policy and municipal administration were at stake. Nevertheless, Malone was not surprised that Councilor Ruthers was present today.

They stopped at the end of the hall in a round room lined with bookshelves. The pattern on the floor mirrored the skylight above, creating circles of sunlight that rippled out from the center of the floor. A slender, older man with a wavy crest of snow-white hair stood at the far end of the room with his back to them, leafing through a volume. He paid no heed as footsteps echoed in the space around him. "Sir," Dominguez called, "Inspector Liesl Malone and her assistant, Inspector Randolph Sundar, are here to speak with you." The latter winced at the use of his proper name.

The white-haired man looked up and turned around. He replaced his book on the shelf and strode toward them, the fine material of his dark blue suit sending echoed whispers about the room. As he drew closer, Malone was startled by his piercing blue eyes and arched nose, which gave him the aspect of a bird of prey.

"Inspectors, the Honorable Councilor Augustus Ruthers," said Dominguez.

Ruthers stretched his hand to the two detectives in turn. It was smooth yet firm. "A pleasure to meet you both. How may I assist you?"

"Sir, we've come to review Lanning Fitzhugh's projects," said Sundar. Even he seemed temperate in the presence of the most powerful man in the city.

The councilor seemed to consider for a moment before answering. "Very well," he said. "But I'm sure you know what I need first." He smiled and held out one hand in a gesture that seemed to suggest that he was as much a slave to the system as they were. Receiving the warrant from Sundar, Ruthers scanned it with a detached expression. "Well, this won't do at all," he said, returning it.

"Beg your pardon?" asked Sundar.

"The files you require are confidential. You'll need the signatures of most of the Council to open them, Inspectors."

"Your Honor," Malone said, "you know better than we do just how important this contract is. We've seen two murders in two days. We don't have time for bureaucracy."

Ruthers waved a hand. "Do not trouble yourselves, Inspectors. This contract is already under investigation."

Sundar blinked, all protocol forgotten. "What did you say?"

"The Council has delegated this contract to some of its own agents who are more familiar with the people and the facts involved," Ruthers said. "Your services won't be needed." He spoke as if dismissing a butler.

"This needs oversight," Malone said. "That's what we do, sir. It's part of our charter and yours."

Ruthers's voice lost much of its gentility as he responded. "Do not lecture me on my duties, Inspector Malone. All public interests are being duly considered. In fact, for this purpose, we're ordering a lockdown in the city, starting tonight, until this problem is resolved. City guards will patrol the streets in the evening with the authority to detain any suspicious parties."

"Sir, when has Recoletta ever handled a murder investigation this way?" Even Malone was beginning to lose her composure.

"It's the Council's duty to set the policy and yours to abide by it, Inspector."

"This is one killer, Councilor. Not an army," Malone said, her voice barely above a whisper.

Ruthers's quick flare of fury echoed in the rotunda. "It is unprecedented! The way this individual is attacking the very peace and stability of our city is intolerable."

"You mean the peace and stability of your neighborhood," she said, shooting him a final cool glare. The conversation was over.

"Inspector, you take too many liberties. Now you will have to leave before I have you and your partner detained for interfering," he said. "Dominguez, if you will."

A spring in his step, Dominguez once again escorted the detectives away, leaving them after he had marched them ten paces into the surface street. Smoothing the wrinkles in his coat, Sundar looked at Malone, his round eyes ringed with anxiety.

"Can he really do that?"

Malone was silent for several moments. "Yes, I think he can. I just never thought he would."

As Malone and Sundar stood in the streets under a bank of gathering stormclouds, the Council's machines were already in motion. The city guards spread throughout Recoletta like the reaching vines of a creeper. Citizens blinked at the shining bayonets, melting into tunnels as the guards took their posts throughout the city. They would exchange whispers and glances with their neighbors until, coming to a notice board, they could read a freshly pasted announcement declaring the following in boldface letters:

"DELINQUENT ON THE LOOSE. CITYWIDE CURFEW AT 9.00PM. REPORT ANY SUSPICIOUS ACTIVITY TO THE CITY GUARD. THESE MEASURES TO CONTINUE INDEFINITELY."

CHAPTER 6

THE OUTSIDERS

The remainder of Jane's week, like her headaches, passed without incident. With the Guard patrolling Recoletta's passages and the rumors surrounding the murders floating atop the public consciousness like a film of scum, the city resonated with tension. Suspicious reports, mostly from the Vineyard, persisted, and agents of the Council hounded the poorer districts in search of the "delinquent". Nonetheless, the Council's investigations led nowhere.

The attacks, however, had stopped. In the current atmosphere, crime had almost stopped altogether. Would-be crooks had as much to worry about from their over-vigilant neighbors as they did from the guards who scoured the streets and tunnels. It was as if the collective paralysis of the sheltered and privileged Vineyard had dripped down and saturated the rougher districts, leaving their denizens stunned and benign. This moratorium would have been a comfort to most people were it not for the pervasive feeling of being watched. Even for the whitenails, a certain vulnerability had invaded daily life.

Jane was still marked by her experience. The throbbing and tingling had left her skull, but a disquiet had lodged in her heart. It followed at her heels on the most mundane errands and settled beside her when she lay in bed at night. Despite Fredrick's suspicion that the Municipal Police no longer had jurisdiction over the murder contracts, Jane gratefully noticed a black-clad officer nearly every time she passed the entrance to her apartment warren, just as Inspector Malone had promised.

But today was the day of the gala, and her lingering fears were eclipsed by that delicious, fluttering sense of anticipation and, she was surprised to note, by a touch of a different dread. Working for the prestigious families of Recoletta gave her an idea as to the appropriate decorum in social settings, but witnessing these manners and practicing them were two separate matters. Fortunately, Fredrick was more accustomed to these situations and had coached her throughout the week:

"Just remember: curtsy, don't bow. You're not a man, and you're not a servant. Not at the gala, anyway."

Jane scowled. "I'm not a servant at all," she said. "I'm a laundress-for-hire. It's different."

Fredrick brandished the first two fingers of his right hand in a theatrical "V". "Mistake number two! Don't correct anybody. If you can't think of anything agreeable to say, just go with, 'How interesting that you should say so'."

Jane looked back at the starched folds of her skirts, attempting to mask her annoyance with another practice curtsy. "I think I'd take all of this a lot better if it weren't coming from you, the most obstinate and least proper person I know."

"I never follow advice, not even my own. But I know what I'm talking about."

She smirked. "How interesting that you should say so."

After a week of these lessons and dancing in Jane's den, the day of the gala had arrived. Restless, she arose early and completed her work by mid-morning. She spent the later part of the morning blighted by that anxious idleness that prevents one from accomplishing much of anything on the cusp of something momentous. After a meager lunch, she began her preparations for the evening: bathing, grooming, and dressing. By the time she went next door to meet her escort, it was hard to imagine how such a slow day had passed so quickly.

Fredrick answered the knock with a shouted "Come in!" and she found him standing by his dressing table, straightening a tie. He wore a trim tuxedo with longish tails that would have looked gaudy on a less ostentatious man. Jane had selected a gown that one of her whitenail clients had discarded and left to her. With her keen eye for detail, she had tailored its fit for her smallish figure and replaced outmoded tucks and stitches with more contemporary alterations. Now, Jane cut an angelic figure, swathed in creamy, diaphanous fabrics that wrapped her frame and floated behind her. Her dark locks were tucked at the back of her head and secured with a complex arrangement of pins. Looking over from his fussing, Fredrick gave a low whistle.

"Well! You can stop worrying that your clients may recognize you tonight. I hardly can, myself."

"I think you mean that as a compliment, so I'll give you the benefit of the doubt."

"Please do. I generally need it."

"But I can't give you any more time to obsess over your hair. Are you really not finished yet?"

Licking his forefinger, Fredrick gave the edges of his mustache a playful tweak and affected a snobbish accent.

"Dear girl, it is but the work of a moment." With that, he tucked his billfold into an inside jacket pocket and, taking Jane's arm in his own, whisked out of the apartment. They reached the surface, and he hailed a horse-drawn cab.

"Fredrick," Jane said, climbing into the coach, "are you sure we can go by the surface streets?" She looked around, her brow lined with worry. "I mean, is it proper?"

He waved a hand, balancing in the open door of the cab with the other. "Don't worry about it. Plenty of people will be doing the same thing. Besides, if you haven't seen the Brummell Hall veranda by night, you really must." He slid into the seat next to her. "And what with the curfew, you won't have many other chances." The festivities would last well beyond the usual 9pm deadline, but, as in most things, the whitenails and their affairs enjoyed some leeway.

Fredrick's skillful banter banished any foreboding Jane felt about the evening. He turned her mind from preoccupations with custom and class to visions of laden banquet tables and dashing young bachelors and, rolling through the streets, her anticipation mounted as the glamour of her surroundings increased. In the Vineyard, tiny lights had been set at every corner in celebration of the evening's festivities, covering the district in a sparkling frosting. The gardens, too, were conspicuous with diamond-like twinkles. Beams of colored light in the distance announced their destination.

They finally came to a halt in front of Brummell Hall, a building that was to pomp and fashion what the Barracks was to might and power. Surrounded by columns of light in the early evening, its rich white marble glowed with an ethereal luster. Pathways lined in low flames led from the drive, where ladies and gentlemen exited their carriages, through a garden of pruned hedge lines and dewy rosebushes. At the entrance, glowing columns supported the open section of the veranda. Her skin prickling in the pleasant, late autumn chill, Jane realized that she was already halfway through the garden but still transfixed on the sights around her. It was just enough to mask the presence of glowering guards.

She and Fredrick followed the stream of people to a wide staircase, its velvet-lined steps curving down and into the main hall. Jane steadied herself with one hand on the thick marble balustrade as the hall came into view. The overwhelming whiteness above was replaced here with shimmering gold and crystal. A sparkling, golden hall, lined with mirrors, stretched before them, the plush red carpet crunching softly underneath their shoes. Jane gasped at the floor-length mirrors she passed, her radiantly draped figure looking like a vision from someone else's dream. A thousand mirrored iterations of her doe-eyed expression gazed back at her with sympathy.

This strange and marvelous passage opened into the ballroom, where delicate, spiraling columns set off the wings. Between these, the dome of the ballroom rose toward the horizon. Chandeliers of glass and crystal dispelled the faintest hint of a shadow, with the grand device in the center of the ballroom burning as high and bright as a beacon. Each ghostly tongue of fire danced in reflections and refractions inside the crystal. Jane's shoes clapped on the tiled floor, barely audible amidst the murmur of conversations.

She felt a not-too-subtle jolt at her arm as Fredrick tugged her in the direction of the banquet table. Crossing to the far end of the ballroom, she saw the orchestra situated on a stage against one wall. Their tranquil minuet served as a backdrop for the chattering groups of invitees. Fredrick loaded a plate for himself, and, seeing Jane's absorption with their surroundings, fixed one for her as well.

Jane picked at a deviled egg as she scanned the clusters of dignitaries and socialites. Her gaze flitted now and then to the trickle of people still filing into the ballroom and swept the smaller halls in the wings where a few came and went. She even watched the curtained doorways through which the attendants passed.

Only vaguely did she hear Fredrick mumble at her.

"Are you going to finish any of this?" Staring at her plate, he waited the obligatory beat. "Mind if I do?" She shook her head as he seized the dish. "Oh, here comes the show," he said between bites of salmon canapé.

A hush fell over the crowd, and the orchestra rushed to their coda. The rooster-like man from the market waited on the stage. He wore the stiff green robes of a councilor, the rigid collar rising behind his neck and opening at his throat. The outer garment fell straight down to his feet, streamlining his figure to a solid pillar of green broken only by the slit down the front where the two halves of the sheath met.

Looking off to the side, Jane saw eight men and women attired in the same manner. She picked out Hollens and recognized Phineas, the egg-like man, his air of studied poise refuted by his shining forehead. She returned her gaze to the man on stage, recalling with a jolt that this was Ruthers, the informal leader of the Council. A little trill of urgency rippled in her stomach as she debated what to do. Silence fell over the room, and her only option for the moment was to listen.

Ruthers folded his hands in front of his chest. The commanding chill in his voice shattered the fatherly image. "Ladies and gentlemen of the city, allow me to express my sincerest delight." He used the word like a knife.

"You represent the finest and most distinguished of our great city. Tonight we welcome our neighbors from South

Haven," he said with a sweep of his arm. Jane followed his motion and saw a handful of men and women in burgundy robes standing in a secluded cluster a little ways off from Recoletta's councilors. They flashed stiff, decorous smiles at their introduction.

Councilor Ruthers continued as the applause faded. "This has been an eventful week in our fair city, but you all have seen how the strong arm of justice descends in protection when trouble arises." He gestured grandiosely at the guards stationed around the room. "And I know you share my joy at the safety and tranquility that has returned to Recoletta." Scattered nods testified to the general agreement. Something was building.

The councilor's voice darkened. "Indeed, it has always been our destiny to seize glory from misfortune. Through strength and determination we can overcome the failures of the past as well as those individuals who would hold us back. We must press forward as a city, and we must recognize those sacrifices that are necessary to ensure our continued survival and prosperity. This is as true today as it was when our city was first born from the ashes of decadence and destruction." He glared around the room, challenging his audience. Mouths were clamped shut and eyes cast down. Even from Councilor Ruthers, such a direct reference to the antebellum past was unsettlingly rare. Satisfied, he continued.

"Thus, it is with a spirit of triumph that we receive our neighbors here today. Let us welcome them in a manner befitting our city's magnificence." Grateful for the change in tone, the audience clapped with gusto.

"Tonight, let us not concern ourselves with the trials that lie before us. This is a night of commemoration, and we celebrate our cooperation as brother territories." Ruthers smiled at the vigorous cheers, and the South Haven representatives nodded quietly. With a magnanimous flourish toward the orchestra, he backed from the stage, and the music swelled.

Jane lowered her eyes from the stage and had turned to look again at the South Haven delegation when her breath caught in her throat. Leaning against one of the winding pillars, in almost the same posture in which she had first seen him, Roman Arnault stood with his long hair slicked back, sipping pale spirits from a vial and lazily gazing about the ballroom. Something in her chest fluttered as she watched him unnoticed.

Her reverie was broken by Fredrick's gentle prompting. "How rude of me, Jane. I keep forgetting that you don't know anyone here. Let me steer you into friendlier waters." Popping a cheese-stuffed olive into his mouth and placing his hand on her back, Fredrick guided her toward a gaggle of older women congregated at the other end of the room.

"They're a little dusty, but they're good people," he whispered. "Stick with them and they'll take care of you. Just watch their claws."

"Fredrick," she said, stopping him. "The man who just spoke..."

His eyebrows lifted from behind his plate of food. "Ruthers?"

"I saw him last week. In the market."

"Even councilors go shopping, Jane."

"That's not what I mean. He was with one of the other councilors – the short, bald one. Phineas. It was just the two of them, and they were whispering about something."

"Be thankful they weren't shouting about it. I've heard the Council sessions can be chaos once they get going." Fredrick swallowed another olive.

"You're missing the point! They'd come all the way to the market to avoid being noticed. Really, how often do you think two councilors actually go by themselves to pick up groceries? If they needed something, they'd send their staff. Anyway, the whole time they were there, they were whispering about something, and Phineas seemed terrified–"

"Hello-o, Jane, did you see the man on stage? And did you listen to a word he said? It's all very innocuous-sounding; Councilor Ruthers practically runs Recoletta, and he just reminded us of that. There may be a you-know-what out there," Fredrick said, "but in here, we're surrounded by guys that look like that." He nodded at one of the guards across the room, a man armed with a bayonet and no apparent personality. "And those guys all follow Ruthers. That's his way of pointing out that while there's only one 'delinquent', there are thousands of guards, so the rest of us had best stay in line."

"But I think they were plotting–"

"Of course they were plotting, Jane! What do you think councilors do? And I know what you're going to say next, so yes, it probably did have something to do with the murders. But so what? That's what everybody's talking about." Fredrick skewered another three olives with a toothpick and slid them into his mouth. "So," he said between bites, "unless you heard them say something about a new mistress or a new quartz vein, there's no news."

Defeated, Jane allowed Fredrick to usher her again toward his destination. When they moved into range, a group of three elderly women looked over and smiled politely, awaiting their introductions. They were older than many of the other attendees, and more showily dressed, dripping with jewels. As Jane noticed their ring-laden fingers, she realized what

Fredrick had meant when he'd warned her about their claws. Their nails were easily four inches long and as strong and sharp as daggers. Jane rarely saw anyone take the whitenail tradition to this extreme, and those who did came from old families and old money. Lots of it.

"Jane, allow me to introduce to you the honored and esteemed Lady Myra Lachesse, Madame Francine Attrop, and Madame Lucinda Clothoe. Ladies, may I present my very dear friend, Miss Jane Lin." They gave Jane a polite appraisal while she executed the much-practiced five-step curtsy. Fredrick glowed with pride.

"How charming," said Madame Attrop.

"It is always a pleasure to meet somebody new," Lady Lachesse said. "We so rarely do at these events." Madame Clothoe only smiled and nodded.

"Where do you come from, my dear?" asked Lady Lachesse.

"I live on the east side, next door to Mr Anders." Jane avoided mentioning its proximity to the factory districts.

"How delightful. And where are your people from?"

Fredrick cut in. "Ah, yes, Miss Lin and I go way back, and you could even say–"

"Hush, Freddie, we're talking to her," Madame Attrop said. The trio looked back at Jane, and Fredrick blanched apologetically, avoiding her eye.

"It's OK, Freddie. I was an orphan," Jane said. "I don't know much about my family."

"I am very sorry to hear that," Lady Lachesse said. "And I'm also sorry that our mutual friend thinks we would shun a nice girl like you based on uncertain connections. Heavens, Freddie, how archaic do you think we are?" she asked, turning to him.

"Well, we're certainly ancient enough," Madame Attrop said.

Fredrick glanced over his shoulder. "Well, as it appears that you are just getting acquainted, I will leave you to it while I nose around the movers and shakers. Ladies, I thought I would leave Miss Lin in your charming company to save her the tedium of following me around."

"Certainly, certainly Mr Anders," chimed Madame Clothoe. Her creaky voice rang with surprising exuberance for her age.

Lady Lachesse smiled. "Do what you must. Our play is your work, after all."

He bowed low and turned to face the rest of the party, his ears pricked for activity. With her advocate gone, Jane felt at a loss surrounded by these benign old tigresses. They eyed her more toothily now, and there was something shrewd behind their pleasant and aloof smiles.

"Is this your first society event, Miss Lin?" Madame Attrop asked.

"Yes ma'am, it is."

"You must be overwhelmed to be surrounded by so many strangers."

Jane didn't bother mentioning that she had encountered more than a few of the partygoers. Even without Fredrick's warnings about well-meaning corrections, she knew better than to volunteer the fact that she was a professional laundress.

"How do the festivities strike you, my dear?" asked Lady Lachesse.

Jane turned her eye to the dancers swirling to the music, many wearing more finery than most of the people in her neighborhood had ever seen; to the hobnobbing backslappers darting between islands of people; and to the hub of councilors, secluded behind a phalanx of guards. This brought her mind back to Ruthers's commanding introduction, which, she realized, had not addressed the purpose of the South Haveners' visit.

Thinking of all of this, she again remembered Fredrick's coaching. "It's very pleasant, Lady Lachesse. I cannot think I have ever seen anything quite like it. I'm enjoying myself very much."

Lady Lachesse had a dark, genteel face that moved only in small gradations. Everything about her suggested exact measurement and calculation. Her finely arched eyebrows twitched precisely and deliberately in response to the people and conversations around her, like two blinds discreetly lifted and adjusted over the soul's windows. Upon hearing Jane, she waved a bejeweled hand. "Come now, that is what you are supposed to say. You're a friend of Fredrick's, aren't you? Surely you must have something more interesting than that."

Jane blinked a couple of times. Though taken aback, she remembered her encounter with Roman Arnault and refused to be flustered by the aging dames. "There's a layer of gloss over people's words, over the scenery. It seems as though everything here takes on a hidden meaning."

Lady Lachesse nodded. "You would do well to keep that sensibility about you in a place like this."

Satisfied with their new companion, the ladies drew Jane into polite chatter. Once she had worked past the initial awkwardness, Jane found them to be disarming, if extravagant. Lady Lachesse was obviously the alpha of the group and, possibly, she suspected, over a significant number of others in the ballroom. Madame Attrop possessed a merry and cutting wit that she exercised throughout the conversation, and Jane noticed her peculiar habit of clutching at her many necklaces with the palm of her flattened hand as she talked. It could have been a dainty gesture but for her thick fingers and timeworn hands, not to mention her formidable fingernails. It seemed as though she were constantly checking to satisfy herself that her many baubles were still in place. Or perhaps she meant to refer to herself, only the modest direction of a few fingers was too simple. She required the whole of a stretched hand.

Madame Clothoe appeared to be the most touched by her age. She had a way of stringing out a nod or an inane bit of conversation until directed by one of her companions. Her tiny eyes sparkled with glee from her crinkled face. Half the meaning of the conversation seemed to float past her, and she watched it go with her constant, oblivious smile.

For all their refined cordiality, however, Jane sensed a more devious instinct coursing through their veins. It was a killer's instinct, selected and trained in them and their caste, and, though the mellowness of age might cover it, it waited just beneath the skin. Jane enjoyed their company and conversation now, but she felt grateful that she had not met them in their younger days.

As they continued to chat, Jane found herself once again scanning the ballroom for her mysterious friend. After several furtive glances toward the banquet table, she saw him standing in another corner, talking with a shorter man in simple dress. Something in her eyes must have given her away, for Lady Lachesse smiled knowingly.

"My dear, I take it you have your own acquaintances at the gala tonight?"

She blushed. "I recognize a few familiar faces, Lady."

Madame Attrop's eyes narrowed with a fierce grin. "Is there anyone you would like to inquire about, Miss Lin?"

Jane felt the heat rise faster in her face, but she sensed her resolve give way before she even opened her mouth. "Perhaps there is something you would deem worthy to tell me about Mr Roman Arnault."

Three pairs of eyebrows arched in unison as Jane pronounced his name, and the women erupted in delicate titters. Jane did not know whether to be amused or embarrassed. Madame Clothoe spoke first.

"I must say, Miss Lin, you manage to make rather interesting acquaintances."

"To better answer your question, might I inquire as to how you met?" asked Lady Lachesse. Jane reviewed the incident of their first encounter, omitting the details of the overheard conversation. The ladies nodded with some kind of understanding, except for Madame Clothoe, who continued to nod at nothing in particular.

"One might best describe him as a classic opportunist, the product of our bureaucracy system and of his own specific upbringing," said Lady Lachesse.

"What do you mean by that, my lady?"

Lady Lachesse tilted her head toward Jane. "I mean, my dear, that when men and women of power need to accomplish certain ends, Roman Arnault can be relied upon to provide the means."

"Oh." Jane's brow creased. Surely the charming stranger she had met did not deserve such a sinister-sounding description. "Do you mean to say that–"

"Mr Arnault and I do not run in the same circles," Lady Lachesse said. "Not anymore. We have a limited acquaintanceship, so far be it from me to paint him as the boogeyman."

Madame Attrop cleared her throat a little too noisily.

Jane eyed him again. "He looks like..." she paused, trying to think of an appropriate term "...a man of leisure."

"Not exactly," said Madame Attrop.

"He's too cynical to be a playboy!" Madame Clothoe said, using the word that had originally occurred to Jane. Jane reached for a vial of sparkling wine as the waiter passed.

"He'd have to have some fun for that," Madame Attrop said. "As careless as he looks, Mr Arnault does nothing without calculating and doesn't leave much room for anything else." The other women pursed their lips sagaciously, and Madame Attrop continued. "But there's more than that. People avoid him. Even disreputable women avoid him. There is something ominous about him, Miss Lin, like a hint of ruin. I would not propose to tell you what to do, but allow me to advise that you exercise caution."

"I appreciate the warning," Jane said, finishing her drink.

"One would almost call him a workaholic," Lady Lachesse said, "were it not for that practiced air of carelessness."

"What exactly does he do?" asked Jane.

Madame Attrop lifted her shoulders. "It is difficult to say with certainty what Mr Arnault does. But rest assured, he does it very well."

Lady Lachesse raised her own glass, holding it steady as she gazed around the ballroom. "He is an agent in the employ of the Council. His official title is 'consultant', whatever that may mean. More precisely, he is the hatchet man of the regime and, as Madame Attrop has assured you, brilliant at his job." Jane nodded with feigned understanding as something inside her growled restlessly.

So absorbed was she in conversation and contemplation that she was startled to hear a voice behind her purr, "My lady." Turning, she beheld Roman Arnault, more familiar to her now through half-conscious and quickly banished daydreams than through real encounters. With a fluttering mixture of delight and chagrin, she smiled and greeted him. Her companions continued to look on through masks of polite neutrality.

"Miss Lin, I'm surprised to see you here," he said.

"I came with a reporter covering the event. A friend," she added quickly.

"Then I'm glad you did," he said with a slow, spreading smile. "Would you like to dance?" he asked, looking toward the center of the white-marbled floor. Couples were already sailing across the ballroom in slow, stately waltzes. The faces of the dancers and, indeed, of nearly everyone in the room betrayed little emotion. Jane felt like she was surrounded by chiseled porcelain masks, painted and weaving amongst one another. The only features that betrayed a life were the eyes, which flitted and flared.

Jane accepted Arnault's offered hand, and they glided across the seamless tiles. Comfortable in the dance and coasting through the steps, he focused on her with the same combination of amusement and intensity that she had noticed at their first encounter. She found his naked gaze unnerving, but the tension dissipated once they began to talk.

"So, Mr Arnault–"

"Roman."

"This isn't your first society event."

He grinned. "Unfortunately not."

"You seem to spend a lot of your time in the company of councilors and their like."

"Correct again. Not unlike yourself, I'd add."

"I've met Councilor Hollens once or twice. You drink with people like him and Councilor Ruthers. It's different."

Roman frowned. "What gives you the impression that I know Councilor Ruthers so well?"

"Well, you work with him. Or for him. Something like that, right?" Slowly turning around the ballroom, they coasted past the stage and the black-clad musicians.

"That's a close enough description of it."

Jane shrugged. "Anyway, you know your way around these crowds. What do you do?"

"I do whatever the Council tells me to do, Jane."

"That sounds pretty vague."

His eyes drifted across the ballroom. "So is my mandate." She grinned despite herself as they continued their dance in slow, sweeping circles. His expression was guarded, but not in the stiff, formal way of the other guests, she noticed as she watched him study the socialites and bureaucrats around them. A fellow outsider, she thought.

"It seems," she said, "that everyone here has secrets."

Roman's eyes darted back to hers. "Why do you say that?"

"I've seen the way you watch everybody."

He smiled in defeat.

"'I knew the mass of men concealed
 Their thoughts, for fear that if revealed
They would by other men be met
With blank indifference, or with blame reproved;
I knew they lived and moved
Tricked in disguises, alien to the rest
Of men, and alien to themselves – and yet
The same heart beats in every human breast!'"

Her face lighted with recognition. "'The Buried Life'," she said. "It's from Matthew Arnold."

He cocked his head. "Impressive, especially for a laundress."

She colored and looked over his shoulder at nothing in particular. "I'm an avid reader, Mr Arnault."

"Roman. And you're quite an observer, too." Jane bit her lip to avoid a nervous smile. His dark blue eyes positively bored into her now. "So tell me," he said, "how does an orphaned laundress become a student of the poets?"

She looked up, startled. "I never told you I was an orphan."

"You forget the extent of my connections."

Jane nodded, not certain whether she should be thrilled or alarmed. "Maybe it's because I was an orphan. My parents died when I was two, and I spent as much of my childhood as I can remember surrounded by strange people and strange smells. The orphanage was miserable, and I was always looking for an excuse to spend time away from it. One day, when I was about seven, I found that excuse. One of the caretakers took a group of us to the Municipal Library – it's right next to the Quadrivium."

"I know it," Roman said. Located near the schools, it kept volumes upon volumes of books deemed safe for public consumption.

"It was quiet as a tomb. I had never been any place before where the sound of my own breathing was loud. It was wonderful." She paused, smiling at the recollection. "It gave me a reason to get away from the orphanage, so I applied for a special permit. Every afternoon after classes, I would leave for the Municipal Library and lose myself in the stacks and shelves until nightfall, when the custodian chased me out. It was orderly, peaceful, and with no one but the characters in the books to trouble me, I felt at home. Is that strange?"

"No," he said quietly.

Emboldened, she continued. "I read whatever I could reach. Stories, poetry, even a bit of science. The library became my haven – whenever I wanted to be alone, I was. And when I needed company... all I had to do was open a book."

"An interesting way to make friends," he said. Jane laughed.

"You have no idea. Actually, that's how I met Fredrick. In the library." Jane looked for Freddie in the crowd and found him quickly, a drink precariously balanced in one hand while the other waved and chopped. He had joined a ring of bureaucrats and was talking with more than his usual animation.

Roman squinted in his direction. "He doesn't look like the bookish type."

"He's not. But he buckles down when he needs to." Even in the glowing ballroom, Jane could still see the crooked shelves and rickety writing tables, all coated with the stains and scars of years. "He'd just gotten a job at the paper, and he found my favorite reading nook. It became his, too, and he was there several times a week, sometimes reading, sometimes working on one of his articles. We started talking, and I guess we took to one another. His mother died when he was fourteen and he didn't have much of a relationship with his father, so we saw eye to eye, if you understand what I mean."

"That's how you became friends?" Roman tilted his head forward, as if surprised that it could be so simple.

"There's a bit more. When I turned seventeen, he helped me arrange an appeal before the Sponsorship Committee so that I could get a temporary housing stipend and a job. One that didn't involve the factories." Many orphans and unfortunates ended up working twelve-hour shifts on factory machines and assembly lines. The most anyone could say for it was that it was an honest paycheck, and that accident rates were the lowest they'd been in decades. "As a successful professional with a good record, he signed himself as my sponsor, and the committee gave me a grant to set up shop as an independent laundress. I didn't have any money, and without him the most I could have hoped for was a maid's position in one of the wealthy houses. More likely, though, I'd be a groundskeeper living in a bunkhouse." Jane sighed, offering a small smile. "Freddie's glib, but he's a good friend."

Arnault nodded. "So it would seem."

"Now I've told you quite a bit about myself," Jane said. "Earlier, though, yours wasn't a real response – your lovely snatch of poetry. One would almost suspect that you have your own skeletons to hide."

He raised his eyebrows. "You're still thinking about that? Dear girl, there was nothing random about what I recited for you," he said. "After all, it's Victorian."

"What's that?"

"Matthew Arnold and his ilk, though who knows when they lived or what they produced beyond their poetry. Based on their writing, though, I can say that the Victorians knew a good deal about facades, though I would venture to say that we've learned more. It's a poem about secrets."

Jane knitted her brows. "Really? I always thought it was about people trying to connect. To figure who they are in relation to those around them."

"A similar idea." He leaned in. "Nothing is more defining than the things we choose to hide." Jane's eyes flitted to her fellow dancers, and she noticed that she and Roman seemed to have carved their own, private space out of the crowd. The other couples orbited at a safe distance.

"And what is it you choose to hide?" Jane asked. Once again, Roman threw back his head and laughed.

"Nothing gets by you, does it, Jane?"

She responded with what she hoped was an enigmatic smile. "I still don't understand exactly what it is you do with these people. You don't seem to have much in common."

"That's what makes our arrangement so simple. I don't have the same ties or interests. As an outsider, I am the perfect... what would you say? Accessory." He watched her nose wrinkle as she tried to make sense of his response. "That's just precious."

"You don't know the first thing about me," she said.

"No?" He chuckled. "Perhaps not, but I can guess quite a lot. You're just like the rest of them."

"The rest of who?"

"The nice girls of the world who try to fit in with the rest of us. You put up a show, but there are some things you'll never understand," he breathed, brushing her ear. Refusing to be baited, she looked over his shoulder and continued dancing as if she had not heard him. Without warning, he threw his arm and spun her outward, and she had to concentrate to keep her balance. Preparing for the return, she counted the steps as he pulled her back, the light skirts of her dress swishing against his knees. Tightening his grip around her waist, he doubled their pace, and she watched his eyes in hopes of anticipating his next move.

She didn't.

Without warning, he swept her legs out from under her, and she fought the urge to plant them back on the marble-tiled floor. Instead, she straightened her posture and trusted his lead, finishing the dip with a gamely kick. He held her barely a foot from the ground.

"You're bold but not too wise," he said, looking down at her.

"You don't intimidate me, Roman."

"You don't know enough to be intimidated." He straightened and returned Jane to her feet.

Jane brushed at her dress. "That's the way you wanted it. You're like the people in the poem. You get others to assume exactly you want because you only show them the tiniest part of yourself."

"For most people, that's enough."

She returned his piercing stare. "I don't care who the Council thinks you are, what it is you do as their enforcer, what the whitenails say about you, or why everyone else runs from you. You don't frighten me, and, for all your fierce looks, you don't have anything on me. Like you said, I'm an outsider."

He held her gaze in his own and smiled faintly. Slowly, he brushed her ear again and whispered. "I could show you who I am, what I do, and why they run. But will you like what you find?" His words lingered like an alcoholic aftertaste, and the lewdness stung her better judgment. She looked up at him as the song ended, and their dance slowed to a halt. His eyes, his whole face was motionless, and it was only as she felt a hand on her shoulder that she turned away.

Fredrick blinked at her, dazed by drink and astonished at her company. "Jane, I was hoping you'd give me the next dance."

She turned back to Roman, who had regained his sly smirk and cavalier posture. "It was a pleasure," she said. He kissed the back of her hand, grinning roguishly.

"Until we meet again." Something respectful fixed his gaze to hers, and they parted as two equals after a truce. Fredrick watched him go and whirled back to face her with the same look of poorly hidden wonder.

He hiccupped. "Some interesting friends you've made tonight."

"You knew we'd met already."

"Yes, the night you nearly got your head bashed in, but I wasn't aware that you two were so... chummy!"

She ignored him. "Come on, Freddie. You said you wanted to dance." She held up an arm, waiting for him to assume the proper position. With a bemused shrug, he grasped her hand and they floated with the current of people.

They danced to a peppery waltz, hopping spryly about the room. Fredrick maintained his uncharacteristic silence, at times avoiding her gaze and at others glancing at her with cockeyed suspicion. Jane avoided thinking about why he would be annoyed with her and turned to her own thoughts. She thought about Roman, about what her new whitenail friends thought about him, and, most importantly, about whether she was as naïve as he seemed to think.

Fredrick spoke up. "Over there. Another friend of yours." Jane turned and saw him staring at a woman in a shimmering silver and gray gown. Liesl Malone was hardly recognizable without her customary uniform, but the short, razor-like platinum locks; the hypnotic, pale eyes; and the statue-like expression set her apart. The slimming gown hugged the womanly curves that Jane was a little surprised to notice Malone did, in fact, have. Judging by his expression, Fredrick was noticing the same thing. Jane had never thought of her as being a woman in a dress, yet Malone blended in with the glamorous crowd. Somehow, this made her more intimidating.

As the song finished, Jane and Fredrick returned to their acquaintances of earlier. The three women watched them with Cheshire-cat smiles and glittering eyes. "So wonderful to see the two of you back," said Madame Attrop with almost exaggerated politeness. "Fredrick, how did your inquiries go?"

He rolled his eyes a little too wildly. "Just the usual, Madame Attrop. Another convention to divide and re-divide the governorship of farming communes in the south. The only thing that's interesting is how well the two sides get along when you put alcohol and crab cakes in front of them," he said, smirking. Madame Clothoe giggled.

"And how did you enjoy the dance, Miss Lin?" asked Lady Lachesse. Her many jewels winked at Jane.

"It was wonderful," said she. "Mr Arnault is an exceptional dancer." The women smiled with still more feline ambiguity, and Fredrick looked again at her in disbelief.

"Such a strange young man," said Madame Clothoe in her creaky voice. "And to think, he could have been a member of the Council. So much potential," she mumbled, trailing off. Jane twisted her head at Madame Clothoe and hoped that someone would continue her thread.

Of course, she had hoped for someone other than Freddie. "I take it you aren't aware of Mr Arnault's history," he said, eyeing her with malicious entertainment.

"I didn't even know he existed until last week."

"Perhaps the good Lady Lachesse would be so kind as to enlighten you. She knows more about these circles and histories than anyone here."

"I know he's got a shady reputation," Jane said with a fierce glance at Fredrick.

"Shady?" He nearly laughed. "That doesn't cover the half of it, my dear." He nodded in the direction of the dance floor, and Jane followed his gaze. She saw Roman now locked in tight footwork with Inspector Malone, and she felt a flash of something uncomfortable that she could not definitely pin as jealousy or fear. To her chagrin, Fredrick was studying her with grim satisfaction, and she turned around, again trying to look as if she had not noticed.

"Roman Arnault is a uniquely static figure in that his history begins with as much mystery as that in which he now abides," said Lady Lachesse, framing her words with painted lips. The others turned their rapt attention to her, and Jane realized that Lady Lachesse was probably accustomed to this kind of audience. "The boy, Roman Arnault, arrived in Recoletta twenty-six years ago with his parents. They came from somewhere overseas, though it was never clear exactly where they came from or why they left. Some speculated that the Arnault family moved to escape an impossible debt, avoid some bloody feud in their homeland, or simply fulfill a strange wanderlust that may have possessed them. Of course, later theories purported that some unknown atrocity or dark secret, attributable to the seven year-old Roman himself, motivated their mysterious relocation, but this is based more in his highly developed myth than in fact."

"What became of the family in Recoletta?" Jane asked.

"Their swiftly acquired titles will give you some hint as to their prudence in the whitenail circles. Duke and Duchess Arnault, as they came to be called, were every bit as enigmatic as their son is now, and shrewd as well. They arrived with a fair sum of money and in the space of less than a year were the toast of the Vineyard. Very quickly the Arnaults became intimate friends with the illustrious Sato family, which, I trust, you have heard of."

Jane nodded. "Of course." Though the last of the Sato family had perished years ago, their name was still more highly regarded in the city than even Councilor Ruthers's.

Lady Lachesse lowered her voice and continued. "Duke and Duchess Arnault were their confidantes, and Councilor and Lady Sato formed an uncommonly close bond with them.

"Despite their enviable political connections, neither Arnault ever aspired to any overt power. Much like their son, they were content, even in their element, working their own potent magic in the background. They had titles, but those are more useful in the marriage market than anywhere else. The only title with real, fungible power in Recoletta is 'Councilor'." She took a breath. "The Arnaults earned a substantial income owning and developing real-estate sites. The first of these were gifts from the Satos, and the Arnaults appeared every bit as suited to business as to behind-the-scenes politics."

"Their removal from the system was part of what gave them so much power," said Madame Attrop. "They stayed out of the political games."

"How do you mean?" Jane asked.

Lady Lachesse shot an irritated glance at Madame Attrop and continued. "Councilors are politicians because they know how to ask and, in some cases, demand favors. The Arnaults were landowners, so they had plenty of favors to give but made a point of asking for few. When you own a cubic mile of the most valued property in Recoletta, there isn't much else you need, after all.

"Twenty-three years ago, both Duke and Duchess Arnault expired from sudden illness, though many conspiracy theorists insist that poison was involved. Their deaths shook the city, and Councilor Sato lost both great strategists and close friends with their passing. Young Roman was already something of a loner, but this unforeseen loss plunged him much deeper into his isolation. The Sato family took him in, adopting the lone remnant of their strange and powerful allies." She paused, a distant look in her eyes. "Whether this was a strategic or sentimental maneuver is still debated. As with most things, it was probably a measure of both. Many of the Arnaults' secrets, including that of their mysterious origins, most likely died with them, but Roman would still have been too valuable to be passed along like a bad debt." Jane felt a sudden pang of empathy for him, yet also wondered that his orphaning had brought him to a position so different from her own.

"I do not mean to paint an overly melancholy picture of Roman's childhood," Lady Lachesse said. "He was good friends with the single Sato child, Jakkeb, who was his junior by a year or two. One must, however, fit these tidbits into the greater context of our political world, where notions of familial affection are often secondary.

"Nevertheless, things went well for the newly extended Sato clan. Councilor Castor Sato, one of the most popular politicians in recent history, continued his personal golden age heading the Council with unprecedented success. Lady Luz Sato was an astute businesswoman, and her endeavors prospered. Jakkeb and Roman benefited from the finest tutors the city had to offer, and both excelled in their studies at the Quadrivium." Here Lady Lachesse sighed, almost with weariness.

"It was at this time, just over fourteen years ago, that misfortune struck again. I am sure you will recall this event for the uproar that followed in its wake. Councilor and Lady Sato were killed one night by a mugger. He was, of course, quickly apprehended and executed by a unanimous vote almost before a trial could be finished, but the public was heartbroken over the loss of its favorite darlings. As if this were not enough, in a stupor of grief, Jakkeb Sato walked into one of his late mother's properties, a textile storehouse, which he set aflame himself. He never walked out.

"And Roma... Mr Arnault?"

"After unforgivably surviving his second family, Roman was doomed to be branded a pariah for the persistence of his reputation," she said.

"You might say he has a variant of the Midas touch," Fredrick said. "Everything he touches dies."

Again, Jane ignored him. "And that's why he's so reviled? Because he's unlucky?"

"That is really only the beginning," said Lady Lachesse. "The Roman Arnault that we see – or at least, that I see," she said with a shrewd look, "– is thoroughly enveloped in a myth of his own creation. He has never said or done anything to discourage his unsavory reputation. In fact, he invites it. It is his identity as surely as mine is a railway heiress and yours is a sweet-mannered laundress."

Lady Lachesse plucked two fluted glasses from a passing tray, handing one to Jane. "But it isn't the same. Because you and I can detach from these public personae at will, whereas Mr Arnault, I sincerely believe, cannot. Whether through grief or for security, he retreated so far into his dark image that it is impossible to tell the man and the myth apart. No, he could not disentangle himself if he wanted to, and it is for that reason that I pity the man who could have been a prince." Her eyes turned upwards, and Jane saw a flash of bronze neck as Lady Lachesse tilted her head back to finish her drink.

"But what about his title and his fortune?" Jane asked. "Surely he could live a comfortable and quiet life if he wanted."

"He relinquished his title after the death of the Satos. You must appreciate the effect that these events had on him – fame and luxury became an anathema to him when he saw how poorly they protected the people in his life. As for the fortune, conventional wisdom is that he has it squirreled away for an emergency, but he lives modestly on his income from the Council."

Jane shook her head, running her thumb along the smooth edge of her own glass. In the background, a group of men and women laughed loudly. "Why even bother? Why get involved with the Council if he has the money to live a quiet life?"

Lady Lachesse gave Jane a long, sideways glance. "Security."

Seeing Jane's puzzlement, Madame Attrop spoke. "I think you're missing the point of our story, Miss Lin. Someone in Roman's position cannot afford to be irrelevant, so he chooses to make himself useful. He's unassuming enough to avoid challenging anyone for power, but he's resourceful enough to be indispensable to those that have it. Knowing what he knows, he has to be."

"And what does he know?"

"That," Madame Attrop said with a smile, "is the question."

Jane paused, mulling over the new information. "You'll forgive my ignorance, but this is all rather shocking. I was under the impression that whitenails lived charmed lives. You can see what a wreck the murders of the past week have caused, after all."

Lady Lachesse smiled. "We live, bleed, and die too. We just try to make everyone forget that."

"Councils change," Jane said. "What happens to Roman then?"

"Oh, I'm sure he'll find a way to manage. He had better."

"You must understand, dear, what he does on behalf of very powerful people," Madame Clothoe warbled, stroking Jane's arm.

"Well, what does he do?" Jane asked.

A nasty sneer crept across Fredrick's face. "I trust you've noticed that a certain… odor lingers about Mr Arnault?"

"The clove cigarettes," Jane said, reluctantly turning back to him.

"Yes, but do you know why he smokes them?" Fredrick asked. Jane waited in the pause that followed. "They kill the gag reflex and cover the stench. For a bottom-feeder, see?"

"It's funnier if you don't have to explain it," Jane said.

Madame Attrop interceded. "Mr Anders has just regaled us with a common, if unflattering, joke about Mr Arnault and the unpleasantness of his work. With the exception of Lady Lachesse and a couple others in this room, few could say with specificity what Mr Arnault does," she said. "This, you will agree, is part of where he gets his power."

Madame Clothoe winced. "They say that he commits murders for the Council," she whispered.

"And he has never tried to deny it," Madame Attrop added quickly.

"Of course he wouldn't," Lady Lachesse said. She smiled slowly. "And as much as he depends on his air of mystery, I can't fault him for guarding it. I doubt he has gone that far, but I can regale you with one story that is true, if you want to know what kind of man he is."

"Please," Jane said.

"It happened several years ago. Councilor Ruthers and certain investors had entered into a bargain with a metallurgist named Oxley to develop a lighter alloy for railcar construction. After the others had financed these efforts, Oxley realized he had developed a much better product than he'd anticipated, and he reneged on his agreement with the intention of selling the composition on his own.

"Expecting retaliation, Oxley hid his notes and samples well before this became known. He had also arranged a chain of middlemen through which he could sell his alloy to factories outside of Recoletta. He planned this scheme for months. The point is, it was obvious that Oxley had protected his creations well enough, so Roman didn't steal from him. He stole from Azari." The look on Lady Lachesse's face was not quite admiration, but it was close.

Jane blinked. "Azari?"

Lady Lachesse nodded. "Azari was a rival metallurgist. Not only did he and Oxley compete in their formulae, but they also competed for patronage from investors such as Councilor Ruthers, so you can imagine Azari's furor when he realized that months of his labor had vanished and that he would have to produce an explanation for a rich and powerful patron. Imagine that furor when news of Oxley's plans surfaced.

"Along with the other members of the metallurgists' guild, Azari believed that Oxley was also selling his alloys to the foreigners. It didn't help matters," Lady Lachesse added with a grin, "that Azari had found a broken pair of Oxley's spectacles in his shop. Before long, Oxley was wondering whether selling his designs would bring him wealth or ruin. When another guild member's formulae disappeared, he began to fear for his life.

"Ultimately, Oxley gave up the scheme. He surrendered the designs to his original investors, and the metallurgists' guild retrieved the missing compositions from his study. He did leave Recoletta, but without a penny of the fortune he had hoped to earn."

"I don't understand," Jane said. "Why go through so much trouble when Ruthers could have had him arrested?"

Lady Lachesse smiled again. "To make an example. Besides, Councilor Ruthers isn't the kind of man that likes to have the Municipals involved in his business when he can help it."

Jane exhaled, and, as her attention broke from Lady Lachesse's tale, she was almost surprised to see the rest of the partygoers still dancing and the attendants bringing out new trays stacked with delicacies. "It's quite a story. You'll pardon my curiosity, but how do you know that Roman was behind it?"

"The new designs were installed on Lady Lachesse's railways, dear," Madame Attrop said. "And she always watches her investments."

Lady Lachesse placed her empty glass on another passing tray. "I told you this story to give you an idea of how Mr Arnault operates – cleverly and in the background. I don't think he's a killer, but I know he's devious. Still, he's no worse than most others here, and I can't blame him when so many of us profit from his exploits. But come now, this is unsuitable talk for a party. Let us continue to merrier subjects, shall we?"

CHAPTER 7

THE OTHER SIDE OF THE BALLROOM

In the week before the gala, Liesl Malone's preparations had begun not with etiquette lessons, but with covert meetings. She could hardly expect the Council to issue her an invitation, so she and Sundar had devised other means.

Like any good machine, a party consisted of several moving parts. For Malone, inserting herself into it was a matter of identifying the weakest of these components and applying leverage. Ticking through her options, she knew it wouldn't be security and it wouldn't be food. Both the guard detail and the catering would run like clockwork. This left service and entertainment. Malone did not relish the idea of taking more orders than necessary from the whitenails, so she and Sundar set the first option aside and explored the latter in her office.

"Seems like our only choice, but going in with the performers isn't as subtle as I'd like," she said.

"It'll be easier than you think. Besides, you've got a cellist's fingers."

"But not a cellist's training. How do you know so much about the orchestra?"

Sundar scratched the back of his head and looked away. "I, uh, know a violinist."

"How well?"

"Old acquaintance from my performing days. Let's just say I'm not in any position to ask favors from her right now." He coughed into a fist. "It's, uh, complicated. Anyway, don't worry about the playing – you won't have to."

"I'm not hiding in the cello case."

"Better," he said. Reaching inside his jacket, he pulled out a folded but crisp sheet of paper and spread it on her desk. "You have an invitation."

"Except that isn't my name."

He shrugged. "That can be fixed. This is just a performer's invite, so it's not printed on the fancy stuff."

Malone bent over the square. "This is how you upset the violinist?"

"All in the course of duty, I'm afraid." Sundar sighed and ruffled his forelocks.

Malone looked at her watch. It wasn't yet eight in the morning. She smiled slowly. "She might not be upset if you'd stayed for breakfast."

Sundar grimaced. "Too right. But then I wouldn't have made it here."

"Is she going to know you took it?"

He relaxed. "Not a chance. I'm surprised she hadn't lost it already, knowing how often she's misplaced her instrument. It's a good thing she doesn't play the triangle."

"Do they check invitations against a master list? If so, we've got another paper to forge."

"No, not the last I heard. There'll be a few stand-ins and changes anyway if someone gets sick. Or if a second-chair performer shapes up. You'll blend in as long as you wear something black. For you, that shouldn't be a problem."

"That takes care of the doorman, but what about the orchestra? Someone will notice I'm out of place."

"Just show up at the door five minutes late and look apologetic. You'll miss the musicians completely."

Malone sat back in her chair and nodded to Sundar, who looked supremely pleased with himself. "There's only one more problem."

"What's that?"

"I don't have a cello."

"Of course." Sundar tapped the edge of the desk. "I know where we can get one, though. On loan. I know someone who runs a shop."

"Another 'acquaintance'?"

"Different kind. But you have to bring it back, or I'll be paying for it over the next year." He sighed, rubbing his chin. "The doormen will point you to a back room when you enter – it's where the musicians gather. You can leave the instrument there and pick it up again on your way out. They're all professionals, so no one will touch it."

"Wonderful." Malone stretched her lean arms, drawing a deep breath and looking around her office and its spartan furnishings.

"Come to think of it, there is something else." Sundar gave Malone a doubtful frown.

"Yes?"

"After you clear the door, if you don't want to look like a fugitive performer, you'll have to... uh... wear a dress."

She swung her arms back down to the desk. "I know."

"I mean, not just any dress, a nice one."

"It's covered."

"A really nice one." He leaned forward, eyes wide and serious.

"Sundar... I've got it."

He sat back, looking unconvinced. "OK."

Malone sighed. "We won't be able to do this forever."

Sundar blinked. "Plan in your office?"

"No. Investigate this contract, right under the Council's nose."

"I thought we were being discreet."

Malone shook her head, but her pale eyes remained fixed on him. "Sooner or later, they'll notice."

Sundar frowned, lines creeping across his handsome face. "What's our endgame? If we don't figure it out and the Council realizes that we're still snooping, they'll... what?"

"Suspend us."

Sundar exhaled dramatically. "Fantastic. They suspend us. And if we do get to the bottom of it, and we uncover the mystery and whatever Council secrets go with it, they'll shake our hands?" He tilted his chin at her.

"I don't plan on getting caught. They'll need more than a suspicion to punish us. Besides, I think we can count on support from certain members of the Council when we reach the endgame if we can prove ourselves. And I've got an idea of where to start."

"And that's what you're going to look into at the gala?"

Malone nodded, pursing her lips. "That's part of it. I'm going to make a few other inquiries."

"Is that safe?" Malone could tell by the wrinkling of Sundar's brow and his frown what he thought of the idea.

"They're not going to suspend us for making conversation. Not as long as the forgery's good, anyway." She tapped the invitation. "It's when we get serious that we'll need to be careful."

Sundar's eyes widened. "I can't wait to see what you consider serious."

Malone planted her elbows on the desk. "Soon, we'll need to find someone we can trust. Someone with access to the whitenails. An informant."

He tapped his temple. "So we can stay out of the Council's line of sight."

"Precisely. I'm looking for someone who comes and goes in their circles without being noticed. Someone with a wide network of contacts. Any ideas?"

Again, Sundar frowned. "Roman Arnault?"

"Try Jane Lin."

A wry grin crossed Sundar's face, half amused and half dubious. "Jane Lin, drugged laundress?"

"The same."

He shook his head. "I don't know, Malone. I can't see her sneaking into directorates or swiping invitations." He waggled the creased paper in the air between them.

"I can. She just needs the right incentive."

Whereas Jane had entered Brummell Hall via the full splendor of the veranda, Liesl slipped in through a quiet back entrance designated for staff and musicians. As Sundar had assured her, the door guards admitted her without too much fuss, and she left her borrowed cello in a quiet salon reserved for the performers. She pulled a smuggled evening dress from the cello case and made her transformation. With a bracing breath, she turned back down the hallway and into the ballroom.

Swirling in the room, she saw secrets. They sulked in corners, they glided across the dance floor, and they stood huddled in discreetly chattering groups. The partygoers who did not recognize her were suspiciously closed to her, and the few who did know her even more so. Secrets, hovering just out of reach and scattering like moths from a lantern.

She saw plenty of familiar faces, but none that would be glad to see her. The buzz was all about the fashionable delegation from South Haven, or rather, how they might pass for fashionable were they not from such a wretched little hamlet, wearing robes the color of dried blood. Malone was finding little of use.

She knew of one lead. The Council, now accompanied by the South Haven delegation, talked animatedly at one end of the room, expertly cordoned off by a ring of hangers-on. Satellite attendants floated in and out, but the tended flock lay just out of reach. Most importantly, the one member that Liesl truly wanted to meet with, Alfred Hollens, stood in the thick of it.

He seemed to her trained eye more insulated than his peers. Appropriately to one so tightly enclosed, he also seemed more uncomfortable. Was it the heat of so many bodies lending the telltale sheen to his forehead, or was it something within? There was a distinctive undertone of tension in the group of politicians, not unusual for such a gathering, but there seemed something hotter and ranker mingled with it – fear? Was it only her own suspicion, or did a number from both sides of the group, including Hollens, seem beleaguered with the sticky-warm churnings of vain, primitive fear?

That would be difficult to determine without a closer look. But Hollens was lodged in the group like a cog in an engine. Hollens, the head of the Directorate of Preservation, the councilor who might have explanations for the secret projects, the man who, in his delicate state, might be prodded into sharing them, seemed at this juncture the hardest to reach. Malone's considerable experience had taught her that in such cases, it was better to lure the target than to chase it.

She watched as he drained a green-tinted martini and broke from his protective throng to signal a passing waiter. Receiving his instructions, the waiter nodded and made a beeline for the kitchen as Hollens retreated again into the human insulation. Malone hovered just out of sight of the Council throng as she waited for the server to return. When he did, she had to step in front of him to get his attention, so focused was he on returning to the councilor. She moaned, a look of painful anxiety on her face.

"The washroom?"

The waiter blinked and pointed to a side corridor, unaware of her hand quickly passing over the martini glass to deposit a clear pastille as she gripped his shoulder. Bobbing her head gratefully, she hurried toward the bathroom with convincing haste. She planted herself in front of the men's room, telling the few baffled guests who approached that they would have to seek relief from the toilets on the other end of the hall until these had been thoroughly cleaned. From that removed position, she monitored her handiwork.

The waiter delivered the tainted martini to Hollens, who promptly transferred it to a larger man with the look of a well-trained ape in a tuxedo. The simian assistant gingerly sipped the martini and, smacking his lips, returned it to Hollens. The pastille, a light emetic, would only just have begun to dissolve, and its convenient lack of flavor and color would escape suspicion.

Hollens had finished his martini well before she saw him cough and sputter, raising a hand in protest to the simian-man's alarm. Nothing too distressing, just the nerves of a long evening finally getting to him, and he begged the pardon of his companions for a moment. With admirable composure, he scurried to the facilities to relieve the sickening churnings of fear, which had at last manifested themselves physically.

Aware that he would not be allowed to follow Hollens into the bathroom, the simian assistant trailed his master to make sure that no one else did.

Hollens reached the toilets without a moment to spare. He heaved his head over the appropriate depository as his restive insides surrendered their contents. After he had finished, he rested a perspiring temple on the cool wall, recovering. His reaction was one of astonishment when he saw a plush white towel held inches from his nose. The protest died in his throat as Malone pressed the towel into his free hand and addressed him coolly.

"You've had a long week, Councilor. I can see the pressure has finally brought itself to bear on you."

"Madam, I don't know who you are, but this is highly inappropriate. I must ask you to leave," he said, rising.

"I want to help you."

"The towel will be plenty. Please go." Hollens crossed to the washbasin and splashed his face with water. He averted his gaze from Malone the way one would avoid looking at a madman.

"I need to know what you know."

In the mirror, Malone saw Hollens's eyes flicker toward her over his cupped hands. "I haven't the slightest idea what you're talking about."

"The murders, Councilor. Something is happening among your ranks, and it's already cost two men their lives." A dark look crossed his features, replacing the embarrassment and confusion.

"Our guards have this situation under control," he said, bringing another handful of water to his forehead.

She gestured at the empty bathroom. "Are you sure?"

"We have protocols, Madam, and they are none of your concern."

"They're also pointless. You know as well as I that your people have accomplished nothing in the intervening week. If I were on the other side, you'd be dead already."

Now realization and rage scalded his words. "You go too far. I could have you arrested for this."

"Councilor Hollens, I'm an inspector of the Municipal Police. I'm trying to help you."

"You're overstepping your bounds, as I understand it," he said, patting his face dry. "Your authority has been suspended as far as this contract is concerned."

"And what good has it done?" she said. "For all the special measures your guards and agents have taken, it hasn't brought you one step closer to apprehending the killer."

"It's a complicated and extensive investigation." He glowered at her. "Besides, you didn't do much better."

"Only for lack of opportunity. We were on the right track, and we were making progress. That's why we were cut out of the contract so abruptly."

"No, you were removed because your people do not have the background or the connections to properly investigate it, Inspector..."

"Malone." She paused, hoping that she wasn't making a mistake. Sundar, she knew, would be disappointed if their gambit failed for her lack of discretion, especially after their last meeting. "And whose fault was that? I tried with your Dr Hask before Fitzhugh was killed."

Hollens blinked in surprise. "It is not as simple as facts and leads, Inspector. The information you want is confidential, and as minor as that detail may seem to you, we maintain these protocols for a reason."

Malone shook her head, the radiance stones shining

across her slicked locks. "This is absurd, especially with a traitor in your midst."

Hollens froze. "What?"

"Why else has your investigation from the inside been so useless? One of your colleagues has been collaborating with the murderer from the beginning. By compartmentalizing and passing the investigation through your hierarchy, you're playing directly into his, or her, hand."

"You know this for a fact?" he asked, almost keeping the quaver out of his voice.

"I'd be blind not to notice it. As your investigators have been, apparently." She cocked her head and leveled her gaze at him. "I suspect that this has at least occurred to you, Councilor Hollens."

"What reason do I have to believe that you can be of any use? Especially if you are correct in these preposterous assumptions."

"You and your peers have cut me off from the contract, and, as far as they're concerned, I'm hamstrung. A lame horse can't kick the coachman."

He snorted. "Nor pull the carriage. What do you expect to accomplish?"

"Give me time and information, and I'll find out who's behind this. It's a process of elimination, starting with those who want to see your directorate fail at its project."

"You think you're that good?"

"Check my record."

Hollens mopped the perspiration from his forehead. "If I help you, Inspector Malone, it stays between us. More than the murderers will be after me if anyone gets wind of this."

Malone shrugged her bare shoulders. "I'm officially off the contract. What you tell me doesn't leave this toilet."

He shot her a cross glare. "Given the circumstances, you will have to trust me when I give you only the information directly pertinent to this matter."

"What may seem trivial to you could be useful to me, Councilor. I need to know what the Directorate of Preservation is doing."

Hollens straightened, his voice regaining some of the authority of before. "I will be the judge of relevancy, madam. Besides, I'm the one who will pay if I am wrong – either way." He trapped a sigh behind his lips and passed a shaking hand through his hair. Guiding her further from the door, he continued in a rumbling whisper. "I cannot tell you much now, and I've been in here too long. The best I can do is advise you to look into the Sato case. You recall the murders of the prominent councilor and lady?"

Malone nodded.

"There is more to the case than was explained, much more. Examine it thoroughly, and you will find there was a reason the murderer was executed so quickly." Hollens looked away briefly, his eyes showing something like remorse. "Contact me when you succeed, and, if you're as capable as you say, I'll tell you more."

He spun briskly for the door, but paused. "If we do not meet again," he began, his back still to her, "there's a vault in my residence, in the cellar, behind the wine. Should it come to that, I trust you can find it. When – if – if you do, much will be explained. Do not under any circumstances attempt to access it before my death."

"How do I open it?"

He turned to her and cracked a twisted grin. "You say that you've met Dr Hask? By which I assume you somehow reached her in her office?"

"Just as I found you in the washroom."

"The writing's on the wall, Malone. If you're as clever as you say, you'll know what to do when the time comes. I'm not so desperate as to reveal all of my secrets to a stranger."

Malone stepped toward him, her feet clacking softly on the tiles. "I need the truth, Hollens. Not riddles and games."

"Truth is exactly what you need, Inspector. But, like the rest of us, you'll have to figure it out for yourself." He strode decisively from the bathroom. Peering around the corner, Malone saw the simian man waiting outside the bathroom to escort Hollens, who marched back toward the councilors without a trace of the fear she had seen. After a pause, she slipped out of the bathroom and again into the mingling crowd.

Malone stopped next to a piece of sculpture, watching the couples dance. After brief observation, she noticed a tall, dark man leading a bright young thing with more than the usual force. The girl responded with sly coyness, allowing her partner to sweep her along. She seemed familiar, and as Liesl continued to watch the boldly roving eyes and delicately insouciant lips, she recognized the earnest young laundress from the hospital. How different she appeared now!

Intense and filled with fiery glee, Jane presented an entirely different vision. She swung and swayed, exhilarated at the rough direction of her dark partner and at their seemingly parallel conversation. Liesl would not have imagined her so spry and fierce. Still, that spark of sincerity set Jane apart from the crowd, lending her an air of gravity and naïveté.

Pleasantly intrigued, Liesl turned her focus to Miss Lin's partner. She did not recognize his patiently menacing stride, his coolly taut features, or anything else about him. Recalling her earlier conversation with Lin, she remembered the shy girl's mention of a Roman Arnault and Chief Johanssen's brief characterization, and something clicked.

Their strange dance ended, and Malone saw Lin and Arnault part. The reporter whisked her away, leaving Arnault to brood next to a table of spirit-filled glasses. Miss Lin, she was sure, would never be too hard to find, but Arnault? This moment presented an unexpected opportunity.

Skirting the edge of the ballroom, Malone reached Arnault's corner and sidled up next to him. "Roman Arnault, in the flesh. I've heard so much about you."

He looked uncertainly down, as if noticing the trim blonde for the first time. "Is that so?"

"No. But if you'll give me a few minutes of your time, we could fix that."

He snorted and took another swig from his glass. "What do you want?"

"A little civility, for starters."

"Civility?"

"The kind a gentleman offers a lady."

Arnault studied her for several moments, swirling his drink between two fingers. "I know you, *madam*. You're no lady. You're a Municipal."

"And you're no gentleman by proper standards," she said. "But we can both pretend tonight, can't we? Just like the rest of these politicians and panderers."

Before Arnault could protest, Malone slipped one arm through his and with the other hand took his drink. She tossed it back and plunked the empty glass onto a passing tray. "I want to dance." One of them – it would be difficult to identify which – led the other back to the center of the room.

Now locked together in a rhythm, Malone had Arnault captive for a few minutes. He must have noticed this himself, for he smiled mirthlessly. "A woman who dispenses with foreplay. You're a rare breed."

"I don't believe in wasting time. Tell me what you know about Werner Cahill and Lanning Fitzhugh."

"If memory serves, you lost that contract. Enlighten me; why should I talk to you about this?"

"Because you're still stuck with me for the next three minutes. And I've got bad pitch and a habit of humming with music."

"You are persuasive."

"So talk to me about Cahill and Fitzhugh."

He rolled his tongue around inside one cheek, creating a thoughtful bulge. "Well, my lady," he said, drawing out the first syllable, "they're both dead."

"Something else."

He gazed over her shoulder, apparently doing his best to ignore her.

"You had some acquaintance with these men before their deaths," she said.

"And how do you assume that?"

"Don't be defensive. There's nothing suspicious in your having known them. Already you play the guilty party, and I haven't accused you of anything." Behind Malone, other dancers scooted away, giving her and Arnault wider berth.

"Interrogate me if you must, but don't bait me. I'm perfectly aware of my reputation and further aware that my job depends on it."

"What job might that be?"

He smiled cryptically. "I'm a consultant."

"And I'm consulting you."

"My employers appreciate my discretion. Who knows, if you had that aptitude, maybe you'd still have a contract."

"At the rate they're going, there may not be too many whitenails left to employ you soon."

Arnault rolled his eyes. "How morbid. Then you know that I would stop these calamities if I could. What do you expect me to do about it?"

"Tell me something useful."

"That dress makes you look hard and shapeless."

Malone's lean, muscled shoulders tensed, and her grip on Roman's arm tightened. "Mr Arnault, if I'm right about you, you could be arrested. If I'm wrong, you could be next. Aren't you concerned?"

"Madam, I'm in politics. I dodge bullets like this daily. Why should I worry about a demoted Municipal or a murdering insomniac?"

"Because I can place you within blocks of Lanning Fitzhugh on the night of his death. Give me time and I can find you closer to Cahill."

Arnault sighed. "Really. Then you'll also know that I have an alibi."

"Don't be so sure," she replied, conscious of the song winding to a stop. The dance halted to scattered applause, and Arnault gave the obligatory, stilted bow of someone who has just completed a disagreeable task.

"My good inspector, I would say it has been a pleasure, but I think we both know better."

"Until we meet again, Roman Arnault."

"Do not count on it." Whirling with casual grace, he swept out of sight, leaving Malone to ponder her next move. Her thoughts returned to Jane Lin, who stood chatting with the reporter and a trio of older women. She waited until she saw Jane break from the group and head for the washroom. On the return trip, Malone swooped.

"Inspector Malone! How nice to see you," Jane said with polite but affected surprise.

"Likewise, Miss Lin. I know you work for these types, but I didn't think you were on their invite lists."

"I'm not. In fact, you're only the second person to recognize me. I came with Fredrick Anders. He was with me at the hospital."

Nodding, Malone shifted her gaze to the left. "It would seem, however, that you and I share a common associate."

Jane's eyes drifted and her complexion reddened. "I promise, I told you everything I know in the hospital. I've no reason to hide anyth–"

Liesl smiled gently. "I'm not here to interrogate you, Jane. I just wanted to say hello. And," she said, guiding Jane by the elbow, "I wanted to inform you of some changes in Callum Station."

"Oh?"

"As your friend the reporter may have told you, I'm no longer on the contract. In fact, the Municipal Police no longer has any jurisdiction over these investigations. I've learned," Malone said, glancing over their heads, "that the Council is handling the contract."

"Why would they do that?"

"To cover something up. Maybe an embarrassment or an administrative secret. At least, that's what I'd like to think."

Jane's features fell and pallor replaced her girlish blush. "What else could it be?"

"For now, let's just hope that's it."

Jane frowned, glancing from Malone to the shifting crowd around them. "What does this mean, then?"

"It means that we will both have to be a little more careful. I still don't think you're in danger, but all the same, you should be careful. Whether or not these murders involve the Council, someone in the upper echelons is part of it. My instincts point to your friend, the 'consultant'."

"Inspector, I think you're being hasty. I'm not prepared to believe–"

"He's not necessarily working with the murderer." Malone hesitated, setting the lure. "He could also be in danger. One way or another, someone with fewer scruples than me will be after him. That's why I ask you to keep an open mind."

Gnawing at her lip, the laundress nodded. "What do you want me to do?"

"Keep your head down and let me know if you notice anything peculiar. I can't officially investigate anything, and you can't openly contact me, so we have to communicate in secret."

Jane nodded again. "Go on."

"If you need to contact me, leave a message at the Dispatch in box thirteen-sixty-four. If necessary, I can meet you at 3 o'clock the day I receive your message, or the following afternoon. At the market. If you were to find any useful information, that box would also be the place to deposit it." She suddenly smiled. "Don't look so alarmed, Jane. These are merely precautions. I would ask the same of any witness."

"I'm a little shocked. You're asking me to help you investigate? Is this routine?"

"Events of the past week have not been routine, Miss Lin. I don't trust the way the Council is handling this, and you need to ask yourself if you do. I can't afford to pass on help if you're willing to give it."

Jane narrowed her eyes. "Why do you trust me, Inspector? How do you know I won't turn you in to the Council myself?"

Malone smiled knowingly. "After Councilor Ruthers's toast? Or the week of martial law? I may be the only one standing between you and a killer who could still decide that you pose a threat. By the same logic, I'm the only one in a position to save your gentleman friend, either way things fall.

"Besides," Malone continued, "if you turned me in, the Council would hold you under suspicion, too, and they wouldn't treat eavesdropping in a councilor's home so lightly. They'd worry about what you know, and, at a time like this, they'd consider you collateral damage."

Jane shook her head as if trying to clear it. "But why come to me? I don't know anything about spying or investigations."

"Exactly because you're an unlikely agent. But I'm not asking you to look for trouble. It may find you, ready or not."

Jane nodded more resolutely. "I hope you're wrong, but I'll keep an ear out, Inspector."

"Take a deep breath, Jane. Think of this as a promotion."

Jane decided that this wasn't the time to ask if it came with a pay raise.

Malone returned her focus to the party where laughing men and women reveled despite the intrigues unraveling around them. "Thank you for your time, Jane. I hope I haven't kept you too long from your friends."

"Not at all." She grinned. "I know I'll never forget my first gala."

Malone tilted her head in the direction of the open dance floor. "From what I saw, you didn't need me to make it memorable. Enjoy the rest of your evening, Miss Lin."

"I would say the most interesting parts have passed – both of them."

CHAPTER 8

DIRTY LAUNDRY

Malone spent the days after the gala keeping a low profile and hoping her younger partner could do the same. While she had bobbed and weaved among the luminaries at Brummell Hall, Sundar had spent the evening on stakeout in the Vineyard, a role that he had accepted with characteristic and dutiful gusto. He had kept his post in the shadows until the wee hours – well after the partygoers had returned home. With the guard contingents in the Vineyard distracted by the gala, he had managed to avoid detection.

Much to Malone's amusement, he retained his zest the next morning when they met at the station and he inquired about the gala.

"It was impressive," she said, "but frightening to think of the kind of business that is settled over so much wine and caviar."

Sundar grinned with vicarious pleasure. "Well, at least you got to have some."

Malone cocked her head, and Sundar blinked back at her. "Wine and caviar," he said. "And truffles, slow roast, and whatever else they had. You did try them, right?"

"I wasn't there to sample the banquet."

Sundar collapsed in a fit of thespian anguish. "Malone! You're telling me you were there four hours and you couldn't spare five minutes for the finest food you'll ever clap eyes on? I can't do this. Next time, you dodge patrols in the cold."

"Calm down. The news isn't all bad."

Sundar perked up. "You had more success with the politicians than the buffet table?"

"Let's discuss it in private." They set off from the main hallway toward her office. "Have you checked in with the chief yet?" she asked.

"As soon as I came in this morning. As usual, he didn't have much to say." Sundar gave her a suggestive glance. Malone understood what he meant. Chief Johanssen had turned a blind eye to their clandestine investigations, and the two inspectors kept up their end of the ruse. The pair continued to check in with their chief every morning, but the visits were always the same. When she and Sundar entered the chief's office, he did not look up, but continued writing in the bright glow of his green-shaded desk lamp.

"Morning, Inspectors," he would grunt.

"Good morning, Chief."

"Anything to report?"

"No, sir."

"Dismissed."

He would sometimes assign them a marginal task, such as moving a file in the archives or making sure that all of the chairs in the meeting room were properly tucked under the table. Just as often, with no instructions at all, they sharply took their leave.

Malone knew better than to take offense. She understood these awkward moments as evidence that the chief felt angrier at the Council's pronouncement than even she did. Unlike

Malone, however, he had no means to oppose the Council. As Chief of the Municipal Police, he endured a level of scrutiny that kept him exactly where the Council wanted him: pinned behind his desk with his boxer's nose out of their business.

Under the circumstances, he did the next best thing: he left the two inspectors to their own devices. With the absence of any meaningful assignments, Malone knew that the chief was aware of her and Sundar's continued investigations. That's why he made sure they had nothing but time on their hands.

Despite his initial bemusement, Malone could tell that Sundar had embraced the freedom of their open mandate. He followed her to her office, close at her elbow, his lips mortared shut and a mischievous twinkle in his eyes. For all the severity of their situation, she could not suppress the glimmer of a smile from her own.

Turning the final corner and gliding into her office, Malone turned and locked the door behind Sundar.

"Such a handy little space," he said, rubbing his hands together. "Though I still think the walls need some color. Of course, I can't expect one of my own for another few years, can I?"

"Five, at least. Enjoy the communal rookies' offices while you can. Things are a lot quieter back here. Even Farrah hardly drops by," she said, eying him.

He coughed. "Anyway, let's hear your big success from last night."

"Beauty before age, Inspector Sundar." She sat behind her desk while he took his seat across from her.

"Then prepare for disappointment," he said with a shrug. "I patrolled the same twenty blocks all night, but nothing. When the pretty birds came flocking back, I managed to find Ruthers, but he went straight home. Trailed, of course, by a contingent of guards." He pulled a wry frown and looked up at Malone.

"Good work anyway. We needed someone waiting in the streets, just in case. Sorry it had to be you."

"Next time, just see if you can slip something from the dessert table into your handbag for me. So, what did you find?"

Malone lowered her voice and recounted her conversation with Hollens, noting the councilor's reluctance and reticence. "He must have a lot to lose if this – whatever it is – comes to light," she said.

"Yes, but he's got a hell of a lot more to lose if it doesn't."

"I think he's beginning to realize that. He was surrounded by more guards than friends last night."

"So what did he give you?"

"He told me to examine an old contract – the Sato murders from fourteen years ago."

Sundar's eyes brightened. "I remember when that happened. I was still in school at the time, but we were all released early when the news broke. The murders and the killer were all anyone spoke about for months, and no one went anywhere alone. When they caught the perpetrator, just a few days later, the entire city went mad."

"Do you remember what happened to him?"

Sundar's eyed drifted toward the ceiling as he searched his memory. "The panel of judges convicted him, and he was executed the same day. I think the neighbors actually lit firecrackers that night in celebration. On the surface, of course."

Malone nodded. The Sato murders had created a wave of public shock and outrage that had not existed on such a scale in any of Recoletta's recorded history. The Vineyard represented not only the pinnacle of luxury, but also the epitome of security. Personal and commercial quarrels took their toll on the reputations and fortunes of the whitenails, but they were nearly immune to threats of bodily harm from lower classes. The Sato murders had broken a deeply ingrained taboo.

In fact, most people felt comfort rather than indignation at the inequitable security standards. The whitenails were living proof that Recoletta's system of governance worked and that it could ultimately maintain order. Therefore, when a hapless mugger murdered Councilor and Lady Sato, he attacked not only two prominent and beloved individuals, but also the very basis for Recolettans' sense of wellbeing. Recalling the panic of those days, Malone sensed a resurgence of the unease and fear of that time.

"Rumor had it," Sundar said, remembering, "the guy even turned himself in. Knowing what the whitenails would have done to him if they'd caught him first, I believe it."

Malone nodded. Their vigilante justice constituted a merciless alternative to a speedy trial and quick execution.

"So," Sundar said, taking a deep breath of the still air in the office, "you spoke to Hollens, and he mentioned the Sato incident. Any other coups?"

"Nothing decisive. I caught Roman Arnault for a few minutes."

"Based on what I've heard about him, that's a coup. How'd you manage it?"

"Foxtrot by force. See what you would have had to do if you'd gone to the gala?"

Sundar squinted and held out two hands, weighing the food and drink on one and close dancing with Roman Arnault on the other. "I think I would have coped. What's he like?"

"As slippery as you'd imagine."

"Did he tell you anything?"

"No."

"Well, that tells me something."

"I'm not sure," said Malone. She rubbed her thumb along the rough wood grain of the desktop. "With someone like him, it's hard to know."

"Anything else?"

"Yes," Malone said. She related her final meeting with Jane.

"I don't know what's more surprising." Sundar leaned on one arm of his chair. "That she was there, or that you got that kind of cooperation out of her. What was your angle?"

Malone smiled. "Arnault."

Sundar popped forward. "You're kidding. I don't suppose he's a client?"

"No, he's something more. I haven't worked it out yet, but I think she has more of a taste for danger than we thought." She gave Sundar a hidden smile with a quick flash of teeth beneath it. "Good for us."

"And the plot thickens. What's Arnault's side of the equation? Did you try this one on him?"

"No, I don't want to give anyone a reason to suspect her. Least of all him."

"Good thinking." He sighed and leaned back in the chair. "Ah, there's the cello. Mr Righetti was probably awake later than we were just thinking about it. I'll take it by later with a nice vintage – who knows what we'll need next time." Stretching an arm to the wall behind him, he ran his fingers down the sleek, wooden curves of the cello case. "So, field trip to the archives?"

"I'm one ahead of you."

Sundar smirked. "I should have guessed. Tell me about the Sato contract."

Malone pulled a file from her desk drawer and shuffled through it. "I'll start with the summary report." Plucking a sheet from the bound leather portfolio, she skimmed aloud. "Eleven at night on December 17th. The councilor and his wife, Fairmount Passage. Both bodies, throats slit, discovered at 4.15 the following morning by a torch lighter. Money and valuables missing from both. The presumed motive was robbery," she said, resting an elbow on her desk.

"Does the report say what the Satos were doing out at that hour?"

She glanced back at the sheet. "Returning from an arts benefit. They had donated five thousand marks to the Carousel Theatre Company."

"Then a lot of people would have known they would be there."

Malone nodded. "Presumably."

"Yet the report indicates that the murderer was a mugger – that he robbed and killed the Satos for the valuables they carried. That doesn't add up."

Malone continued to watch her partner with a prompting expression.

"Nobody would be desperate enough to rob and kill people like them for their pocket change. Either he didn't recognize the Satos, or he recognized them after he accosted them and killed them in a panic." He twirled a fingertip through the air, tracing a twisting path of thought. "He was in trouble either way, so perhaps he thought he stood a better chance by eliminating the witnesses." He drummed his fingers and broke his gaze. "Still, it doesn't make a lot of sense."

"Which may be why we've been directed to this contract."

"What does the file say about the mugger?"

Malone thumbed through several more pages. "Mortimer

Stanislau. A freight worker born in Recoletta and connected with several smuggling operations but never convicted. The inspectors handling the contract picked him up less than thirty-six hours after the murders on a tip. An anonymous tip." Malone paused, reading further down the page. "He was in possession of one hundred and fifty-seven marks and valuables belonging to the Sato family. A knife in his domicile matched the cuts on the victims, and he had no alibi for the night of the 17th. He was brought to trial on the 21st and appointed a lawyer, and a bench of five judges unanimously convicted him and sentenced him to death by firing squad."

Sundar gaped. "All in one day?"

"Over two days. But that's fast."

"Even for a crisis."

Malone pinched a thick sheaf of paper. "There's a transcript of the proceedings, and it looks thorough. There were no surviving witnesses, so that might explain the lack of delays."

"Character witnesses?"

"A couple," she said. "Foremen from his loading team. Given Stanislau's reputation for unscrupulous behavior, it's no surprise that these testimonies were not in his favor."

"No long, pleading statements from the accused?"

"None. Stanislau's lawyer, Edmund Wickery, handled his end of the proceedings and provided all of Stanislau's statements."

Sundar took the sheets detailing the transcript and skimmed through them. "This doesn't leave us with much."

Malone was reading through Stanislau's dossier. "No wife, no children, no surviving family, and no friends to speak of. After the execution, Stanislau's assets were absorbed by city coffers."

"In other words, there's nothing left on this guy." He slumped in his chair, sighing. A long pause followed during which Malone continued to flip through the pages.

"Well, this is interesting," she finally said.

Sundar leaned forward. "Did you find something?"

Malone reread a passage of interest. "According to the files, Mortimer Stanislau was mute."

Jane had spoken correctly at the gala: the remainder of the party passed uneventfully. Fredrick remained silent throughout the carriage ride home, leaving Jane to her thoughts. "Good night," he finally said when they parted at her door. "I'm forecasting a late morning with a chance of hangovers, so, whatever you do, don't knock before noon." She nodded and bade him good evening.

The following day elapsed with the same sort of quiet. Jane washed, sewed, and mended without any remarkable happenings. The only excitement arrived in the form of Fredrick, who arrived late in the evening with a vengeful appetite. If he was still cross with her for her imprudence the previous evening, she couldn't tell. His customary jauntiness made it clear that she should anticipate no rehashing of the previous night's argument and no apology for it. As always with Fredrick, his humors changed with the tides of the day.

Over dinner, she had little trouble drawing him into their usual rhythm of conversation, so thankful was she to have overcome the awkwardness from the end of last night.

"So, the editor liked your story about the gala?" she asked, loading her plate.

"Quite a lot, if I may say so. Of course, she didn't have a whole lot of choice – it had to run today one way or another, but I prefer to think it was better than your average drivel."

"Did Burgevich say anything about it?"

"Hah!" Fredrick looked up between bites of broccoli, his eyes gleaming. "That sorry hack couldn't make eye contact with me all day. Serves him right – he nudged Chiang for the Vineyard murders." Jane didn't mention that by "nudged" he meant "bribed" and that he, Fredrick, would have done the same thing if Chiang's price weren't so high. Fredrick continued. "Now he doesn't have a thing to write about. I guess that's something to appreciate about the Council's secrecy." He merrily turned his attentions to the salted cod on his plate.

Near-silence passed as both focused on dinner. When they had picked their plates clean, Jane cleared the table and brought tea, which enlivened Fredrick again. "How were your house calls? See anyone from last night?"

She started as she looked up, but she realized that he was not talking about Roman. "I just had a couple of stops as far as the Vineyard, but I didn't see anyone from the gala. Even if I had," she added, pouring her cup, "I think the recognition would have been one-sided."

"Ah, such sweet irony," he mused with a wry smile. "And yet you were the toast of the evening, m'dear."

Jane coughed into her tea. "I was?"

"Oh yes," he said, lifting his eyebrows and fixing his stare on a spot on the table. "You were quite the topic of conversation. I hope you don't mind being so objectified."

"Who was talking?"

He waved his hand. "Everyone."

"Well, what did 'everyone' say?"

"Oh, this and that. You know, the usual. Charming girl, lovely smile, interesting friends, very elegant in red..."

Jane frowned, passing the sugar bowl. "My dress was white."

"Whatever, same thing."

She could not tell if he spoke seriously or if he was toying with her. She was inclined to believe the latter, and she set her jaw, resolved not to take the bait.

Fredrick, as if sensing this, nodded earnestly over his own tea cup. "Honestly, those ladies you met last night liked you very much. They told me you seemed like a pleasant young woman. And that's gushing, coming from them." He hesitated, as if on the verge of a corollary, but he seemed to think better of it. When they finished their tea and Jane walked Fredrick to the door, she allowed her relief at their pleasant banter to eclipse the lack of closure with which it ended.

Perhaps as a result, she awoke the next morning with a sense of unease. She bathed and dressed early and had churned through much of her morning's work by nine, when Lena arrived with a parcel of suit jackets for Councilor Hollens.

"The councilor needs the spot removed from this jacket on top," Lena said, pointing to the offending stain, "but the other had a split in the seam, so I brought it along, too. They're rather urgent," she added, managing to make it sound more like a suggestion than a specific request.

Jane examined the two articles. "Thanks, Lena. I'll have these back by tonight."

Lena dipped her head, relieved. "You have a good day, Miss Lin."

"You, too."

The door closed behind her, and Jane set to work on the two jackets. The stain on the first, some kind of dark grease, came out easily with a compound of mineral spirits and careful brushing. As she reached for the second jacket, her door began to resound with knocks, and her threshold became a momentary epicenter of activity.

Her less exclusive clients arrived with bundles of laundry to be processed en masse, and Jane thought it prudent to begin at once with the washing to allow for adequate drying time. The early hours of the afternoon had come and gone by the time she had strung the linens and clothes around the front parlor, pumping a bellows in front of the glowing fire to circulate warm air. The aromatic infusion of crushed herbs and flowers inside the bellows gave off a light, fresh scent akin to a warm spring breeze. Anticipating the heat, she cracked the window by her door, which faced the apartment warren hallway, and she opened the vents located around the room.

This completed, she returned to the workroom where Hollens's two jackets hung. The second was more of a light overcoat than a standard suit jacket, she reflected as she turned it on its hanger. It showed fading around the hem and a frayed stitch under the right arm, yet like everything Hollens owned, it seemed meticulously cared for. She had to search to find the tear, but, running her fingers along the inside-front seam, she detected a split about three inches long where the fabric of the liner separated from the heavier stuff of the coat.

Jane marveled that Lena could have noticed such a minor defect, but a councilor's servant was nothing if not meticulous. Jane laid the coat on her desk and set to work. She pinned the parted edges together and smoothed the liner fabric just beyond the tear with her fingertips. As she traced the satiny material, she felt something unusual. She pressed her fingers more slowly into the fabric, and the effect was like a phonograph needle jumping at a scratch.

Suspecting that a scrap of material had somehow fallen inside, she unpinned the liner and slid her fingers into the gap. They found a folded sheet of paper. The compartment itself, she realized, was a deliberate contrivance, a pocket sewn discreetly inside the coat and several inches deep. With her index and middle finger, she grasped the paper and slid it out of the pocket as professional qualms and curiosity played table tennis with her conscience.

The paper was folded in several times on itself and was soft with age and use. Ignoring that it had been concealed in a secret pocket, it almost seemed too plain to hold any information of real importance. It was probably a receipt or a shopping list. Still, Jane wouldn't know what to do with it until she read it, and there could be no harm in simply reading the paper, could there? She unfolded it and read:

1. A Ruthers
2. A Hollens

At number 3, someone had crossed out "L Fitzhugh" and written in "P Dominguez".

4. C Hask

Below this hierarchy were two separate columns of names. She read through the eighty or so names listed, recognizing only "W Cahill", a probable match with the murdered historian. Reaching the bottom of the list, she gave a start to see "R Arnault" scrawled in the bottom margin and separated from the others, as if added in afterthought.

A jumble of names with a handful she recognized and several dozen she did not. She was familiar with the two councilors and the two murder victims, and she knew of only one Arnault. Without knowing the other names or understanding the connection between them, the list meant nothing. But it evidently held enough importance to hide in the seam of an old coat, she thought. Her dilemma now was how to fix it. She could not sew this compartment shut, or

Hollens would know that she had found it. Yet what could she say to Lena? It would be obvious if she did not fix it, but equally incriminating if she explained why she didn't.

Jane did not have to ponder for long. Someone pounded frantically at her door just before bursting through it. At the sound, she dropped her pins and thread with a yelp.

"Jane! Jane, where are you?" Fredrick shouted as he stumbled over the threshold, groping at the hanging sheets and clotheslines. "Jane!"

She slid the paper back into the jacket. "In here," she called. She shoved through the drying clothes and rushed to him, trembling. Both breathed in heaving sighs of relief. "What on earth are you doing here? You scared me to death," she gasped.

"I was so worried," he said. He blinked and stared with a kind of fearful concern so utterly removed from his usual irreverence. "Have you heard?"

Much to her later chagrin, she stamped her foot in exasperation. "No, Freddie, I have not heard. You come bursting in here and shouting like the world's going to end, and you ask me if I've heard. I gave you that key for emergencies, not for—"

"Jane, he's dead," he whispered. "Just now. In the middle of the day."

"Dead? Who...?" Her frustration sizzled in a cold pool of dread.

"That councilor. Hollens. Stabbed in his own house little more than an hour ago. The maid found him in his sitting room – Jane, she thought he was napping! The domicile full of servants, and someone got to a councilor in the middle of the day."

The weight of his statement hit her with an almost physical force. "Freddie, are you sure?"

"I was in the office when our man rushed in, and I ran all the way here." He was still panting from the combination of exertion and panic, a hapless expression on his face. She felt a pang of guilt at her earlier outburst.

"Oh... this is..." Words ground to a halt in her mind as she searched for something meaningful to say. But what? Unexpected? Shocking, yes, but no one could have thought that the architect was the end of it. The week of patrols and curfews had seemed more like a pause than a conclusion in the increasingly alarming series of murders, and the city had bathed in denial. Now, the news cut through the week of haziness like a sharp beam of light, dispelling any illusion of security.

Jane was barely aware of the reeling sensation as her head dipped and her body sagged downwards, crumpling at the knees. She was even less conscious when Fredrick caught her under the arms, reaching behind her to stop her descent, and carried her gently to the sofa. She did not regain consciousness until moments later when he patted her cheek, crouching on the floor in front of her. She blinked dizzily, trying to piece together the moments between swaying on her feet seven paces away and lying slumped on her couch.

"You fainted," Fredrick said, his jutting elbows and knees silhouetted by flames as he perched. The firelight cast his recently shaven jaw in a sympathetic glow, and she could see the day's growth of stubble.

She glanced around the living room, embarrassed. "I'm sorry, Freddie."

He shook his head slowly. "Don't think of it. This is a tough bit of news to receive and a hard way to hear it." He pushed himself up with his hands on his thighs and sat beside her. She opened her mouth to speak, but he waved a hand to quiet her, fluttering his fingertips. "Besides," he said, "you have a lot at stake." His eyes focused on her and his mouth hardened into a line. "Which brings me to something else we need to discuss. You've known both of the last two victims, and I'm concerned for your safety."

Jane's eyes widened to unnatural dimensions. She took his hand. "I need to show you something." Without a word, he followed her out of the den and down the hall.

Returning to the workshop with its dangerous little mystery gave Jane a tiny shiver. The light reflecting from the wooden table and workbenches and spilling into the hallway had a yellowish hue that Jane normally associated with warmth, but now it carried a noxious tinge. She imagined that the folded paper, endowed with an importance disproportionate to its size, now radiated a yellowish color like a toxic fume.

Jane pulled the paper delicately from its compartment and placed it in Fredrick's outstretched hand. He whispered the first ten names slowly, barely enunciating as he scanned the page. "Jane, I don't understand. What's this supposed to mean?"

"Councilor Hollens's maid dropped these suits off this morning. I was looking over this one when I found a secret pocket – very well hidden – in the lining. When I reached inside I found that paper."

Fredrick's eyes narrowed to points as he studied the page. "Do you have any idea what this is?"

"No."

"But you weren't supposed to find it. Anything so thoroughly concealed was meant to remain so. Has it occurred to you that three of the people listed here have died in the past week and a half?" He shook the paper in his thumb and forefinger, and her blood froze. "I doubt Hollens was murdered over a scrap of paper, but I know we aren't supposed to have this." He closed his fingers around it and moved for the door.

"Where are you going?"

"I'm going to burn this, Jane. Hollens is dead, and no one ever needs to know we've seen this."

Jane leapt forward, catching Fredrick in the hall. "Wait. Give it back to me, please."

He blinked incredulously. "What could you possibly want with it? You already know what it says. You can't mean to keep this."

"I'm showing it to Inspector Malone."

"Jane, have you lost your mind? If the rumors of corruption are true, that's the last thing you should do."

"Nonsense. The Council threw the Municipals off of this contract, remember? The City Guard practically shut them down."

"And there may be a very good reason for that. Jane, has it occurred to you that you might be trusting the wrong people? Based on that look you're giving me, I assume not." He shot her a paternally disparaging expression that irked her more than his words. "Plus, like you said, they're off the case. What good could the inspectors do for you even if they are clean? Besides, whoever's responsible may be watching the station. We have to assume that they know who you are and what you look like. If you go in there, whatever mysterious grace you may or may not have from them will be gone," Fredrick said, his voice lowered to a furious rasp.

She looked down and pondered for several seconds. Only the crackling fire in the den made a sound. "I trust Malone. She needs to see this."

"Have you heard a thing I've said? Whether or not you trust her is beside the point."

"I don't have to go to the station. There's another way."

"What's that?"

"There's a drop box."

He threw his hands forward and clenched his eyes shut. "Jane, are you listening to yourself? That's even more suspicious. Do you have any idea why she would be so secretive about this?"

"You've already given a great list of reasons. Maybe she's corrupt, or maybe she's hiding from people who are. A minute ago, we can't trust the Council, and now you don't trust anyone else. What could I possibly do right?"

"Burn that paper."

"Besides that. You're not giving me any options." Jane realized that, while Fredrick had retreated into a hoarse whisper, she had begun to raise her voice.

"That's because this is crazy. You don't need to get involved, and you run a real risk of getting yourself killed over a hunch."

"That's your opinion, isn't it? But it's my decision," she said, thrusting her flat palm toward him. "It's my find and my choice. It's evidence."

"Says who?"

"You can't really believe that this problem will solve itself, can you? I need to do something. If I'm wrong about the right people," she said, thinking, "then I imagine this won't change too much in the long run."

In the hall between the dim glow of the workroom and the distant radiance of the fireplace, Fredrick's face was cast mostly in shadows, but Jane could still see the dark look that crossed it. "How gruesome," he said. "You don't mean that."

"No more than you mean to have me sit by while people, including people I know, are killed. I want this whole mess to be over too." She pointed to the little paper. "I need to do

what I can to stop the killers before they decide I'm a liability."
Her breathing slowed as the pace of their argument slackened.

He winced as she said it and grudgingly dropped the creased
paper into her hand. His hand froze over his thigh as he
resisted an urge to wipe his palm on his pants leg. "I can't
argue with that. Do what you have to do."

Despite her thudding heart, she smiled a lopsided little grin.
"Hey, I'm surprised at you. If you were in my position, you
probably would have published it."

He returned a strained smile, smoothing his hair back with
the heel of one hand. "But you're in your position. Besides, the
Council's lackeys are practically editing the paper nowadays.
Look, I'm not going to argue about it anymore. Just promise
you'll get rid of that thing as soon as possible."

"Tomorrow, Freddie. I'll take care of it first thing in the
morning. I can't imagine that anyone would raid the apartment
over that scrap, though."

"No, but if they searched your place based on your
connections and found it, that wouldn't be good for you."

"There are plenty of people in Recoletta with similar
connections," she said, tucking the scrap away before he could
change his mind.

"Yes, but none who have stumbled upon a fresh murder."
He walked back into the den.

"Point taken, Freddie."

He spun on his heels. "That reminds me of something else,"
he said, his voice resuming a matter-of-factly bossy tone with
which she was more familiar. "You should get a boarder.
Things would be that much safer if you had someone else
living here with you, and you could rest easier."

"Which of us are we talking about? I sleep just fine. Besides,
considering that the murderer snuck past several attendants to

get to Hollens, how would one more warm body keep me safe?"

Fredrick rolled his eyes and leaned with both hands on the table. "What harm will it do? You can split your rent, and this might even be fun," he said. "Just until everything cools down."

Jane shrugged. "I suppose you're right. But where would I find someone?"

He sniffed and waved a hand. "That should be the easy part. The factory districts are swarming right now with recent arrivals looking for decent quarters. The recent immigration boom, you know."

"I hadn't heard about it."

Fredrick shrugged. "Some say it's drought in the south, some say it's seasonal labor, but this kind of influx happens from time to time. Now we might at least get a little news from some of our neighbors. Anyhow, we'll find a boarder. I'll put an ad in the paper right away and send some notices out to the bulletin boards, and we can expect some responses within the next week. If we don't, we can make some visits to the bunkhouses, and I'm sure we'll find someone."

She suppressed a wince. "Thanks, Freddie."

He smiled back. "Don't mention it, Jane. My, it's late. I need to look in at the paper, and you've got your laundry to finish." She could tell that he wanted to advise her to make her rounds early tonight, but he held his tongue. His expression became graver again as he continued. "Promise me, though, that you're going to be careful. That you'll let me know what you find."

"I will, and I will. Look, don't worry about me, OK? I'll come by later and we can have dinner at your place. Even bachelor stew is fine by me," she said, referring to Fredrick's haphazardly concocted surprises.

She followed him to the door and he rested his hand on the knob before turning back to her. "If I don't see you tomorrow, if anything happens, I'll know where to look first." The sentence hung in the air like an incomplete threat.

Jane could not restrain the fond smile from her lips, but she kept the condescension out of her voice. "Freddie, you're not a Municipal, you're a journalist. But I'm touched all the same."

He patted the back of his hair. "No, but I can still do something. You've said it already. You have your resources, and I have mine. Until later."

"Take care, Fredrick." The door closed behind him with a gentle snick, which she prudently complemented with the heavier click of the lock and, after a moment's thought, the thud and slide of the bar.

CHAPTER 9

CORRESPONDENCE

Liesl Malone did not hear of Hollens's death for a full two hours and thirty-seven minutes after Fredrick rushed into Jane's apartment. Malone had returned from an unproductive afternoon at the train station and in the slums, pursuing connections to Stanislau, while her partner had stayed behind, researching related contracts. After a series of dead-end interviews, she concluded that either no one remembered Stanislau, or no one wanted to. Both possibilities seemed plausible.

Dusk had already settled, and the police station was next to deserted on Monday evening. Lights shone from under doors and through shaded office windows, but Malone passed no one in the silent hallways. Her footsteps reverberated in the stone corridors, and besides the trembling flames above her, she saw no other movement. When she reached her office and turned the key in the lock, a hand shot out of the darkness and clamped onto her wrist. She gasped and twisted out of the stranger's icy grip, raising an elbow to strike when she recognized Sundar's wide-eyed stare. Following his finger to his lips, she nodded and led him into the office behind her.

Once they were safely inside, Sundar told her what he had discovered over two hours ago. A contact from the papers had slipped into the station earlier and informed Johanssen of Hollens's murder. Johanssen, in turn, had sent for Sundar, who had been thumbing through old smuggling contracts. When Malone finally arrived at the station that evening, it was his turn to break the news, which he did with a quaver in his voice. Though the murders of a historian and a whitenail had consequences enough, the murder of a councilor was something else, entirely.

Sundar recounted every detail, from the butler who had brought Councilor Hollens his tea at 3.30, to the maid, a quiet girl named Lena, who had come to remove the tray at 4.15. Tiptoeing around the silent, still man, Lena did not see the blood on his shirt front, and what she saw spilled on the tray she first took to be marmalade. It was not until she nearly tripped in a slick of it that she realized her master was not sleeping. The crash of the tray and the wailing scream brought the rest of the household thundering into the sitting room in seconds. Not one servant noticed a cracked window or a door ajar.

By the time Sundar had finished itemizing every detail from Hollens's last afternoon and his servants' frantic, fruitless search, all of the other lights in the station had been extinguished. Malone felt her own innards flutter, knowing what she and Sundar must do next.

A woolly fog lumbered over the surface streets the following morning as Jane crossed town to deliver the list. Much to her annoyance, the news of Hollens's murder and Fredrick's anxious warnings had spooked her, and her imagination endowed the streets around her with a sinister quality. Despite the cold, her palms and feet felt warm and clammy.

Even through the fog, her breath formed visible puffs in front of her. The beginnings of morning traffic were just stirring in the streets, and the clatter of veranda gates, muffled footsteps, and creaking carriage wheels formed a comforting cacophony in the obscuring mist.

Jane imagined that she could feel the weight of the list, which she had tucked into an envelope in her bodice. It seemed to press into her flesh, an urgent reminder. In that moment, it recalled the memory of a similar errand some fifteen years ago.

In that now-distant moment, she'd wandered through a dusty hallway with cracked, peeling walls and a pervasive musk. Then, also, a tremor in her legs reminded her of the distressing task she had set out to perform. The dirt caked on the skylights made it difficult to tell the time of day, but as she neared the end of the hall, she saw dust fluttering in murky shafts. To seven year-old eyes, the swirling particles looked like dull will-o'-the-wisps.

She was grateful to see the daylight glow crest the haze.

The sun's rays began to cut through the thick fog, crowning passing people and horses with blurry halos. Nearing the Dispatch, Jane could already see messengers darting along alleys and between buildings. Messengers were typically men and women of a small, sprightly build, and they spent the better portion of their days traveling between various offices and homes at a pace somewhere between a jog and a sprint, delivering messages. Their bright, fitted suits and distinctive orange sashes could part most crowds. Despite their petite stature, messengers had been known to bowl over larger men and dart under horses in a pinch. Flitting in and out of the mist, they looked like tongues of flame leaping through smoke. By the time Jane reached the Dispatch, so many messengers filled the block that the mist appeared to burn from within.

In her memory, Jane tiptoed into another office, which was brighter than the children's quarters below, but dark nevertheless. She did not marvel that the taunts of peers had urged her that far; she only wanted to prove that she was not scared, even though every nerve and tissue within her quaked. By retrieving a token from the headmistress's office, she would prove to the others that, for all her reserve, she was not a coward.

Descending a curving staircase, Jane had to back against the railing four times to dodge passing messengers. She wished she had taken the elevator, but the Dispatch encompassed several levels of postal boxes, and she did not know where she would find Malone's. Fortunately, a sign at the first landing directed her to the second floor, where a hall branching from the stairway phased into antique green tiles and brass fixtures. Recognizing this floor as her destination, her pulse quickened, and the hidden letter weighed heavier yet.

In the headmistress's office, it dimly occurred to Jane that neither she nor her mockers had settled on an appropriate token, but she felt herself drawn to the cabinets in the back of the room, behind the desk. Inside, she saw a series of boxes, each covered with dust and printed with the name of a child in the orphanage. Since the children were not allowed personal possessions, the headmistress stored whatever had been dropped off with the orphans. Jane could read well enough to recognize her own name, and she reached for it.

Jane only saw a few torches lining the passage in the Dispatch, but the brass paneling made the walls flicker and jump with firelight. The hall she traversed ran the full length of the oblong level, and at its terminus she saw another large stairway and set of elevators. To her right was a series of desks spaced against the glowing wall where helpful employees waited to assist visitors and prevent anyone from tampering with the boxes. She wondered if any of them were monitoring Malone's mail drop, ready to apprehend her after she delivered the list. In her mind she could see a phalanx of city guards waiting in the stairways and stoically marching her off to a pitch-black prison cell in the Barracks on the charge of treason.

In a more gruesome scenario, a slinky, hooded figure dogged her steps, obscured by the morning fog, and now waited in the shadows to execute her after the completion of her ill-fated errand. In any case Jane's fevered mind envisioned, she felt at the mercy of forces already set in motion. For the first time since her harrowing encounter in Fitzhugh's house, she felt helpless.

Young Jane's small hands slid the top off of her box in a cloud of dust. She pulled a small book from inside, the title *Grimm's Fairy Tales* emblazoned on the front. Tucking the thin volume into the folds of her dress, she heard footsteps coming toward her from down the hall.

Jane closed her eyes, took a deep breath, and expelled fluttering panic, turning her thoughts to the postal boxes in front of her.

Patting the letter beneath her clothes, she followed the numbers to her left, which marked the numerous corridors stemming from the main hall. Almost halfway down it, she ducked into one of these smaller passages, which was lined with boxes set into the stone. Reading in the dull, brassy glow, she followed the numbers on the front until she came to box 1364, an unremarkable receptacle that was identical to those around it except for its particular pattern of tarnishing.

Jane peeled the letter from her layers of clothes, slipped the envelope into the mail slot and eagerly made her way back.

Back in the orphanage, Jane had just enough time to return her empty box, close the cabinet, and scurry away from it when the headmistress entered the room. Two eyes blazed at Jane from under a grime-colored sweep of hair, and, after leaving their impression, they darted to a half-empty jar of candies on the desk.

"How many?"

Jane noticed the candy box for the first time, but she understood that she had to give the headmistress a reason to punish her to her satisfaction if she wanted to conceal her prize.

"Five."

"Your hands, Miss Lin."

When Jane took them back, they were striped red and raw. Jane was banished to her cot at dinner, and she hid her book beneath the lumpy mattress. Seeing her hands, none of her classmates asked to see what she had taken, and she was glad to keep it to herself.

Since hearing of the latest murder, Malone was racing to keep abreast of the implications. Her wanderings and Sundar's readings on Mortimer Stanislau had turned up nothing, but now, with Hollens dead, she was not even sure that the Stanislau connection was relevant anymore. Worst of all was the Council's reaction to Hollens's death. In the hours following the murder, armed men had broken into bunkhouses and union headquarters across the factory districts, showing the kind of delicacy that marked the City Guard. Four "suspects" had been killed in the ensuing interrogations, and it had become an even contest between the Council and the murderer to see who would tear the city apart first.

Malone remembered Hollens's contingency instructions, so her next goal was to follow them: to slip into his residence and find the safe in the wine cellar.

Of course, this was much more easily said than done. The block would be swarming with city guards in the aftermath of the murder, none of whom would take well to meddling by rogue inspectors. Malone was confident that Hollens had hidden his safe well, but she grimaced to think of what might happen, and what might be lost, if the Council found it first. As she and Sundar pondered their situation, a very relieved Jane Lin was returning unhindered from her errand at the Dispatch.

"Surely Hollens would have imagined this scenario," Sundar said, settling into his now-familiar chair across from Malone's desk. "Grim as it is, right? I mean, what would be the point in telling you about the safe if you would never be able to reach it?"

Malone took her own seat. "He wasn't convinced that I could. Besides, it's not his problem now. And the more time we lose waiting for opportunities to open up, the greater the risk of our leads disappearing and of another assassination."

"But the assassin isn't the only one we have to dodge," Sundar said. "If the Council gets wind of what we're doing, they'll book us an extended stay at the Barracks."

"You know the stakes."

Sundar was not ready to admit defeat. "What if Hollens had a confidante – someone he trusted who could get us in? There must be someone on his staff that he knew well enough to give a contingency plan."

Malone shrugged. "Even if we knew who that was, he couldn't let us in the front door now. The Council has removed Hollens's staff for interrogation and replaced them with the guards."

Sundar rubbed his chin. "What about another role-playing scenario? If it got us into the Directorate of Preservation and the gala, we could pull it off again."

Malone shook her head. "Not there. They'll have more than a secretary guarding the door. Besides, after our last trick, they're going to be more careful. Our best option is stealth."

Sundar grinned and flicked an eyebrow at her. "Your way, then. Are we going in through the chimney?"

"I was thinking we'd try the other end. Pull schematics for a radius of two blocks from the house, and tonight we can stake out the place and plot a way in," Malone said. Sundar had turned to go when she stopped him.

"Sundar."

"Malone?"

"This is what I consider serious. Since you asked." She paused, watching his expression. "Breaking into a councilor's house. It's over if we're caught." He nodded, and when she said nothing further, he continued out the door.

Malone read through the Sato contract again, and Sundar returned an hour later with several rolls of blueprints and a stack of papers.

"It's more than we need," he said. "But I had to pretend I was looking for smuggling tunnels." Malone nodded.

The pair spent the next ninety minutes poring over the designs, searching for neglected passages and concealed crawlspaces. Malone had mapped out a plausible route to the house when a station messenger came to the door with a plain, gray envelope. Sundar watched as Malone extracted the paper inside and slowly read the list that Jane had sent that morning. Too slowly, his fidgeting fingers suggested.

"So, what is it? Another invitation?" he asked.

Malone showed him the paper and watched as he read it, focusing on the familiar names.

"It's interesting. Whatever it is," he said.

"That's the question."

"A hit list?"

"Too ambitious. Besides, only one name is crossed off, and it's been replaced with another. It looks like a hierarchy," Malone said.

"That makes sense, particularly with Ruthers at the top."

Malone circled back around her desk. "There are two councilors on the top of the list, but the other eight are scattered in the section at the bottom."

"How did we get this?"

Malone pointed to a note scribbled on the mostly-blank side of the paper. "Whoever got it found it in Hollens's things. I've got a guess," said Malone, thinking of Jane.

Sundar nodded. "Now what?"

"Now, we find a way into Hollens's wine cellar."

CHAPTER 10

UNEXPECTED GUESTS

Jane had not expected to hear anything further from the inspectors, and her nerves had cooled by Wednesday morning, a full twenty-four hours after her clandestine delivery. Nevertheless, her heart skipped a beat when, well into her first load of laundry, she heard a knock at her door. The face on the other side of it, however, replaced Jane's panic with curiosity.

A large-eyed woman with long lashes and an oval face stood on the steps carrying two worn canvas bags. When Jane opened the door, the woman flashed a row of perfect teeth from between plush and pouty lips and looked around with a kind of half-wild relief.

"You are Jane Lin?"

"Yes..."

The woman smiled wider still. "Wonderful! Can you show me?" she asked, pointing over Jane's shoulder and into the apartment. She had a vaguely familiar accent with a tripping, peppery cadence.

"I'm sorry, who did you say you were?"

"Of course. I am Olivia Saavedra. I saw your ad in the *noticias* yesterday."

It took another beat for Jane to remember Fredrick's promise to advertise for a subletter. When she did, she was relieved to understand the reason for Ms Saavedra's visit but perplexed by the speediness of her arrival. Clearly, Fredrick had not understated the recent influx of outsiders. Still, Jane had not expected an answer for at least a week, and she had been counting on the time to get used to the idea.

However, if Ms Saavedra's easy charm was any sign of her usual disposition, then she seemed promising. "I'm sorry, I didn't realize anyone had seen it yet. Please, come in." Jane stepped aside for her and took one of the bags. It was heavier than it looked.

"Thank you," Olivia said. "I saw the notice just this morning. I was staying in a community hostel east of here, and I packed my bags as soon as I saw it."

"How long have you been in Recoletta?"

"Three weeks," she said. "I came from Bremmond, where I was living for the last seven years. But I am originally from San León."

Now Jane recognized the accent. The orphanage in which she lived as a child had stood next to a bakery. The proprietor, a loquacious man the children knew as "Mr Pedro", spoke with a similar rhythm and gave them sweet rolls to share if they happened to visit after a fresh batch had been baked. If Jane remembered correctly, he had come from Nuevo Laredo, a dusty city to the southwest. For all his talking, though, he had never explained why he had moved.

The women set the bags in the corner of the den. Jane stopped to work out a kink in her spine and finally had a moment to look Olivia over. The first thing Jane noticed, to her mild embarrassment, were the exceptional curves that outlined Olivia's figure. With her long, dark hair pulled into a smooth ponytail, and her soft, dusky features, she embodied a voluptuous loveliness that Jane found both fascinating and intimidating. As Jane looked at Olivia, Olivia looked around the room with quick, calculating glances.

"It's not that big, but I can show you around if you'd like."

"Yes, please."

Glad to leave the bags in the den, Jane took Olivia around the apartment, showing her the kitchenette, workshop, bathroom, and her bedroom at the end of the hall.

"I'm familiar with Bremmond, but I'm not sure I've heard of San León. Where is that?"

"Almost twelve hundred miles southwest of here. It's just past Ciudad del Mar."

Though Jane had never traveled there, she knew the name. Bordered by stretches of jungle and desert, Ciudad del Mar occupied a balmy nook on the coast and enjoyed warm temperatures year round. Now in the first frigid nips of mid-autumn, Jane had to wonder why anyone would forsake that kind of comfort. "What brought you so far north?"

"My family left San León with me when I was young. More people than jobs, and my grandfather had cousins in the north. When I was older, I left for Bremmond."

"For work?" Jane tried to keep her tone conversational, but she found her curiosity growing rather than diminishing.

"For a change of scenery."

Jane counted three moves, including Olivia's most recent transition to Recoletta, which was more than most families made in thrice as many generations, and the woman did not yet look thirty. Fighting the urge to intrude further, Jane realized that she was losing.

"And then you came to Recoletta three weeks ago?"

Olivia tilted her head, wincing. "Things in Bremmond have not been so good for the last few years."

Thinking of the current troubles in Recoletta, Jane wanted to ask more, but she noticed the anxious manner in which Olivia turned away, and she dropped the issue.

Habitual movers were rare. In underground society, they were almost as much of a curiosity as surface-dwellers. Jane guessed that something harder lay beneath Olivia's easy, carefree smile, like sinew under smooth flesh.

Jane led her back to the kitchenette and offered Olivia a conciliatory cup of tea. "I don't mean to badger you; it's just that I've never been outside Recoletta. I'd love to hear more about your travels some time. For now, it's just nice to have company." Jane stopped short of adding, "Especially these days."

Olivia brightened again. "And it's good to be out of the hostels. I would feel safer surrounded by so many people, but too many of the residents are, ah, not the type I like sleeping close to."

"I understand. Well, I can set you up in the workshop if you'd like. I haven't had the chance to clear it out, but if you'll give me a hand, we can pull the worktable and tools into the den."

Having lifted one of Olivia's bags, Jane was not surprised at the ease with which Olivia hauled and heaved the table and accessories. With the workroom cleared, Olivia hoisted her luggage into the room while Jane swept the dust lurking in the corners.

"It's not exactly spacious, but we could fit the sofa in here until you've had the chance to find a mattress."

Olivia pointed at her luggage. "I have some bedding already."

Jane nodded, relieved to avoid further heavy lifting for the moment. "Oh, and about rent. You haven't been here long, so we can settle weekly starting this Friday if you need some time to…"

Olivia plunged into one of her bags and pressed the resultant cash into Jane's hands. "This covers the month, yes?"

Jane counted the bills, trying to hide her astonishment. She wondered where Olivia had acquired that sum of money, and in Recolettan marks, no less. Currency exchanges between cities were notoriously difficult. Still, Jane marveled while looking again at the canvas bags: with her strength, she probably could have worked two factory jobs in her three weeks and earned almost that amount.

Holding the roll of cash, Jane felt suddenly self-conscious and tucked the bills into the folds of her dress. "You seem to know your way around Recoletta, Olivia. What do you do?"

"I'm a maid uptown. There are a few openings for part-time cleaners in the Vineyard."

Jane hoped, for both their sakes, that the population of the Vineyard did not continue to decline at the rate of the past week. She understood now how Olivia could come by so much cash in a few weeks, but a new mystery replaced the old: how was she finding work in the Vineyard so quickly without connections in town? "I have a few clients in that neighborhood as well," Jane said. "They're a rather insular lot, so I'd be happy to ask around and introduce you."

"Thank you, but I have a full schedule. And not to be rude, but I have an appointment there in an hour. Perhaps you could give me some time to set up here?"

"Of course." Jane returned to the washing while Olivia unpacked and arranged her travel-ready possessions. With a parting smile, Olivia left Jane to her laundry and her thoughts. Foremost among these were gratefulness at having found someone as capable and easygoing as Olivia, and perplexity at the mysterious woman's habits and history.

Nightfall came as a long-anticipated opportunity for Inspectors Malone and Sundar. Having spent the previous evening and early morning monitoring the former councilor's residence, they knew the guard rotations and their possible means of entry. Now, clothed once again in their usual black, they were ready to convert observation into action.

The subterranean blocks adjacent to the Hollens mansion maintained a light patrol of plainclothes guards. Malone and Sundar snuck past them with good timing and old-fashioned stealth. In front of the house itself, a guard stood at every corner and in front of every entrance. If Malone's hypothesis was correct, their constant presence meant that the Council had not yet found what it was looking for inside. That, or this was an elaborate trap to catch a returning killer or clumsy snoop.

Sundar looked at Malone and pointed to a spot on the ground five yards away. A drainage grill set into the street lay just within range of one of the patrols. It provided access to the sewage tunnels of the Vineyard and, more importantly, one of its branches surfaced seventy feet away, two steps from Hollens's place, in the next block. Just beyond that outlet lay the key to their plan.

In keeping with the grandeur of the Vineyard, the exposed facades of the residences around them were high and heavily decorated, nothing like the window-pocked rock faces that marked more common dwellings. Not wasting a moment, Sundar cast a rope with a soft, weighted knot at one end over a gargoyle perched on the building next to him. He scurried fifteen feet up the wall and into the shadows, making nary a sound as his feet found purchase in the relief work and sills. The wide, soaring construction of the tunnels in the Vineyard created more visibility for someone watching from the right position, and with the skylights overhead darkened, that position was suitably obscured for the inspectors' purposes.

Now perched on a shadowed ledge, he edged to the corner of the building and peered around, the Hollens residence and squad of guards clearly visible.

At the base of the building, Malone waited for his signal. After a few moments, she saw Sundar flash his open palm, and she hurried to the grating with a heavy key. Sequestered from the offices of the Municipal Police, the key provided access to all of the sewage tunnels and gratings of the Vineyard. With a turn of the key, the grill slid easily into its recess, and she found a series of rungs descending to the sewers.

Malone produced a small hand lantern that provided just enough light for her to follow the narrow walkway rising above the mire. Remembering the schematics, she followed the main channel for about fifty feet and turned into the fourth access tunnel on her left. She could see a bluish glow from the grating above her head, and she knew that she must have reached the point just below the house.

Upon reaching the end of the tunnel, she would have identified the water main and followed it down to where it punched into the domicile's reservoir. Ducking into an adjacent crawlspace, she would have centered herself underneath the grating that directed runoff from the basement into the sewers. Between her crowbar, her lock pick set, and the master key for the sewers, she was confident that some combination of the resources would get her from one side of the grating to the other and then from the basement to the cellar. However, all of her elaborate planning became worthless once she saw the heavy alloy gate separating her from the crawlspace below.

The schematics were five years old, so she reasoned that the gate must have been a recent construction. The gate was moored to the rock face of the sewer tunnel, and a boxy, fist-size lock kept it shut. When the master key failed, Malone examined the lock under the light of her hand lantern. She rummaged in her pocket and found a few unofficial tools of the trade. Setting her light in the piping overhead, she focused on the lock and went to work. After a few practiced maneuvers, she heard a soft click, which she took as a signal of quick success. When she heard a gassy hiss, she knew she'd been wrong.

. Malone just had time to jump back from the gate when she began to smell heavy fumes. She stumbled back along the tunnel, dimly aware of the dull splashing of her boots in the sewage. Her vision had already begun to blur, something in her throat was constricting, and her knees were starting to buckle.

When she reached the grate by which she had entered the tunnels, she leapt up the rungs and clung to the grill, sucking at the fresh air through the bars, no longer mindful of stealth or silence. Over the pounding of her heart, she could not hear the footsteps of patrols or the distant whisper of the gas. She did, however, hear a shout from the direction of the domicile. Seconds later, Sundar's coat swished in the corner of her vision as he took off at top speed, and she nearly fell from the ladder as two guards thundered over the grill, chasing after him. Weakly, she turned her key in the lock and peered into the street as the grate slid open above her.

She didn't know what had happened, but, for the moment, there was not a soul present in the street. Climbing out of the sewer, she quickly skirted the adjacent building where Sundar had been roosting and looked around the corner.

Malone could hardly believe her luck. The east end of the house was completely deserted, but she knew this opportunity would not last long. Though her legs still felt like pudding, she sprinted to the side of the house under one of the circular windows. Peeking inside, she saw only darkness, and she rotated the window open and slipped inside.

Malone landed on soft carpet and crouched low. Outlines of a desk and chairs suggested that she had dropped into a study. She felt her way along the floor and crept catlike toward the door where she could see a faint glow from further down the hall. Waiting just at the edge, she produced a matte-surfaced mirror to check around the corner. When Malone saw no one, she stepped into the hall, flexing the feeling back into her legs.

She recalled studying the house plans with Sundar and began reconstructing the blueprints in her mind. She had just stepped out of a small office, and the hallway in front of her looked narrow and unimportant. To her right and around the corner, she could see more light, and she guessed this way must lead to the main hall. If she was correct, then to her left she should find a small stairway in an arched recess leading to the bottom levels of the domicile.

She followed the dimly lit hallway to the left, reaching a darkened nook with a circular staircase. Out of the corner of her eye, Malone saw a spark of light and ducked against the wall. Her blood froze as her eyes traced the faint outline of a guard leaning against the wall in the stairway, just on the other side of the arch. She felt a surge of panic as his hand dropped to his side, and, sure that he had seen her, she prepared to spring at him. To her surprise, he turned his head away and inhaled deeply, an orange point hovering like a firefly in front of his face. Her mind raced as she weighed her chances of incapacitating him and completing her mission before someone sounded the alarm. As she prepared to move, she heard a voice calling from a lower level in the stairway.

"Oy, Marrek, is that you again?"

The man with the firefly only sighed.

"For the love of– Put that damn thing out! How many times do I have to tell you, you can't smoke in here! If the captain catches you, he'll have your head."

"Captain's not here," drawled Marrek.

"Well, it won't be long; I can smell that thing a mile away." He paused. Malone heard the other man ascending the staircase, his boots producing a metallic clunk on the steps. Timing her footfalls with his, she crept into the room to her left.

"You done your rounds yet?"

"I'll get to it," Marrek said.

"No, you'll stand here puffing that twig and I'll take the heat when Captain finds out that nobody's walking this level."

There was another pause, and Malone knew that Marrek must have shrugged.

The second guard stormed down the hall and Malone heard a long silence broken only by Marrek's relaxed breathing. She could smell the bitter odor of smoke from his cigarette. After a few moments, she heard the other guard returning, his pace quickened.

"Dammit, Shen and Rivas are gone."

"So? You know how those two are."

"I know there's no one watching the east side of the house, which means you and me have to search!"

Marrek muttered an expletive.

"Give me that!" Malone heard the second guard snatch the cigarette and grind it against the metal railing. "Keep your mind on the job. Start at the other end of the hall and search every cabinet and closet. I'll take this side."

Marrek's heavy footsteps plodded down the hall, and Malone realized with dismay that the second guard was coming around the corner. She groped the wall behind her, searching for someplace to hide. She scrambled around a hefty block of furniture just as the lights came on. The second guard was checking each corner of the room with mechanical precision and slowly making his way toward her. Recessing herself further into her nook, Malone backed into a wooden panel with a small knob protruding. Carefully, she turned and lifted the panel by the knob, hoping the hinges wouldn't squeak. A narrow, vertical shaft rose a couple levels above her head and plummeted a few more to what looked like a bin of whipped cream. She had found the laundry chute.

The guard took a detour into the connecting bathroom, buying Malone precious seconds. Crawling into the chute, she braced herself with her feet against the smooth stone and eased the panel shut as the guard's boots came into view. With a final glance at the pile of linens below her, she bent her knees and dropped feet-first down the chute.

Malone landed in the sheets, and shock waves reverberated through her bones. Submerged in laundry for the moment, she took the opportunity to gather her thoughts.

By any sensible estimate, she had just dropped into the laundry room. It did not connect directly with the cellar, but both sections occupied the same level in Hollens's domicile. In order to walk to the cellar, however, she would have to leave the laundry room, follow a basement level hall, ascend one floor, and follow another hallway (which, if she knew anything, contained a guard or two). Fortunately, she knew of another way.

Climbing out of the linen bin, Malone paced to the far wall. Instead of marble and wood paneling, these walls were of plain stone block, free of embellishment. Positioned in the wall just above her head was a grill covering the laundry room's air vent. Malone wedged it open and vaulted inside. One consequence of life underground was that vents and shafts riddled most buildings like termite trails, making clandestine travel possible for someone who did not mind a squeeze. All the same, she was beginning to feel like a sewer rat.

Malone continued straight down the shaft, counting the side tunnels as she passed them. Finally, she took a right and, as she expected, found herself face to face with another grating. Peering beyond it, she saw nothing (and no one) but a few rows of barrels lit by torches. She crawled out, her descent eased by a stack of crates just under the grill.

"In the cellar, behind the wine." Malone knew she was searching for something, but she did not know exactly what. Luckily, the cellar was only three rows deep and six yards wide. She took a torch from its sconce and began examining the bottles and barrels, row by row.

The first row was filled with barrels of spiced rum and ale. In the second row, she found only bottles of spirits and imports labeled in strange scripts. When she reached the third row, she had a feeling she was much closer to her goal.

Wines, from sherries to chardonnays, lined the third and final row, which rested against the wall. Malone began the painstaking task of examining them all, bottle by bottle. The corks protruded from their recesses like dozens of buttons, all aligned in neat rows and columns. Once she saw the cork marked with an A, she knew she was moving in the right direction.

It was easy to miss in the middle of a grid of bottles forty wide and twenty tall, but the emblazoned A stared back at her, a dark mark in the flickering torchlight. She examined the corks surrounding her new discovery, and each one bore another letter following standard alphabetical progression. At random, she selected the N bottle and pulled it out of the shelf. The label was plain and white, and a dark fluid sloshed beneath the green glass. She removed bottle F and saw much of the same thing. As she slid the two bottles back into their slots, however, she heard a click as something fell into place. Gingerly testing the C bottle, she felt it recess deeper under pressure. She needed a password.

Malone thought back to her final conversation with Hollens in the washroom. "The writing's on the wall, Malone." It was on the bottles, too, but something he had said must have been a clue about the password. She needed something true and concrete.

She considered what she knew about Hollens, facts and rumors alike. He had never been the subject of much scandal or speculation, unlike others in his circle. For a politician, he was remarkably clean. Never married, a family history of public service, citizenship in Recoletta dating back more than a dozen generations, and of course, head of the Directorate of Preservation.

Malone thought back to her covert visit to the directorate with Sundar, recalling the hundreds of texts and manuscripts that would never see the light of day and the carefully selected scholars who analyzed them. She remembered meeting Dr Hask, studious and smug in the comfort of her office. And Hollens had asked about her office. As she played back the scene in her mind, the answer became clear. Deciphered truth, writing on the wall. Veritas.

Hoping the connection was as good as it sounded, she spelled "VERITAS", pushing the marked bottles in order deeper into their recesses. A barely audible thump followed each bottle in the sequence, elevating Malone's hopes. After the seventh, silence.

Malone waited with bated breath, listening for the telltale click or alarm. Recalling the trap in the sewers, her insides gave a little wrench at the thought of what might happen if she had failed.

Intending to at least cover her tracks, Malone tugged at the S bottle to pull it back into place. When she did, the wall moved with it. The rack containing the lettered bottles and the section of wall behind it swung open, and Malone found herself staring at a squat cabinet ensconced in an alcove about five feet tall, five feet wide, and three feet deep. Judging by the layer of dust covering it, she was the first person to find it since Hollens's death. Malone began her search in the top compartment.

It was full of financial documents that were private but not immediately relevant. She passed over deeds, correspondence, and certificates that she felt foolish leaving but did not have the time to examine. As much as she would have liked to take everything, she did not want to make it overly obvious to the Council, if they found the safe, that someone had already searched it. Malone could only carry so much, and she was counting on the notion that she would know what she needed when she found it.

At last, her hands fell on a leather-bound folder marked with a single title: "Prometheus". Malone recalled Jane's mention of the name during their first meeting. She removed the leather straps and rifled through its contents to check her hunch.

Before she could inspect her prize, she heard footsteps and voices approaching from the stairs above the cellar. Quickly assessing her options, she considered for a split second hiding in the secret compartment itself. In even less time, she dismissed the idea of shutting herself in a confined space, which was probably not built to open from the inside, as beyond stupid.

In two rapid motions, she shut the compartment and pushed the folder into her overcoat. With a quiet snap, the bottles popped back into position behind her, and, replacing the torch, she dashed to the vent by which she had entered the cellar. As the footsteps outside the door grew louder, she got a better idea.

Huddled inside one of the crates below the vent, Malone blessed her luck when the door opened seconds later. She heard two pairs of feet and two new voices drawing near.

"What in the blazes are we doing down here?"

"After the alarm outside, we're checkin' every corner. You know the drill." The second guard spoke with a slightly higher voice.

"Well I'm gonna have a drink while we're in the neighborhood."

"I've seen you nursing that hip flask of yours all night. You don't need any more sauce in your system."

"I've got three more hours doing basement shift, and I'll be damned if I'm gonna do them without a drop."

"Just watch yerself."

The first man shuffled down the same racks that Malone had examined minutes earlier, clearly taking his time. She could hear the other guard, whom she guessed was female, pacing the rows.

"So, what was the fuss all about, anyway?" asked the first, uncorking a bottle.

"Nothing, man. Some kid throwing rocks."

"They catch 'im?"

"Naw, he got away. They lost him after a mile or so and gave up the chase."

Inside her crate, Malone breathed a silent sigh of relief.

"Bloody hell!" exclaimed the woman. "What's that smell?"

"I don't smell nothin'."

"Take that bottle away from your nose and go over to the crates!" Malone had not noticed any unusual smells, but, with so much attention now focused in her direction, she became aware of an unpleasant odor emanating from her clothes. Wincing, she recalled her frantic run through the sewage tunnel earlier. She could hear the boozing guard breathing loudly over the crate.

"What are you doing?" asked the second guard.

"I'm gonna open it."

"Don't do that!"

"Why not? I wanna see what's inside."

"Well I don't wanna smell it! Keep it closed and let's haul these boxes up to the trash."

Malone had found her means of escape.

CHAPTER 11

RUMORS AND HALF-TRUTHS

Jane was surprised at how quickly she and Olivia were settling into a routine together. Olivia kept strange hours, but when she was around Jane found her unfailingly pleasant and helpful around the apartment. Only a couple of days had passed since the commencement of their new living arrangement, but Jane was grateful for the good start.

This evening, Jane was preparing dinner for Olivia, Fredrick, and herself. Olivia was still out working, but Fredrick had insisted ever since passing her on the landing that he be invited to dinner to formally meet the new arrival. Jane could hardly object when the whole arrangement had been his idea in the first place.

It was five until seven and Jane had just set potatoes to boil when she heard Fredrick at the door. He let himself in with his spare key and strolled into the kitchen, a look of anticipation in his eye.

"Don't get too excited; she won't be back for another hour or so," said Jane. His expression fell. "But let's pretend," she said, "that we're friends, and you just stopped by to visit."

He smiled. "Need a hand?"

"I'm about done, but thanks. Everything just has to cook now." Drying her hands on the dishtowel, she took a seat on the sofa next to the fireplace. "What's the news today?"

"I'm afraid there isn't any, my dear. You know the expression."

"'No news is good news'?"

"Try, 'My head was pounding like a steam engine and I didn't go to the office today.'"

She laughed. "Don't wear yourself out. Olivia may not know what to do with all of that charm."

"Well, if you're not feeling up to the banter, you could always take the night off and leave me to entertain," he said, sitting down and regarding her with a half-hopeful expression.

"Not a chance."

He shrugged. "Can't blame me for trying."

"Nor me for having Olivia's best interests at heart."

"Ouch."

Almost two hours had passed before the pair heard another key turning in the lock. Both perked up to see Olivia sweep through the door, as cheerful as ever but a little disheveled.

"So sorry! My appointment took longer than I expected."

"Don't think of it, Miss Saavedra," said Fredrick, rising to his feet.

"Allow me to make introductions," Jane said. "Fredrick, this is my new roommate, Olivia Saavedra. Olivia, this is my friend, Fredrick Anders."

"Charmed."

"*Igualmente.*"

Fredrick was still standing, halfway between electrified and dumbstruck, when Olivia smiled politely and rushed off to her quarters. "If you will give me a minute to change clothes, I am ready."

Against Jane's whispered admonitions, Fredrick dragged the table closer to the fireplace, which he regarded as the most romantic corner of the apartment, while Jane arranged the plates on the moving table. Though unaccustomed to accommodating three, the solid cedar table fit the plates of chicken, potatoes, and greens with plenty of space still for the diners and their dishware. By the time Jane and Fredrick had everything ready, Olivia had changed out of her gray dress and waited by the kitchen, an eager smile on her face. "It smells wonderful."

Jane handed her a plate. "Roasted chicken with vegetables. Please, help yourself."

Seated around the fireplace and enjoying a hearty dinner, Jane was pleased to find her old friend and her new roommate getting along well. Fredrick was describing his work at the paper with characteristic exaggeration, and Olivia listened, leaning her chin on a fist.

"What a fascinating job. But how are things now that there is so much trouble in the city?" As Olivia blinked her large, round eyes, Fredrick puffed his chest and straightened his back.

"I shouldn't say too much," he said, lifting his eyebrows, "but it's been quite a rush. Intrigue and investigative journalism at its best, all packed into long days and late nights."

Jane froze mid-chew and frowned, reflecting that Fredrick's recent late nights had been spent chasing a whiskey buzz. Olivia remained rapt.

"How thrilling to investigate these mysteries! And how bold to do it behind the Council's back." She smiled, one finger skating the rim of her glass, and Fredrick reddened. "How do you keep it a secret?"

"Keep what a secret?"

"That you're looking into the murders."

Fredrick glanced at Jane, who shot him a warning look. "Ah, well, I'm not so much investigating them myself..."

"So modest! But without your help, I'm sure your colleagues would not be able to."

Thinking about the hidden list that Fredrick had almost burned, Jane continued to stare holes into his forehead. As much as he tried, he couldn't ignore it.

"We're not really investigating the murders at all. The Council's had these scandals in lockdown since the first week and, as we all know, you don't cross the Council." Here he looked up at Jane, shooting her his own meaningful glare.

"Nonsense," Olivia said. She patted his arm, seemingly oblivious to the staring contest between her companions. "The paper has run stories about the murders. I've read them."

Deflated, Fredrick stirred the greens on his plate. "What you've read are the puffs authored by the Council. Since they can't exactly hide the murder of a councilor, or any other whitenail, they write their sanitized version of events and send it to us to print."

"So you do the best you can," Jane said, trying to sound heartening.

"Selling out."

Olivia cut back in. "But she's right, Freddie. What can you do?" She paused, her perfect lips taking a ginger sip from her glass. "It can't be all bad. Even if you can't write about it, you must hear some interesting information."

"We'll always have our sources, if you understand me," he said between bites, warming to the encouragement. "In fact, I'd venture to say that we have some of the better information outside of the Council. Better, even, than the Municipal Police." Still stung, he glared at Jane.

"Bit of an exaggeration," Jane mumbled.

"Hardly. They're either incompetent or corrupt, and I don't know which is worse."

Between Jane and Fredrick, Olivia slapped the table. "Corrupt is worse, of course!" She looked pleased to contribute to the debate.

"Aha." Fredrick dabbed at his mouth. "You might think so. But someone who is corrupt can at least be bought. You can't do anything with a fool. Incompetence is useless." Olivia nodded slowly, focusing on this wisdom with a furrowed brow. Reaching some mental conclusion, she turned to Fredrick with renewed interest.

"Do you have any idea who is behind the murders?"

"Nothing certain. However, there are a few newsroom theories, and I have my own suspicions," he said, with another glance at Jane, who sawed furiously into her chicken.

Olivia prompted him with an indulgent smile. "And?"

"Well, one of the more popular theories attributes the murders to a gang of the dissatisfied and unemployed. As you know, a few of our neighbor territories are going through something of a recession, which is thought to have caused the recent immigration boom. The usual scapegoats and, not surprisingly, the Vineyard's pet theory." He paused to savor the attention. "Others among us, however, feel that the crimes are too methodical for a band of angry laborers. There are rumors of intrigue within the upper circles and backstabbing in their ranks."

"What kind of intrigue?"

"Dunno. That's what makes it intriguing."

"They may be 'backstabbers', but none of the whitenails would actually want a blood feud," Jane said. Fredrick leveled a skeptical stare at her. "Come on, it's common sense. They have too much to lose to squabble violently. No one at the top is going to threaten the whole structure by knocking out a few loose bricks."

Fredrick twirled his fork over the vegetables. "Not everyone enjoys quite the same benefits. Besides, as they say, power corrupts."

"And who in the Council would want to do this?"

"Not necessarily within the Council itself." Fredrick turned from Jane to Olivia. "As you may know, there are quite a few cronies and underlings that exist barely outside the absolute power of the Council and that enjoy more freedom for it."

"Don't be such a conspiracy theorist," said Jane.

"Conspiracy theorist? Jane, we're in the middle of a crisis. I've got my suspicions about who caused it, and I know I'm not the only one."

Olivia watched them both intently now. "Who?"

Fredrick ignored Jane's steely glare. "Roman Arnault."

Jane let her fork clatter to her plate. "Oh really, Fredrick."

"Yes, I've heard of him," said Olivia.

Fredrick appeared surprised. "You have?"

"You forget that Olivia and I cater to much of the same clientele," Jane said.

"Besides, it's impossible to spend three weeks in the factory district without hearing something," Olivia added.

Jane shook her head. "Fredrick loves a good scandal. Me, I just can't see it."

"That's because you've put on blinders where this one's concerned," Fredrick said. "Your detective friend feels the same way I do."

"Fredrick!"

"Wha-at? Oh, don't be silly, Jane, we're among friends."

It was Olivia's turn to interject. "Then this Roman Arnault is the prime suspect?"

Fredrick answered before Jane could protest. "It's not as simple as that. See, the investigation is being handled by the Council's own agents, and there's no telling what they think. As of last week, they certainly weren't giving him a curfew," he said, scowling. Fredrick continued too fast for Jane to add that no one at the gala, themselves included, had faced curfew. "Investigations aside, I will say this: I've worked for the news for over ten years now, and it's my job to know the climate in Recoletta. People are talking, and among those who would know, the name is Roman Arnault." He concluded with a fierce stab at a chunk of potato.

Jane found her opening. "Roman Arnault has a suspicious reputation, but he's not the only possibility. Fredrick has his 'sources'," Jane said, pronouncing the word as if it were a polite term for something less reputable, "but it's all speculation. The fact is, no one knows, so people are eager to assign the blame anywhere they can, and Roman Arnault is also a convenient scapegoat," she added, watching Fredrick's expression.

Olivia smiled and patted Jane's arm. "Jane, I thank you for your assurances, but don't worry that I take rumors too seriously! I know that Mr Anders is only looking out for us. You should be grateful for such a friend, so interested in your wellbeing." Fredrick did not attempt to conceal his satisfaction.

Jane softened and could not help grinning herself. "I guess you're right. But here we've been going on about our work without even asking you about yours."

Olivia smiled again. "Never mind that! Just another day of soap and polish."

"You work in the Vineyard too, am I right?" asked Fredrick.

"Mostly." She stirred her meal with a fork.

"And what exactly do you do?"

"I clean house, Mr Anders. I'm afraid it's not that interesting."

"Nonsense! You must come across all kinds of mysterious stains and scandalous messes."

Olivia laughed. "But none of it's nice to mention at dinner."

Fredrick held out his hands and dropped them onto his thighs. "And here, after you've gotten all of my secrets out of me."

Jane stared at the bottom of her glass as she drained it. "Wasn't exactly hard," she muttered.

Fredrick smiled at Olivia. "Well, if you can't tell us about your day-to-day now, how about something from your previous life abroad? Can't be any harm in spilling the goods on some whitenails from Bremmly, Belmond–"

"Bremmond," Jane said.

"–or wherever."

Again, Olivia laughed. "I've had some scandalous clients, but nothing that would shock a reporter. In fact, I'm eager to hear more about the scandals here."

Needing no more encouragement, Fredrick spun stories from the rumor mill as the three picked at the scraps on their plates. Dinner ended with the stretches and yawns that signify tired bodies and full stomachs. Olivia disappeared while Jane and Fredrick were clearing the table, and when she returned moments later, they were surprised to see her again decked out in her plain gray dress.

"Leaving so soon?" Fredrick asked.

"I'm afraid so. I have one more appointment tonight, and I didn't realize how late it was."

"You really do keep odd hours."

"So do my clients," she said. "Jane, I'm sorry to go now, but I can help tomorrow night with dinner."

"Don't worry about it. Look, it's nearly eleven, and you know there's a curfew..."

"It's OK. My client gave me a note to get me past the guards." Olivia patted a pocket. "I have my key, so I can let myself in later tonight." She buttoned her jacket and tugged at her sleeves. "Don't wait for me." She nodded to Fredrick. "Wonderful to have met you, Mr Anders."

"The pleasure is all mine." She was out the door before he finished. "Well, Jane, it's official," he said.

"Is she your next future ex?"

"Your new roommate is a lady of the night."

Two days after Malone's adventure in the wine cellar, she and Sundar were still deciphering the Prometheus report. Everything they read confirmed that she had grabbed the correct file from Hollens's safe.

The report itself contained an odd network of connections and gaps, raising at least as many questions as it answered, but it fit with the list that Jane had provided. With the exception of "R Arnault", each name on Jane's list was accompanied by a number, and each number had an assignment in a sister list of the Prometheus file. For instance, 1 ("A Ruthers") was cross-listed as "Project Director". If "A Ruthers" did indeed refer to Councilor Augustus Ruthers, Malone had no doubt that they were on the right track. Number 2 was "A Hollens" on Jane's list and "Assistant Project Director" in Prometheus. After the first two numbers, the list got more interesting.

"C Hask" held the position of "Chief Historian". Studying the rest of the assignments, Malone saw a fair variety, from "3rd Historian" and "Records Specialist" to the last twenty names, all of which were classified as "Security". The most intriguing was still the number 3 position: "Director of Excavation".

This slot matched "L Fitzhugh" on the first list but would now be "P Dominguez", she recalled crossly. Scattered throughout the list were quite a few other slots labeled "Excavation Team". Here lay one information gap: a team devoted to digging, but no evidence or record of the bounty.

"Probably to prevent someone from doing what we're doing now," Sundar said, his boots resting on the edge of Malone's desk.

Malone snorted.

"We wouldn't even know who this involved if it weren't for the laundress's list," he said. "I'd do it that way, and I bet you would too if you needed to keep records but wanted to preserve secrecy – split 'em up." He gnawed on the end of a pen. "It's smart."

"Only if you can trust the people holding the pieces, and I don't think the Council can." She did not have to remind Sundar of her theory that someone in the inner circle had given the murderer access to the victims' homes. "Besides, there's a hole."

"In my theory? Never." He kicked his feet off of the desk and brought them down with a small thud. "What is it?"

"If this is about segmentation, why did Hollens have this portion of the report and the list of names?"

"The list was in his jacket. Maybe he was passing it along to someone else."

A log from the Prometheus folder displayed the times and dates that certain members of the team had worked, though the inspectors could only guess at what. The log also included information on changes in the team, but no names were given, only the numbers that corresponded.

"They really do know how to keep a lid on things, don't they?" Sundar said.

"No telling how many other files there are." Flipping to the first page of the log, Malone checked the date of the first entry. It was fourteen years old.

"How could they take fourteen years on this?" Sundar asked.

"They don't exactly have a lot of people working on it, and I'll bet that's intentional."

"I love a private party."

Malone sighed. "Diggers, politicians, and historians."

"Don't forget security."

"And this somehow ties in with the Sato case... also fourteen years ago."

"Well, we know the who and the when," Sundar said.

"But not the what, where, or why."

He shrugged. "Someone's got to be the optimist."

A ghost of a smile flickered across Malone's lips. She paused. "We know they're digging. So what are they recovering?"

"Or storing," Sundar said.

"True." She turned back to the page. "Well, how did we miss this before?"

"What?"

"The log. Take a look." Malone passed the flimsy book to Sundar. Opened to the first entry, he could see that several pages had been ripped out of the front.

"So much for the when," Sundar said.

"And we still don't know how Roman Arnault fits into this."

"Ah, but that's no surprise."

Malone paused again, thinking. "Did you ever look up 'Prometheus'?"

He brightened, tapping the air with an index finger. "As a matter of fact, I did. A mythological figure: the fire-bringer. Not sure what to think of that."

"And Edmund Wickery?"

"A better success. His office still exists, but as to whether or not he does, I haven't a clue."

Malone checked her watch. "It's past curfew already, but at least we've got something."

"Yep, a handful of loose ends."

Malone gathered the papers from Prometheus and slid them into a desk drawer. "Meet me here tomorrow morning, and we'll see about visiting Edmund Wickery."

"Or at least his files."

She nodded. "Since we don't have a contract, we won't be able to do an official interview, but, if he worked closely with the Council before, something tells me he'll be cooperative."

"Yeah, but the Council wouldn't want us looking into the old Sato murder."

Malone locked the desk drawer with a gentle snick. "He won't know that."

CHAPTER 12

THE HOUSE CALL

When Malone arrived at the station shortly after six the following morning, her plans for the day centered around the visit to Edmund Wickery's office. However, Farrah's unexpected visit brought a more interesting prospect, and Malone would later be thankful that she had arrived so early.

Malone tilted the open Prometheus file away from the door when Farrah nudged it open, but Farrah wasn't looking.

"Chief needs to see you. Immediately." She flashed a sheet of paper at Malone. "I'll have the temporary contract waiting for you."

"On my way," Malone said, waiting for Farrah to turn back into the hall. She locked the file in her desk and left her office, latching the door behind her. When she reached Chief Johanssen's office, Farrah nodded her in without another word. The chief looked up as Malone entered. He had something purposeful in his manner, which was unusual as of late.

He motioned for her to sit and spoke in a husky whisper. "We don't have more than an hour. There's been another disturbance outside the Vineyard. Entry and assault, but no deaths. Here's the address," he said, passing her a slip of paper. "This incident hasn't been connected to the murders, which means you need to act before someone tells me otherwise. I'll send Sundar to that address when he arrives, but I need you to get to the hospital and interview the victim first. He won't be there long."

"Who is it?"

"Roman Arnault."

Johanssen read the question in Malone's face. "Yes, he's conscious and coherent, not that it's going to help you deal with him."

"My thoughts exactly."

"Get a copy of the temporary contract from Farrah on your way out. Arnault'll have to talk to you until the Council rejects it. Dismissed." Malone bowed and slipped out of the office, rolling the aforementioned contract into her jacket.

At her brisk pace, the hospital was only a quick walk from the station. Urgency lengthened her stride. If this attack was indeed related to the three murders, it would not be long before the Council sent its own investigators to keep her away. And, knowing the victim, she expected robust opposition.

She would not be disappointed.

After showing her badge to the hospital staff, Malone allowed a young nurse to lead her to the quiet room where Arnault was recovering. "We've kept him in one of the more secluded wings," she said. "We thought it best to, ah, keep him separate. For various reasons." As they approached the room, the nurse's muscles tensed and her back straightened. Malone surmised that she had enjoyed the dubious pleasure of treating Arnault personally.

"Mr Arnault should be waking up any moment now," the nurse said.

"How long has he been here?"

"A neighbor escorted him in at 4.30 this morning, and the doctors went straight to work."

"What happened?"

"He was very badly beaten: one blow to the face and an eight-inch long knife wound in his side. The cut wasn't too deep, otherwise you wouldn't be talking to him now. We gave him stitches, but he wouldn't take anything for the pain." She hesitated and looked back toward the room. "Nothing except for the bottle."

"Thank you," Malone said, and the nurse left her. She entered the chamber, prepared for whatever manner of incivility she was about to receive.

The room was small and neat with little in it except for a bed and a side table supporting a bottle of amber liquid. Arnault was reclined in the hospital bed, his eyes closed. As Malone passed through the door, his eyes slowly opened, as if he had been waiting. By the displeasure on his face, he had evidently not been waiting for her.

"Good morning," Malone said. He grunted. "I have several questions for you."

Arnault stretched in his bed and folded his arms over his chest.

Malone pulled the form out of her jacket, unrolling it. "And my contract says you'll give me answers."

"Temporary contract," Arnault said. "And you have no authority with the Vineyard murders, so I'm not under any obligation to humor you."

Malone cocked her head. "And here I thought this was an isolated assault. Do you know something I don't?" Roman grimaced, sensing defeat. "Then you do have to humor me. Unless you think your handlers will enjoy bailing you out of trouble for failure to cooperate."

"Just get it over with."

"Give me as much detail as you can about this morning."

"Forty stitches, three nurses, two physicians, two glasses of bourbon, and one unpleasant inspector." Arnault ticked each item off on an outstretched finger.

"Related to the attack, Mr Arnault."

He sighed. "Last night, then. I returned home and went to bed early."

"What time?"

"1.30, about."

Malone frowned. "That's early? Where were you returning from?"

"Yes, it is, and that's none of your business."

Malone tapped the contract in her jacket.

Arnault rolled his eyes. "The Gearbox. A bar near the factory districts. Anyway, I awoke in the middle of the night and thought I heard someone in the domicile."

"Could you be more specific about the time? And what did you hear?"

Arnault clenched his jaw, raising knots behind his molars. "Shall I tell my story or not? I wasn't taking notes, so you'll have to be satisfied with what I remember." He paused and slicked back his hair with one hand. "It must have been after three. I got out of bed, took my pistol, and went to the hall, where someone gave me this." He gestured to the welt on his cheekbone. "I jumped back, dropped the gun, and grabbed my attacker's arm and twisted. He sliced me with the knife in his other hand, and I let go. By the time I had my gun in hand, he was disappearing down the street. I made it almost to the door before losing consciousness. A neighbor heard the commotion, saw me lying in blood, and helped me to the hospital. And that's all I know."

"You dropped the gun?" Malone asked.

"That's what I said."

She looked at him in disbelief.

"Why so surprised? Isn't that the kind of thing that normally happens, Inspector?"

"It is with home-defense amateurs, but not with men like you."

Roman snorted. "I don't use it as much as you seem to think, Inspector. Certainly not as often as you use yours," he said.

"Did you see your attacker?"

"No."

"Can you tell me anything about him?"

"Not really. Seemed smaller than I." Given Roman Arnault's considerable frame, that was a reasonable assumption. "It could have been a woman, for all I know."

"You didn't see him at all?" Malone asked.

"It was dark. We didn't spend much time face-to-face, in case you couldn't tell." The polished stone walls behind Arnault glowed in the bright hospital lights, but a scowl shadowed his face.

"How did the attacker get into your domicile?"

He sighed. "If I knew that, he wouldn't have."

"Do you know of anyone who would want to harm you?"

"Plenty," he said with a grin, "but none who would dare try."

She glared and paced closer to his bedside. "Mr Arnault, you aren't being very helpful."

His nostrils flared, and he gritted his teeth audibly. "Madame Inspector, I was awakened in the middle of the night, hit over the head, and drained of five pints of blood. You will pardon me if my memory is not as sharp as yours would be."

"That's not the problem. I don't think you want to help me."

"Such powers of deduction."

Malone squeezed her hands into fists. "I'm not asking favors. You're the one in the hospital bed."

He sat up and brought his face close to hers. She could see the glassy sweat beads at his temples and the blood vessels snaking across his eyes. "Inspector Malone, do you think I don't know that my life is in danger?" For the first time, Liesl Malone saw him look truly unsettled. "If I had anything useful to tell you, I would. Doubt no longer. I am terrified for my life." Looking at his wide eyes and pale, perspiring cheeks, Malone believed him.

"Then let me help you," she said. "Tell me what you do know and let me protect you."

"Inspector, you haven't the slightest idea of what you're getting yourself into. The truth is, neither do I." He continued before she could interrupt. "Besides, there's only one person I trust, and I'm sure you can guess who that is." He tapped his chest.

"I can't protect you from your own paranoia, Arnault."

"You saw Hollens just before he died, Inspector. Tell me, did he give you what you wanted?" Malone's face darkened and creased. "Oh, I seem to have touched a soft spot."

"For a man afraid for his life, you have a dark sense of humor."

"You Municipals are so much like the criminals you pursue: deceptive, manipulative, and heedless of any authority outside your own." Arnault watched as Malone stood in silence, biting her tongue. He smiled, and his bright eyes gleamed in his blanched face. "When was the last time you broke into a suspect's home? Stole evidence? Forged an identity? Browbeat a witness?"

White teeth flashed from behind Malone's drawn lips. "We've never been elegant, but we have limits. That's what makes us different from the lawbreakers... and from you."

Arnault barked with mirth, wincing as his sides heaved. "No, it's your self-righteousness. You're so certain that you know what's wrong and how to fix it. You're ignorant and headstrong, and one of these days, you're going to get someone killed. I just hope that it's you."

"Easy for you to criticize when the only one you have to look out for is yourself."

Roman settled back into the bed, allowing his eyelids to droop as he prepared to return to sleep. "How are you always so sure of everything, Malone?"

Malone stood back from the bed. "You've been as helpful as ever." The nurses looked on wordlessly as Malone stalked out of the ward, her face set in an impassive mask.

At the station, she did not have to wait long for Sundar, which didn't bode well for his end of the investigation.

"The place was already swarming with the City Guard and the Council's 'official' investigators. They were checking papers at the door, and, as you can guess, I didn't have an invite. I certainly hope you had better luck," he said.

"In a way." Malone flicked her head in the direction of her office, and they walked through the station in silence, their eyes fixed to the ground and their minds on their respective defeats. After reaching sanctuary, Malone gave him the rundown on her exchange with Arnault. "He's afraid, but he's determined not to cooperate," she said, resting her head on her hand. "If he were anyone else, and if this were any other contract, we could force more cooperation out of him."

"Through the Council, you mean."

"Right." She signed. "I don't know what to make of him anymore."

"Target practice would be one thing."

Malone looked up. "Be careful where you say that."

"Don't tell me you haven't thought the same thing."

She smiled.

Sundar sighed and clasped his hands, resting on elbows. "What now?"

"Now, we see what Edmund Wickery can tell us, whether on paper or in person."

As promised, Olivia prepared dinner that evening. Jane sat by the warm fireside, mending a pair of trousers. She could not forget Fredrick's comment from the other night, and despite years of friendship, she still never knew when to take him seriously. Sharing a walk earlier in the day, she had tried to pry the candor out of him.

"You know, just because she's gorgeous and uninterested in you doesn't make her a... um..."

"A prostitute?"

"Yes."

"Of course not. It's the schedule she keeps and her way with people." Furrowing her brow, Jane nearly tripped over a flagstone. "Do you know anyone else who makes 'house calls' after ten at night? It's obviously a euphemism," he said, his tone airy yet authoritative.

"I'll admit that's odd, but what do you mean about 'her way with people'?"

"Did you notice that she rarely talks about herself?"

Wheeling her laundry cart around traffic, Jane considered the question. "Maybe she's shy."

"She dodged all the questions we asked about her, but she

asked plenty about us – our work, our day, our opinions. And she found it all fascinating. What does that tell you?"

"That she's a nice person."

"Wrong. She knows how to make people feel good. Her trade isn't just about providing clients with physical pleasure. It's about holistic satisfaction."

Jane frowned, watching the clothes shift and bounce on the cart in front of her. "You make it sound like an art form."

"Ah, Jane, don't be such a prude. She pays the rent early and keeps you company. What do you have to worry about? After all, she brought her own bedding."

Now, sitting in front of the fire, Jane pushed the memory from her mind. It was still early, but she was looking forward to a quiet evening at home, her deliveries for the day already done. Savoring the smell of simmering herbs and the heat of dancing flames, Jane set the needle and pants beside her and flexed her fingers, rolling her wrists from side to side. The turn of a key at the door and subsequent rumbling of the bar interrupted her peace. "Hold on," she called. Checking the window, she saw Fredrick and hastened to let him in.

"Hi," she began. He pressed a newspaper into her hands with an impenetrable expression. As she unfolded it, he moved to sit on the couch.

"Be careful, there's a–" she began.

Fredrick leapt up, muttering an expletive and feeling his backside. He produced the needle between thumb and forefinger, but his gaze faltered as he looked back at Jane. Returning to the paper, she opened it to the first page and a headline that stopped her breath: "PROMINENT SOCIALITE FOUND HALF DEAD IN HOME OUTSIDE THE VINEYARD." Beneath it was a picture of a scowling Roman Arnault.

"I don't know if that's a good description of the man, but I certainly can't think of anything else that's printable," Fredrick said from the couch. Jane continued reading a lurid description of Roman's bloodstained doorway on Carnegie and his dramatic entrance to the hospital. The author had seasoned the account with graphic statements from the nursing team about Roman's injuries and treatment, each stitch like a gory exclamation point on the page.

"If it's any comfort, I think the article exaggerates his condition," Fredrick said more softly, seeing Jane's pallor. "I'm fairly certain that he was only at the hospital a brief while this morning, and I happen to know that the reporter who wrote that article has a knack for embellishment." Olivia had paused in her cooking for a moment, and the apartment was silent but for the crackle of the fire and the bubbling of pots.

"I do not understand. What has happened?" Olivia asked.

Fredrick saw Jane's eyes still glued to the page and answered, keeping his recounting brief and free of detail. "It's not serious," he added, watching both women.

"Not serious?" Now it was Olivia's turn for surprise, not only at the news, but also at Fredrick's seeming nonchalance. "How can you say it is not serious if someone is in the hospital?"

"Was in the hospital," he said. "And I say it by considering the totality of the circumstances. In fact, I'd go so far as to say that he's terribly lucky. Three men have died, and he's managed to get away with a bruise and a scrape."

Olivia reddened, shaking an accusing spoon at Fredrick. "Yes, we'd see if you call it 'a bruise and a scrape' if you were the one–"

Fredrick held up two placating hands. "It could be much worse."

"Much worse! How can you–"

"Because he survived," Fredrick continued, gathering steam. "He's younger and in better shape than the other victims. It seems our murderer was overconfident after preying on graying bureaucrats."

Olivia threw up her hands and returned to the pots.

Fredrick sighed and ruffled his hair, looking down into the fire. "And it would appear that I was, er, mistaken in my earlier accusations. He's still an odd trick, but I didn't see this happening. So I'll say it once and let it rest: I was wrong. How's that, Jane?" He looked over his shoulder, expecting a response, but she was gone. The door hung ajar and the discarded newspaper marked the spot where she had stood only moments ago.

Dashing through passages and sprinting down tunnels, Jane had left her apartment warren before she knew where she was going. She slowed at Tanney Passage to catch her breath and clear her head. The newspaper had said that Roman was home, and Fredrick had said that he was all right, but she needed to see this for herself. Her pulse thumped a rapid pace in her throat, and she assessed her options.

It would be nine o'clock in several minutes, which meant curfew. Jane didn't have an excuse to be out, but she thought that she could invent something suitable if it became necessary. She had an idea of where Carnegie was, and, on the outskirts of the Vineyard, it wouldn't be hard to find. Her only problem was getting there, and without getting caught… by the guards or anyone else. She hoped that she knew the subterranean passages well enough from her laundry runs to evade anyone that she might not wish to meet.

Jane sprinted along the passages on padded feet, skirting the major thoroughfares and on the lookout for guards.

She had not decided what she would do when she reached Arnault's domicile, but she resolved to trust her feet for now and her wits later. Her pulse steadied as she sprinted, crept, and listened. She nearly ran in front of a pair of patrollers, but she ducked behind a corner just in time and watched them pass unaware, close enough for her to tug their coats.

She glimpsed the few trolleys and railcars still running, hearing their growls and hums below her feet and above her head. They could save her thirty minutes of travel, but she did not want to answer any questions.

Her pace slowed as she neared the Vineyard, expecting to find more guards. She wandered the grid of tunnels on the outer rim of the Vineyard, convinced that Carnegie was somewhere nearby. Rounding a corner, she heard someone shout.

"You there!" a man directly behind her called. She froze, and, as she heard footsteps draw closer, turned.

The guard was standing five yards down the passage, his hands folded behind his back. "It's half an hour past curfew, you know. Where are you off to this late?"

Jane looked up at the nearest tunnel marker and read "Carnegie." "Home," she said. In the low lighting, she saw the hint of a smile.

"You'll pardon my saying so, miss, but you don't exactly look like you live around here."

"A maid. I'm a maid, officer." Looking down at the worn hem on her skirt and her disheveled garments, she could see what he meant.

"I see. And what are you doing out?"

This was the question she had hoped to avoid. None of the explanations that she had invented along the way seemed plausible now that she was standing in front of an actual guard, pistol, uniform, and all. As she made a final effort to think of an excuse, she blushed and her eyes darted to the ground. The guard seemed to take meaning from this and laughed aloud.

"Oh-ho-ho, I see what this is! Don't you worry, missy – your little secret is safe with me. But you'd best hurry on 'fore someone else notices what's missing at home, right?" He gave her a wink that was a little too familiar.

Nodding, she turned and hurried down the next passage, eager to be out of the guard's sight for more than one reason. Thinking back to her conversation about Olivia, she wondered how many others like her were out past curfew making their rounds.

Fortunately for Jane, most of the doors were marked with plaques bearing the names of the occupants or businesses. She walked quickly, scanning them. Carnegie was a serpentine passage with a high ceiling and sturdy, varnished doors that spoke of position, so when she reached the plaque gnawed by tarnish, she knew she'd found the right one. The printed name "ARNAULT" confirmed her suspicions and, brushing a few stray locks from her face, she rang the bell. The tasseled cord left a fine film of crumbling red velvet on her palm as the bell sounded on the other side of the door. The radiance stones set in the passage glowed dimly, their white light reflected off of the smooth gray walls. She began to count them as she waited.

After a few moments, she heard a click on the other side. Roman opened the door, and his face betrayed his astonishment at seeing her there.

"Miss Lin, this is an unexpected surprise." He looked her up and down and glanced all around her, as if anticipating someone else. "It's well after curfew, you know?"

"That wouldn't stop you."

He laughed. "No, it wouldn't. Please come inside, and forgive my poor manners." She followed as he ushered her in and led her to the drawing room. His hair hung free to his chin and, as seemed his custom, he was dressed loosely and comfortably. Jane noted a slight limp in his right step.

"Sit and rest. I don't entertain many guests, but I hope you'll make yourself comfortable."

She took the offered seat next to a crackling fire. She sank into the plush armchair, letting her heels slide down the scroll-patterned area rug at her feet, and looked around.

The drawing room was not large, but it was well furnished. The wood paneling and flooring lent a warm touch and a rich scent to the room. Bookcases, packed full with multicolored spines and assorted oddities, framed the fireplace and ran the length of that wall. Foreign-looking artifacts and hangings nestled between the books and adorned the walls, reflecting the tastes of an explorer or eccentric more than a sinister misanthrope. A map decorated one segment of the wall, and a pair of microscopes sat in a corner, next to a shelf holding orbs of various sizes and designs.

"The one on the left shows the world bisected by the magnetic poles," he said, following her gaze. "And next to it is a globe map of the constellations."

Looking down, Jane realized that the carpet alone must cost more than her apartment. Now trying to lift her feet from it, she looked to the ancient telescope sitting against the far wall.

"And that doesn't work indoors," Roman said. He spread his hands and turned back to her. "It doesn't compare with the luxury of the Vineyard, but it's at your disposal."

"It's beautiful." Her gaze rested on the wall of bookshelves, the embossed covers winking at her in the fire's glow. In the light, she could just make out the titles of the copies nearest her.

Roman circled to the chair across from her and sat, resting on one elbow. "What brings you here this late?"

Fingering the nap on the arm of her chair, Jane realized that she had not fully answered that question for herself. "I read about your incident in the paper, and I wanted to see how you are."

"A house call?" he asked with feigned shock.

"I suppose so."

"I'm touched. Did you have any trouble getting here?"

"Not really." She hesitated. "Well, I ran into one guard."

"He didn't stop you?"

Jane blushed. "I told him I was on my way home."

His eyes widened even further and he leaned forward. "You lied to the City Guard? Jane, I'm shocked... and proud. This is unlike you."

"I'm a little surprised, myself." Smiling, she relaxed. "Funny, though, it wasn't as hard as I thought."

"You fooled him?"

"I got lucky, I'd say. I suppose I still have some learning to do to really trick anyone." She looked back at him and saw his grin spreading, his gaze intent. Embarrassed, she glanced back at the fire. "It hardly compares with your adventures, though. How are you feeling?"

He touched the welt above his cheek. "Not too bad. But I will have to ask you to keep your wit at a minimum," he said, running a hand over the cut in his side.

Jane was surprised to notice how contentedly she had reclined in her own chair, relaxing at his good humor. Something in the shape of his posture or the slant of his smile suggested a different man from the one she had met at the gala or even at Hollens's place. If this was the change that a knock on the head could produce, she could not bring herself to regret his misfortune.

He stretched in his own chair and spoke again. "I'm relieved to see you here, Jane. After facing doctors, councilors, and inspectors all day, it's good to see a friendly face."

The word "inspectors" stung her with a tiny but precise force, and she realized part of what had driven her here: a desire to investigate. Basking in warmth from more than the hearth, she cringed at the thought of betraying this charming new Roman, but she remembered her conversation with Malone. Besides, even he had admired her newfound cunning, hadn't he?

She squinted vaguely, assuming a look that, she hoped, suggested she had just thought of something. "Did you say 'inspectors'? That's funny, I thought they weren't supposed to investigate the Vineyard murders anymore." She looked over at Roman, hoping that he would think nothing of the heat rising in her face. "Fredrick told me," she added. "He hears all sorts of things at the paper, and he generally doesn't keep them to himself."

"He's right. Unfortunately, some people are as dogged as they are ignorant." A dark expression clouded his features, and Jane decided to move the conversation along.

"I'm sorry about what happened to you, but I'm glad you're alive."

"That makes two of us."

"Do you remember anything about how it happened?"

"Only vaguely. It was over in a flash." He looked down at his right side and touched his cheekbone again. "I kept reminders of the significant events, though."

Jane grinned. "It's just still so hard to believe all of it. Who could do something like that?"

"I wish I knew."

"You mean you didn't get a look at him during the attack?"

"I could be asking you the same thing," he said. She swallowed and wondered if she was pressing too hard.

"But wait, Fredrick never published my name. How did you know about–?"

"Jane, you forget who I work for. The Council knows everything. Almost everything," he added gently.

"But not the name of the murderer."

A crooked smile spread from one cheek to the other. "No, not the name of the murderer." Jane blinked away the image of Roman's toothy grin. Her lack of subtlety felt like a weight around her ankles.

"I suppose Ruthers isn't too happy about that," she said. An instant of shock registered on Roman's face, and she corrected herself. "Councilor Ruthers, I mean."

"No, I can't say he is."

"I shouldn't be so nosy. But going through the whitenails' dirty laundry for five years now, I never would have guessed that there was so much I didn't know."

Roman took an iron poker from a stand by the fireplace and stirred the burning logs. "You get a rather intimate view of your clients' personal lives, wouldn't you say?"

She watched the iron probe the flames. "That's true."

"Do you ever snoop on them?" As Jane opened her mouth to answer, Roman turned his head and regarded her with a knowing gaze. She thought back to their meeting at Hollens's residence.

"Sometimes you can't help but notice things."

He nodded. "Well put. And do you think you notice more than most people?"

"I've never thought about it. A lot of my job is about attention to detail, though." She looked up at him, but he stared back, expectant. "I suppose yes, then."

"And what," he said, replacing the poker, "do you supposed distinguishes people who notice things from people who don't?"

Her eyebrows came together on her forehead. "I couldn't begin to say. It has a lot to do with what people are like, doesn't it?"

"Take a step back. What makes you a good laundress? I'm assuming, of course," he said with a smile and a gesture in her direction, "that you're an excellent one."

"I know how to fix problems – stains and rips."

"And how do you know when to fix a problem?"

"Well, first..." She cocked her head and looked up at the mantel. "I know what I'm looking for."

"Yes." Roman leaned back in his armchair and propped his left heel on his opposite knee. "You know what you're looking for." He smiled at her. "You've gotten at the heart of that question. But here's another: does someone tell you what you're looking for, or do you figure it out yourself?"

"A bit of both, I guess." In the silence that followed, Jane feared the unspoken question, *and what are you looking for here?*

Instead of asking, Roman kicked his left leg to the floor and sat forward again. "You seem to have a taste for secrets, Jane. If you're still feeling bold, I'd like to show you something." Roman tilted his head at her, the question dancing in his eyes. Jane blinked her surprise, a thrill of anticipation swirling in her stomach.

"OK."

He rose from his chair and moved to the far side of the bookcase, and she followed. "I won't ask about the most dangerous item you've ever come across in a client's residence," he said, running his finger across a row of spines, "because I guarantee it won't top this." He pushed several volumes aside, revealing blank paneling at the end of the shelf. Pressing against one edge, he slid the dark wood aside to uncover a hidden compartment stocked with an assortment of books and papers. He extracted a thick tome and placed it in her hands.

"*The Riverside Shakespeare,*" she read. "What is this?"

"A collection of plays." He watched her examine the cover. "Many of them historical."

Her head snapped up, and she instinctively held the book away from her body. "This can't be legal," she whispered.

"Of course not. It's one of the most dangerous books around."

She marveled at the cover, hard and worn, with no indication of the sinister enigmas beneath it. It gingerly rested on her fingertips, and she realized that she was holding it out to Roman. He made no move to take it back. "Why?"

"Why is it dangerous? Besides containing history, many of the works inside it demonstrate a disturbing contempt for authority. Rulers are installed and unseated about as often as they sneeze." His eyes rolled quickly in their sockets, and his even voice rose in pitch. "Heaven forbid people should get the idea that leadership is seized rather than bred."

"No, why are you showing this to me?"

"You like books. And secrets." He took the volume from her, replacing it in its compartment. As he leaned it back into its place, her eyes fell on the stack of papers wedged behind it. Shuffled and dog-eared, they stood out from the straight-backed books sandwiching them. A worn folder barely kept them together, and Jane could just make out "Prometheus" in faded lettering across the spine. "And I like sharing both with you."

"Does the Council know?"

"They let me get away with a lot, but they don't know about this. Are you going to tell them?"

She tried to laugh. "Of course not."

His eyes softened as he squared his shoulders and regarded her. "And again the poor host. You walked all the way here, and I haven't offered you any refreshment. May I make you some tea?"

What Jane really craved was a minute alone with the sheaf of papers. "I'd love some."

He turned toward the kitchen and looked back at her, smiling with something that looked like regret. "We can't hide from what we are, each of us. I'd like to tell you that we're instruments of a destiny written in the stars, but I don't believe in plans. We only follow what's in our blood, and I hope you don't judge me too harshly for what's in mine," he said with strange tenderness. "I have to heat the water, so you'll have to excuse me for a few minutes." He crossed the room and she heard him opening cupboards in the kitchen. Jane glided to the shelf and swept the loose pages from between the books, glancing back at the hall where Roman had disappeared.

Flipping through the pages, she saw a long list of names and phrases, none of which she recognized. As she thumbed through several sheets of the same, she realized she was looking at a long list of titles. An inventory – too extensive to relate to Roman's personal bookshelves, but perhaps a catalog of the Department of Preservation? It seemed to fit, especially since Roman maintained his own collection of clandestine literature. Still, she found herself vaguely disappointed until she reached the last sheet.

It was a map, worn and covered in mottled colors that could have been geographic features or stains. Recoletta sat at the center, but the map's last owner had been more interested in a place called "Fairview", a commune several inches south of Recoletta. That, and a large, circled dot in an otherwise empty portion of the map. Someone had written in the margin:

"IBRA Y RES – 80 miles south of Fairview Commune, due E of river from giant veranda."

"Is this how you usually repay hospitality?"

Jane whirled to see Roman standing inches away, his eyes boring into her. There was no tea.

"I was—"

"What you were doing is obvious, and you're a fool to think you could sneak it past me."

"I know how this looks, but—"

"Yes, Jane, please enlighten me. Exactly how does this look?" His fury was withering, his voice rising over the pounding of her heart.

"Roman, I'm not a spy, I swear."

"You forget that I am, and I'll always be two steps ahead of you. In fact, I'm insulted that you could think otherwise." He snatched the papers from her grasp and thumped them on a side table with menacing deliberation. Clamping a hand on her shoulder, he led her back toward the fireplace. Jane began to feel terror rising like bile in her throat.

"No, please don't." She tugged feebly against his grip.

"Don't what?" Roman spun her to face him. "What exactly are you afraid of?" His voice was dangerously low, but she could still hear its obsidian edge. "Not so brave anymore. What am I going to do with you?" He pulled her closer until she could count the blue rays in his irises. "Answer."

"You're hurting me," she said, not daring to speak above a whisper. Her shoulder was losing feeling under his iron grip. Looking down, he released his hold, and she took two tentative steps back. The man facing her was not the same one who had admitted her into the domicile thirty minutes ago. The warmth was drained from his expression, and, glaring at her in the firelight, something deadlier than his old venom simmered under the surface. She expected to read fury in his eyes and a snarl on his lips, but everything about him radiated calculated coldness and perfect calm.

"What did you come here looking for?"

She opened her mouth with an answer but stopped. "I didn't know," she finally said.

He almost smiled. "That's the first thing you've said that's true." His voice oozed condescension.

"I didn't mean any harm. I just wanted to help."

"Of course you did. The problem is, I don't think you really know who you're helping or why."

"Listen, can't we–"

In one quick movement, he drew a pistol and brought it to bear on her. "Stop. You forget that you're not made of the right stuff. You may be an angel, my dear, but you can't fly."

The sight of the gun aimed at her chest silenced her. Then he spoke again. "If you aren't careful, you're going to end up just like your parents."

Jane's blood froze. "How do you know about my parents?"

"How do you think, Miss Lin?"

"Are you telling me that you...?"

"Don't be ridiculous. I was thirteen years old when your parents died. But someone else did."

Jane was struggling to speak. "My parents were..."

"Murdered." The word sounded like something cold and metal in Roman's mouth. "They were writers, but, more importantly, they were snoops."

Her voice quavered. "And you've known..."

"Yes, since I met you. I recognized your name immediately."

She paused, absorbing the new information. "I've never heard of any writers named Lin."

"They wrote under a *nom de plume*. The Brownings." He saw recognition dawn in her eyes. "Yes, like the ancient poets.

Unfortunately for your parents, some of their writings were too political."

Something inside Jane was changing. Anger began to replace her fear. "How—"

"I've nothing more to say on the subject. Your parents were reckless meddlers, and you would do best not to follow their example."

"Tell me." The heat returned to her face.

"Enough." He thumbed the hammer on his gun. "Your parents got what was coming to them, and if you don't learn when to abandon a line of inquiry so will you."

Her entire body shook as she glared at him. "You're a monster."

"And you're a fool." A sadistic grin twisted his mouth. "Did it ever strike you as odd that the maid found you so quickly? And the hours she keeps!" He stared at her, relishing her bewilderment. "She does much more than clean houses. I sent Olivia Saavedra. And if you don't exercise discretion, you'll find out why."

Jane blanched, shocked into silence again.

"You'll find a carriage waiting at the surface," he said. "I don't need to tell you not to mention this night to anyone."

"Are you going to shoot me if I do?"

"I won't have to. Stay out of this, Jane. You don't know what you're interfering with. Now get out." He nodded at the stairs.

She began to take a step toward the landing, but she stopped. "You still don't frighten me."

"It's just the adrenaline talking. Go." Jane turned toward the stairs and he lowered his gun.

"Jane." She stopped on the threshold at the sound of her name. "If you ever try anything like this again, I will not be so lenient. With you or the reporter." Without another word, she

ascended and found the hansom waiting. It rolled forward as
soon as she stepped in, the horse's hooves pounding a heavy
tattoo. The ominous rhythm thundered in her head all the
way home.

When the carriage stopped above her apartment she got
out, and it started away with a jolt. She waited until it was
out of sight before patting her bodice, where she had tucked
the map. She turned toward the city center with a final errand
in mind. It was risky, but Jane decided it was also necessary
if she was going to make this fresh peril worth anything. She
had one thing left to do before Roman Arnault and his spies
tightened their hold on her.

CHAPTER 13

TURNABOUT

Malone arrived at the station the next morning to the sounds of the early shift traffic: shuffling footsteps, mumbled greetings, and stifled yawns. Given yesterday's events, she was surprised not to find Sundar already at his desk or, more likely, waiting by her office with stacks of notes in hand. They had enjoyed a tantalizing measure of success at the Wickery office the day before, a much-deserved victory after their individual defeats investigating Arnault, but she was still stunned by the implications of what they had found.

Arriving at the law office by mid-afternoon the previous day, they had been astonished to find it still operating and under the management of Edmund Wickery's son, Edmund Jr. He'd greeted them with the matter-of-fact dourness of a man who both loathes his occupation and believes that his feelings on the matter are universal. When the inspectors had introduced themselves and their purpose, he'd seemed only moderately surprised.

"My father retired from the practice eight years ago, and he passed away two years later," he told them as he stacked and shuffled papers.

"I'm sorry to hear that," Malone said.

"You clearly didn't know him. Now, what is it that you're here for?"

Furnishing a contract, Malone had explained that she and Sundar were fixing some gaps in the station's files and would need to see the records. Edmund Jr had led them to a moth-infested room full of shelves and files and gave the inspectors a quick rundown of their quasi-alphabetical order. As he'd retreated to the comfort of his office, he'd informed them over his shoulder that if they should need anything, he was at their disposal. The door had closed behind him almost before he'd finished his leave-taking.

"With the tracks he just made, you'd think we were going to ask him to count these," Sundar had said, nodding at the shelves of files.

"I don't think he wants anything to do with them, counting or otherwise. Judging by the dust, I doubt anyone's been in here for a few years," Malone had replied, showing him a furry coating on her fingertip.

Sundar had raised an eyebrow. "Well, watch where you stick your hands. I think some of those things are ready to feed." He'd nodded at the ceiling where several moths of fearsome proportions nested.

Wiping the dust layers off of the protruding file tabs, they'd gone down the row. After combing through the Ss, a few Rs, and even a scattered B and L, they'd found the Stanislau file, more or less where it should have been. Its perfect envelope of dust had confirmed that no one else had examined it in a long time.

"Really?" Sundar had said. "That easy? No half-drunk guards, no short-tempered bureaucrats?" He'd looked around as if expecting to see them surrounded on all sides.

"Just moths."

Heaving the file out of its spot in the shelves, they'd been pleased at its thickness.

"After all the trouble we've had finding everything else, I'd say we've had this coming to us," Sundar had said.

"Let's see what's in it first."

"And what's missing."

They'd cracked the folder open, its ancient adhesive popping and snapping. The biographical information provided on Stanislau corroborated what they had seen in the police files and also filled in a few blanks. Stanislau had been fifty-two years old at the time of the trial, had been a suspect in various smuggling and robbery operations, possessed a reputation for a violent temper, and had been mute and illiterate. They'd each taken a sheaf of papers, following their fingertips down the yellowed pages as they searched for useful nuggets. Sundar had found the next link.

"Look," he'd said, tracing a page with his index finger. "According to these records, Wickery met with Stanislau once before the trial... in an interrogation cell, accompanied by guards." He'd squeezed his eyebrows together. "On the other hand, Wickery met with representatives of the Council... twelve times."

"And they selected him to represent Stanislau."

Sundar had gnawed his tongue. "According to procedure, yes. The Council has the jurisdiction to select lawyers in a trial for any party who cannot afford to pay for his own. And Stanislau fell under that category."

"Clearly. Does the file say how much Wickery was paid?"

"Yes, it was... wow. Fifty thousand marks for all of three days' work. That's the real crime." He'd pulled the file closer, blinking into it. "His contract states that the additional conditions of his assignment were total confidentiality on his part before, during, and after the trial and his agreement to the presence of an armed guard during his contact with the accused... at all times."

"What for?"

Sundar had thumbed through several more pages. "For restraining Stanislau. He appears to have developed a habit of going ballistic from time to time over the course of the proceedings."

"Where do you see that?"

"An early letter from Stanislau's handlers at the Barracks to Wickery. They wanted to inform him that Stanislau was a danger to himself and others and that he required an 'armed and capable presence' at all times. We also have several outbursts throughout the trial transcript," he'd added, thumbing through red, circled portions of the next ream of papers. He'd looked up at Malone with an eager, dazed expression.

"Tell me if I understand this correctly," Malone had said, clasping her hands behind her back and pacing the narrow row of shelves. "A dock worker with a dubious past is charged with murdering two of Recoletta's most famous citizens for a few valuables and pocket change." She'd looked at him from under knitted brows, and his own had shot back a question.

"One hundred and fifty marks," she said. "Not pocket change for him, but not enough to warrant becoming an enemy of the city-state. Anyway, he meets with his appointed lawyer once before the trial, even then accompanied by a contingent of city guards. He is under strict restraint at all times and makes no statements. He does not speak or explain himself because he is mute... and he cannot communicate to anyone in writing because he is illiterate. From the time of his arrest, all statements on his behalf are made by his lawyer, who is selected by the Council and paid, we can both agree, handsomely. The five judges unanimously found him guilty and approved the death sentence." She'd paused and stopped pacing, turning to face Sundar. "Does this sound procedural to you?"

"About as procedural as Dominguez's indefinite appointment." Sundar had scratched his chin. "The Council really, really wanted to make sure that he was convicted."

"More than that, they wanted to ensure that he couldn't talk. So to speak," Malone had said. "But what were they worried he would say?"

"That's the question. Do you think a guy like that was really a threat after he was already locked up?" He'd rested his back against the shelf behind him, leaning into it.

"If so, it would certainly explain the lawyer's payment. And the other terms of his contract." Malone had scowled, the sharp lines of her face standing in hard relief against the galaxy of dust swirling around the room. "A year's income on one case in exchange for his silence and complicity with extreme terms. It would appear that fifty thousand marks were enough to buy Edmund Wickery."

"That, or a concern for his family's safety. If the Council wanted Stanislau's conviction so badly, do you think they wouldn't have applied a little pressure?" Sundar'd asked. When Malone had looked back at the door to the office, Sundar had continued. "Fine, Junior didn't think much of him as a father, but does that mean Wickery didn't love his family?" Sundar's eyes softened.

Malone had been a breath away from asking Sundar more, but something about the territory felt too personal. Instead, she'd said, "They may have threatened him, and that's a troubling possibility." Malone cleared her throat, briefly turning her attention to the dust motes. "So why eliminate Stanislau? What did he know, what had he done, that they wanted him silent and dead? If the Council wanted to avenge the Satos, they shouldn't have worried. There was no shortage of evidence and prejudice against him, so why silence him?"

Sundar had looked back at her, his eyes softer still. "Maybe he was innocent."

She'd shaken her head. "No. The Council wouldn't knowingly condemn an innocent man." Whatever else she might have believed or felt about the Council, that was one step too far.

Sundar had tapped his temple and frowned. "Unless they needed a scapegoat."

Malone had frowned. "Why this man?"

"Because they could silence him and no one would doubt his guilt. The five judges who delivered the ruling apparently didn't." He'd set the file aside, resting dusty hands on his thighs. "You don't kill a councilor and his wife over a pocketful of valuables, and you don't worry over the fate of a man who's presumed guilty before his trial begins." His voice had sounded rusty and tired, and two ghost handprints had stood out on his dark slacks as he shifted again.

Malone had tasted a sharp bitterness as Sundar had laid out his suspicions. "Are you suggesting that Stanislau was framed?"

"That, or hired. I used to think the councilors were locking down because they feared for their safety. Now, I think they're trying to hide their guilt."

If he was correct, the problem was much worse than they had feared.

"If that's the case," she'd said, "how is it that we're reading these files now?" She'd looked back in the direction of Edmund Jr's office.

He'd followed her gaze, a somber curve haunting the corners of his mouth. "They don't seem like a pair that talked much."

Today, she and Sundar had planned on visiting the judges who'd ruled on the murder case. The city kept a pool of scholars educated in law, ethics, forensics, and logic, and for any given trial or arbitration, five were selected at random to hear the testimonies and provide a ruling. Plenty of safeguards, including handsome salaries and a meticulous selection process, were in place to prevent the bribing of a judge or any other variety of dishonesty, but Malone's faith in the system was dissolving as her investigations progressed.

The inspectors had copied the names of the judges from the case file in Wickery's office the previous day with the reasoning that the judges might be able to point out any anomalies in the proceedings. And if they didn't, their reticence would be more telling. Unfortunately, only one of the five was still practicing. Malone hoped that their luck from yesterday would hold and that the other four would be living and locatable.

Sifting through her notes, Malone was vaguely aware of morning's advance by the increased foot traffic. She had been sitting at her desk for roughly an hour when she heard a rapid tapping at the door.

"Police courier, madam."

"Come in."

A man in a bright sash popped in, dropped a sealed message on her desk and, bobbing his head in a truncated bow, retreated as suddenly as he had arrived. Listening to the quick cadence of his footsteps, Malone broke the wax and unfolded the paper.

It was a map showing terrain and features between Recoletta and South Haven. It looked old, although a few scribbles were smudged and fresh. Someone had circled a spot east of a blue thread of river and written, in hurried hand, "He is watching me".

Jane had not signed the note, but Malone recognized her handwriting from her last message. She left the note in a drawer and rushed to the chief's office. The judges would have to wait.

Rounding the corridor and turning into the main hall, she approached Johanssen's office at a brisk pace. Farrah was visible at her desk from the doorway, and, looking up at Malone as she caught her eye, she slowly shook her head. Malone stopped twenty paces from the office and watched the secretary. With a discreet glance in the direction of Chief Johanssen's office, Farrah tapped her extended forefinger on the desk and stared absently at a pile of papers.

Malone took the cue and withdrew to the corridor, waiting in shadows. She brewed a cup of tea in the service room and swirled it in one hand as she waited. After a few minutes, Farrah came out and found Malone around the corner. Her voice was edged with cool urgency.

"You've got to get away. There's a pair of guards with Captain Fouchet in the chief's office."

The cup stopped swirling. "Fouchet, here? Why?"

Farrah hid neither her surprise nor her ire. "For you, of course. They're going to arrest you for treason. For your interference."

Malone nearly dropped the teacup. Captain Fouchet was the head of the Guard and a man with no love for the Municipal

Police. A longtime critic of Chief Johanssen, he regarded the Municipal Police as the Guard's rival for martial authority in Recoletta. His reputation as the Council's ruthless enforcer was well known, and if he was here in person, Malone knew he did not intend to end the day without her arrest.

She and Sundar had kept their investigations discreet. Not even Chief Johanssen knew the details, which was a very good thing, she reflected, as now he could truthfully deny any knowledge of their involvement. They had been careful to keep a low profile and operate under plausible cover, but Malone had suspected that it would be only a matter of time before the Council rapped their knuckles again. The question was how hard.

Malone didn't need to ask how Johanssen had managed to delay them, nor did she need to ask why Farrah now regarded her with such undisguised resentment. Their beloved chief's neck now hovered near the noose, and it was her fault. But she couldn't keep one heated question from her own lips.

"And you were going to warn me when?"

"I couldn't disappear in the middle of the interview, could I? I had to wait until one of those apes asked for a drink. Just thank your lucky stars that they were too lazy to start with a sweep. Now, do you really want to be standing around squabbling about this when they come to arrest you?"

Malone snorted. "They can't have anything substantial."

"Doesn't matter," Farrah said. "The chief's been arguing with them for the past twenty minutes, but they're not going anywhere. Now, go while you still can."

"Go where?" Malone asked, gripping the saucer. "And for how long? I can't do much good hiding in a smuggler's den and waiting for the Council to forget about me, can I?"

"Figure it out, Malone. You can feel sorry for yourself when they catch you. In the meantime, do what you can for as long as you can. You owe the chief that much."

Malone felt as though Farrah had slapped her across the face, and she was oddly grateful. "And Sundar?"

"No word on him. They're after you right now."

"I have an important lead. I need you to–"

"Don't tell me. Just get out of here before they start searching for you, and lay low. Don't go home, either."

Malone nodded. "If Sundar shows up…"

"He's got a smuggling case waiting for him. Don't worry about him, just take care of yourself and let Chief Johanssen smooth things out. With any luck, this'll blow over soon enough." The tone of her voice did not convince either of them.

Farrah glanced over her shoulder toward her office. Malone pressed the teacup into her hands, and Farrah nodded her thanks, turning back to Johanssen and his inquisitors. As Farrah left her, Malone headed in the direction of a back route, watchful for guards. She followed the hall around its slow curve to the point where it converged with an entry hall, and she saw other inspectors and clerks passing her at a hurried pace, looking over their shoulders. Their agitated murmurs revealed what she should already have guessed: guards checking the exits. These were not the actions of a Council that was only moderately interested in her arrest.

She did not think at this moment that her run-in with the Council would "blow over" any time soon. But later, when there was time to review the events of the past weeks, she would reflect that Farrah was more right about this than either of them could have known.

For now, it was enough to have an idea of what to do next. Turning back down the hall, she set out for the coroner's office.

Malone passed the pooled offices of the younger inspectors, the desks clustered together and their occupants huddled in conversation. She saw no sign of Sundar. Malone could not afford to wait, nor could she risk leaving him a detailed message. Pressing on, she had to trust that Farrah would take care of him when he arrived. With any luck, he would manage to stay out of trouble and talk to the judges on his own.

After a quick pass through the supply room for traveling equipment, she ducked into the coroner's office where Dr Brin sat, hunched over his desk. He blinked owlishly when she entered.

"This is an unexpected pleasure, Inspector Malone."

"I have a favor to ask, Doctor, and there isn't much time. If you're willing to help, know that you may spend the next decade in the Barracks if we're caught. If that sounds like too much, then carry on as if you never saw me."

He rose, the pale light of the office's torches shining like a halo on his balding pate. "Inspector, insofar as I can help you, you may assume that I am brittle, ill-tempered, and decades past my prime, but you may not assume that I am a coward. Not another word except for your instructions."

Malone explained that she needed a way past the guards and out of the station. Brin tapped his shining head.

"Just the thing. Follow me." He led her out of his office and to a long room lined with metal tables under bright, low-hanging radiance stones. As they crossed into the mortuary, Brin's left hand darted behind him and shoved Malone back into his office with surprising force.

"David! What are you doing here? Have you any idea what time it is?" Brin's voice carried all of the hard authority of a schoolmaster, and the unseen David responded to it.

"Sir, I just wanted to get an early start on the examination."

Malone heard a startled quaver in his voice, and she could picture the speaker clearly: young, diligent, and clean-faced, a shock of tousled hair forever obscuring his glasses.

"You know that I cannot concentrate with you banging around in here. Give me an hour of peace, and then you can have as much time as you'd like. Agreed?" Brin's voice softened as he finished, and David stuttered an apology and retreated to the hallway at the other end of the mortuary. When they were alone, Brin looked back at Malone.

"I dislike scolding him, but I like less the idea of his complicity in this if we're caught. Now, you'll go into that cart."

Sitting in the middle of the room, as if awaiting their purpose, stood a well-worn gurney the length of the tables on either side of the room. Malone pulled a long, white sheet from the top and gazed at the cold metal surface below.

"Not onto it, Inspector, into it. But first, you can help me with the cadaver." He wheeled the cart next to the nearest table, and she helped him ease the body of an older woman onto it. She felt heavy and strangely unyielding as they settled her into place.

Brin pulled the long shroud over the woman's face. "And now it's your turn."

As Malone climbed into the storage space just above and between the four wheels of the gurney, she reflected that, by comparison, resting on the metal bed above would not have been as uncomfortable as it first seemed. Stretched in the compartment with her pack resting over her hips and an assortment of shrouds and sheets covering her, she was safe as long as no one decided to search.

Fortunately for Malone and Brin, no one did. The trickling currents of people in the station parted at the sight of the gurney, and Malone did not feel their progress slow until they reached the exit.

"What's this here?" a voice above her asked.

"A cadaver. We're sending it for cremation."

"Is that so? Pull back the sheet, then." In a soft rustle overhead, Malone heard Dr Brin expose the face of the dead woman.

"Satisfied?" Brin did not quite keep the irritation out of his voice.

"Now that you mention it, no. Let's see what's underneath." A little more light reached Malone's eyes through the screen of sheets as Brin lifted a corner of the shroud on top. "Cremating your laundry as well, old man?"

Malone felt a spike of adrenaline, but her nerves cooled at Dr Brin's commanding tone. "We've used these linens to cover, handle, and clean cadavers showing signs of dysentery. So, yes, of course we're going to burn them, but, if you really want to dig through them first, be my guest," he said. "I suggest that you use gloves."

The shroud dropped back into place, and the guard sounded like he had discovered one of the sheets on his own bed. "That will be all. Move along." Malone felt grateful for Dr Brin's imagination, but she nonetheless tasted a hint of bitterness rising in her own throat.

The next time they rolled to a halt, it was in a quiet passage several minutes from the station. Brin pulled back the sheets and looked at her through his bottle-thick spectacles.

"You'd better get out here. Unless you really do want to visit the crematory."

"Not today. I can't thank you enough for your help, Dr Brin."

"Don't mention it. It isn't often that I get this much excitement before ten. Good luck with the rest of your day, Inspector Malone." With that, he wheeled the gurney down the empty tunnel, a spring in his step and a meandering tune on his lips.

Shouldering her pack, she set off in the direction of Recoletta's main train station, almost due south. Avoiding public transportation and keeping an eye out for patrols, she calculated that she could reach the station in an hour.

When the gilded arch of the station swung into view overhead, she glanced at the clock in the center: a quarter to ten. Fairview lay almost halfway between Recoletta and South Haven. With any luck, she could find a train bound for the latter and book passage out. She passed under the arch and into the fog of steam and smoke that, despite Recoletta's sophisticated ventilation, still managed to choke the train station.

In fact, because of that haze, she did not realize that she had been caught until she was standing in front of the ticket counter, reserving a seat on the steam engine leaving in the next forty-five minutes. She heard a familiar and unwelcome voice.

"Going somewhere?"

She whirled around to see a phalanx of guards already surrounding her. In the middle stood Dominguez, as sickeningly smarmy as ever. In an instant, Malone realized that she almost would have preferred to surrender in Johanssen's office than face arrest by Dominguez. "Captain Fouchet has issued orders to arrest you on sight for treasonous interference, and here you are at the train station. A coward as well as a fool, then?"

"If you're going to arrest me, you'll need some charges to go with your new rank, Interim Director."

Dominguez reddened. "Which part do you not understand, Inspector: the treason or the interference?"

"The evidence."

"You received an ultimatum less than two weeks ago, that under no circumstances were you to continue your investigations of the Vineyard murders."

"So?"

"You questioned Roman Arnault in the hospital..."

"Following up on an assault. It's standard procedure."

"...and dug around the Wickery office in the same day. It's almost like you were looking for attention."

"Those cases have been closed and filed for ten years. Is there a connection?"

Dominguez began to purple. "Inspector Malone, please. Don't be so coy."

"If you want to accuse me of breaking my orders, then you'll have to link the Vineyard murders to those cases," she said.

"Well, if we need more evidence, perhaps we should arrest your partner as well. Of course, we were hoping to avoid complications." Subdued, Malone glared at him. "Then again, you could always accompany us to the Barracks, and we could keep this simple." He drew himself up beside her, speaking directly into her ear. "Are you going to give us trouble, Inspector?" Dominguez waited, watching her. He stepped away from her and addressed the nearest guard. "Lock her up. She's coming with us."

Malone held out her wrists and allowed herself to be cuffed and marched back into the city. The small crowd that had gathered to watch from a distance dispersed as Malone and her captors filed into a prisoner transport carriage, heavy with bars and bolts.

Inspector Malone had escorted many a criminal to justice by similar means, but this was her first time on the other side of the shackles. She found it distinctly unpleasant.

She sat on a hard bench, the bars that separated her from the guards just inches from her knees. There were six in the carriage with her, and they gazed at her with hostile uncertainty as their conveyance bounced along the cobblestones. The bars that spanned the windows cast shifting shadows across the guards' faces, and they seemed to constantly weave and whisper as they slid from darkness into light. Ahead, Dominguez and his own contingent rode in a grander carriage befitting their triumphant return.

As the carriage slowed to a stop, Malone tilted her head to peer between the bars. Before her rose the impenetrable facade of the Barracks. Whereas Callum Station housed Recoletta's law enforcement, the Barracks was home to Recoletta's military – the guards and agents under the direct control of the Council. Like a massive, geometric octopus, it rose up and spread grasping bastions into the open cavern around it. The veranda was a formation of obelisk towers that emerged over the horizon like thick fingers.

Nearby was the political seat of Recoletta, Dominari Hall, which overlooked the underground networks from its rise at the western terminus of the Spine. Its gleaming marble surfaces seared the eyes after the dull gray of the Barracks. Majestic spires punctured the earth to mark the capitol building aboveground. Dominari Hall and the Barracks made up the control center of Recoletta, with political grace backed by brute force.

Malone could not help but look up as she was led across the featureless stone courtyard to the Barracks. So solid was the building and so ingenious its construction that it did not appear to have any entrances at all, only square faces and block arms that seemed to absorb and emit guards at random.

Inside, her escorts directed her through several corridors and finally down many flights of stairs until they arrived at what, for its cultivated gloom and memorable odors, had to be the dungeon. The guards relieved Malone of her possessions and undid her shackles, shoving her into a lone cell.

Dominguez followed them, stopping just inside the cell. From the way he looked around him, Malone guessed that he didn't feel comfortable going farther than that, guards or no. "I'm going to leave you here a little while to reflect on your actions," he said, recovering some of his bluster. "But don't make yourself too comfortable. We'll call on you soon enough."

Malone did not break her gaze. "For my trial?"

He cocked his head. "What trial?"

"The one where you demonstrate the evidence against me. So you can keep me in jail."

He tented his fingers in front of his lips and smiled indulgently. "Inspector Malone, I'm afraid you're looking at this all wrong. We're not charging you as a criminal, we're charging you as a traitor, and you're not being jailed, you're being held. Indefinitely."

"When will you inform my department of my arrest?" she asked quietly. Chief Johanssen would know that she had escaped the guards at Callum Station, but he would not know that they had apprehended her an hour later. If he believed that she was in hiding, it could be quite some time before anyone came looking for her here.

"I really don't think that will be necessary. Your Chief Johanssen has enough to worry about without having your treason on his mind, do you not agree?"

Malone glared back at Dominguez.

In the doorway, his silhouette lowered its head. "Now, Malone, bitterness does not become you. If you'll quit being so selfish, I know you'll come around in a few days. If not, I'm sure we can help you with that."

Malone felt the futility of argument, but she feared what would happen inside her if she stopped fighting. "When the Council gets word of this, you'll lose more than your title."

The guards backed away and stood behind Dominguez. He glanced at them as the space between him and Malone cleared. "And where do you think I get my orders? Your fate has been decided by the highest authority, and, after your imprudence, I'm afraid you're out of allies." He paused, sighing and straightening his jacket. "I cannot waste any more of my time like this. Should you require anything, you may summon room service with a shout." Dominguez turned and strode out of the cell, a pair of guards slamming the heavy door and locking it with a disheartening series of thuds and cranks. Malone flew to the door's barred window and pressed her face to it as she watched the men retreat the way they had come, leaving a lone guard to monitor the cellblock.

Leaning into a corner, Malone surveyed her new accommodations. The cell measured about nine by seven feet with no apparent outlet except the heavy iron door through which she had entered. Smooth and without a handle, it sealed the wall, and she could discern no way to pry it open, pick its lock, or remove it from its hinges, and certainly not without alerting the guard outside. The barred window at chin level was barely wide enough to see through, and the slit for the food tray was secured from the other side.

A straw cot with a single moth-eaten sheet sat in the farthest corner of the room. Malone searched the large, rough-hewn blocks that formed the walls with stretched palms and probing fingertips and then their counterparts in the floor on hands and knees, but she found nothing except a thick layer of grime. Every block was solid and every seam filled flush with the rest of the wall. Listening in the near-darkness, Malone heard only the intermittent pacing of the lone guard echoing in the otherwise empty cellblock. Even here, she was alone. She slumped onto her cot and sighed, feeling defeated for the first time since Cahill's murder.

Lying on the hard plank and staring at the ceiling, Malone listened absently to the stirring of the guard outside. As she counted his steps, she thought she heard them double. She sat up and realized that another guard had joined the first and that the two were conversing. She silently slid off of the cot and crept to the door, poised just under the window to listen.

"…between you 'n' me, but I'm a bit nervous about it," said one guard.

"What's to worry about? It's just another job."

"It's my first time out at the site, you know."

"Oh, I get it. Look," the other said, "just keep to your post and stay on alert. And mind you stay out of everyone else's way."

"Nothing I'd like more."

"If you see anyone unfamiliar approaching the site, kindly escort them to the captain on duty. No sweat, easy as pie." Malone did not like the sour emphasis that the guard put on the word "kindly".

The first guard shifted as he worked up a response. "It's just that, well, I heard they caught someone snooping around last week…"

"And?"

"And what happened to him?"

"I don't know, and I don't want to. The site's a secret for a reason," said the second, quickly. The direction of his voice wavered, giving Malone the impression that he was looking around as their conversation lingered on the subject of the mysterious site.

"But why?" asked the first. "Do we even know what this place is?"

"Look, mate, that ain't for you or me to know, alright? You're asking too many questions. Just keep your mind on the job and forget about the rest," the second man said. "Hey, they're paying us enough for that, don't you think?" he added, trying, with minimal success, to lighten the mood.

The other guard mumbled something in reply, and when they concluded their conversation, Malone shuffled back to her cot and returned to counting the first guard's footsteps. In a matter of moments, her eyelids drooped shut and she fell soundly to sleep.

She awoke suddenly with a mixture of guilt and surprise. Blinking, she guessed that several hours must have passed, and she listened for sounds of the guard outside. Silence. She rose from the lumpy cot, ignoring the kink in her back, and tiptoed to the door to listen again. Still nothing. She straightened her knees to peer through the tiny window.

"Malone."

A husky whisper startled her, causing her to jump back half a foot. She returned to the narrow window and peeked out from all directions, but she couldn't see anyone from her angle. "Who's there?" she whispered back to the empty hall.

"Quiet. Listen carefully, Malone. The guard rotation begins in two minutes. For now, the cellblock is empty. When I open the door, climb the stairs by which you descended and take an immediate right at the top."

"Hold it. Who are you and what are you doing?"

"No questions. That tunnel will lead you out of the Barracks, and from there you will skirt the complex until you reach the passage running south. This will take you back to the train station, and from there, you can..."

"What makes you think you know where I'm going?"

The disembodied voice on the other side of the door chuckled. "I certainly know where you were arrested, and there's only one place you would have been headed from there. I can only assume you mean to finish what you started. And I suggest that you do it quickly." He cleared his throat and continued.

"Once you have left, don't stop or turn back for any reason. You will have five minutes from the time you leave this cell before someone returns and finds you missing. If anyone sees you along the way, I trust you know what to do. The door is unlocked," Malone heard a rattle and a muffled thud as her mysterious benefactor turned the key and unbarred the door, "and you may count to twenty once I leave."

He hesitated. "And one more thing. At all costs you must avoid being seen at the site. There's a river fifty minutes after leaving the third farming commune – Fairview. Jump the southbound before the train crosses the river and follow it southeast until you reach the ruined veranda with the giant man, then follow the broken arrow another two miles east. You can observe from an elevated position, but stay away from the main entrance."

"Wait! What do you expect me to do once I get there?" she asked, still craning her head to get a view of the stranger.

"Start counting, Malone." She heard the soft rustle of fabric as her nameless ally hurried away, still out of sight. Resisting temptation, she dutifully counted down before slipping out of her cell and into an empty hallway. No one stood at the guard desk, and she replaced the keys on their nail in the wall. Her things were scattered on the desk. She quickly threw on her coat and secured her equipment, turning up the stairs and ignoring the wrenching of nerves in the pit of her stomach.

She passed no one on her ascent and, after a much longer journey than she remembered, she reached the level from which her captors had led her. To her right, as promised, was a narrow passage, which appeared virtually unused. Malone decided to take advantage of her opportunity while this was the case.

Guiding flames set on parallel tracks in the walls led her through the winding tunnel and, amazed at her good fortune, she passed no one. A grayish blob of an exit appeared as she rounded the last bend.

Malone stopped when she reached the end of the tunnel, her nose not quite flush with the open doorway, and listened. Someone paced twenty-five feet above her head. Another pair of footsteps joined the first: the new guard on duty coming to relieve his predecessor. Looking up, she saw that the walls rose straight to the polygonal ridge where the exchange was taking place. She glanced over her shoulder as she heard footsteps echoing down the previously deserted hall and heading in her direction. There was no cover from the guards up top, so she would have to hug the walls and ease around the corners as her unknown friend had instructed her, hoping that the guards would not wander any closer to the edge of their lookout.

She edged along the wall, pressing herself as close to it as possible. She moved steadily and silently, sliding along the stone. Malone heard a choking sound from above and froze, prepared to bolt, when a wad of phlegm landed inches from the toe of her boot.

Not daring to crane her head upwards, she remained still for a moment more before stepping over the spot on the ground and continuing her shuffle.

Another set of footsteps echoed in the direction that she had come from, spurring her to creep faster. When she reached the south edge of the building, she knew she was free. A crude tunnel ran up to the side of the Barracks where the walls of the building merged with the cavern. She sprinted for the tunnel and traced a maze of half-empty passageways back to the transit station without incident.

The honeycomb of streets and passages merged into a hub of activity as Malone reached the station, where the damp tunnel walls glistened as the night sky surely did outside. Instead of returning to the ticket desk, she made her way to the back cars of the southbound lines where laborers were loading freight destined for South Haven, Morsefield, Juny, and beyond. Riding in the passenger cars up front was no longer an option, so she would again have to content herself with the cramped company of crates and cargo.

Ducking between the hulking boxcars and in and out of plumes of steam, Malone located a series of linked cars carrying cargo marked for South Haven. Securing passage unnoticed was simply a matter of slipping into a half-packed car while the laborers were otherwise occupied and settling into a nook between the boxes, sacks, and barrels. When the door to her car rolled shut with a clank and the angled diamond of light disappeared from the wall next to her, Liesl Malone breathed a sigh of relief.

She emerged from her cranny as the train slid to life beneath her feet. Steadying herself against the walls, she weaved to the other end of the car, where clouded windowpanes conveyed the ghost of movement. Malone sat on a burlap sack of something that felt like grain, watching the flurry of twinkles outside as the train rushed through tunnels with gleaming dewdrop points, an imitation sky. When the metal behemoth lurched out of its warrens and into the natural night, she could only tell the difference by the stillness. She settled onto her sack, watching the dark patches of scenery fly by and aware for the first time that she had never before seen so many trees.

CHAPTER 14

MISUNDERSTANDING AND MISFORTUNE

Jane did not sleep on the night of her confrontation with Roman. His carriage had left her at the entrance to her apartment warren, but when the driver turned the corner a block away she had faded back into the shadows and returned to the Dispatch to leave the map for Malone. Jane was still surprised that she had managed to take it. When Roman had first confronted her, her fingers had tightened around it out of fear more than anything else. When she had dropped the rest of the pages in his stack and let them flutter past her skirts, she had realized that he was so intent on intimidating her that he wasn't paying attention to the small, quick movements of her hands behind her back. He probably didn't think she was capable of them.

Still, after her run-in with the patrol earlier that night, she was more cautious and found herself calculating and anticipating the movements of guards blocks away rather than just checking for what was around the next corner. When she reached the Dispatch, she found it as empty and as quiet as the streets winding around it. The lone desk clerk never looked up at her coming or going, and Jane was only certain that he even knew she was there when she heard him speak.

"Best hurry along," he had said. Or so she thought. His lips did not seem to move, and the words came out more as a reflection than a comment. Still, it was enough to stop Jane in her tracks.

"Best hurry along," the clerk repeated, still showing Jane no more than the gleaming dome of his bald head as he gazed dreamily down at his papers. "Lots of activity tonight. The guards are getting restless." She lifted the hems of her skirts and took his advice.

By the time Jane reached home, her skin was covered in a cold film of sweat, and she was certain that she would find Olivia waiting for her with questions on her lips and accusations in her eyes. Instead, Jane found the apartment empty, tumbled into her room, and buried herself in her bed, fully clothed. She lay awake, staring at the blackness between her face and the wall and half expecting to feel cold steel at her neck. A few hours later, the faint thud of footsteps overhead and whispers from pipes in the walls announced the morning.

The day trickled by. Olivia had somehow arrived in the night, and she greeted Jane with a bright smile and tea. Jane accepted both warily, wondering when Olivia would surprise her with a warning confrontation. It never happened.

For Jane, everything Olivia said and did assumed a double meaning. Idle chatter about their daily chores disguised lures and snares that Olivia would use to trap her when the time came. As much as Jane wanted to boot her out of the apartment, doing so would have been a direct challenge to Roman's threats.

Jane went to bed early that night, staring at the blank palette of the ceiling and shuffling through her thoughts. The mention of her parents had thrown her emotions into a spin, but she would not be able to get any more information from Roman about them now, and she pushed that issue from her mind.

Her next question, of course, was what to do about Fredrick. She had not seen him since Roman's revelation, and she had not yet decided whether ignorance or knowledge put him in greater danger. Despite his conviction that Olivia was indeed a prostitute (and of the first-class variety, he was sure), his interest in her showed no sign of abating. With the threat of retaliation still fresh in Jane's mind, she hesitated to tell him anything that might put him in a compromising situation.

When Jane finally drifted to sleep, her mind thoroughly exhausted from a restless night and day of preoccupation, she slumbered more soundly than she had since the beginning of the murders. She arose with her mind and body refreshed and left her room for the day's routine, prepared anew to face Olivia.

But when Jane saw Olivia that morning, she knew that something had changed.

Busying herself with the morning chores, Olivia seemed no less lively but more watchful. Unless it was Jane's imagination, those large doe eyes peered at her over the rims of soapy dishes more than usual, and every time Jane seemed on the verge of leaving the room, Olivia assaulted her with a fresh barrage of conversation: a charm offensive if ever there was one. Finally, Jane excused herself to complete her own morning routine. When she returned to the common room, Olivia's tone changed abruptly.

"Where are you going?" she asked, as Jane, washed and dressed, stopped at the door with her cart. The question must have come out sharper than Olivia had intended, which Jane realized when she looked back at her in surprise. She also realized that Olivia still stood over the same pile of dishes that she had begun washing almost an hour ago.

"I have to pick up a few things," Jane said. "It's almost nine and I haven't made it out of the apartment yet."

"But you will be back by one, yes?" Olivia asked. "I have made reservations for us at a restaurant I know. The owner is an acquaintance of mine, and he has been begging me to bring some fresh tasters." She smiled, drying her hands with her apron in an oddly motherly way. "I also wanted to thank you and Fredrick for being such good neighbors."

"Fredrick's coming?" This time it was Jane's turn to attempt to keep the alarm out of her voice.

"He'll meet us here. I didn't think you would mind that I invited him," she added, with what Jane thought was a none-too-subtle note of insinuation.

Jane's heart sank at the notion that she had lost her chance to warn Fredrick away, but she also felt something inside her steel. "I'll be here."

"That's good," said Olivia, pleased. "But where are you going now? Why don't I come with you?" she said, abandoning the spotless stack of dishes and hanging her apron in the kitchen. She must have noticed the puzzlement on Jane's face, and she smiled again. "I'm at loose ends this morning, and, between our schedules, you and I haven't had much time together."

Olivia already stood by the door, so Jane agreed with her best attempt at a smile. Still, she meant to stay in public and, under the circumstances, could not imagine that her roommate planned to do anything viler than keep an eye on her. Whatever scheme Olivia had prepared would wait until lunch.

Despite Jane's misgivings, Olivia was pleasant and helpful company as she ran her morning errands, picking up and delivering bundles of laundry. At half past twelve, she began

to look anxious, so the two headed back. As they traced the
jagged and winding tunnels back to the warren, Jane tried to
think of a way to tell Fredrick everything she had learned.
Too soon for her liking, they returned home to find Fredrick
waiting for them, oblivious and mischievous.

"Right on time and lovely as ever," he said, marveling
at their common cotton work dresses as though they were
evening gowns. He turned to Olivia. "Miss Saavedra, I'm
charmed and delighted at your proposition, er, proposal for
lunch. Where are we going?"

"A charming place called Cassandra's, north of Turnbull
Square. It's quiet and out of the way." Jane did not like the
way Olivia emphasized these features.

"Should we catch the tram, then? There's a stop just below
the apartment."

Olivia frowned. "Let's not. It's a short walk, and I don't like
being stuck in those at lunchtime."

Fredrick accepted her preference without question, and
Olivia accepted his crooked arm. Jane had no choice but to
follow along. Olivia led the way, appearing to choose the most
twisted route of tunnels possible and seemingly aided in this by
a small army of construction and maintenance crews shunting
traffic out of half a dozen different tunnels. When Fredrick
remarked on the number of projects, Olivia shrugged and said
something about redirecting sewage lines, which ended any
further conversation on the matter. For all Olivia's assurances
of a short walk, nearly forty-five minutes had passed before
they arrived. Then, the crowds began to thin and only a
quiet trickle of people mingled in the round, cozy streets. The
tunnels intersected more tightly, with sloping rabbit holes
meeting and parting at irregular angles and reinforcing the
image of the subterranean as an immense warren.

The restaurant Olivia had selected was a cozy little bistro with a subterranean balcony. Seated upstairs, the trio had a view over the quiet underground plaza where a small fountain bubbled and pedestrians milled with sandwiches and ale.

"My dear Olivia, what an excellent choice," Fredrick said as they sat at their table, pulling crisp white napkins into their laps. "And perfectly inconspicuous. How did you find it?"

"I met the owner when I first came to town," she said, looking down at the plaza. Jane was tempted to press the question further, but she bit her tongue, waiting instead to see what the rest of their lunch would hold.

"Well, I've hardly been to this area of the city. It's nice," Fredrick said.

"And quiet," Jane added.

Olivia glanced up from the plaza and smiled. "Yes, that's what I love about it."

Their meal arrived promptly and did not disappoint, and, as they tucked into bowls of lamb stew, plates of sautéed squash, and leek and mushroom tarts, Jane wondered if she would have the opportunity to get Fredrick alone. Olivia was as polite and pleasant as ever, but she kept a watchful eye on both of them.

Dusting the pastry crumbs from her fingertips, Jane rose from the table.

"Where are you going?" Olivia asked.

"To the facilities. They're just around the corner, right?"

"Yes, that way," said Olivia with a nervous glance.

When Jane returned, Olivia and Fredrick were chattering animatedly. She was describing some of the delicacies of her homeland in succulent detail while Fredrick listened with rapt attention. Jane had to stand by the table for almost a minute before she found an opening. "Lunch was wonderful,

Olivia, but I'm due with a stack of linens this afternoon." She looked over at Fredrick, who appeared all but oblivious to her exit strategy. "And I think Fredrick has a deadline, right?" she added, hoping he would hear the desperate suggestion in her voice.

"Only a bit longer, Jane," Olivia said. "You and Freddie must try the chocolate soufflé." That was all it took to win Fredrick over, and Jane was unwilling to leave him alone. Lunch settled like a stone in her stomach.

The waiter had not yet returned when they heard thundering crashes in the distance and felt reverberations beneath their feet. After a split second of total silence, the plaza below collapsed in an uproar.

Cries of horror and panic rose from the plaza as people fled blindly, uncertain of where to run, only convinced that they must. Looking like a sick swarm of bees from the balcony above, they dashed in all directions, bowling over one another and trampling the slow underfoot. A few people froze, clutching the fountain or a signpost for support while they attempted to stand against the tide.

"Wha– what's going on?" Fredrick gripped the edges of the table and looked wildly around as if expecting to see the responsible party sitting at the next table. But Jane knew the answer was closer, had been with her all day and had cornered her and Fredrick in a restaurant for reasons she was about to discover.

"You," she said to Olivia, her voice quavering as it rose. "You knew this was going to happen."

Fredrick blinked at Jane, wild and clueless. Around them, a cacophony of clattering dishes and thumping tables joined the shouts below as the rest of the late lunch crowd fled the restaurant.

Olivia did not look away. Now, Fredrick stared at Jane in open amazement.

"Jane, have you lost your mind?" His mustache twitched above his trembling mouth.

"She's right," Olivia said, her eyes moving to Fredrick. Either she had lost her accent or it suddenly sounded much less musical.

"This is nonsense! How could anyone possibly know something like this?" Fredrick said, his gaze flickering between the two women. "We don't even know what that was!"

Jane's attention remained focused on Olivia. "I need to know."

"It's better you don't." For the first time, Olivia dropped her gaze.

The ruckus continued from the plaza below. "I knew something wasn't right and kept quiet because I was afraid. Now I need to know what I allowed to happen."

"Jane, there was nothing you could have–"

"Just tell me."

Olivia took a deep breath and laid her hands flat on the table. In the sudden stillness of the restaurant, Jane felt the ragged sighs and gasps of her own breathing as she fought tears. Fredrick's wan face hovered over the other end of the table, and the din of panic sounded far away.

"Bombs. Set throughout the city last night. What you just heard we've been planning for months. It's called 'the Catalyst'," said Olivia.

For once, Fredrick was speechless.

Jane's eyes stung. "Why?"

Olivia shook her head. Feeling the tears finally roll down her cheeks, Jane pushed back from the table and started to rise. Olivia clamped a warm hand on her wrist and motioned her to sit.

"I know this is a small comfort, but we didn't want to hurt anybody. We picked the least crowded places we could find and waited until after the lunch rush. And the work crews were there to redirect most of the traffic." Olivia paused, relaxing her grip on Jane's wrist and drawing a deep breath. "We only wanted to draw out the guards." She hesitated. "So they'd get people off the streets early."

Fredrick shook his head, but when he spoke, it was from behind a thick fog. "Off the streets for what?"

Olivia ignored the question and continued with her eyes still on Jane. "Please believe me when I say that this kind of warning is better than the alternative."

A numb lump formed in Jane's throat. "How many?"

"Twenty-three. Of various sizes. One was half a mile from your apartment," she said in what sounded like an apology.

Fredrick at last seemed to emerge from his fuddle. "I don't understand. You're behind this?" There was a pity and disgust in his voice that shamed even Jane.

Still, she turned to him with urgency and with relief that she could finally share what she knew. "She's been in on it all along." When he turned back to her, his eyes still tinged with doubt, she almost pounded the table in frustration. "I know, Freddie," she said before he could protest. "I've known for two days now."

He waved his hands in the air between them as if clearing it of all of the extraneous questions to settle on one. "How?"

"Because Roman Arnault sent her." Jane glared back at Olivia. The plaza below began to clear as people hurried indoors.

Olivia's expression softened. "You know? Then you understand why we're here."

"I don't understand," Jane said. "And I don't want to."

Fredrick cleared his throat, still regaining some of his voice. "I'd like to, actually."

Again, Olivia ignored him. The maid rested her head on her hand, a weary gesture that seemed out of place amidst the chaos. "You may not sympathize with our actions, but I hope that you will at least think a little more kindly of him, if not of me," she said.

Jane felt her features twist. "So the hatchet man has a hatchet woman. Does that make him less guilty?"

"What *are* you people talking about?" Fredrick shouted.

Jane whirled to face him. "Roman sent this woman to watch us, Freddie," she said. "She's been spying on us the whole time."

"Whatever the hell for?" he asked. Somewhere in the exchange, his blind confusion had changed to blind anger. Now, he seemed to yell at no one in particular.

"Arnault sent her as a safeguard. To kill us if we became a liability."

Olivia shook her head, her eyes wide. "Jane, no. Please understand. Roman Arnault sent me to protect you."

Liesl Malone had remained hidden on the train as per her instructions. Still on her sack of grain, she had watched as the train pulled into the first two farming communes during the night and had taken cover behind the crates in her car when the rusty squeals signaled a stop. The boxes around her were emblazoned with bright red letters stating their destination as "South Haven", and true to her change in fortunes, no one had yet come to check her car. Now emboldened by her arrival at the third farming commune, she balanced atop some of the crates near her boxcar's window and observed the laborers as they exchanged freight. In the cities, commune farmers had a reputation for being wild, anarchic, and eccentric due to their exchange of civilization for brain-boiling sun. Malone had never met anyone from the communes, but, watching the farmers now, they looked nothing like she had expected.

The men and women lugging equipment and supplies from the train, and talking with the railcar operators, appeared vigorous and strong-bodied. The sky was just beginning to lighten with the first pre-dawn shades, casting a healthy glow on the skin and brows of the farmers. Stretched out behind them was an outpost of sprawling fields, clumps of wood and stone block buildings, and the silhouettes of grazing livestock. Malone had heard it said that the people who lived on the farms chose to build their houses aboveground out of a love for open spaces and a desire to awaken with the sun. She could not imagine trading the security and order of tunnels for the chaos of the elements, but gazing at the vast empire of sky and field, some primal recognition stirred.

She stayed at the window until the train lurched to a start again and rolled away from the farming commune. Still fascinated, and curious to see it in the full colors of the day, she was sorry to watch it slip past her window. Almost forty minutes into the resumed journey, she rolled open the sliding door in her boxcar and was momentarily deafened by the roar of the tracks. Climbing the metal rungs to the top of the car, she shivered as the early November chill drew gooseflesh from her skin and the biting wind swept back her hair.

More jolting than the morning wind or the clattering train was the view. The landscape rolled out farther than her eyes could see in the fading dark, and she fought an urge to return to the train and the tight spaces that she had been bred to live in. The sight of so much open expanse made her feel tiny and helpless, as if the sheer immensity would swallow her up and she would simply dissolve, pulled apart and negated by vast emptiness.

Malone gripped the surface of the boxcar and trained her eyes on the distance, where a silver-surfaced river cut through the landscape. At this point, she could expect to reach it in just a couple of minutes. She pulled herself from the frosty sweep of wind and returned to the railcar, where the air now tasted stale and dank. Grabbing the grain sack that had served her well those past hours, she decided to put it to one last use.

As the train neared the river, she gripped the sack by its sides and stood poised in the open door. She clutched the sack tighter to her chest for padding and leaped clear of the train, burying her face in the smell of dried barley.

She landed flat on the sack and rolled down the knoll and away from the train, each thumping contact with the ground emptying her lungs in visible puffs. Malone at last tumbled onto a flat, and her velocity decreased until she ceased spinning altogether and lay catching her breath, her face skyward.

Heaving and staring up, she pushed the grain sack off of her and noticed the dawn colors uncluttered by a mausoleum skyline. Rolling to her elbows, she picked herself up and dusted off her knees. Liesl Malone then turned to the ridge and, noting the time, raced toward the rising sun.

All of the colors Malone saw in the fields and the blushing horizon existed underground, but in fabrics, paintings, and other manmade objects rather than in earth and sky. She had ventured aboveground many times before, but not without cobblestones beneath her feet and marble or granite to mark the land. Adjusting to the sink and spring of grass underfoot, she put such observations from her mind. Duty still took the first priority. For whom she acted was becoming an increasingly complicated question.

The ridge next to the river was bare on the initial ascent, and Malone was careful to remain on the northwestern side and out of sight of any patrols below. As the rise leveled, she could see for miles to the east. A carpet of dark green foliage spread out before her in the hazy sunrise, and somewhere beyond it lay the secret that would claim more lives before the sun rose again.

After covering a few miles, Malone began to descend again and slowed her pace. The windswept hilltops flattened, and bare, bristling forests sprang up. Though leafless, the trees grew thick and wild enough to provide cover. She remembered Jane's map with its sparse arrangement of cities and farming communes and the forbidding blankness in between.

She reached a plain where the trees grew more thinly and spread across a broad field of ruins. Chunks of white marble and forsaken structural remnants marked what must have been a city in the distant past. In the east, a familiar shape rose on the horizon.

Broken columns jutting like crooked teeth surrounded a rectangular veranda. Crossing to the other side, Malone saw a bearded statue enthroned in what was left of the pavilion. Creeping vines nearly covered what time had not already worn away. Malone found no entrance to the underground, and she followed the giant's gaze east.

Continuing through the ruins, she found a toppled obelisk pointing still further down her path. Malone marveled at its size and the clean line of its taper, shattered and separated in several places from its fall, and she realized that this must be the broken arrow the stranger had mentioned. She proceeded along the indicated path, gazing up at the wide and broken world that was springing up around her. Her cover had grown scanter, and the clearing amidst the ruins seemed to form a broad avenue. Crumbling buildings and free-standing walls formed skeleton rows on either side of her and sank gradually into the earth toward the horizon. A set of fresh footprints caught her eye in a bare patch of dirt, and she moved further into the shadows as she continued east.

It appeared that someone had excavated around some of the better-preserved structures and abandoned them after only a very brief exploration. Malone could not even see an entrance to any of them. Passing the metal skeletons of buildings that protruded from the ground like broken bones, she noted that the excavators had ignored many other mysteries that sank deeper into the ground, some sealed by dirt and others apparently in fragments.

At the end of the avenue lay great piles of rubble, the remnants of destruction and decay strewn like bunkers in a war game. Slinking between boulder-sized hunks of debris, she saw the flash of blue uniforms: guards combing the ruins for uninvited guests. Malone crouched still lower, wondering what she should be looking for, when almost beneath her feet she saw an exposed portion of an immense, flat slab. She followed its edge through the labyrinth of rubble, where the ground dropped sharply to an entrance, excavated from beneath several yards of soil.

It was an ancient building, much of which was still submerged under the loamy earth. The excavators had dug a broad ramp leading down to the entry. Rows of pillars and windows dropped from the top of the building to the recovered entrance, which was a series of three arched doorways, and angled staircases emerged from the dirt to reach it. There was something impressive and majestic about the building and the way it rose from the earth. Though soiled by centuries of dirt, it seemed to defy decay, its corners and faces showing much less damage than the other buildings Malone had passed. A tarnished copper plaque, still affixed to a broken hunk of stone, sat near the excavated entrance like a signpost. The words "IBRA Y   RES" rose from the copper like a fading dream, the only letters that time had not rubbed away from the ancient plaque.

Malone remembered the words of her benefactor and crept away from the entrance, looking for another way in. Something caught her eye in the morning sunlight. A silhouette loomed a short distance away, directly on top of the hill covering the rest of the partially excavated building. She had at first taken it for more rubble, but, upon closer examination, she realized it was actually the topmost part of the structure. Climbing and circling the mound brought her to an uncovered portion of the building's dome, where a narrow gap in the soil hugged it and descended to its base. She slipped down the fissure to a spot where a landslide had broken through a window and a considerable portion of the wall below it. Malone dropped through the opening and ducked low as her eyes adjusted to the dimness.

She was perched on a balcony that encircled a great, round room beneath a series of semicircular windows identical to the breached specimen by which she had entered. The absence of proper lighting left her balcony in relative darkness, but the Council's team had set up enough torches and radiance stones to work by below. She crawled along the balcony for a better view of her surroundings. Though now dusted in cobwebs, the room must have been magnificent in its day. The faded plaster wall behind her hinted at a deep crimson past, and the apex of the dome above her still sported a squadron of painted angels watching the proceedings below with distant stares. Antique desks arranged in a circular pattern supported a handful of men and women busily writing, and statues in the galleries across the room from her gleamed evasively with the light from below.

Striking something with her foot, Malone looked down and noticed a book, fugitive from a nearby cart that had been overturned and forgotten. She picked it up, the ancient hardback binding unfamiliar in her hands. The cover read *The Prince*, and below, "Niccolò Machiavelli." Her curiosity further aroused, she opened the front cover and read, stamped in faded blue ink, "Library of Congress".

The missing pieces of the puzzle began to reassemble. Malone followed the gaze of the statues perched atop the banister and noticed halls leading from the circular room to others lined with books. But it was the person she saw entering from one of those halls that caused her the greatest surprise.

Rafe Sundar followed an immaculately clad man, who looked more like a researcher than a guard, into the reading room, his coat draped over an arm and craning his neck to take in his surroundings. The researcher had an air of agitation about him, but Sundar was as cool as ever.

"Dr Hask," the researcher began, approaching the petite woman at the center of the room, "please forgive the interruption, but we found this man in the stacks." Even far above the scene, Malone could read the annoyance in Hask's posture and the unspoken question as to how an intruder had gotten there in the first place. Perhaps sensing this, the researcher pressed on. "Now he's demanding to see the person in charge." He obviously hoped that this would be the end of the matter as far as he was concerned.

"Yes, I see," she said. "You may return to your station. Inspector Sundar and I are already acquainted." Sundar's guide stormed off with a final look over his shoulder, but the researchers gathered at the tables all around ignored the new arrival. "I thought I smelled something rank," said Hask.

"That's probably from my horse, although I prefer to think of it as an earthy musk. We've gotten pretty well acquainted since we met at the commune a few hours ago. Alas, we can't all travel in style. Some of us have to get our hands dirty on the job."

Hask grinned. "Why, Inspector Sundar, you understand me better than you think. I'm surprised."

"Not nearly as surprised as I am, Doctor. I've chased trails across the city and now beyond it... to find a library?"

"A *library*, Inspector. Utter the word with the respect it deserves, as a repository of words, of ideas that you and I... well, that *you*, at least, can hardly fathom," she said in a voice tinged with disdain and colored with awe. "There are names in this place that have endured for centuries – millennia, even – surviving war and dust and forgetfulness. We stand in the presence of greatness." She circled their rounded aisle at the center of the desks, gazing around her with a beatific expression.

Sundar dropped his coat onto the nearest desk. "The only names that interest me right now are the ones related to this project. I have reason to believe that the discovery of this library is related to the deaths of Dr Cahill, Lanning Fitzhugh, and Councilor Hollens."

She sniffed. "You detectives are so predictable, and you would do well to take some cues from your deservedly more famous predecessors living in these shelves." Hask paused, as if on the verge of suggesting a reading list. Abruptly, she spun back to face Sundar. "Except, I am surprised to see you here alone. What happened to your dear partner, Malone?" she asked.

"That's Inspector Malone," he said. "Utter the title with the respect it deserves, identifying a soldier of justice, a word that *you* seem to have forgotten in the midst of all these others." Listening above, Malone felt an uncomfortable swell of pride and affection. "She was detained," he said. For a moment, Malone wondered how he could have found the place, but in an instant she remembered: the map. She had left it in her desk before she left, and Sundar must have searched it.

Hask crossed in front of Sundar in long, slow paces. "Ah, how unfortunate. And yet you found your way here, all by yourself, without the guidance of your mentor?" In her voice was the silken edge of a vindictive schoolmarm coaxing a secret from an errant child. Malone only hoped that Sundar could hear it.

He paused. "I may not read, but I can do math."

"But surely you told your most respectable chief of your little detour?" Scanning the rotunda below, Malone saw almost a dozen guards surrounding it and a few more filing in and out of the stacks.

"We both know that this investigation is off the books. So to speak."

Hask nodded in one downward motion as she continued pacing. "Yet you came." Malone had six shots loaded in her revolver. Even if she made all six, Sundar would be surrounded, and the guards had most likely disarmed him.

"In the hopes that we could work something out. That we could talk more outside the city."

"All alone. How very commendable." She stopped and looked up at him with the most frightening smile Malone had ever seen.

"Only my civic duty. Which, at this moment, is to discover your purpose here."

"My purpose, as you so aptly put it, is to recover and guard the secrets that have survived, to restore the knowledge around us to proper use and authority, and to piece together a history that was forged long before your oldest memories and that will persist beyond your pitiable life... which may not be very long."

A familiar crease crossed Sundar's smooth brow. "What?"

At that moment, a guard who had been waiting in the wings materialized behind Sundar and jabbed a dagger into the young inspector's back. Sundar's eyes flew wide in confusion and pain, and a scream rattled pitifully in his throat. He sank to his knees, the guard easing him down. "I am sorry, Mr Sundar," Hask said. "But it's a pity you didn't read more." None of the researchers looked up from their work as the guard dragged him out of the reading room, a trail of blood smearing beneath his limp legs.

Malone knelt in her spot behind the banister, frozen. A scream stuck in her throat, leaving her as helpless to free it as she had been to save Sundar. She looked up at the statues, as if hoping that their eyes had witnessed a different scene. Suddenly, the sight of the statues, the faded paint, the musky desk and forgotten books filled her with an unspeakable revulsion. Numb, but for the tremors zipping through her body, she crawled back to the rockslide and clambered up the debris and back through the window. Malone gasped at the brisk morning air as sunlight hit her face and clawed her way out of the pit, which now felt like a grave. Reaching the surface, she hunkered down on her hands and knees and vomited. Her face was already wet with tears, and frozen in her mind was the final image of Sundar's face as he fell to his knees, stricken with terrible understanding.

"I truly am sorry for your loss, but believe me when I tell you that he was gone the moment he set foot in that place."

Malone stumbled around to face a man she had never before seen. He was thin and tall, though it was hard to tell how tall, crouched as he was. His wispy, bright red hair framed an elegant face, but what caught her attention were his eyes, shrewd and motionless. "Almost no one who has discovered Project Prometheus has lived to tell about it," he said, seeming to hold back a conspiratorial wink, "and I believe you'll understand why." She dimly realized that she was still bent over a pile of her own sick, trembling.

"I suppose that you'll require an explanation. Sit down, let's get you out of that mess... that's better." Pulling her away from the dome, he sat across from her in a fresh patch of grass and tilted his head with the matter-of-fact air of someone about to share common knowledge. "Inspector Malone, we've much to talk about. Yes, I know who you are, and my name is Jakkeb Sato."

CHAPTER 15

THE REVELATIONS

Jane fought her way through the crowds and headed toward the Vineyard. Confusion swept the streets as the masses swarmed in panicked tides and scattered squads of the City Guard attempted to stem them. She had rushed from the restaurant, deaf to Olivia's protests and Fredrick's questions. Foreseeing Jane's destination, Olivia had gone so far as to try to stop her, but Fredrick had restrained Olivia as Jane set off at a swift jog.

Her mind whirled as she pushed her way through streets and tunnels. Olivia's latest revelation had left Jane dazed, but she was inclined to believe it. If Roman had really assigned Olivia to eliminate her, the savvy maid could have easily done so, and she certainly would not have bothered to treat her to lunch and a safe haven that afternoon. But as much as she wanted to feel gratitude toward her protectors, she was appalled by the implication of their role in the bombings. She did not want to believe that Roman himself was responsible for the murders… or could it have been Olivia, making outings at strange hours? Jane needed answers and she only knew of one person to ask. She would only have to hope that she could overcome his usual predilection for dodging questions.

As she raced through town, she wondered about the actual damage of the bombs. So far, she had only seen the secondary effects manifest in citywide hysteria, but a dark corner of her mind dreaded the moment that would thrust her up against the bloody face of the tragedy. Rounding a corner and rushing directly into a knot of panic, she saw the cause of the uproar.

Nearly half of the block ahead of her was smashed. Where once a hive of offices had stood, a pile of smoking rubble and bodies now lay. Ordinary citizens and whitecoat medics alike heaved moaning and screaming bodies from the wreckage and lay them in what open space they could find, no doubt praying for the swift arrival of the ambulance carriages, while a crowd of useless onlookers stood by in shock. The area where the offices had stood was cleft open like a cross-section, showing halls and rooms that now led nowhere. Jane hoped that the bombs of "various sizes" had been mostly smaller.

When she neared Carnegie, she slowed her pace. The crowds had thinned drastically as she approached the Vineyard, leading her to believe that the whitenails and their associates had either fled or hidden in their mansions. Stranger still was the sudden absence of guards. The few Jane had seen had been busy redirecting the crowds. Jane covered the last leg of her journey at a lope before that could change.

She pounded on Roman Arnault's door, struggling with the possibility that he might be elsewhere. The tide of recent events – from the bombings and Olivia's subsequent revelations to her own intrigues and attack (which now seemed distant and minute by comparison) – had left her with enough to sort out through many sleepless nights, but the thought of bearing it without any idea of what it all meant was too much. Out of breath and shaking with nerves, she leaned against the doorpost and continued beating an irregular rhythm on the door. She relaxed when Roman opened it, looking, if possible, even more surprised than he had at her first visit.

"Roman, I–"

"I warned you against coming back." He sighed, sounding more weary than angry. "Quickly, before someone sees you," he said, taking her arm and not waiting for a response. He guided her back to the drawing room with neither the hospitality nor the wrath of before, but with a sense of urgency. He brought her once again to the crackling fireplace and turned her to face him. "Jane, I cannot tell you what a mistake you've made in coming here. What can I say to make you understand that you have to stay away?"

"You lied the other night, didn't you?" Jane said. Roman blinked, mystified. "You didn't send Olivia to kill me."

"Oh, that… Is that what you came all the way to tell me? Thoughtful, but I'm afraid this was unnecessary," he said, a strain of emotion coloring his dark voice. "You've put yourself in more danger by coming here."

Jane dropped into the chair next to her. "Danger from what? The Council?"

Roman grasped her hands and gently pulled her to her feet again. "No, it's much worse than that. For you, anyway. The Council will soon be among the least of your worries, and for that reason you must leave. Tonight."

"Leave where?"

His eyes flew wide and he leaned closer to her, his hands shaking hers with emphasis. "The city! Recoletta. After tonight, this place will no longer be safe for you." He watched her eyes for understanding and continued more calmly. "I have exercised what little influence I have, but you know too much, and they will kill you for it if you remain. I wanted you to stay out of the murders and the rest of this mess, but you're too close to be safe," he said, awkwardly, avoiding her eyes.

"Who are 'they'? And what could I possibly know?"

Roman hesitated. "The Council's replacements. And you know that the Council didn't break down on its own."

"There was a murderer. Everyone knows that."

"Do they?" Roman raised an eyebrow. "People believe it because they've been told so. But when this is all over, they'll be told another story: that the Council cannibalized itself, and that the councilors and their most corrupt cronies turned on one another when their machinations spiraled out of control."

"And that's how the murders happened?" said Jane.

Roman nodded. "And the replacements figured it out and came to clean house."

"People will never believe that."

"People allow themselves to believe a lot of things, Jane. And once this all plays out, it will make more sense than you think. But you're one of the few people in Recoletta who knows better."

Jane bit her lip. "I could go along with it."

"Not convincingly."

"No one knows who I am," Jane said. "No one even knows I was in Mr Fitzhugh's house." She paused, wrinkling her brow. "Well, almost no one."

"These things have a way of getting out. We can't take that chance."

"But this doesn't make sense! If 'they' wanted me dead, the real murderer could have easily killed me two weeks ago."

He still held her hands in a surprisingly warm and soft grip. "It was not the murderer who drugged you," he said, watching her. He looked down at his hands and quickly dropped them to his sides. "Don't make me say it."

She hesitated and regarded him. "You mean that you…? It was you in the house that night?"

"You said that you had more errands in the Vineyard, and of course I knew what had already been arranged at a certain address and time," he said. His gruffness sounded as artificial as Jane now knew his threats to be. "The assassin only had one target, but any complications would necessarily be eliminated. I followed you and, after some difficulty in that darkness, incapacitated you." He cleared his throat and looked away, frowning. "I later explained that I had followed the assassin to keep an eye on things, which, after the way he nearly bungled the first job, was not unreasonable," he added crossly, "and that in his carelessness, a young housekeeper had followed him in… and was no longer a threat. By the time they learned that you were alive, it was too late to do anything. They had been convinced that it wasn't worth the effort to get to you." Roman did not have to tell Jane who had done the convincing. The faint color in his cheeks said everything.

Jane rubbed the smooth edge of a thumbnail, letting the information sink in. "You left the door open."

"Of course I did," he said, eying her oddly. "You might not have been discovered for another day or two had I not." Given the tangle of mysteries, she was pleased to have answered at least one question almost by herself. Another soon occurred to her.

"What about Hollens? How did the assassin kill him without any complications?"

"Hollens kept a staff." He looked at her, waiting.

Her eyes widened as realization dawned on her. "And you've had people on the inside." He only nodded. "People like you."

"It wasn't me. But yes, people like me."

She frowned, deep creases lining her forehead and the area around her mouth. "You didn't do it, but you knew about it. All of these people dead, and you let it happen."

He stared back at her. "You assume they were innocent, Jane. Don't."

"Whether they were innocent is a different question from whether they deserved to die, Roman. Who deserves to be murdered?"

"Those who allow others to be murdered." His nostrils flared, but his voice lacked the fire of a zealot's conviction. Instead, Jane heard controlled reason and exhaustion.

"Does that mean you'd count yourself in that group?" Jane asked. The question sounded peevish when it left her lips, and as soon as she saw Roman's sad smile she regretted it. Jane shook her head. "But what about the bomb victims? Or do you expect me to believe that they were also guilty of something?"

Roman's features darkened with a quiet fury. "There weren't supposed to be any. The bombs were intended to scatter the guards and force people indoors... and they were supposed to detonate on the outskirts of town. I suppose I was a fool to believe that the plan would be so clean." He stared into the fire, fidgeting with something in his right pocket.

She hesitated, watching Roman's fierce distraction before deciding on another line of questioning. "And the other night..."

He looked up again, his features almost relaxed. "An attempt to drive you away. Unsuccessful, apparently," he said with a rueful smile.

"And your attack was staged?"

He rested a hand on the mantel, gazing back into the fireplace. "Olivia realized after speaking with you and that reporter that my name was under suspicion, and something had to be done to remove it. The attack was staged, but the wounds were real," he said, drawing a finger across his side and turning the fading bruise on his face to her. "It had to be convincing."

Jane winced. "That's quite a commitment to your cause."

"Only what was necessary. They have the plan, and I'm prepared to see it through to the end."

Jane shook her head, feeling her impatience build. "But I still don't understand who 'they' are or what your part in all this is."

"Keep your voice down," he said. Roman held a hand to her and waited, listening. "You're dead if they catch you here, do you understand?"

She gritted her teeth. "That's why I'm leaving tonight, remember? Leaving home for a place where I'll have no money, no job, and no ties to anyone. And since I am, you might as well tell me all of it."

He took a deep breath. "I'd hate to send you away with unanswered questions, especially knowing how far you'll go to resolve them. This begins fourteen years ago with the deaths of Councilor and Lady Sato, which I trust you are old enough to remember."

"Yes."

He looked slightly relieved. "The Council had, through the research of its historians, learned of an ancient library from antebellum civilization. The Library of Congress, as it was called, was reputed to have the largest collection of books, essays, and information in the world at the time of the catastrophe, and its stores included all subjects: history, philosophy, science, technology. It was the latter category that interested the Council most. The Council learned that the Library, if it still existed, would not be far from Recoletta. Less than two hundred miles, among the ruins of a forgotten capital.

"The majority of the councilors, under the leadership of the already powerful Ruthers, were in favor of finding this Library and its hidden stores of knowledge. The only opposition came from Councilor Sato, who not only resisted the plan, but forbade it. As Councilor Sato was the head of the Directorate of Preservation and highly respected among peers and citizens, this posed a problem for Ruthers and the other seven." Roman pawed a stubbled cheek before continuing.

"They tried to persuade him, but he declared that if they pursued the project he would announce it to the public. His decision was final, and the rest of the Council realized that there was no way to excavate the Library with Sato in place. So, a handful of councilors, led by Ruthers, arranged for his assassination. The others turned a blind eye."

That pit of suspicion in her stomach hardened like a stone. "They killed one of their own?"

He nodded. "For a secret which they saw fit to use and he wanted to keep buried, yes. And they covered their tracks. They ensured the speedy execution of their instrument and proceeded with the excavation. But there was one figure they grossly underestimated."

"You?"

A ghost of a smile crossed his lips. "Hardly. Jakkeb Sato was the councilor's only child, and suspicious of a plot, Councilor Sato broke his oath of secrecy and told his son of the Library and the dispute. Days later, Castor and his wife were assassinated, and Jakkeb was left with his grief and knowledge of the betrayal that had caused it."

Again, Roman smiled joylessly. "We had been friends since boyhood, but his behavior was inscrutable to me. He accepted no comfort and ceased speaking almost entirely. I didn't know what to say to him."

Jane frowned. "You mean he didn't tell you about his plan?"

"No. I don't even know exactly when he figured it out. But one night, he walked into a burning storehouse and everyone, including me, took it for a suicide.

"He was far too shrewd for that, and I should have known it. But I remembered the pain of losing my own parents and believed him dead until he reappeared to me seven years later." In Roman's wide eyes, Jane detected a hint of mingled fear and respect. "Jakkeb explained the truth behind his parents' deaths as well as how he had spent his time since then, wandering and mixing with a resourceful breed of lowlifes: smugglers, assassins, thieves, and rabble rousers. He was already planning his retaliation against the Council, and he wanted me to know about it. Since that time, he has been growing in strength and using his considerable influence to build a following. He's advancing to take Recoletta with his army tonight. They're surrounding the city and moving on Dominari Hall, where most of the Council will have holed up."

"A coup?" The word stuck like peanut butter in Jane's dry mouth.

"Much more. Not only a shift in the regime, but an all-out revolution that will change the way Recoletta is governed forever. Never in our history, nor in the known history of any other city, has the top been replaced by the base." Again, Jane heard awe tinged with low-frequency terror in his voice. His eyes returned to hers, and he seemed to recognize the cautious dismay in her face. "If it eases your mind, Jane, consider this vengeance for your parents."

"What?"

"Ruthers, who orchestrated the Sato murders, was also behind your parents' deaths. They wanted to see him removed from the Council, but they dug too deep for his liking." He held up his hands. "If I knew more, I'd tell you, but that's all." Jane swallowed, limbering her tongue before asking more.

"And what's your part in all this?" She dreaded what the answer might be.

"I've been Jakkeb's informant and inside man from the beginning. We were friends through our childhood and youth, so he relied on my abilities and my sympathies when he explained his plan. Once this conversion reaches its bloody conclusion, I'm to serve as his lieutenant and right-hand man."

"So you're doing this for a promotion." She felt a stab of pain somewhere indefinable, as if he had betrayed her as well as his colleagues.

Roman scowled. "Miss Lin, you surely cannot think me so base. You of all people should know that I don't savor the limelight. Jakkeb has good reason, and I would be cold-hearted indeed not to sympathize. After all, his parents raised me as their own."

"Yet Councilor Sato didn't tell you anything about the Library."

He ignored her. "Furthermore, his revolution has a certain sense to it. The current regime is on its way down, and the Council can smell it." Roman looked at Jane's puzzled expression. "Corrupt, inept, and desperate. If you haven't noticed it before, consider how they've handled the crisis of the past few weeks."

"And what are you going to do tonight? Are you staying here to ride it out?" she asked, hopeful.

He bowed his head. "No, I have a part to play as well. I've been here, awaiting the appointed time and preparing."

"Preparing?" Wordlessly, Roman pointed to a small table where Jane saw a crystal decanter filled with brandy and a matching tumbler. "That hardly seems prudent," she said flatly.

He stiffened, his mouth set in a firm line. "I'm not a drunkard, Jane, but I don't look forward to what I must do tonight. Still, I know the role I've been assigned."

"So you're going to jump from being the hatchet man of one regime to the hatchet man of the next."

"I know my strengths."

She took a step toward him. "Jakkeb Sato and his followers may have murdered the guilty, but they've also sacrificed innocent people to their cause. You can't pretend that they're the good guys."

He squared his shoulders against her, gazing down and into her eyes. "I don't. But tell me this: when there are no good guys, which bad guys do you choose?" She fell silent. "There are no heroes, Miss Lin. Only survivors."

"If that were true, you wouldn't be risking yourself to save me."

Roman glared intently at a spot on the carpet. "You should be going now, Jane."

Instead, she pressed her advantage. "Roman, you don't have to get caught in this violent cycle. You talk as if you have no choices, but you're free to go whenever you want. People aren't fixed in one place from birth, and their fates aren't written in the stars. You're only a victim to the traps that you let yourself stay in," she said.

"Then why do people live out their lives in the same miserable cycles? If we can choose, why do we always choose so poorly? Do you really think that whatever catastrophe sent our world underground was so different from the one that we're embarking upon now?"

Jane could feel hot tears of frustration beginning to boil up behind her eyes. "Just come with me tonight. You don't have to spend your life gambling on the lesser of two evils. You could still redeem yourself. Let me help you get out."

Now she was looking away in an attempt to hide her misery. Tenderly, he raised her chin with a knuckle. "Don't you understand, Jane? You are my good deed."

Hours before, Jakkeb Sato had recounted the same history to Liesl Malone with, necessarily, a different perspective. She had listened in silence as the whole mystery of the past sixteen days unraveled before her in a way that even she had not foreseen. The double surprise of Jakkeb Sato and his revelations numbed her pain, and she was able to put Sundar's death out of her mind for the moment.

"What I still don't understand," she said, trying to put everything in its right place, "is why Councilor Sa– your father opposed the rest of the Council."

Sato shot her a crooked grin. "The councilors wanted to uncover the Library's secrets, but only for themselves. These are the tyrants who would entertain us with Shelley's odes but keep from us his 'Queen Mab'."

"Who?"

Sato seemed to ignore the question. "A visionless oligarchy. No respect for the history they would unearth and no discipline in using it. They would create storehouses of vaccines only for themselves if they could. Textbooks on suppression and propaganda, but none on philosophy." He paused, tempering his fervor with a thoughtful, confiding turn. "Before the catastrophe, people had weapons that you and I can hardly imagine: bombs capable of destroying the Earth in a single detonation and plagues that could wipe out all life in a matter of days, grown like crops and kept in glass. Some believe they still exist, also buried in remote locations. Can you imagine these weapons in the hands of a man like Ruthers?"

"But it wasn't to be just Ruthers. There's the partnership with South Haven."

Sato's wild red hair waved and trembled. "The South Haven delegations are a farce. The Council only invited them as a show of power, to convince them to submit quietly. Ruthers wants to reconstruct an empire, and that's what my father opposed. He believed that these secrets had been buried for a reason and that the conflicts and the fear that they recall are best left forgotten. To him, the remembrance was a disease, and if we were to allow it to drive our ambition or taint our good sense, we would become as corrupted and as damned as the ancients." Again Sato paused, a quiet grin spreading across his face while his eyes flashed with inner fire. "But he was wrong, too.

"The Council was corrupted by their greed, but my father was naïve in his reluctance. He failed to see how this Library can advance civilization. The antebellum peoples engineered their own downfall with their addiction to power and their dependence on weapons, but we know better." He picked up speed, his voice rising in pitch as he brought Malone to his thesis. "There is so much that we can learn from them, and, with the record of their mistakes, we can surpass them. Instead of hiding in our pitiful caves, keeping to ourselves, we can return to enlightenment and once again open ourselves to the world. That knowledge is a birthright – not just of the few, but of many." The blaze of the fanatic burned behind his words.

Careful not to douse him with her doubt, Malone edged into an objection. "But it's done that way in every city-state I've ever heard of," she said, watching his eyes for a dangerous flare. "Perhaps we aren't ready to open Pandora's box."

"Long ago, I would have agreed, but I spent fourteen years traveling, planning, and seeing the world. Once you've seen all the lands between the mountains and the oceans, you can never go back to the cave. I was born into privilege and I completed my education as part of the chaff. I've lived both extremes, and I know that a person isn't born into his station, he becomes it. And we can become the people that restore civilization." He leaned in, a few red wisps swaying in front of his eyes. "Would you like to know something else? This isn't the first revolution in which the substrate overthrows the top. That's another thing the whitenails and their Council don't want you to know. History isn't stable, and revolution has been done before, and successfully." He gazed beyond Malone with a distant, hungry look.

"And you think Recoletta is prepared for one now?"

"Not just prepared, but ripe. The Council has proven its feebleness and its depravity," he said. "They began the murders, but I will finish them. You know, I could never even bring myself to hate Mortimer Stanislau. He may have killed my parents, but he was just another instrument of the Council."

"How exactly does Roman Arnault figure into this?"

Sato smiled knowingly. "My old friend had risen in the ranks without quite joining them by the time of my first return to Recoletta. I know that you've been following him. He is a truly brilliant man, and the Council saw that. He served them well, of course, and they were eager to make use of his unorthodox talents. Of course, the problem arises when you begin to see a weapon like Roman Arnault as distinctly your own. The Council had relied so heavily on him as their spy that they could not ever envision him as anyone else's spy."

"Then he was the one providing the keys," Malone said. Sato nodded. Malone asked the next natural question. "And what makes you so sure that he'll always be your spy?"

"Who says I am? He's my friend, but I know better than to believe that I can control him. He's a fierce individualist, and I respect that. I have to. Roman Arnault will stay by my side as long as he believes that it best serves his purpose, whatever that may be. Permit me to say that I know his limits – where I can push, and what he would not allow." He paused, meditating. "I'll allow him the freedom he requires, and I'll keep him close. I know him well enough to make sure that I never give him a reason to betray me. He's not prone to slavish devotion, and it is partially for that reason that I value his alliance so highly... and his friendship." He smiled at Malone, looking sly and pleased at sharing a confidence. "I know that you don't harbor a high opinion of him, but there is no one I would rather have loyal to me than Roman Arnault. Almost no one, that is." He turned a sharp eye on her as the fall breeze rippled between them.

"Inspector Malone, I've been following you for months now, and I am impressed. In fact, it was downright flattering that the Council had to take you off the case. I'm offering you a place among my ranks. Like Roman, I want to keep you close."

Malone was speechless. At first she thought he was joking, but the seriousness of the situation began to sink in, along with the realization that Jakkeb Sato did not seem like a man accustomed to joking. "I am an inspector of the Municipal Police," she replied, measuring her words carefully. "For all intents and purposes, I still serve the regime you want to tear down."

The jump in his voice suggested a laugh of surprise. "The same regime that just murdered your partner?"

"And where were you and your army?" Malone said suddenly. Her throat tightened.

Sato's fierce look softened. "I came to intercept you as soon as I heard you were coming," he said. "I didn't know about your partner until it was too late, or I would have brought reinforcements. But I didn't know what this was going to turn into, and neither did he."

Malone nodded dumbly.

"Inspector, the regime stopped serving *you* a long time ago. The order you believe in has been feeding off of Recoletta like a parasite."

As Sato waited for her reaction, a startling realization came over her that she would not have so much as entertained a mere week ago. He was right.

Seeing the understanding dawn on her, he rose and offered his hand. "There is a long night ahead of us, and I have allies from all corners waiting in the city. There is nothing left for you in the Council's Recoletta, but I have a special place for a woman of your genius in the new government. Will you join me?"

She looked at his proffered hand with her last shred of skepticism. "Do I have a choice?"

Again, Jakkeb Sato smiled. "There is always a choice, Malone."

It hardly surprised her that she accepted the hand and the future it entailed, and when they met the train with Sato's cheering and hooting faction, waiting almost at the spot where she had jumped another like it hours ago, it was as though there had never been a choice, only this next inevitable step for her and for the city. As they returned to Recoletta under the sheen of the late morning sun, Malone sharing her berth with energized radicals rather than crates, she began to appreciate what that new step might bring.

CHAPTER 16

THE MACHINE IN MOTION

Jane was running again, this time from Roman Arnault's domicile. His matter-of-fact yet tender words resounded in her ears, making her hasty exodus even more difficult than it would have been half an hour ago, but he had succeeded in instilling the proper sense of urgency. Now that he had revealed his maneuvers on her behalf, all she could think of was returning home to find Freddie and flee for the safety of all three of them.

Passages that had been a crush of panic and people only a little over an hour ago were now deserted, leaving eerie, abandoned streets that spoke of human presence in the past tense. The tunnels she traveled, wide and narrow, straight and crooked, smooth-faced and rough-hewn, cast irregular echoes of her footfalls, reminders that she should be moving faster. Jane had the uncomfortable feeling that her departure was already overdue.

Even the public transportation, normally a metronome for Recoletta and its way of life, had stopped running. The rail shuttles that crossed the city and the suspended cars that ran along the major thoroughfares were all still, many stopped with their doors askew at the last exit their drivers had reached after hearing the explosions.

The sun was setting. Jane could see its last slanted rays entering through the skylights, and the feeble light they cast on the walls of tunnels and buildings was distinctly sanguine. Heaps of rubble and gaping holes blown into passageways and edifices that had attracted mobs of the morbidly curious before were now as empty as dried honeycomb.

Night had fallen by the time Jane reached the apartment. The hints of movement behind her neighbors' doors and the poorly hidden glow of lamplight behind drawn curtains were the first reminders since leaving Roman that others still inhabited Recoletta, and she found these small tokens comforting, if bittersweet. She moved quietly now, uncertain of what to expect. Jane tapped softly at Fredrick's door and listened for the same stirrings she heard elsewhere. After several moments, she pulled out the spare key he had given her and slipped inside.

The place itself was in its usual state of disarray. Papers littered the floor, spillover from the writing desk against one wall. Jackets, overcoats, and unbuttoned shirts were also scattered about the room, draped over chairs and hung on any available corner. With a rising dread, she continued her search in the back rooms.

The closet, bedroom, and bathroom all showed signs of a total lack of upkeep, but nothing more serious. Drawing deep, steadying breaths, Jane convinced herself that he must have gone across the hall to her apartment to await her return.

Yet when she came to her own domicile, only her piles of abandoned laundry greeted her. In the context of the impending transformations in her life and the city around her, it was jarring to see her home exactly as she had left it, and probably for the last time. Ashes in the fireplace and kettles on the stove, but no sign of Fredrick. Or Olivia.

The bathroom was clean, polished, and empty. The workshop was full of clothes and bedding but devoid of people. It was not until she reached her bedroom that her search returned any clues. What she found left her numb with dread.

Placed upon her nightstand next to the made bed (a stark contrast from Fredrick's disordered quarters) was a note written in his familiar, hurried hand.

Jane,

If you've gone where I think you have, then I have the comfort of your safety, but I have my own leads to pursue. Olivia left shortly after you and refused to elaborate on what is happening. She told me to stay here and wait for you, but I can't be sure when you'll return. If you read this note, know that something very big is about to take place, and I have gone to Dominari Hall to find out what.

Her heart sank as she read the last sentence. Knowing what she knew, she could not possibly leave Fredrick in what was about to become the epicenter of the battle. Her flight would have to wait. She glanced at the clock: barely after 5.30. The official curfew did not matter anymore, but she worried about another that might descend without warning.

She filled a satchel with a few articles of clothing, some food, and the money and valuables she kept stashed in her nightstand. She would have to hope that whatever city she landed in would accept her currency. On a second fleeting thought, she grabbed a couple pairs of trousers and button-up shirts from the drying line for Fredrick. They would be among the least of their original owners' worries, and planning for Fredrick's eventual flight with her restored a measure of hope. She returned to the streets, praying that she was not too late.

Jane was running faster now, racing against an unseen army descending upon the city and the doom it spelled for her and Fredrick. Given the Council's desperation in the final hours of its reign, her friend was walking into a volatile situation.

The streets were darker than usual, owing to the absence of groundskeepers... or anyone, for that matter. Most of the city's radiance stones still glowed bravely, and the fire-trench lighting remained strong in the larger halls, but a few untended torches had begun to go dark, casting perilous shadows. Jane struck her foot against an uneven curb and stopped, gasping in pain. That was when she heard the gunshots.

Echoes resounded through the passage, and she could not tell where they were coming from. When she heard second, third, and fourth rounds, she was certain they were in different locations. Looking up at the line of skylights in her high-arched, oval-shaped tunnel, Jane saw only blackness. The lit torches flickered ominously in their sockets, but she was sure they were the only things moving.

Mayhem erupted in pockets around the city. Jakkeb Sato's army was trickling into Recoletta from all sides, and supporters already in place were coming out of the woodwork. The City Guard was distracted and scattered by the afternoon bombs and unprepared for the guerillas that advanced from the shadows. Confused guardsmen alternately fired blindly at the darkness and fled into the traps their attackers had set up. Though trained as a fighting force, Recoletta's erstwhile stability with neighboring powers had kept them out of any major skirmishes.

The mysterious attacks threw them off balance and cut them off from their commanders and one another.

In the chaos that ensued, the guards fired at anything that moved.

Chief Johanssen had heard the shots as well. One battle had erupted outside Callum Station, and, though he could not tell who was firing, the combatants were getting closer. Most of the inspectors and officers had set off throughout the city in the wake of the bombings. Of the few that remained, some were listening intently in their offices, and many others were standing in the halls. Farrah poked her head into Johanssen's office, an expression of concern clouding her normally calm features.

"What's happening, Chief?"

"No telling. Wait here," he said, moving into the hall. He heard a scream come from somewhere in the rotunda, followed by yelling and several more shots. "They're inside the station," he said. Already the haze of gun smoke was making it difficult to determine who was firing... or being shot. "Stop! Hold your fire!" he yelled down the hall. The shots continued and the cloud of musket smoke advanced closer. A bullet whizzed past his nose, and he ducked back into the office. Across the hall, one of Johanssen's officers fell under a volley of bullets. The thick layer of smoke, combined with the unknown scatter of his own men, kept him from adding his own shots to the fray.

"Cease fire!" he bellowed at the unseen attackers. "Stop shooting, dammit!" But still the advance continued. "Miss Sullivan, get into the office," he said over his shoulder.

"But Chief–"

"Get into the office and open my bottom-right drawer. Toss me one of the hand-mines inside."

"A *what*?"

"Bottom drawer. Now." He extended his hand toward her, his eyes glued to the open slit of the doorway.

Farrah reached into the specified drawer and produced a small, roundish ball about the size of her fist. She held it almost as far from her body as her extended arm would allow, as if a few extra feet of distance would spare her the disaster of an accidental detonation. She looked back up at Johanssen, certain that he must not have realized what he was asking her to do. "Chief, I don't think this is–"

"Then don't miss," he said, finally turning his head to her. Those unsmiling eyes and that firm-set mouth told Farrah all she needed to know about his earnestness in the matter.

Catching her breath, and not for the last time, she hoped, she lobbed the mine to her chief in her softest underhand. Johanssen caught and cradled it with more delicacy than his massive paws had seemed capable of. He checked the hallway once more, but the other officers were either retreating or had already fallen under the gunfire. Pushing the door to the hall most of the way closed, he snaked his arm above the frame and balanced the mine atop the remaining wedge. He pulled Farrah's desk into his office, pushing it against the heavy double doors as he shut and locked them. His fortifications complete, he crossed back to where Farrah waited behind his desk as if barricading the office were a daily bit of business.

"Nice arm," he said.

Her lips curled in a kind of shocked rage, and she wondered how long he had kept a box of mines in his desk, which sat not twenty feet from hers. "You can say that again. Because if I'd thrown just a couple feet short…"

"We'd probably be breathing through our handkerchiefs. It's a smoker, Miss Sullivan." His eyes glittered at her, and

Farrah found herself taken aback, as usual, by the chief's rare flashes of humor.

Reaching into a cabinet, Johanssen handed her a howdah pistol and a bag of ammunition. "You know how to use this?"

She knitted her brows in exasperation, her eyes only leaving his to check the breech as she loaded and cocked it. "Chief..."

He threw a hand in front of her. "Get back." They knelt behind the heavy oaken desk that faced the double doors.

"What's the plan?" Farrah asked.

"The smoker should scatter and string 'em out on their way in. With the red-eye they'll get, they won't be shooting straight, either. Get ready. I think they're about to come through the–" He stopped at the loud hissing in the other room.

"Door?"

"They're in your office now. Keep your sights level." He reached under the desk and pulled out a double-barreled shotgun, steadying it on the desk. He set a box of shells by his knee. The shouts they heard from the other room, though, were both more numerous and more ordered than either of them had expected.

"Chief?" Farrah was just beginning to lose her cool. "What's going on?"

"I don't know, but I want you out of here." Johanssen pulled a small lever under the desk, and the fireplace at their backs swung open to reveal a secret passage.

"I can't leave you here!"

The first shot tore through the double doors, and Johanssen returned fire.

"You have to. Get to Malone and tell her what happened. If she got as far as I think, she's the only one of us who understands what's going on." A bullet lodged itself in the mantel above their heads. "Go!"

Nodding mutely, Farrah hurried down the passage as Johanssen pulled the lever again to seal it and snapped it at the base. Johanssen managed to exchange two rounds with the attackers before the first of the band broke into the office, and it would be impossible to say whose confusion was greater: Captain Fouchet's or Chief Johanssen's.

"Fouchet! What the hell are you doing here?" Forgetting that he was under assault, Johanssen almost rose to his feet in disbelief.

"Putting an end to your little insurrection."

"You think this is us? Have you lost your mind?" He slid two more shells into the breech.

"No, I followed my ears. Rather telling when the attackers strike from the vicinity of your station and retreat into it, don't you think?"

Johanssen felled a gunman that had knelt just inside the doorway and taken aim. "Fights are breaking out all over the city, you moron," he said.

Fouchet ducked back into Farrah's office, yelling through the haze. "And where else would a small army have gotten so many weapons, eh?"

"Your Barracks, that's where!" Johanssen saw a shadow shift in the doorway and fired into the wall just to the right of it. He was rewarded with a gasp of pain from Fouchet. Johanssen reached for his box of shells and grabbed two more.

"You Municipal scum," Fouchet muttered, stumbling around the wall and training his sights on Johanssen through the smoke. Farrah was halfway down the passage when she heard two final shots, one the blast of a shotgun and the other the report of a musket.

Jane had reached the Spine, where the firing seemed more remote. The flames ribbing the walls burned red, and the distant shouts and rumbles of gunfire furthered the impression of standing inside a great, dormant beast on the verge of awakening. She was alone with fading radiance stones like dying stars, and the emptiness was immense and the darkness barely warded off by the sputtering torches and the reddish glow from the wall.

The tiles appeared molten under Jane's flying feet in the low, shifting light, but they led inexorably to Dominari Hall and the Barracks. She was running along one of the lower tiers of the Spine, and, other than the soaring ribs and floating points of light, she could discern nothing in the darkness above. Her legs burned when at last the towers of Dominari Hall came into view, rising to the surface like the roots of a mammoth tree.

Lights shone from behind windows, and bright torches illuminated the plaza around the hall. A tangle of shapes ran in every direction across the plaza, and in the patches of shadow and light it was impossible to tell who was coming and who was going. The only thing evident was massive confusion.

When at last she reached the overhang where Dominari Hall, and beyond it, the Barracks, was perched, she ascended in the shadows. In the frenzy of activity, no one stopped to question Jane.

Inside were fewer people but they were still running in all directions. The mayhem seemed to defy the ordered, pristine interior of Dominari Hall. Ivory and porcelain-enameled walls rose to chandeliers of gold and crystal that hung over a scene out of a pauper's opera. With only a little choreography, the leaps over upturned tables and the semi-musical sprints through shattered mirror-glass would have fit perfectly in several productions that Jane had seen in what she already thought of as her former life.

It would have been pointless to call for Fredrick and, in any case, she doubted it would be a good idea to advertise her presence, regardless of the disorder. Nevertheless, searching Dominari Hall from top to bottom would surely take more time than she had and likely bring her to one of her antagonists before Fredrick. Realizing this, she stepped into the path of a woman heading straight in her direction.

Jane made eye contact, or she thought she did. "Excuse me, I need–"

The nameless bureaucrat continued looking through Jane as she galloped along in a beeline, slamming into Jane's shoulder. Jane crashed against the wall, barely straightening her back again before attempting to hail another clerk mid-flight.

"Hello, I just–"

This time, Jane swung out of the man's path before he could collide with her, but he paid her no more notice than the woman before him had. If she wanted to get anyone's attention, she would have to seize it more forcefully.

Fortunately, Jane only had to wait seconds for the arrival of her next target. A middle-aged, bespectacled man sped toward her, the red blooms on his cheeks standing out against his spotless, white shirt. As he reached her level, Jane extended her foot in time to send him sprawling.

Hearing the thud that his body made as he hit the carpet and seeing his confusion and terror, Jane's first impulse was one of deep guilt and regret. She extended a hand to help the man to his feet, but as she did so, she reminded herself that Fredrick's life depended on her quick action.

"You! Where did you come from?" Jane attempted to sound authoritative; to her own ears, she only came across as crabby. But to the man she had tripped, she was evidently convincing enough.

"F-from my office. In the north wing."

"What's going on?" she asked. But the man only stared at her with a wide-eyed panic that pained and frightened her, and she realized that if she did not maintain some kind of command over the situation he would bolt like a mare in a fire.

"I'm here to get everything under control," she said, and saying the words even made her feel it a little. "When did everybody start running?"

The man licked his lips and jiggled the frames of his glasses. "Bombs. And shooting. Then Dominguez came, said everyone was to leave–"

"Did you see a reporter?" Again the blank look. Of course not, she thought; what are the chances that Fredrick would just march into Dominari Hall and announce himself as "The Reporter", come for the story? Pretty good, actually. "Who's in charge?"

"Dominguez. And R-Ruthers."

"Are they still here?" He nodded. "Where?"

The man pointed a shaking finger straight down the hall. "East wing. All the way at the end. Brought g-guns..."

Jane was off before she could hear the rest, and she hurried down the main hall toward the offices and reception rooms, where the pack thinned further. In a matter of moments, she was clear of any detectable human presence.

The tumult behind her was only a din, and she reached a grand double staircase that descended further into the heart of Dominari Hall. She could neither see nor hear movement in that direction, but a faint glow spilled onto the bottom steps, and it seemed as likely an avenue as any. Tiptoeing where red velvet crept over white marble, she edged down the stairs.

Emerging into a new hallway, this one more impressive than its predecessor, she slowed her pace. The faces of cherubim emerged from the creamy marble, staring down at her from the shadow of the vaulted ceiling. Below them hung portraits of Recoletta's long line of councilors, the men and women affecting regal poses within their golden frames. A dim glow reflected off of the smooth polish of the mahogany doors lining the hall, looking warm to the touch.

The only light came from much further down the hall, and Jane's position was in semidarkness. Picking her way down the hall and peering into darkened corridors, she chided herself for not having thought to bring a lamp but decided that the advantages of stealth outweighed those of visibility. Listening more carefully, she continued.

As she watched the floor for snags in the carpet, something caught her eye: a patch where the velvet carpet appeared to run outside its bounds and pool against the wall. With closer observation, she saw that the pool was a good deal darker than the carpet. Blood.

The puddle had spread to just less than six inches in diameter, and it trailed in drops and streaks down a side corridor. She followed the track a few feet down the corridor, around a corner, and into a dim office, sickness and dread rising in her throat. Just on the other side of the doorframe, Fredrick sat propped against the wall. Gasping, she rushed to the slumped figure and knelt in front of his bowed head.

His upper half was bent over his knees, which angled imprecisely upwards and outwards. His right hand clenched something on his abdomen, and red bloomed between the white fingers and knuckles. His face was turned downwards and obscured by limply hanging hair. She lifted his head gently, feeling the sweat that slicked his brow and temples and noticing, even in the low lighting, that he had achieved a dangerous pallor.

"Freddie? Can you hear me?" she whispered. To her unparalleled relief, he let out a low moan, and she had to stop herself from squeezing him in a joyful hug. "Thank goodness, you're alive." Watching the listless way that his head and limbs swayed, though, she wondered how long that would be true. She took his hand, feeling more warmth than she expected. "Listen, we have to go, it's not safe for us here."

Groaning, he lifted his head and it lolled out of control, thumping against the wall. "You don't say."

"Save your witticisms for later, Freddie; we've got to get out of here. What happened to you?"

Fredrick heaved a few labored breaths. "Short. Bulgy eyes, creepy mustache. I came, after you'd left, to get answers. Whole place in an uproar. Found Ruthers and a few other councilors; said something about hostile takeover." Fredrick paused, briefly overtaken by a fit of coughing. Jane was pleased to see that none of it came out red. "They asked me who sent me; I said 'Roman Arnault', and this guy shot me. Name's Dominguez, I think." With his left and relatively clean hand, he reached into his pocket and pressed something cold and hard into Jane's palm.

"What's this?"

"It's a gun. I brought it for a worst-case scenario," he said, chuckling weakly. Holding it up to the light and, with a little trouble, pushing out the cylinder, she could see that it was a six-chambered revolver, fully loaded. "Cock that little catch on the back to shoot," Fredrick added. She pocketed it.

Jane hesitated, looking at the bleeding mass under Fredrick's hand. "I'm going to

need–"

"No."

"Fredrick, I have to see how bad it is." She peeled his hand away, and he gasped. The wound was a mess of half-crusted and oozing blood, and Jane couldn't discern much except that it wasn't bleeding as profusely as she'd feared. Also, the wound was closer to the side than the center of his abdomen, and while she couldn't have said what organs were in the path of the bullet, or which had been missed, this seemed like a good thing.

"Can you walk?"

"Do I have a choice?"

"Come on." Jane tore a strip from her billowing skirt and tied it under Fredrick's chest as he winced. Pulling his arm around her shoulder, she hoisted him to his feet.

"OOOOOOOW,   ohpleaseohpleaseOHHHH!"   Fredrick squeezed his eyes shut as Jane straightened her legs and stood him upright. She took slow, shuffling steps and he painfully dragged his feet beside her. "Just leave me," he moaned. "It's not worth it. You'll have to go without me."

She stopped. "Freddie?"

"Yes?"

"Shut up."

Picking up speed, they shuffled back into the hall. Up the stairs and back the way Jane had come, the din had grown louder. Shouts, scuffles, and gunshots echoed down the hall toward them.

"Not that way," Fredrick sighed. Jane nodded and directed them away from the stairs, toward the radiance, as the carpet grew ever brighter under their feet. In less than two minutes, they had reached a great rotunda and the source of the light.

A massive chandelier sat in the center of the rotunda, anchored and glowing wanly. The ropes and chains descending behind it from an oculus in the ceiling gave it the appearance of a giant, crystalline spider, its multitude of eyes winking at them. Jane stood, transfixed by the sight and forgetting their danger until she caught the odor of smoke and spice in the air. Standing to one side, his back against the wall, was Roman Arnault.

"They brought it down for cleaning. Interesting, isn't it? It takes all those ropes to keep it up, but just one to hold it down," he said, pointing to an anchor in the wall where a lone rope was tied, taught as a bowstring. His voice sounded wearier still than it had earlier in the evening.

"What are you doing here?" Jane asked. He dropped his cigarette to the floor and smothered it in his stride.

"I could ask you the same thing, but it appears that, once again, you've been caught in the pursuit of a noble mission," he said and paced around, looking at Fredrick. The reporter glowered back with all the distaste his pained features could manage.

"How do we get out?" Fredrick asked.

"You don't. As you probably heard, they came in behind you and are filling the palace as we speak, casing every office, closet, and filing cabinet. Ahead lies a secret passage to the surface, but it would be impossible to crawl through it in your current state of encumbrance." He glared at Fredrick, as if holding him responsible for their condition. "In a few minutes, Sato and his army will be upon us, and I'll have more than a little explaining to do. I fear that nothing I can do or say will be enough to save you two. Or me, for that matter. For your entanglement in this, I am sincerely sorry."

"Sorry?" Fredrick said. "If we're about to die, at least do us the courtesy of a little honesty. You're a lying, murderous pig, and you led us into this."

"Right on the first two counts, Mr Anders, but mistaken on the last," Arnault said, his wrath rising. "If she'd listened to me, Miss Lin would have safely fled and I'd only be apologizing to you. Instead, she came back. To rescue you." He snorted. "And this has to be the most inept bandaging I've ever seen, Jane. Is this supposed to stop the bleeding or hold his trousers up?" he said. He deftly retied the swathes and added a wad of fabric from his own shirt to improve it. "At least he won't bleed to death before Sato arrives."

Fredrick looked down at the fresh dressing as if he expected it to bleed him even faster. "What's with the 'us' anyway? You're on their side, as I found out the hard way."

Roman rattled a sigh from somewhere deep in his throat and looked away. "You don't really expect me to stand by while they massacre the two of you, do you?" His voice rang with annoyance, and Fredrick fell silent.

"You still haven't told me what you're doing here," Jane said.

"I have unfinished business down the hall."

"Is that what you've been dreading all evening?" She noticed a faint tremor in his hands.

"Run, Jane." His voice had adopted an unfamiliar quaver. "Hide your friend, and perhaps I can draw them off."

"Why did they send you here?"

In the pause that followed, Roman brushed a strand of hair from his forehead with a shaking hand. "Locked in the office at the end of the hall is Councilor Ruthers. One of our moles in the Guard left him there, supposedly for safekeeping until the rioting subsided." He drew a shaking breath. "As a final test of loyalty, my job is to kill him."

Fredrick recovered from his astonishment and remembered some of his loathing for Roman. "Can you be serious? You, of all people, are worked up because you have to kill someone you've been betraying all along?"

Roman's face was nearly as ashen as the reporter's as he glared back. "Working against someone and murdering him in cold blood are two different things. It's true, I share responsibility for the other murders, though I did not commit them with my own hands. While I cannot sympathize with the Council's actions in the past, I would never have wished for this position. I'm many things, Jane, but not a murderer." Already a fearsome change took place in him as he struggled to accept his duty. "There's another thing," he said, his voice and his eyes hardening. "I cannot forgive Ruthers for what he did to the Sato family, and to many others, but, no matter his crimes, it would never be easy for me to kill him. Augustus Ruthers is my great-uncle." He gave a sad little laugh. "The only family I have left. But Jakkeb will accept nothing less as proof of my loyalty... and in return for your safety, assuming you've left. He thinks that once I've done this I'll be indelibly under his control."

Jane paused. "Do you have the key on you?"

He fished in his pocket and held up a thick, shiny key. "Our contact in the Guard passed it to me on his way out. A double betrayal, though I suppose Ruthers deserves nothing less. I know well what kind of man my uncle is."

"But heaven forbid you should become the same."

"I wish I had a choice."

"I know," she said with real sympathy. "And I hope that you can forgive me for this one day and understand what I'm doing for you." Arnault looked up at Jane with mild bemusement, which grew to wide-eyed alarm when he saw the small revolver she was pointing at him. Meeting his gaze with all-but-banished regret, she fired.

He fell to the ground, clutching his leg and bellowing in pain. "Are you insane? What have you done?"

"Sorry," she said. "But I think I've got more right to this chore than you." Rushing to his side, she retrieved the key he had dropped and ran down the hall toward the locked door. Fredrick watched the series of events unfold as if in slow motion, and only the subsiding sounds of Arnault's gasps and growls brought him back to realtime.

"Oh, shut up," he muttered, hobbling to the chandelier.

Jane's own pulse was surprisingly steady as she dashed to the end of the hall, the rotunda disappearing in a final curve. A lone door, gilded and carved masterfully, was set into the left-hand wall. She knocked.

The sounds of stirring reached her through the thick wood. "Sergeant Gorham? Is that you?" The voice was firm and commanding, and she recognized it well from an afternoon at the market that seemed like years ago. She unlocked and opened the door with the stolen key.

The man on the other side of the door looked from her disheveled figure to the revolver in her outstretched hand with open wonder, though not a hint of fear. Those pale blue eyes settled back on hers, daring her to be done with it. Feeling a touch of dread herself, Jane detected something unpleasantly familiar in the cold, malevolent stare, and she fired.

The report of this second shot sounded louder in this small room, but Jane's hands were still steady on the gun when she lowered it. She took a moment to catch her breath, gazing at the motionless man through the gunpowder smoke, before sprinting back to the rotunda where the ruckus had grown louder. Roman had regained something of his composure and was kneeling awkwardly where he had fallen, having staunched his wound. His eyes met hers with pity. Crouching beside him, she looked at his leg.

"Never mind it." He took her face in his wide, surprisingly smooth hands and inspected it with sadness and awe. "I never meant for you to be in this position, Jane. What have I done to you?" He brushed a lock of dark hair from her cheek. "I'm so sorry." Drawing her face closer to his rough jaw, she kissed him.

As their lips met and searched, holding on to that tender moment as the world fell around them, Jane's senses took her back to the orphanage, where a single jar of honey gleamed golden against bowls slopped with insipid, grayish porridge. The honey was reserved for the headmistress and her cohorts to drizzle on their bread, but, when no one was looking, Jane would dip her own spoon into the jar so that she ate the bland porridge with the taste of honey on her lips. In this moment, she thought of nothing so much as bitterness refined by a touch of sweetness.

The bursting of gunshots in the rotunda broke them from their reverie. "Jane, I think they're firing at me!" Fredrick said, ducking behind the chandelier as crystal and glass exploded around him. "Oh, I don't want to get shot... not again!"

Jane looked at Fredrick clinging to the chandelier, and an idea occurred to her that would have seemed foolish a few minutes ago. "Go," Roman said, giving her hand a final squeeze. She tumbled behind the chandelier, holding Fredrick against one of its golden rings.

"Hold on," she said, pulling out the revolver.

"Why?" he asked, fearful. Jane aimed at the anchor on the wall. Seeing her, Roman drew his own gun and did likewise. Two shots erupted simultaneously. One embedded itself in a section of plaster near the fastening, and the other splintered it, sending the chandelier rocketing skyward as Sato and his men erupted into the rotunda. The only sound louder than the hissing of the rope was Fredrick's terrified scream as he and Jane shot toward the ceiling.

"Stand down," Sato said as the chandelier bounced one hundred feet above their heads. "It's finished."

Jane managed to rock the mass of gold, crystal, and glass to the outer edge of the oculus, where a railing and fastenings permitted her to anchor it steadily enough for her and Fredrick to climb to safety. A short flight of stairs later, they were at the surface and running as fast as Fredrick's injury would permit. The skylights under their feet flashed and rumbled like the gates of hell as the fighting continued below them.

"Jane?" Fredrick's voice sounded stronger now, and the color began to return to his cheeks as they hurried.

"Yes?"

"You remember back there when I told you to leave me?"

"Yes."

"I really didn't mean it. I'm glad you came back."

"I know, Freddie."

Back in the rotunda, Jakkeb inspected Arnault and his leg wound. "Who did this?"

"The laundress. She'd brought a revolver with her," he added, seeing Sato's incredulity. Sato continued to look between Roman's eyes and his wound, as if waiting for the rest of the story.

A voice, feminine, chimed in from somewhere behind Sato. To Roman, it sounded familiar but impossible to place. "She's a laundress, not a marksman, Sato. And Roman's lucky. Another foot, and he'd have more than a limp to worry about."

Sato nodded, still mesmerized by the wound.

Leaning closer to him, Roman whispered. "That's not all she did. I told her the truth about her parents."

Sato's eyes went wide in astonishment. "I see. That's just as well." Sato paused, looking back at Roman's leg. "Does this change things? Shall I...?"

"No," he said. "Let her go."

"Are you going to be alright? Your leg..."

"It's fine," Roman said. "I'll get it properly dressed once this is over."

"It very nearly is, my friend," Sato replied. "And as such, it's time you met our newest associate. Roman Arnault? The former Inspector Liesl Malone." Sato stood aside as the pale blonde drew from the assembled group, and Roman recognized the speaker from moments ago. The two regarded one another with undisguised hostility.

The arrival of a panting militiaman cut the tension. He hurried to Sato and whispered something in his ear. Nodding with concern, Sato drew the messenger aside and questioned him. After several minutes of anticipatory silence, he dismissed the soldier and beckoned Malone with a bony finger. "Malone, please." She came and he took her aside, his features drawn. In the echoing rotunda, the action seemed more like a gesture than a real moment of privacy, but she understood that it portended something grave all the same.

"I'm afraid I have some bad news. It appears that the initial outbreaks of fighting caused some confusion among several squads of the Guard. One platoon set upon Callum Station under the supposition that your people were responsible, and several officers were killed. Including Chief Johanssen. I'm sorry, Malone."

She nodded dumbly, and he left her standing alone as he returned to the mass of followers gathered at the entrance to the rotunda. "In less than an hour, we will celebrate our victory as the new and rightful governors of Recoletta. All of the councilors have been accounted for. Our only remaining chore is to check Mr Arnault's progress with the task appointed to him." When he spoke, Sato lifted his arms and raised his chin, addressing his listeners with a demagogue's grandeur. "Roman, is it done?"

Arnault gestured to the curved hallway opposite them where a rosy light tumbled forth. Sato checked over his shoulder where Malone stood, silently gazing at a seam in the floor. "Inspector? Will you be so kind as to tell us what you see at the end of the hall?" He beamed as she trotted to the room to check. Her footsteps receded to a dull echo as she reached the end of the hall, disappearing from the view of those in the rotunda. They stopped, and silence fell while Malone surveyed the room.

"It's a small parlor," she said, looking inside.

"But what's in it?" Sato paused, waiting for Malone's reply. He cleared his throat. "The body, Malone," he said, retaining admirable poise. "Augustus Ruthers's lifeless corpse."

"Is not here, sir."

His face fell and the triumph evaporated from his voice. "What?" Dashing over with every attempt at maintaining self-possession, he ducked into the room. "Not here? Arnault just said that little scrubber did it herself!" Overturning chairs and desks in a rage, he uncovered nothing but dust, and his nostrils were already irritated by the dissipating smell of gunpowder. He slammed a gloved fist into the wall and let out a bellow of rage that echoed into the crowded rotunda.

From his seat in the middle of the floor, Roman Arnault threw back his head and laughed at an outcome that even he had not foreseen.

Several layers of dirt and stone above them, Jane and Fredrick continued their flight, barely having reached the northern boundary of Recoletta. On the edge of a forest of towering pines, they crossed to where the squish and crunch of soil and vegetation replaced the thunder of paved streets and fled north under the cover of a starless night.

EPILOGUE

Jane and Fredrick tripped and dragged each other through the woods, breathing heavy plumes of steam, until they found the farming commune. Or rather, the commune's farmers found them. A pair of game trappers in the woods heard something crashing in the underbrush that was too talkative to be an injured deer. They found Jane and Fredrick and took them back to the commune, the larger of the two men carrying Fredrick like an injured lamb. Inside the cabin and next to a crackling fire, Jane was surprised at how cozy the aboveground dwelling actually was.

An elderly woman joined them within minutes of their arrival, shepherding Fredrick to a nearby table and examining his wound with startlingly clear eyes. Her leathery face remained impassive as she removed his shirt and surveyed the wound, and when she administered a shot of whiskey and placed a gauze-wrapped spoon in his mouth, he swallowed and bit down obediently. Yet he felt less pain than he would have thought as the woman's nimble fingers worked over his body, removing the bullet and cleaning the hole it left. His body felt distant, and he focused on the faces hovering over him, Jane and the two trappers. Hers was a pale moon next to nebulae of swarthy skin and tangled beards.

No questions were asked, and the exiled pair spent a week in the company of the surface-dwellers while Fredrick recovered. Their hosts were cheery and hospitable, and crowds of small children showed up every morning, their bright faces peering through windows at the new arrivals. Jane was awed by the simple temerity of the children, questioning them both about the underground with wide-eyed interest (generally about the monsters and ghosts that supposedly lived below the earth) until parents and older siblings came by, smiling shyly, to shoo them away. As Fredrick's health improved, Jane began to take leisurely walks with him, the cloud of children always following a few yards behind.

Even more striking to Jane was the intensity of the smells and tastes around her. She had rarely experienced more than the taste of salt- or ice-packed meat, preserved for sale and consumption in Recoletta, but twice a week the communers ate freshly slaughtered game and livestock, a delicacy generally only affordable to the whitenails. The fruits and vegetables, too, had a hue and a flavor Jane had rarely tasted in her years in the city, and she found herself chewing slowly to savor every bite.

Fredrick's humor began to return, and he went so far as to quip about the pedestrian taste of the customer from whom she had filched his clothes. "If you're so picky, you can keep wearing your own, but don't expect to lean on me much longer," she said, waving the air in front of her nose.

At the close of the week, when Fredrick seemed healthy enough to continue their journey, Jane judged it best that they move on in case Sato's men came looking for them. When at last they left, many of the hundred-odd communers gathered to see them off, providing them with satchels of fresh food for the trip, clean dressings for Fredrick's wound, and a guide to lead them to the next farming commune en route to the next city, almost one hundred miles away. Part of Jane was sorry to go, and as they set out, she noticed that the smell of grass and trees had already settled on her own clothes.

Augustus Ruthers was not a man accustomed to surprises, but he received three monumental ones on the night of Sato's invasion. The first was when an aide, frantic and frenzied, burst into his office and informed him in sentence fragments of the battles springing up around the city and of the scruffy contingents slowly making their way to Dominari Hall. Sergeant Gorham, with the usual cool, had taken over from the aide and, guiding Ruthers to a safe room, had explained that a coup was suspected. Gorham assured him that the other councilors were being similarly tended to. Locked in the office off the rotunda and awaiting Gorham's return, Ruthers could not imagine any rivals who would act so boldly.

The second great surprise came when the door opened again, but not for anyone Ruthers had ever seen. Her round face was like a child's, but, full of tension and fury, it seemed to shine. Most startling were her eyes, fixed on him with a directness he first attributed to hatred. When she raised her revolver, he did not fear. He waited.

The last and possibly greatest surprise was when she fired into the floor at his feet. Standing in the doorway for a few seconds longer, silhouetted in golden light from the rotunda and wreathed in gun smoke, she looked like a ragged angel of mercy, and Ruthers understood that the look in her eyes had nothing to do with hate.

"You know the way out?" she asked. The real question was how she knew it, but that was now beside the point. He only nodded, his eyes never leaving hers.

When she left and Roman held her face in his hands and no more attention was given to the hall where Ruthers should have died, he slipped out of the office and felt the wall molding at the end of the hall for a tiny switch, which he pressed. The ground opened at his feet. A block of tiles slid away, and he descended into the crawlspace while Jane and Fredrick mounted the chandelier above.

Ruthers felt in the darkness as the tiles moved back into place, and, ripping at the levers and jamming the gears, he locked the trapdoor in position before turning to the long, climbing passage. He had never begged for anything in his life, but it was on his hands and knees that he crawled to freedom outside of the city.

Farrah Sullivan, however, remained in her tunnel until the battle stopped. She knew how to fight, but outside she could not tell friend from foe. When she emerged hours later, blinking in the sunlight above the hospital, she might have been the only person in Recoletta. The streets were empty, except for the occasional pile of rubble or corpses: refuse from the sudden skirmishes. Most of the bodies were clothed in the uniforms of city guards and a few others in nondescript civilian dress.

While she surveyed the damage, veranda gates began to swing open around her as others came out from hiding. Belowground, it was as if the city breathed, and hundreds of doors and windows swayed open in a collective sigh. Then eyes blinked and lips began to move, slowly at first. Everyone asked the same question.

What next?

Jakkeb Sato did not make them wait long for an answer. His emissaries were in the streets, proclaiming the glorious revolution to a bewildered public. They also announced the appearance of their new leader that very day, a man to guide them out of the darkness, and when Jakkeb Sato himself emerged for the gathered crowd they hailed him as a prince. Announcing the glory of Recoletta and the return of justice to the city, he spread his arms wide like a messiah and stepped into the crowd, as the parting of a sea. The insecurity that had gnawed at them earlier dissipated as a new figure filled that void of power and ceremony. The return of Recoletta's most favored and aggrieved son proved that, for the truly exceptional, miracles are possible.

Liesl Malone watched her new boss with a remote awe. Standing on the stage where he had left her for the crowd, she saw him only a dozen yards away but felt a much greater distance between them. As his new lieutenant and Recoletta's youngest ever head of law enforcement, she had a new set of responsibilities to distract her from the ache that persisted inside. With Sundar and Johanssen dead, it was a hollow promotion.

Sato had assured her that his rear guard had executed Hask as well as the guards and administrators at the Library responsible for Sundar's death, and though he'd offered to show her the bodies she'd declined. Somehow, the thought offered little comfort.

As the fanfare rose around Malone, her mind retreated to the quiet room in her quiet domicile where a cello now lay. In the first hours of the morning, as the smoke had cleared and early light had broken the gray sky, she had ventured to the music shop. When she knocked, it was hard to say who was more surprised: Malone at the presence of the shopkeeper, or the elderly shopkeeper at the presence of a customer. Malone instantly recognized the cello that Sundar had procured for her, and when she pointed to it, her hand trembling with agitation, the shopkeeper mistook her meaning and made as if to hand it over to a bandit. She shook her head, and only after several gestures to the money on the counter did he understand that she meant to buy it. Now it sat, tucked in the seclusion of her study, and she ached with bittersweet longing to think of the moment when she would finger its bow and strings with the exploratory touches of a new lover.

For now, her mind had to return to business. The force that she led was composed of some of Sato's followers from outside, most of the surviving members of the old Municipal Police, and even several city guards. Sato had wanted a regime change, not a massacre, so he welcomed most of the old guardsmen and aides of the Council who agreed to accept his authority. Most of the old Municipals, as Malone herself understood, now felt hostility toward the Council and did not protest the usurper that was, in any case, already firmly in place.

She did not quite comprehend why the laundress and the reporter had fled, but, as Sato's celebratory address rang on, some dim corner of Malone's mind heard it stuck on the strident note of triumph, and she began to understand. Sato's cause was just enough, but she still felt too numb to savor his victory. At least, she hoped that was it.

Glancing to her left, however, she caught sight of the other, his chin-length black hair brushing his cheeks as he scanned the crowd. He stood offstage, less conspicuous, as befitted his position. Looking at Arnault, Malone felt a refreshing surge of aversion, and she took a measure of satisfaction in the knowledge that one thing would never change. Chance may have placed them together, but it did not alter the way she felt about his underhanded methods or smug contempt. In him, she retained at least the shadow of a moral compass.

Roman Arnault had little difficulty adjusting to his new position as Sato's right-hand man and spymaster, except for the proximity to Liesl Malone. Though they now worked for the same side, he would never trust her any more than she him. Still, he knew he was lucky.

He had not had to murder his great-uncle. In fact, Ruthers had escaped, thanks to his most surprising and resourceful laundress. He did not have to bear the burden of such an irrevocable crime, and Sato could not punish him. Certainly he had believed Roman's story. Had he not heard the gunshot echoing down the hall, smelled the acrid air in the office? Had he not examined the leg wound itself, which was now bandaged and cleaned but destined to leave Roman with a scar and a limp? And lastly, had he not seen the laundress rising on the chandelier, a mortal lifted to near divinity in Roman's eyes? Sato had most of his revenge and his city. Roman could keep his peace of mind.

But first in all his fortunes was Jane's continued safety. Roman did not know where she would seek haven or when Recoletta would return to a semblance of normalcy, but he would find her then. In the meantime, he would try his best to deserve that moment.

ACKNOWLEDGMENTS

Thanks to the entire Angry Robot team for taking a chance on a debut, with special gratitude to Lee Harris and Mike Underwood for indulging an impromptu pitch at a busy WorldCon. Caroline Lambe's publicity assistance was invaluable, as was the encouragement of Robot-for-a-Day, Nikki Walters.

Every first book needs first readers. Josh Sabio and Will Moser kept me writing when I was still wondering how (and whether?) I'd reach the end of the first draft.

This book needed several other beta readers, too. Thanks in particular to Jacqui Talbot, Michael Robertson, and Bill Stiteler for their insightful critiques and writerly camaraderie.

Thanks to my agent and advocate, Jennie Goloboy, for shepherding this book (and me!) through the publication process.

Thanks to all the friends and family whose faith and encouragement kept me going. To my sisters, Sydney Thompson and Julie Lytle; my brother-in-law, Ryan Thompson; and my parents, Richard and Jackie Lytle, for not making crazy faces when I told them I was going to give this writing thing a try. Most of all, to Hiren Patel.

ABOUT THE AUTHOR

Carrie Patel was born and raised in Houston, Texas. An avid traveller, she studied abroad in Granada, Spain and Buenos Aires, Argentina.

She completed her bachelor's and master's degrees at Texas A&M University and worked in transfer pricing at Ernst & Young for two years.

She now works as a narrative designer at Obsidian Entertainment in Irvine, California, where the only season is Always Perfect.

electronicinkblog.com
twitter.com/carrie_patel

Talking about a revolution...

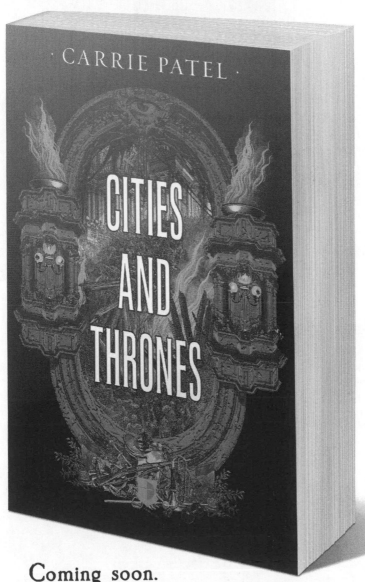

Coming soon.